FORGOTTEN REALMS®

R.A. SALVATORE

THE LAST THRESHOLD

THE **NEVERWINTER**™ SAGA
BOOK
IV

COVER ART
TODD LOCKWOOD

The Neverwinter™ Saga, Book IV

THE LAST THRESHOLD

©2013 Wizards of the Coast LLC.

Published by Wizards of the Coast LLC. Manufactured by: Hasbro SA, Rue Emile-Boéchat 31, 2800 Delémont, CH. Represented by Hasbro Europe, 2 Roundwood Ave, Stockley Park, Uxbridge, Middlesex, UB11 1AZ, UK.

Cover art by Todd Lockwood
First Printing: March 2013

9 8 7 6 5 4 3 2 1

ISBN: 978-0-7869-6364-5
ISBN: 978-0-7869-6429-1 (ebook)
620A2245000001 EN

Cataloging-in-Publication data is on file with the Library of Congress

---

For customer service, contact:
U.S., Canada, Asia Pacific, & Latin America: Wizards of the Coast LLC, P.O. Box 707, Renton, WA 98057-0707, +1-800-324-6496, www.wizards.com/customerservice

U.K., Eire, & South Africa: Wizards of the Coast LLC, c/o Hasbro UK Ltd., P.O. Box 43, Newport, NP19 4YD, UK, Tel: +08457 12 55 99, Email: wizards@hasbro.co.uk

All other countries: Wizards of the Coast p/a Hasbro Belgium NV/SA, Industrialaan 1, 1702 Groot-Bijgaarden, Belgium, Tel: +32.70.233.277, Email: wizards@hasbro.be

Visit our web site at **www.dungeonsanddragons.com**

Welcome to Faerûn, a land of magic and intrigue, brutal violence and divine compassion, where gods have ascended and died, and mighty heroes have risen to fight terrifying monsters. Here, millennia of warfare and conquest have shaped dozens of unique cultures, raised and leveled shining kingdoms and tyrannical empires alike, and left long forgotten, horror-infested ruins in their wake.

A LAND OF MAGIC

When the goddess of magic was murdered, a magical plague of blue fire—the Spellplague—swept across the face of Faerûn, killing some, mutilating many, and imbuing a rare few with amazing supernatural abilities. The Spellplague forever changed the nature of magic itself, and seeded the land with hidden wonders and bloodcurdling monstrosities.

A LAND OF DARKNESS

The threats Faerûn faces are legion. Armies of undead mass in Thay under the brilliant but mad lich king Szass Tam. Treacherous dark elves plot in the Underdark in the service of their cruel and fickle goddess, Lolth. The Abolethic Sovereignty, a terrifying hive of inhuman slave masters, floats above the Sea of Fallen Stars, spreading chaos and destruction. And the Empire of Netheril, armed with magic of unimaginable power, prowls Faerûn in flying fortresses, sowing discord to their own incalculable ends.

A LAND OF HEROES

But Faerûn is not without hope. Heroes have emerged to fight the growing tide of darkness. Battle-scarred rangers bring their notched blades to bear against marauding hordes of orcs. Lowly street rats match wits with demons for the fate of cities. Inscrutable tiefling warlocks unite with fierce elf warriors to rain fire and steel upon monstrous enemies. And valiant servants of merciful gods forever struggle against the darkness.

FORGOTTEN REALMS

A LAND OF
UNTOLD ADVENTURE

PROLOGUE

The Year of the Reborn Hero
(1463 DR)

"YOU CANNOT PRESUME THAT THIS CREATURE IS NATURAL, IN ANY SENSE OF the word," the dark-skinned Shadovar woman known as the Shifter told the old graybeard. "She is perversion incarnate."

The old druid Erlindir shuffled his sandal-clad feet and gave a great "harrumph!"

"Incarnate, I tell you." The Shifter tapped her finger against the old druid's temple and ran it delicately down under his eye and across his cheek to touch his crooked nose.

"So, you're really in front of me this time," Erlindir cackled, referring to the fact that when one addressed the Shifter, typically one was actually addressing a projected image, a phantasm, of the most elusive enchantress.

"I told you that you could trust me, Birdcaller," she replied, using a nickname she'd given him when she had met him at his grove many months before.

"If I didn't believe you, would I have come to this place?" He looked around at the dark images of the Shadowfell, his gaze settling on the twisted keep and tower before him, with its many spires and multiple—likely animated—gargoyles, all leering at him and smiling hungrily. They had just journeyed through a most unpleasant swamp, reeking of death and decay and populated by undead monstrosities. This castle was not much of an improvement.

"Why, Erlindir, you flatter me so," the Shifter teased, and she grabbed him by the chin and directed his gaze back to her face. Her spell wouldn't last forever, she knew, and she didn't want any of the unnatural images to shake the druid from his stupor. Erlindir was of the old school, after all, a disciple of the nature goddess Mielikki. "But remember why you are here."

"Yes, yes," he replied, "this unnatural cat. You would have me destroy it, then?"

"Oh, no, not that!" the Shifter exclaimed.

Erlindir looked at her curiously.

"My friend Lord Draygo has the panther," the Shifter explained. "He is a warl—*mage* of great renown and tremendous power." She paused to watch the druid's reaction, fearing that her near slip-up might clue the old one into her ruse. There was a reason that swamp teemed with undead creatures. No druid, charmed or not, would be so eager to help a warlock.

"Lord Draygo fears that the cat's master is crafting other . . . abominations," she lied. "I would like you to grant him affinity to the cat, that he might see through her eyes when she is summoned home, and cut her bindings to the Astral Plane and anchor her here instead."

Erlindir looked at her suspiciously.

"Only for a short time," she assured him. "We will destroy the cat when we're sure that her master is not perverting nature for his ill intent. And destroy him, too, if needed."

"I would rather that you bring him to me, that I might learn the damage he has already caused," Erlindir said.

"So be it," the enchantress readily agreed, since lies came so easily to her lips.

⁂

"The gates were harder to maintain," Draygo Quick whispered through his crystal ball to his peer, Parise Ulfbinder, a fellow high-ranking and powerful warlock who lived in a tower similar to Draygo's in Shade Enclave, but upon the soil of Toril. "And my understudy told me that the shadowstep back to his home was not as easily accomplished as he had expected."

Parise stroked his small black beard—which, to Draygo, seemed curiously exaggerated in the contours of the crystal ball. "They warred with drow, did they not? And with drow spellspinners, no doubt."

"Not at that time, I don't believe."

"But there were many drow in the bowels of Gauntlgrym."

"Yes, that is what I have been told."

"And Glorfathel?" Parise asked, referring to an elf mage of the mercenary group Cavus Dun, who had disappeared quite unexpectedly and quickly in Gauntlgrym right before the important confrontation.

"No word," Draygo Quick said. And he added quickly, "Yes, it is possible that Glorfathel created some magical waves to impede our retreat. We do not know that he betrayed us. Only the dwarf priestess."

Parise sat back and ran his fingers through his long black hair. "You don't think it was Glorfathel who hindered the shadowsteps," he stated.

Draygo Quick shook his head.

"You don't think it was the work of drow mages, either, or of the priestess," said Parise.

"The shadowstep was more difficult," Draygo argued. "There is change in the air."

"The Spellplague was change," Parise said. "The advent of Shadow was change. The new reality is now simply settling."

"Or the old reality is preparing to return?" Draygo Quick asked. At the other end of the crystal ball, Parise Ulfbinder could only sigh and shrug.

It was just a theory, after all, a belief based on the reading by Parise, Draygo Quick, and some others, of "Cherlrigo's Darkness," a cryptic sonnet found in a letter written by the ancient wizard Cherlrigo. Cherlrigo claimed he'd translated the poem from *The Leaves of One Grass*, a now-lost tome penned nearly a thousand years before, based on prophecies from almost a thousand years before that.

"The world is full of prophecies," Parise warned, but there seemed little conviction in his voice. He had been with Draygo when they had retrieved the letter, after all, and the amount of trouble and the power of the curses they had found along with the page seemed to give its words some measure of weight.

"If we are to take Cherlrigo's word for it, the tome in which he found this sonnet, was penned in Myth Drannor," Draygo Quick reminded Parise. "By the Dark Diviners of Windsong Tower. That is no book of rambling delusions by some unknown prognosticator." "Nay, but it is a book of cryptic messaging," said Parise.

Draygo Quick nodded, conceding that unfortunate fact.

"The proposition of the octave calls it a temporary state," Parise went on. "Let us not react in fear to that which we do not fully comprehend."

"Let us not rest while the world prepares to shift around us," the old warlock countered.

"To a temporary state!" Parise replied.

"Only if the second quatrain is decoded as a measurement of time and not space," Draygo Quick reminded.

"The turn of the ninth line is a clear hint, my friend."

"There are many interpretations!"

Draygo Quick sat back, tapped the tips of his withered fingers together before his frown, and inadvertently glanced at the parchment that lay face down at the side of his desk. The words of the sonnet danced before his eyes, and he mumbled, "And enemies that stink of their god's particular flavor."

"And you know of just such a favored one?" Parise asked, but his tone suggested that he already knew the answer.

"I might," Draygo Quick admitted.

"We must watch these chosen mortals."

Draygo Quick was nodding before Parise began to utter the expected reminder.

"Are you to be blamed for the loss of the sword?" Parise asked.

"It is Herzgo Alegni's failure!" Draygo Quick protested, a bit too vehemently.

Parise Ulfbinder pursed his thick lips and furrowed his brow.

"They will not be pleased with me," Draygo Quick admitted.

"Appeal privately to Prince Rolan," Parise advised, referring to the ruler of Gloomwrought, a powerful Shadowfell city within whose boundaries lay Draygo Quick's own tower. "He has come to believe in the significance of 'Cherlrigo's Darkness.' "

"He fears?"

"There is a lot to lose," Parise admitted, and Draygo Quick found that he couldn't disagree. At a sound in the corridor outside his door, the old warlock nodded farewell to his associate and dropped a silken cloth atop his scrying device.

He heard the Shifter's voice—she spoke with one of his attendants still some distance away—and knew that she had brought the druid, as they had arranged. With still a few moments left to him, Draygo Quick picked up the parchment and held it before his eyes, digesting the sonnet once more.

> Enjoy the play when shadows steal the day . . .
> All the world is half the world for those who learn to walk.
> To feast on fungus soft and peel the sunlit stalk;
> Tarry not in place, for in their sleep the gods do stay.
> But care be known, be light of foot and soft of voice.
> Dare not stir divine to hasten Sunder's day!
> A loss profound but a short ways away;
> The inevitable tear shall't be of, or not of, choice.
> Oh, aye, again the time wandering of lonely world!
> With kingdoms lost and treasures past the finger's tip,
> And enemies that stink of their god's particular flavor.
> Sundered and whole, across the celestial spheres are hurled,
> Beyond the reach of dweomer and the wind-walker's ship;
> With baubles left for the ones the gods do favor.

"Of which god's particular flavor do you taste, Drizzt Do'Urden?" he whispered. All signs—Drizzt's affinity to nature, his status as a ranger, the unicorn he rode—pointed to Mielikki, a goddess of nature, but Draygo Quick had heard many other whispers that suggested Drizzt as a favored child of a very different and much darker goddess.

Either way, the withered old warlock held little doubt that this rogue drow was favored by some god. At this point in his investigation, it hardly mattered which.

He replaced "Cherlrigo's Darkness" face down when he heard the knock on the door, and slowly rose and turned as he bade the Shifter and her companion to enter.

"Welcome, Erlindir of Mielikki," he said graciously, and he wondered what he might learn of that goddess, and perhaps her "flavors" in addition to the tasks the Shifter had already convinced him to perform for Draygo.

"Is this your first visit to the Shadowfell?" Draygo Quick asked.

The druid nodded. "My first crossing to the land of colorless flowers," he replied.

Draygo Quick glanced at the Shifter, who nodded confidently to indicate to him that Erlindir was fully under her spell.

"You understand the task?" Draygo Quick asked the druid. "That we might further investigate this abomination?"

"It seems easy enough," Erlindir replied.

Draygo Quick nodded and waved his hand out toward a side door, bidding Erlindir to lead the way. As the druid moved ahead of him, the old warlock fell in step beside the Shifter. He let Erlindir go into the side chamber before them, and even bade the druid to give him a moment, then shut the door between them.

"He does not know of Drizzt?" he asked.

"He is from a faraway land," the Shifter whispered back.

"He will make no connection with the panther and the drow, then? The tales of this one are considerable, and far-reaching."

"He does not know of Drizzt Do'Urden. I have asked him directly."

Draygo Quick glanced at the door. He was glad and a bit disappointed. Certainly if Erlindir knew of Drizzt and Guenhwyvar, this task could be troublesome. He could recognize the panther and such a shock might well defeat the Shifter's dweomer of enchantment. But the gain could well outweigh the loss of his services, because Erlindir might then have offered, under great duress of course, the information regarding Drizzt's standing with the goddess Mielikki.

"He could not have deceived me in his response," the Shifter added. "For even then, I was in his thoughts, and a lie would have been revealed."

"Ah, well," Draygo Quick sighed.

The Shifter, who had no idea of the larger discussion taking place between Draygo Quick, Parise Ulfbinder, and several other Netherese Lords looked at him with some measure of surprise.

The old warlock met that look with an unremarkable and disarming smile. He opened the door and he and the Shifter joined Erlindir in the side chamber, where, under a silken cloth not unlike that covering his crystal ball, paced Guenhwyvar, trapped in a miniaturized magical cage.

Outside of Draygo Quick's residence, Effron Alegni watched and waited. He had seen the Shifter go in—her appearance, at least, for one never knew when one might actually be looking at the tireless illusionist. He didn't know her human companion, but the old man certainly was no shade, didn't look Netherese, and didn't look at all at home in the Shadowfell.

This was about the panther, Effron knew.

The thought gnawed at him. Draygo Quick had not given the panther back to him, but that cat was perhaps Effron's greatest tool in seeking his revenge against Dahlia. The Shifter had failed him in her dealings with the drow ranger, trying to trade the panther for the coveted Netherese sword, but Effron would not fail. If he could get the cat, he believed he could remove one of Dahlia's greatest allies from the playing board.

But Draygo Quick had forbidden it.

Draygo Quick.

Effron's mentor, so he had thought.

The withered old warlock's last words to him rang in his mind: "Idiot boy, I only kept you alive out of respect for your father. Now that he is no more, I am done with you. Be gone. Go and hunt her, young fool, that you might see your father again in the darker lands."

Effron had tried to return to Draygo, to remedy the fallout between them.

He had been turned away by the old warlock's student servants, in no uncertain terms.

And now this—and Effron knew that the Shifter's visit had been precipitated by the old warlock's plans for the panther. Plans that did not include Effron. Plans that would not help Effron's pressing need.

Indeed, plans that would almost certainly hinder Effron's pressing need.

The twisted young tiefling, his dead arm swinging uselessly behind him, crouched in the dark brush outside of Draygo Quick's residence for much of the day.

Grimacing.

"You play dangerous games, old warlock," the Shifter said later that night, when she was collecting her coins from Draygo Quick.

"Not if you have done your research and enchantments correctly. Not if this Erlindir creature is half the druid you claim him to be."

"He is quite powerful. Which is why I'm surprised that you will let him return to Toril alive."

"Am I to kill every powerful wizard and cleric simply because?" Draygo Quick asked.

"He knows much now," the Shifter warned.

"You assured me that he did not know of Drizzt Do'Urden and was nowhere near to him in the vast lands of Faerûn."

"True, but if he harbors any suspicion, isn't it possible that he put similar dweomers on himself as he did on you—to allow you to view the world through the panther's eyes?"

Draygo Quick's hand froze in place halfway to the shelf where he kept his Silverymoon brandy. He turned to face his guest. "Should I demand my coin back?"

The Shifter laughed easily and shook her head.

"Then why would you suggest such a thing?" Draygo Quick demanded. He let that hang in the air as her smile became coy. He grabbed the bottle and poured a couple of glasses, setting one down on the hutch and taking a sip from the other.

"Why, tricky lady," he asked at length, "are you trying to pry motives from me?"

"You admit that your . . . tactics would elicit my curiosity, yes?"

"Why? I have an interest in Lady Dahlia and her companions, of course. They have brought great distress to me, and I would be remiss if I did not repay them."

"Effron came to me," she said.

"Seeking the panther."

She nodded, and Draygo Quick noted that she held the brandy he had poured for her, though he hadn't handed it to her and she hadn't come to get it—or at least, she hadn't appeared to come and get it. "I know that Effron desperately wishes this Dahlia creature killed."

"More strength to him, then!" Draygo Quick replied with exuberance.

But the Shifter wasn't buying his feigned emotion, as she stood shaking her head.

"Yes, she is his mother," Draygo Quick answered her unspoken question. "From the loins of Herzgo Alegni. Dahlia threw him from a cliff immediately after his birth, the fiery elf. A pity the fall did not show mercy and kill him, but he landed amongst some pines. The trees broke his fall and broke his spine, but alas, he did not succumb to death."

"His injuries—"

"Aye, Effron was, and remains, fairly broken," the warlock explained. "But Herzgo Alegni would not let him go. Not physically, and not even emotionally, for many years, until it became clear what little Effron would be."

"Twisted. Infirm."

"And by that time—"

"He was an understudy, a promising young warlock under the watchful eye of the great Draygo Quick," the Shifter reasoned. "And more than that, he became your bludgeon to crumble the stubborn will of the ever-troublesome Herzgo Alegni. He became valuable to you."

"It's a difficult world," Draygo Quick lamented. "One must find whatever tools one can to properly navigate the swirling seas."

He raised his glass in toast and took another drink. The Shifter did likewise.

"And what tools do you seek now, through the panther?" she asked.

Draygo Quick shrugged as if it were not important. "How well do you know this Erlindir now?"

It was the Shifter's turn to shrug.

"He would welcome you to his grove?"

She nodded.

"He is a disciple of Mielikki," Draygo Quick remarked. "Do you know his standing?"

"He is a powerful druid, though his mind has dulled with age."

"But is he favored by the goddess?" Draygo Quick asked, more insistently than he had intended, as the Shifter's response—stiffening, her expression growing concerned—informed him.

"Would one not have to be, to be granted powers?"

"More than that," Draygo Quick pressed.

"Are you asking me if Erlindir is of special favor to Mielikki? Chosen?"

The old warlock didn't blink.

The Shifter laughed at him. "If he was, do you think I would have ever attempted such trickery with him? Do you consider me a fool, old warlock?"

Draygo Quick waved the silly questions away and took a sip, silently berating himself for so eagerly pursuing such a far-fetched idea. He was off his game, he realized. The intensity of his talks with Parise Ulfbinder were getting to him.

"Would this Erlindir know of others who might be so favored with his goddess?" he asked.

"The head of his order, likely."

"No—or perhaps," the warlock said. "I seek those favored ones, the ones known as 'Chosen'."

"Of Mielikki?"

"Of all the gods. Any information you can gather for me on this matter will be well received and generously rewarded."

He moved to pour another drink when the Shifter asked with great skepticism and great intrigue, "Drizzt Do'Urden?"

Draygo Quick shrugged again. "Who can know?"

"Erlindir, perhaps," the Shifter replied. She drained her glass and started away, pausing only to glance at the room where the captured Guenhwyvar paced.

"Enjoy your time on Toril," she remarked.

"Enjoy. . . ." Draygo Quick muttered under his breath as she departed. It was not advice he often took.

PART
I

BROKEN CHILD

I did not think it possible, but the world grows grayer still around me and more confusing.

How wide was the line twixt darkness and light when first I walked out of Menzoberranzan. So full of righteous certitude was I, even when my own fate appeared tenuous. But I could thump my fist against the stone and proclaim, "This is the way the world works best. This is right and this is wrong!" with great confidence and internal contentment.

And now I travel with Artemis Entreri.

And now my lover is a woman of . . .

Thin grows that line twixt darkness and light. What once seemed a clear definition fast devolves into an obfuscating fog.

In which I wander, with a strange sense of detachment.

This fog has always been there, of course. It is not the world that has changed, merely my understanding of it. There have always been, there will always be, thieves like farmer Stuyles and his band of highwaymen. By the letter of the law, they are outlaws indeed, but does not the scale of immorality sink more strongly at the feet of the feudal lords of Luskan and even of Waterdeep, whose societal structures put men like Stuyles into an untenable position? They hunt the roads to survive, to eat, finding a meager existence on the edges of a civilization that has forgotten—yea, even abandoned!—them.

So on the surface, even that dilemma seems straightforward. Yet, when Stuyles and his band act, are they not assailing, assaulting, perhaps even killing, mere delivery boys of puppet masters—equally desperate people working within the shaken structures of society to feed their own?

Where then does the moral scale tip?

And perhaps more importantly, from my own perspective and my own choices, where then might I best follow the tenets and truths I hold dear?

Shall I be a singular player in a society of one, taking care of my personal needs in a manner attuned with that which I believe to be right and just? A hermit, then, living among the trees and the animals, akin to Montolio deBrouchee, my long-lost mentor. This would be the easiest course, but would it suffice to assuage a conscience that has long declared community above self?

Shall I be a large player in a small pond, where my every conscience-guided move sends waves to the surrounding shores?

Both of these choices seem best to describe my life to date, I think, through the last decades beside Bruenor, and with Thibbledorf, Jessa, and Nanfoodle, where our concerns were our own. Our personal needs ranked above the surrounding communities, for the most part, as we sought Gauntlgrym.

Shall I venture forth to a lake, where my waves become ripples, or an ocean of society, where my ripples might well become indistinguishable among the tides of the dominant civilizations?

Where, I wonder and I fear, does hubris end and reality overwhelm? Is this the danger of reaching too high, or am I bounded by fear that will hold me too low?

Once again I have surrounded myself with powerful companions, though ones less morally aligned than my previous troupe and much less easily controlled. With Dahlia and Entreri, this intriguing dwarf who calls herself Ambergris, and this monk of considerable skill, Afafrenfere, I have little doubt that we might insert ourselves forcefully into some of the more pressing issues of the wider region of the Sword Coast North.

But I do not doubt the risk in this. I know who Artemis Entreri was, whatever I might hope he now will be. Dahlia, for all of those qualities that intrigue me, is dangerous and haunted by demons, the scale of which I have only begun to comprehend. And now I find myself even more off-balance around her, for the appearance of this strange young tiefling has put her mind into dangerous turmoil.

Ambergris—Amber Gristle O'Maul of the Adbar O'Mauls—might be the most easily trusted of the bunch, and yet when first I met her, she was part of a band that had come to slay me and imprison Dahlia in support of forces dark indeed. And Afafrenfere . . . well, I simply do not know.

What I do know with certainty, given what I have come to know of these companions, is that in terms of my moral obligations to those truths I hold dear, I cannot follow them.

Whether I can or should convince them to follow me is a different question all together.

—Drizzt Do'Urden

CHAPTER 1

ECHOES OF THE PAST

DARK CLOUDS ROILED OVERHEAD, BUT EVERY NOW AND THEN, THE MOON-light broke through the overcast and shined softly through the room's window, splashing on Dahlia's smooth shoulder. She slept on her side, facing away from Drizzt.

The drow propped himself up on his elbow and looked at her in the moonlight. Her sleep was restful now, her breathing rhythmic and even, but shortly before she had flailed about in some nightmare, crying out, "No!"

She seemed to be reaching out with her hands, to catch something perhaps or maybe to pull something back.

Drizzt couldn't decipher the details, of course. It reminded him that this companion of his was truly unknown to him. What demons did Dahlia carry on those smooth shoulders?

Drizzt's gaze lifted from her to the window, and to the wide world beyond. What was he doing here, back in the city of Neverwinter? Biding time?

They had returned to Neverwinter after a dangerous journey to Gauntlgrym, and on that journey had found many surprises, and a pair of new companions, dwarf and human. Entreri had survived unexpectedly, for the sword, which he had been convinced was the cause of his longevity, had been destroyed.

Indeed, when Drizzt had tossed Charon's Claw over the rim of the primor-dial pit, he had done so with the near certainty that Artemis Entreri would be destroyed along with the blade. And yet, Entreri had survived.

They'd ventured into the darkness and had come out victorious, yet neither Drizzt nor Dahlia had relished the adventure, or could now savor in the victory. For Drizzt, there remained lingering resentment and jealousy, because Dahlia and Entreri had shared much over the last days, an intimacy, he feared, even deeper than that which he knew with Dahlia. Drizzt was her lover, Entreri had merely kissed her—and that, when Entreri was certain that he was about to die. Yet it seemed to Drizzt that Dahlia had emotionally opened herself to Entreri more than she ever had to him.

Drizzt glanced back at Dahlia.

Was he here in Neverwinter distracting himself? Had his life become nothing more than a series of distractions until at long last he would find his own grave?

Many times in his past, Drizzt had given himself to the Hunter, to the fighter inside seeking battle and blood. The Hunter smothered pain. Many times in the past, the Hunter had kept Drizzt safe from his torn heart as the days passed and the wounds mended a bit, at least.

Was that what he was doing now, Drizzt wondered? The notion seemed obscene to him, but was he, in fact, using Dahlia the way he had used battle-field enemies in times past?

No, it was more than that, he told himself. He cared for Dahlia. There was an attraction based on more than sexuality and more than a need for companionship. The many layers of this elf woman teased him and intrigued him. There was something within her, hidden—even from her, it seemed—that Drizzt found undeniably appealing.

But as his gaze again lifted toward the window and the wider world, Drizzt had to admit that he was indeed doing nothing more than biding his time—to let the sting of the final dissolution of the Companions of the Hall fade away. Or likely it went even deeper.

He was afraid, terrified even.

He was afraid that his life had been a lie, that his dedication to community and his insistence that there was a common good worth fighting for was a fool's errand in a world too full of selfishness and evil. The weight of darkness seemed to mock him.

What was the point of it all?

He rolled to the side of the bed and sat up. He thought of Luskan and Captain Deudermont's terrible fall. He thought of Farmer Stuyles and his band of highwaymen, and the gray mist in which they lived, caught somewhere between morality and necessity, between the law and the basic rights of any living man. He thought of the Treaty of Garumn's Gorge, which had established an orc kingdom on the doorstep of the dwarven homeland—had that been King Bruenor's greatest achievement or his greatest folly?

Or worse, did it even matter?

For many heartbeats, that question spun in the air before him, out of reach. Had his life been no more than a fool's errand?

"No!" Dahlia said again and rolled around.

The denial rang out within Drizzt even as it reached his ear. Drizzt glanced back over his shoulder. She lay on her back, at peace in slumber again, the moonlight splashing across her face, bright enough to hint at her blue woad tattoo.

No! Drizzt heard again inside his heart and soul, and instead of the failures and the losses, he forced himself to remember the victories and the joys. He thought of young Wulfgar, under his and Bruenor's tutelage, who grew straight and strong and who brought together the barbarian tribes and the folk of Ten-Towns in peace and common cause.

Surely that had been no pyrrhic victory!

He thought of Deudermont again, not of the final defeat, but of the many victories the man had known at sea, bringing justice to tides run wild with merciless pirates. The final outcome of Luskan could not erase those efforts and good deeds, and how many innocents had been saved by the good captain and crew of *Sea Sprite*?

"What a fool I've been," Drizzt whispered.

He threw aside his indecision, threw aside his personal pain, threw aside the darkness.

He rose and dressed and moved to the door. He looked back at Dahlia, then walked back to her side, bent low, and kissed her on the forehead. She didn't stir, and Drizzt quietly left the room, and for the first time since the fall of King Bruenor, he walked with confidence.

Down the hall, he knocked on a door. When there came no immediate response, he knocked again, loudly.

Wearing only his pants, his hair a mess, Artemis Entreri pulled the door open wide. "What?" he asked, his tone filled with annoyance, but also a measure of concern.

"Come with me," Drizzt said.

Entreri looked at him incredulously.

"Not now," Drizzt explained. "Not this night. But come with me when I leave the city of Neverwinter behind. I have an idea, a . . . reason, but I need your help."

"What are you plotting, drow?"

Drizzt shook his head. "I cannot explain it, but I'll show you."

"A ship sails for the south in two days. I plan to be on it."

"I ask you to reconsider."

"You said I didn't owe you anything."

"You don't."

"Then why should I follow you?"

Drizzt took a deep breath again the incessant cynicism. Why was everyone around him always asking "what's in it for me?"

"Because I ask this of you."

"Do better," said Entreri.

Drizzt stared at him plaintively. Entreri started to close the door.

"I know where to find your dagger," Drizzt blurted out. He hadn't intended to say it, indeed he'd never planned to help Entreri retrieve it.

Entreri seemed to lean forward just a bit. "My dagger?"

"I know where it is. I've seen it recently."

"Do tell."

"Say you'll come with me," Drizzt said. "The road will lead us there soon enough." He paused for a moment, then had to add, for his own sake if not for Entreri's, "Come with me no matter what, setting aside the dagger or anything else you might gain. You need this journey, my old enemy, as much as I do." Drizzt believed that claim, for though the plan formulating in his thoughts would take him on an important personal journey, the approach might prove even more important to Artemis Entreri.

This conflicted and deeply scarred man standing before him might well be the measure of it all, Drizzt thought.

Would the journey of Artemis Entreri vindicate him, or make a greater lie of his life?

Entreri seemed to be trying to unwind that last sentence when Drizzt turned his focus back to him once more.

"Any road is as good to me as any other," Entreri replied with a shrug.

Drizzt smiled.

"At first light?" Entreri asked.

"There is something I must do first," Drizzt explained. "I will need a day, perhaps two, and then we will go."

"To retrieve my dagger," Entreri said.

"To find more than that," Drizzt replied, and as Entreri swung the door closed, he added under his breath, "for both of us."

Drizzt's stride was much lighter as he returned to Dahlia's side. Outside, the night continued to clear, the moon shining brighter.

That seemed fitting to Drizzt as he glanced out the window, for he looked out at the world now with a new light and a new hope.

Suddenly.

Drizzt and Dahlia meandered along the forest road south and east of the city of Neverwinter—meandered because the eager drow had allowed Dahlia to set the pace. Drizzt hadn't expected her to accompany him out here this day, and hadn't asked her to do so. He sought the house of a red-haired seer,

Arunika, who had once offered—and hopefully would again offer—insights about Guenhwyvar.

Pale sunlight cast long shadows through the tree branches and speckled the ground before them, shining orange among the many fallen leaves. Winter had not yet arrived, but it was not far off. Some of the trees had turned to their autumn colors and now lay bare against the chill wind, while others stubbornly clung to the last leaves of the season.

"Why are we here?" Dahlia asked, and not for the first time.

The words brought Drizzt from his contemplation, and annoyed him more than a little. He thought to remind Dahlia that she had come out of her own volition, and perhaps even to add that he would have preferred it if she had remained in the city with the others.

He thought about it, but he knew better than to say it.

Still, he let her words go. This was his realm, the forest, the domain of his goddess, the place where he was most reminded of the vastness of nature. Such a humbling notion allowed Drizzt to keep perspective on those problems and issues that troubled him. In the grand scheme of the world, the cycle of life and death, the vastness of the celestial spheres, so many "problems" seemed not to matter.

But Dahlia prompted him again with the same question.

"You could have remained in Neverwinter," Drizzt replied before he could consider his words.

"You don't want me beside you?" Dahlia said, a rough edge coming quickly to her voice, and Drizzt could only sigh, realizing that he had fallen into her trap. He was trying to make sense of his relationship with Dahlia, perhaps most of all, and so was she, he understood. But alas, logic and reason seemed oft trumped by more basic and powerful emotions in issues of personal relationships.

"I'm glad you're here," Drizzt told her. "I only wish that you were glad too."

"I never said—"

"You have asked a dozen times why we're here. Perhaps there is no purpose, other than to enjoy the sunlight through the forest canopy."

Dahlia stopped and stared hard at him, hands on hips, and Drizzt could not help but pause and return the look.

Dahlia shook her head. "This last few days you've been full of thought. You hardly hear my words. You're here beside me and yet you aren't. *Why* are we here?"

Drizzt sighed and gave a nod. "The journey to Gauntlgrym has left me with more questions than answers."

"We went to destroy the sword. We destroyed the sword."

"True enough," Drizzt admitted. "But—"

"But Artemis Entreri remains," Dahlia interrupted. "Does this trouble you so much?"

Drizzt paused and considered the myriad questions in his mind, after dismissing the question Dahlia had just asked. In the end, the matter of Entreri really was a minor thing when weighed against the true purpose of this day in the forest: to discern anything he might about Guenhwyvar.

"Is there a purpose to your life now?" he asked. She fell back a step and assumed a more defensive posture, studying him carefully.

"Since we have joined together, we have moved through several quests," Drizzt explained. "All urgent. We put the primordial back in its magical trap. We sought revenge on Sylora, and on Herzgo Alegni, and then we went and freed Entreri from the insidious enslavement of the sword. Our roads have been a matter of small, but important needs, but what is the greater purpose binding them together?"

Dahlia looked at him as if he'd just grown a second head. "To survive," she replied sarcastically.

"Not so!" the drow countered. "We could have left the region to the primordial forces. We could have walked far away from these enemies."

"They would have followed."

"In body, or simply in your dreams?"

"Both," Dahlia decided. "Sylora would have tried to find us, and Alegni. . . ." She spat upon the ground.

"And so our road has been determined by immediate needs."

Dahlia shrugged and continued to look rather unimpressed.

"But what now?" he asked.

"You're not asking me," Dahlia replied. "You're merely preparing me for whatever road you deem worthy."

Drizzt could only laugh and shrug at that for many heartbeats. "I'm asking," he said at length. "Asking you and asking myself."

"Let me know when you find an answer," the elf woman replied and turned back to the north, toward Neverwinter.

"A bit farther," Drizzt said before she had gone more than a couple of steps.

Dahlia stopped and turned. "Why?" she demanded.

"Arunika the Seer," Drizzt admitted. "I wish to speak with her again regarding Guenhwyvar." He stared at her for just a moment longer, then turned and shrugged and moved along to the south. Dahlia was quick to catch up.

"You might have told me that when we left," Dahlia said.

Drizzt merely shrugged. Did it even matter? He wasn't even sure where Arunika's house might be. Somewhere in the south, Jelvus Grinch had told him, but no one seemed to know precisely.

On his previous meeting with her, after the defeat of the Shadovar in Neverwinter and before the journey to Gauntlgrym, the seer had claimed that she could sense no connection at all between the statuette Drizzt carried and the panther it was used to summon. Nothing had changed, as far as Drizzt could tell.

Still, before he left this place, he had to try one last time. He owed that, and so much more, to his most loyal companion.

With all of those thoughts stirring in his mind, Drizzt nearly walked right past a side trail marked by a recent passage of a large band, something the astute ranger would rarely miss. He spun around at the last moment and moved back to the side trail, bending low to examine the soft ground. Dahlia moved up beside him.

"Not so old," the elf woman remarked.

Drizzt crouched lower, feeling the solidity of the ground, inspecting one clear print more carefully. "Goblins." He stood and looked into the forest. Perhaps this side trail led to Arunika's house, he thought. Had she been assailed by the filthy little beasts?

If so, he'd likely find a bunch of dead goblins scattered about Arunika's undamaged house. The woman was deceptively formidable, by all accounts.

"Or Ashmadai," Dahlia replied, referring to the devil-worshiping zealots who had formed Sylora Salm's army in Neverwinter Wood. Since the fall of Sylora, this force had scattered throughout the region, or so the Neverwinter guards had told them.

"Goblins," Drizzt insisted. He took a few steps along the small trail, then looked back to Dahlia, who didn't follow.

"They could strike at any of the caravans coming up from Waterdeep before the winter snows," Drizzt said, but Dahlia merely shrugged and seemed unimpressed.

Her indifference stung Drizzt, but it was not unexpected. He understood that he had a long road ahead of him indeed if he ever hoped to encourage her to look out for the needs of others.

She smiled, however, and took up her walking stick, the magical stave known as Kozah's Needle, and moved past Drizzt, heading along the small trail, deeper into the forest.

"We haven't fought anyone in a tenday and more," she remarked. "I could use the practice . . . and the coin."

Drizzt stared back at the road for some time as the elf woman moved away from him. There wasn't much altruism flowing forth from her in words, but perhaps it was there nonetheless, buried under the chip that weighed upon her strong shoulders.

She had returned to Gauntlgrym and the primordial, after all, and though she could pretend she had done so simply to strike back at Sylora Salm, Drizzt knew better. Guilt had driven Dahlia back to that supreme danger in that dark place. That guilt was wrought of her need to right the wrong she had helped facilitate, for she had played a role in freeing the monstrous fire being and thus a role in the catastrophe that had obliterated Neverwinter a decade before.

Buried within Dahlia was compassion, empathy, and a sense of right and wrong.

Drizzt believed that, though he feared that he believed it because he had to.

A short while later, the sun still high overhead, Drizzt crouched low and peered through the tangle of branches before him. He held up his fist, signaling Dahlia to stay back. The goblins were ahead, not far, he knew, for he could smell them. Likely, they had set a camp just ahead, buried in the shadows of a grove of thick maples and a few boulders, for goblins did not like the sunlight and traveled only rarely in the daytime.

He motioned for Dahlia to move off to the right flank, then held his breath as the elf woman started away, her footsteps crunching in the leaves. Was she even trying to be careful, Drizzt wondered? Or was she just being petulant?

Drizzt shook his head, trying to let it go. The brown carpet of autumn lay thick about the ground. Even Drizzt, dark elf and skilled ranger, would have trouble moving silently in this region. So, no matter, he told himself. He drew Taulmaril, set an arrow, and crept ahead, trying to gain a better vantage. At last, he spotted the camp—or what was left of it.

Drizzt stood up straight and glanced over at Dahlia, his expression telling her that she need not take care to be silent any longer. Someone, or something, had beaten them to the camp—and had destroyed the place and the inhabitants.

Dead goblins lay scattered haphazardly about the ground, their shredded, bug-ridden blankets all around. Wisps of smoke still rose from several small logs, the remnants of a cooking fire, likely, which also had been thrown around in the apparent scuffle.

Drizzt removed his arrow, placed it back into the quiver, and slid Taulmaril over his shoulder, as Dahlia appeared at the side of the camp. She came in with a wide smile on her pretty face, and Drizzt found himself unable to look away from her in the morning light—indeed, in a different light than he had known during their recent conversations.

Her black, red-streaked hair was in that pretty bob again, bouncing lightly around her shoulders under her fashionable wide-brimmed black leather hat, its right side pinned up. The sun speckled down on her through the trees, dancing around the woman's blue-dyed facial woad. In the morning light, those markings didn't seem fierce to Drizzt, but somehow soft and even innocent, like freckles on a dancing child.

The drow reminded himself that Dahlia was a master of disguise and manipulation. She was, in all possibility, manipulating him even then. But still, he could not pull his eyes away from her.

She wore her black raven cape thrown back from her shoulders, with her white blouse unbuttoned low, to the tip of her black vest that stretched tight about her lithe torso. Her black skirt, cut short and angled, revealed much of her shapely legs—that which wasn't covered by her tall black boots.

She was the perfect blend of apparent innocence and promising sensuality—in other words, Dahlia was dangerous. And he would do well to always remember that, especially after their adventures with Artemis Entreri.

But Drizzt couldn't wrap his thoughts around Dahlia in any cohesive way. Not now, not ever. He watched her walk into the camp, casually prodding a dead goblin with Kozah's Needle, still formed into a thick walking stick, four feet in length. All at once, she seemed sweet, sexy, and vicious, like she wanted to kiss him, or kill him, and as if it wouldn't matter to her which it might be. How was that possible? What magic surrounded her? Or was it in his mind, Drizzt wondered?

"Someone got here before us," she said.

"It would appear so. Saved us the trouble."

"Stole our fun, you mean," Dahlia replied with a wry grin. She drew a small knife from her belt. "They are offering a bounty on goblin ears in Neverwinter."

"We didn't kill them."

"That will hardly matter." She bent with the knife, but Drizzt stepped over and caught her arm, and brought her back up to stand before him.

"They'll want to know who, or what, did this," the drow said. "Ashmadai? A Netherese patrol?"

Dahlia considered his words for a moment, then glanced back down. "Well," she said, "I know what did it, if not exactly who."

Drizzt followed her gaze to the dead goblin she had rolled. The way it had flopped had exposed its neck, showing two puncture wounds, as if made by fangs.

"Vampire," Dahlia remarked.

Drizzt stared at the wound, seeking a different answer. Perhaps a wolf, he told himself, though he knew that to be ridiculous. A wolf would not have bitten a victim like that only to leave the throat intact. Still, the notion of another vampire was not something Drizzt wanted to embrace. He had seen more than enough of one such creature in the bowels of Gauntlgrym; indeed, Bruenor and Thibbledorf Pwent had been slain by just such a creature.

"You cannot be sure," Drizzt replied, and not just out of a desperate hope, for something seemed amiss to him. He moved to the side, where a broken tent lay tangled around a small branch.

"I have some experience in these matters," Dahlia said. "I know what such wounds look like." Indeed, Drizzt suspected the same vampire, Dor'crae, who had attacked Bruenor in the anteroom to the primordial pit had been Dahlia's lover.

Drizzt tried hard not to focus on the recollection of Dor'crae. He tried to wash that thought away with the image of the pretty elf walking into the camp, tried to bury it under the sheer attraction the woman elicited in him.

And when that didn't work, he fell back on that pervading sense of detachment.

Drizzt drew out a scimitar and used it to flip the torn tent aside, revealing more goblins, or more accurately, goblin parts, strewn on the ground before him. He studied the garish vision, the jagged tears in the clothing and skin. These were wounds better known to Drizzt, who had traveled beside just such a fighter for so many decades.

"Battlerager," he whispered, confused.

"No," Dahlia said. "I've seen these fang marks before . . ." Her voice trailed off as she walked over to him, as she noted, no doubt, the very different carnage at this section of the broken camp.

"Vampire," she insisted.

"Battlerager," Drizzt replied.

"Must you always argue with me?" She asked the question casually, but Drizzt detected an undercurrent of true anger. How many times had that edge crept into Dahlia's voice of late?

"Only when you're wrong." Drizzt tossed her a disarming grin—and he realized it was likely the first lighthearted look he'd offered Dahlia since they'd left the bowels of Gauntlgrym, or more accurately, since he had seen Dahlia and Artemis Entreri share a passionate kiss. "I suppose that might seem like always to you," Drizzt teased, determined to push past his own negativity and jealousy.

Dahlia cocked her head. "Are you finished with your pouting at long last?" she asked.

The question threw Drizzt off balance for a moment, for it seemed to him to be a matter of Dahlia projecting her own foul mood on him. Or perhaps it was a matter of Dahlia admitting that her own pouting—or grieving, or shock, or whatever combination it might be—needed to end.

But the question teased Drizzt on a much deeper level, and likely more deeply than Dahlia had intended. Drizzt couldn't deny the truth of her words.

To Drizzt, Dahlia remained this great contradiction, able to tug his emotions any which way she desired, it seemed, as easily as she changed her hairstyle. But to Entreri . . . nay, her tricks would not work for her with Entreri. For Artemis Entreri knew her, or knew something of her, that went past the hairstyles, the clear skin or woad, her clothing, seductive or sweet. Before Drizzt, she had stood naked, physically, perhaps, but before Entreri, Dahlia had been naked emotionally, stripped to the core trouble that so haunted her.

Drizzt had only glimpsed that briefly, in the form of a broken and twisted young tiefling warlock and Dahlia's reaction to that creature, Effron.

"What about you?" Drizzt replied. "You have said little in the tendays since we left Gauntlgrym."

"Perhaps I have nothing to say." Dahlia clamped her jaw, as if she were afraid of what might come spilling out should she lose the tiniest bit of discipline. "I have the ears," Dahlia said and began to walk away.

He followed her out of the camp and into the forest once more, moving slowly and bending low, looking for broken stems or footprints. For a long while she walked, finally coming to rest in a sunny clearing where a single, half-buried stone provided a comfortable seat.

Dahlia reclined, removed her hat, and ran her fingers through her hair, allowing the sunbeams to splash over her face.

"Come along," he bade her. "We must learn who or what killed those goblins. There's a vampire about, so you claim."

Dahlia shrugged, showing no interest.

"Or a battlerager," Drizzt went on stubbornly. "And if it is the latter, then we would do well to find him. A powerful ally."

"So I thought of my vampire lover," Dahlia said, and she seemed to take some pleasure when Drizzt grimaced at the reference.

"Will we never speak of what happened in Gauntlgrym?" Drizzt asked suddenly. "The twisted tiefling accused you of murder." Dahlia's expression abruptly changed. She snapped a glare over him.

Dahlia swallowed hard and did not turn her stare from Drizzt for an instant as he took a seat beside her.

"He claimed Alegni was his father," Drizzt pressed.

"Shut up," Dahlia warned.

"He called you his mother."

Her eyes bored through him, and Drizzt expected her to reach out and claw at his face, or to explode into a tirade of shouted curses.

But she didn't, and that, perhaps, was more unsettling still. She just sat there, staring. A cloud passed overhead, blocking the sunlight, sending a shadow across Dahlia's pretty face.

"Implausible, of course, likely impossible," Drizzt said quietly, trying to back away.

Dahlia held perfectly still. He could almost hear her heartbeat, or was it his own? Many moments slipped past. Drizzt lost count of them.

"It's true," she admitted, and now it was Drizzt who looked as if he had been slapped.

"Cannot be," he finally managed to reply. "He is a young man, but you're a young woman—"

"I was barely more than a child when the shadow of Herzgo Alegni fell over my clan," Dahlia said, so very softly that Drizzt could hardly hear the words. "Twenty years ago."

Drizzt's thoughts spun in circles, very easily coming to the dark conclusion of Dahlia's leading words. He tried to respond, but found himself sputtering helplessly in the face of a horror so far beyond him. He thought back to his own youth, to his graduation at Melee Magthere, when his own sister had advanced upon him so lewdly, forcing him to run away with revulsion.

For a moment, he thought to tell that tale to Dahlia, to try to claim some kinship to her pain, but then realized that his own experience surely paled beside her trauma.

And so he sputtered, and finally he reached out a hand to her to pull her close.

She resisted, but she was trembling. The tears that rolled from her blue eyes were formed in profound sadness, he knew, even as she issued a low growl to cover her weakness.

But denial couldn't hold, and anger couldn't cover the scar.

Drizzt tried to pull her close, but she spun away and scrambled to her feet, walking off a few steps, her back to him.

"So now you know," she said, her voice as cold as winter's deepest ice.

"Dahlia," he pleaded, rising and taking a step her way. Should he go to her and grab her, and crush her close against him, and whisper to her that she might let the pain flow freely? Did she want that? She didn't seem to, and yet, she had let Entreri kiss . . .

With a growl of his own, Drizzt dismissed that ridiculous jealousy. This wasn't about him, wasn't about his relationship with Dahlia, and surely wasn't about her moments with Entreri. This was about Dahlia, and her pain so profound.

He didn't know what to say, or what to do. He felt like a child. He had grown up in a place of deceit and murder and treachery as a way of life, perhaps the vilest city in all the world, and so he thought that he had fully inoculated himself against the scars of depravity and inhumanity. He was Drizzt Do'Urden, the hero of Icewind Dale, the hero of Mithral Hall, who had fought a thousand battles and killed a thousand enemies, who had watched dear friends die, who had loved and lost. Ever level-headed, hardened to the dark realities of life . . .

So he had thought.

So he had lied to himself.

This combination of emotions roiling within Dahlia was quite beyond him at that strange moment. This was darkness compounded in darkness, irredeemable and outside any comfort zones Drizzt might have constructed through his own less-complicated experiences. Dahlia had suffered something to her core, a violation beyond even an enemy's sword, with which Drizzt could not empathize and of which Drizzt couldn't even understand.

"Come," Dahlia bade him, her voice even and strong. "Let us find this killer." She walked off into the forest.

Drizzt watched her with surprise, until he recognized that she was now eager for the hunt for no better reason than to find an enemy to battle. The emotions Drizzt had stirred went too deep and Dahlia couldn't find comfort in Drizzt's hesitant embrace and awkward words, and so she needed to find someone, something, to destroy.

He had missed his moment, Drizzt understood. He had failed her.

The monk stood in the main square of Neverwinter, staring at his hands as he turned them around before his eyes.

"That a fightin' practice?" Ambergris asked.

"I'm looking for hints of shadowstuff," Brother Afafrenfere replied curtly. "What have you done to me, dwarf?"

"I told ye," said Ambergris. "Can't have ye lookin' the part of a shade if ye're to walk the lands o' Toril, now can I?"

"This is not illusion," Afafrenfere protested. "My skin is lightening."

"Is yer heart, then?" the female dwarf asked.

Afafrenfere glared at her.

"How long was ye a shade?"

"I gave myself to the Shadowfell," Afafrenfere protested.

"Bah, but ye fell in love an' nothin' more," the dwarf chided. "How long?"

"You cannot—"

"How long?"

"Three years," Afafrenfere admitted.

"So ye spent the better part of a quarter-century here, and living where, I might be askin', except that I'm already knowin'."

"Oh, are you?"

"Aye, ye got yer training in the mountains aside Damara."

Afafrenfere stepped back as if she had just slugged him. "How could you—?"

"Ye got a yellow rose painted inside yer forearm, ye dolt. Ye think I'm for missin' a clue like that? And I telled ye true back there in Gauntlgrym. Meself's from Citadel Adbar, and Adbar's knowing o' the Monastery o' the Yellow Rose."

"It doesn't matter," Afafrenfere insisted. "I gave myself willingly to Cavus Dun."

"To Parbid, ye mean."

"To Cavus Dun and the Shadowfell," Afafrenfere growled at her. "And now you would take the shadowstuff from me."

"Ye ain't no damned shade," Ambergris insisted. "No more'n meself. Ye're a human, as ye was afore ye ran to darkness. Ye're actin' like I'm stealin' from ye, but know that I'm savin' ye, from yerself, so it'd be seemin'. Ain't nothin' there in the darkness for ye, boy. Ye ain't a born shade, and so ye ain't to get yer desserts there among them grayskins."

"And you were just a spy," Afafrenfere said. "A traitorous spy."

"Might be," said Ambergris, though it was surely more complicated than that. She didn't feel much like explaining herself to the young monk at this time, however. Amber Gristle O'Maul hadn't chosen to go to the Shadowfell to serve as a spy for Citadel Adbar. The adjudicators of Citadel Adbar had sentenced her to that mission for serious indiscretions—it was that or a ball and chain, a mining pick, and twenty years of breaking stone in the lowest mines of the dwarven complex.

"Be happy I was," the dwarf said. "For if not, then be knowin' that Drizzt Do'Urden'd've carved yerself into little monk bits."

"So now I'm supposed to forgive him?" Afafrenfere asked incredulously. "Forgive the fiend who killed Parbid? And I am supposed to forgive you, the traitor, the fake shade? You expect me to change my skin color and pretend that none of that happened?"

"If ye're smart, ye'll be trying to forget the whole o' that last three years," Ambergris replied.

Afafrenfere took a threatening step toward her, but the powerful dwarf didn't back away an inch, and didn't blink.

"Look, boy," she said, waggling a thick finger in Afafrenfere's scowling face, "and while ye're looking, look into yer heart. Ye was never of that dark bunch, not as kin or kind. And ye're knowin' it. Ye might not be no paladin-monk, like them others o' Yellow Rose, but nor are ye any gray-skinned assassin, killin' yer own at the demands o' them Netheril dogs."

"He killed Parbid!" Afafrenfere yelled, and Ambergris was glad to hear that argument alone, for it confirmed her suspicions nicely.

"Parbid attacked him and got what most attackin' that particular drow are sure to be gettin'," Ambergris snarled right back, and now she went up on her toes and put her fat nose right against Afafrenfere's as she spoke. "Are ye holdin' a blood feud against one who did no more than defend himself from yer own attack?"

Afafrenfere straightened a bit, moving his face away, but Ambergris pursued stubbornly.

"Well, are ye? Are ye really that stupid? Are ye really that ready and eager to die?"

"Oh, fie!" Afafrenfere wailed, throwing his forearm across his eyes as he turned away.

"And don't ye give me none o' them Afafrenfere dramatics!" the dwarf scolded. "I got no time for 'em!"

Afafrenfere turned on her, scowling more than ever.

"Good enough then!" the dwarf roared, and she stomped her booted foot on the cobblestones. "Ye wantin' a gate to the Shadowfell and I'll make ye one, and good enough for ye, and on yer word alone that ye won't be rattin' me out to Cavus Dun or any others."

That had Afafrenfere off-balance, obviously. "Send me back?" he asked rather sheepishly.

"Not soundin' like music to ye, is it?" the dwarf pressed. "Now that yer Parbid's dead, what grayskin's to stand beside ye, human?"

Afafrenfere swallowed hard.

"Ye ne'er was o' that place," Ambergris said quietly. "Quit lying to yerself the way ye're lyin' to me. Harder to do that, ye know. Ye never wanted to go to the Shadowfell. Ye never was one o' them, and ye're likin' yer skin lighter than darker."

"You presume much."

"Be glad that I do, for if I didn't, I'd've tossed ye into the primordial's mouth behind Glorfathel," Ambergris replied, and now she was grinning widely, for she knew that she had won, that her presumptions had been correct. For all her threats and bluster, Ambergris truly liked this overly-dramatic, high-prancing young monk. Wherever love, or passion, or confusion, or whatever it was, had led him, Afafrenfere was not a bad sort. He could do a dirty deed if he had to, but it wasn't the course of first choice for him, as it would have to be were he to survive among the hoodlums and murderers of Cavus Dun.

"I wish you had," a third voice replied, and the two turned to see the approach of Artemis Entreri.

"You were listening to our private conversation?" Afafrenfere accused.

"Oh, shut up," the assassin replied. "Half the damned city was listening, no doubt, and I would be quite grateful if you held such conversations truly in private. I have little desire to remind the folk of Neverwinter of my own origins."

"How grateful?" the dwarf asked, rolling her fingers eagerly.

"Grateful enough to let you both live," Entreri replied.

Maybe it was a joke.

Maybe.

"Where is Drizzt?" Entreri asked.

"Went out this morning with Dahlia," Amber replied.

"Bound for?"

The dwarf shrugged. "Said he'd be back for dinner."

Entreri glanced up at the sky, the sun already nearing its zenith. Then he swiveled about to regard the port, several tall ships bobbing out in the harbor beyond where the river spilled into the Sword Coast.

"Ye're leaving us, then?" the dwarf asked.

"Do have a fine journey," Afafrenfere added, his tone both sarcastic and hopeful.

Entreri stared at him for a moment, locking the monk's gaze with the intimidating expression that had sent so many potential enemies scurrying for dark holes.

But Brother Afafrenfere did not shy from that look, and met it with one equally resolute.

That brought a wicked smile to the face of Artemis Entreri.

"Ah, but ain't we got enough enemies to fight already?" Amber asked, but the two continued to stare at each other, and both continued to smile.

"Tell Drizzt to find me if he can when he returns," Entreri instructed. "Perhaps I will still be within the city, perhaps not."

"And where might ye be if not in Neverwinter?" Amber asked.

"Were that any of your concern, you would already know," Entreri said, and he turned and walked away.

Drizzt allowed himself some space from Dahlia as they wove their way through the forest, his emotions still reeling from their troubling conversation. Dahlia pressed ahead, eager for some tangible enemy, some way to free her anger. She didn't waste a look back a Drizzt, he noted, and he understood that she did not wish to peel the scab from her emotional wound. He had hit her hard with his discussion of Effron, the twisted tiefling. He had pried her tale from her, but perhaps, he now realized, she had not been ready to divulge it.

Or worse, perhaps Dahlia needed something from him that he didn't know how to give.

Drizzt felt very alone at that moment, more so than at any point since Bruenor's death. Dahlia was more distant, quite possibly forevermore, and Drizzt couldn't even call upon that one companion he had known and counted on since the day he'd left Menzoberranzan.

With that troubling thought in mind, the drow dropped his hand into his belt pouch and brought forth the magical figurine. He lifted it up before his eyes and stared into the miniature face of Guenhwyvar—loyal Guenhwyvar, who would not come to his call any longer.

Without even really thinking about it, he called softly to the cat, "Guenhwyvar, come to me."

He stared helplessly at the figurine, feeling the loss profoundly yet again, and so entranced was he that he didn't even notice the gray mist gathering nearby for many heartbeats, so many indeed, that Guenhwyvar was nearly fully formed beside him before he even noted her presence!

And she was there beside him then, fully so. Drizzt fell to his knees and wrapped her in a great hug, calling her name repeatedly. The panther nuzzled back against him, replying in kind as only she could.

"Where have you been?" Drizzt asked. "Guen, how I've needed you! How I need you now!"

It took him a long while to calm down enough to yell out, "Dahlia!" He feared that she'd gone beyond earshot.

His fears proved unfounded, though, for Dahlia came rushing back through the underbrush to his call, her weapon at the ready. She relaxed immediately when she came through the last line, to see Drizzt and the panther together once more.

"How?" she asked.

Drizzt just looked at her and shrugged. "I called to her and she came to me. Whatever magic was hindering her must have dissipated, or perhaps a tear in the fabric between the planes has repaired itself?"

Dahlia bent low, stroking Guen's muscular flank. "It's good to have her back."

Drizzt answered with a smile, and the warmth of that expression only grew as he considered Dahlia stroking the cat's soft fur. There was serenity on her too-often troubled face, a genuine warmth and kindness. This was the Dahlia that Drizzt wished for as a companion. This was the Dahlia he could care for—perhaps even love.

For some reason, he thought of Catti-brie, then, and in his mind's eye, he interposed his memory of his dead wife with the image of Dahlia before him.

"So we do not need to find the seer," Dahlia reasoned.

"So it would seem," Drizzt agreed and he continued to brush and hug Guenhwyvar.

"Well, send the cat off on the hunt, then," Dahlia proposed, her voice and her expression going chilly. "I'm tired of this walking already. Let's find the goblin killer and be done with this adventure."

The suggestion, reasonable as it seemed, rang out like a broken bell in Drizzt's heart. He wasn't about to separate from Guenhwyvar if he could help it. And more than that, Dahlia's tone struck him badly. She didn't think of this hunt in the forest south of Neverwinter as any grand or important adventure. She was up for a fight—when was she not?—but that was purely for selfish reasons: the need to let free her rage, or more goblin ears for coin. For personal gain of one sort or another.

Like their lovemaking, he mused. Earlier he had pondered that he was using Dahlia, but was that insincerity not mutual?

The safety of the road, the betterment of those around her . . . these emotions did not resonate within Dahlia's scarred heart. Not to any great degree, at least, and certainly not enough for Drizzt to see her in the same light in which he had once viewed his beloved Catti-brie.

He looked up at the sky.

"Night draws near," he said. "If we hunt a vampire as you suspect, we're better off meeting it in daylight." He looked back at Guen and scratched her neck. "We'll return here tomorrow morning."

Dahlia looked at him skeptically for just a moment and seemed ready to argue their course. But then she replied, as if in epiphany, "You fear that you will have to dismiss the cat to her home and will again have trouble recalling her."

Drizzt didn't argue the point. "Can you give me this much at least?" he pleaded.

His question seemed to hit the elf woman hard. She held out her hand to him, and when he took it, Dahlia pulled him to his feet and crushed him in a hug, whispering, "Of course," into his ear over and over again.

And there was desperation in her tone, Drizzt knew, and he knew, too, that he really didn't know how to react.

She was, yet again, not the person he had just decided she was.

CHAPTER

2

PETTY PERSONAL STRUGGLES

T HE YOUNG TIEFLING CREPT THROUGH DRAYGO QUICK'S RESIDENCE. HE knew that the Netherese lord was out at a gathering of his peers, but having lived in the residence for all of these years, Effron also understood that Draygo didn't have to be here to keep the place well-guarded, both with magical wards and with capable and dangerous underlings.

He fell against a wall and held his breath, hearing the conversation of a pair of warlocks. He recognized the voices and knew these two as his peers in age, though surely not in ability. If it came down to a fight, Effron was confident that he could defeat both with little trouble.

But where would that leave him with Draygo Quick?

Panicked by that thought, the young warlock glanced around for some hiding place or avenue of escape. But he was in a long and bending corridor with few side rooms, all private chambers, and thus all likely locked or warded. Fleeing back the way he had come would cost him too much time.

His indecision made the choice for him, as he came to realize that trying to scamper away now wouldn't get him far enough ahead to remain out of sight. The warlocks were too close.

So he stepped out and openly approached them, as if nothing were amiss.

They both nodded and continued their conversation, one pausing in his discussion to remark to Effron, "Lord Draygo is not in residence."

"Ah," Effron replied "Do you know when he will return?"

The two looked to each other and shrugged in unison.

"I will leave him a note," Effron said. "If you see him, pray tell him that I wish to speak with him."

They nodded and continued on their way, and Effron breathed a sigh of relief. Obviously, Draygo Quick had not informed the residents of the falling out, or of Draygo's dismissal of Effron from his tutelage.

His relief was short-lived, though, for his instructions to the young apprentices would of course reveal to Draygo Quick that he had been in the residence. He could likely talk his way out of that indiscretion if Draygo Quick confronted him, but he had come here to steal something, after all, and now that plan seemed perfectly suicidal.

He pressed on anyway, trying to sort it out as he went, rushing through the main room of the keep, a vast foyer with a checkerboard black-and-white tiled floor. He crossed from there into the main library, a room of potions and an alchemical workbench and a distillery, and from there to the wide curving stairs encircling the castle's main tower.

Many steps later, Effron paused at Draygo Quick's private door. He knew the password to get safely beyond the magical wards, but knew, too, that if Draygo Quick had bothered to change that password, the glyphs would almost surely burn through all of the magical defenses Effron had erected upon himself. How meager his counter-measures would be against the bared power of Draygo Quick!

He almost threw up his hands in defeat then, but just growled out the expected password and stubbornly pushed through the door.

He didn't melt.

Surprised, relieved, shocked even, Effron collected his thoughts and closed the door behind him, then rushed into the adjoining room, Draygo Quick's vaunted menagerie.

The cage was in place upon the pedestal, under the silken cloth, as he had expected, but the bars were not glowing with power and the cage was empty.

Effron bent low and peered around the bars, unable to comprehend the sight before him. Had the panther escaped? How could that be?

And who might have released the magical bindings of the cage?

Effron held his breath and stood up fast, spinning, his broken arm flying around him like a scarf in a gale. He expected to see a six-hundred-pound, angry black panther standing right behind him.

It took him many minutes of scanning the room, his gaze piercing the shadows, before he was able to relax in the confidence that he was indeed alone. He moved to one of the grand cabinets along the wall and gingerly opened it, brushing aside the mist and examining the many bottles on the shelves within. Each contained a tiny representation of some powerful monster, which were, in fact, the bodies of those actual creatures in miniaturized stasis. Effron himself had sorted these items and kept them cleaned, as per his duties for Draygo Quick, and so he recognized immediately that nothing was amiss and no new additions had been made.

He closed the cabinet and turned back to the empty cage, soberly now, and tried to wrap his thoughts around this unexpected turn. Where had the cat gone? A myriad of possibilities rushed through Effron's mind, but only two seemed plausible: Either the panther had been handed back to Drizzt Do'Urden in some bargain concocted by Draygo Quick, or the cat had been slain, or had died of its own accord, perhaps due to the severance of the connection to the Astral Plane.

It took him many heartbeats to steel himself against the implications of both of those possibilities. Either way, he had likely forever lost a valuable tool in his quest to confront and kill his mother.

He thought back to the previous day, when he had watched the Shifter approach Draygo's residence with an elderly Toril man in tow. He had thought then that the visit concerned the panther, and this seemed to confirm it.

"A druid," he muttered under his breath, considering again the dress of the human accompanying the Shifter.

He looked at the empty cage. So what, exactly, had this druid done?

Effron realized then that he had to move quickly. Draygo Quick would learn of his visit, obviously, and the withered old warlock wasn't known for his merciful tendencies. The tiefling was out of the castle in short order, not even bothering to hide from any of the other residents he passed along the way. When he crossed the courtyard and exited the great gates surrounding Castle Quick, Effron couldn't deny the wave of relief that washed over him. He had called this place his home for many years, but now it brought him only dread.

But where to go? He thought that perhaps he should just head to Toril, out of the realm of shadows, and begin the hunt, though he had certainly counted upon having the panther as a bargaining tool. Should he just try anyway, without the cat, and pretend as if none of this mattered?

As with his choices regarding the two approaching warlocks in the hallway, and because of that very encounter, it came clear to him that the decision had already been made.

Draygo Quick would find him, wherever he chose to go.

Information alone would save him, Effron decided, so he set out with all speed to find that most elusive of Shadovar.

She was waiting for him, sitting on a bench set out in front of her modest home, amid her black-petal roses and dull flox. A small fountain sat off to the side of her, the water playing a rather entrancing tune.

Effron didn't ever remember hearing the water song before and wondered if this was an added guard or deception put forth by the Shifter.

He looked at her—at the image of her that was probably not her—as he approached.

"It took you longer than I expected," she greeted him. "Draygo Quick's home is not so far, after all."

"Draygo Quick's home?"

"You just came from there," the Shifter answered smugly.

Effron started to protest, but the woman's smirk mocked him to silence.

"Were you going to steal her, or simply try to harm her that you might harm Lord Draygo by extension?"

"I do not know of what you speak."

"And I am sure that you do. So where does that leave us? At the end of our conversation, I expect, so please leave."

Effron felt as if the ground was rising up about him to swallow him where he stood. He desperately needed to speak to the Shifter, but her tone had left little room for debate.

"Where is the panther?" he pressed.

"I just told you to leave," came her voice from the side, and the image before him shimmered to nothingness, a not-so-subtle reminder that she could strike at him from any angle she chose.

Effron brought his good hand to his face, feeling so very small and so very over his head at that terrible moment. He had thought himself clever, and daring even, for going into Draygo Quick's private residence uninvited, and yet even this person watching from the side had him all figured out. If that was the case, how could he possibly avoid the falling axe of Draygo Quick's judgment?

"You are still here," the Shifter remarked, now from the other side.

"To steal her," Effron admitted. A long silence ensued. Effron dared not speak further, and dared not move.

"Say that again," the Shifter demanded, and Effron looked up to see her sitting comfortably on the bench once more.

"To steal her," he admitted.

"You would dare to so betray Draygo Quick?"

"I had no choice," Effron replied, his voice taking on a tone of desperation. "I have to get to her—do you not understand?—and I cannot hope to fight my way through her growing number of allies!"

The image of the Shifter looked over to Effron's left, and he turned his head just in time to see a pouch flying through the air, moving back behind him. He spun with it, to see the Shifter, now appearing behind him, catch the purse. Effron spun back around to see her sitting on the bench once more, jingling the coins.

"You had every choice," Draygo Quick remarked, coming out of the brush to the left, first in wraithform, then quickly becoming fully three-dimensional.

"Master," Effron breathed and he bowed his head. He thought that he should fall to his knees and beg for mercy then, though it would surely prove futile. He was caught, by his own admission, and there seemed no road to freedom before him.

"Thank you," Draygo Quick said to the Shifter.

"My work is done here?" she asked.

Draygo nodded.

"Then please get this broken creature far from my home," the Shifter said.

Effron looked at her, his expression revealing that he was truly wounded by her harsh words. For he had hired her and paid her well, after all, even when she had failed him.

She returned the look with a helpless shrug, then simply vanished.

"Walk with me," Draygo Quick bade him, and the old warlock started along the swampy road toward his home.

Effron fell in line, obediently behind him, until Draygo Quick waved him up.

"You actually believed that you could walk into my house and steal something as valuable as Guenhwyvar?"

"Borrow, not steal," Effron replied.

"You would trade her to the drow to get him away from Dahlia," Draygo Quick reasoned.

"I meant to threaten the drow with her destruction if he did not move aside and remain aside," Effron replied.

"Did not the Shifter do exactly that in the tunnel outside of Gauntlgrym?" asked the old warlock. "And to no avail?"

"It would be different, I expect, if the one holding the cat had the means and intent to kill her before Drizzt Do'Urden's very eyes."

"So that was your plan?"

Effron nodded and Draygo Quick laughed at him.

"You do not understand this Drizzt Do'Urden creature."

"I have to try."

"Guenhwyvar is beside him at this time," Draygo Quick explained.

Effron's eyes went wide. "You gave her back to him? He murdered my father! He and his friends defeated us at Gauntlgrym! And before that, in Neverwinter! They destroyed the sword! You would reward an avowed enemy of the Empire of Netheril?"

"You presume much."

The calm tenor of Draygo Quick's voice stole Effron's bluster.

The old warlock stopped and turned to face his former student directly. "The panther is my spy within Drizzt's group," he said. "I should like that to continue. In fact, I insist upon it."

"Spy?"

"I know that you intend to go after Dahlia. I cannot stop that, foolish as it seems, but perhaps I was too hard on you. There are forces at play within your heart that are beyond my comprehension, and so I forgive you this transgression."

Effron nearly fell over with relief, and shock.

"But I tell you this in strictest confidence, and on penalty of a most horrible death should you ever reveal a word of it," Draygo Quick said. "Drizzt Do'Urden is a curiosity, and perhaps much more than that, and I intend to find out. He among others might well provide us with clues to important events that will affect the whole of the empire, and indeed, of the Shadowfell itself. I offer you one more chance, foolish young warlock. Abandon your quest to find your revenge against Dahlia at this time—perhaps in the future, if she separates from Drizzt Do'Urden, I will even assist you in destroying her. But not now. The issue before us is too important for petty personal struggles."

"You gave me permission to hunt her," Effron quietly protested.

"I dismissed you out of hand, and cared not," Draygo Quick replied without hesitation. "And now I have more information, and so I rescind that dismissal. You are my understudy once more. I should expect some gratitude that I have forgiven you."

Effron wanted to scream at him, or just yell out in unfocused frustration. He wanted to deny the old wretch and demand that he would no longer serve in Draygo Quick's residence.

He wanted to, but he hadn't the heart or the courage. In that event, he had little doubt that Draygo Quick would obliterate him then and there.

Furthering that sense of dread, Draygo Quick stared at him with that intense, withering glare, and Effron bowed his head and said, "Thank you, Master."

The warlock chuckled victoriously, each wheezing laugh mocking Effron. "Come back and to your work," he said. "You have much to do to regain my respect."

That alone stung profoundly, but then Draygo Quick grabbed him roughly by the chin and forced Effron to look him directly in the eye—and how wild those eyes looked to Effron!

"Understand me in no uncertain terms, young and foolish Effron Alegni: If you harm the drow ranger in any way, I will completely and utterly destroy you, and I will do so in such a manner that you will beg me for your death for many tendays before I finally allow it."

Effron didn't begin to try to pull away, as painful as Draygo Quick's surprisingly strong grip proved, for he could well imagine a plethora of things Draygo Quick might do to make him hurt a lot worse.

"This is too important for petty personal issues," the old warlock reiterated. "You do understand me, and are we agreed?"

"Yes, Master," Effron squeaked.

Draygo Quick let him go and began walking again, but when Effron started out beside him, the old warlock held out his arm and pushed Effron back.

Two steps behind.

CHAPTER 3

MOONLIGHT

D RIZZT HELD THE STATUETTE UP BEFORE HIS EYES, STARING AT IT WITH trepidation. He hadn't wanted to dismiss Guenhwyvar the previous night, fearing that her arrival had been an anomaly, and one not to be repeated. But the cat had appeared haggard to him, and she had needed rest.

The sun had not yet risen outside the window of his room in Neverwinter, and he had dismissed the cat long after sundown the previous day.

But despite the short time, he had to try to call her again.

"Guenhwyvar," he whispered.

On the bed behind him, Dahlia stirred but did not awaken.

"Guenhwyvar."

Even in the darkened room, Drizzt could see the gray mist rising around him, and could feel the presence of Guenhwyvar growing. In the span a few heartbeats, though it seemed like a long while to Drizzt, she was there again, right beside him. The drow wrapped her in a hug, overjoyed. He needed her now, perhaps more than at any time since he'd walked with her out of Menzoberranzan those many decades before.

He hugged her closer, his head against her flank.

He noted her ragged breathing.

Too soon, he realized, and he silently berated himself for his impatience. "Be gone," he whispered into her ear. "I will call you again soon."

The cat obeyed, pacing in a circle and diminishing fast to insubstantial mist, then to nothing at all.

Drizzt started for the bed where Dahlia lay, but changed his mind and went to the window instead. He took a seat and looked out over the city of Neverwinter, still a shadow of what it had been. But the settlers were industrious and determined to rebuild Neverwinter from the ashes of the cataclysm.

41

Drizzt fed off that thought, determined to rebuild his own life. He reflexively glanced at Dahlia as he considered that. Would she be a part of that? She was an elf, and young, and surely would outlive Drizzt unless an enemy's blade cut her down. Would she walk beside Drizzt for the rest of his days?

He couldn't know.

He turned back to the darkened city and thought of his other three companions, and he couldn't help but consider them in light of the four friends he once traveled beside.

Would any of this group measure up to the standards, the character, of any of the Companions of the Hall?

The question stung the drow. Surely in terms of skill, with blade or fist or even magic, the group around him had proven their capabilities. Were these four to battle the previous four companions he had known, the victor would be long in doubt.

But that hardly mattered, Drizzt understood, for the more important measurement was one of morality, of purpose.

In that regard . . .

Drizzt sighed and began to rise, thinking to return to his bed and Dahlia's side. He changed his mind and remained at the window instead. He fell asleep in the chair, staring out at the city of Neverwinter, rising from the ashes, for the sight brought him comfort and hope.

"Ye best be gettin' him out o' the city if ye're wanting to keep him beside us," Ambergris told Drizzt later that morning in the common room of the inn. The night had been cold, and the chill had found its way inside, so Ambergris threw another log on the fire.

"Soon," Drizzt assured her.

"Boats're putting out for the south every day," Ambergris warned.

The drow nodded absently as he stared into the flames.

"Ye got him anxious, though I'm not for knowin' how, but ye understand that one well enough to know that puttin' him on the edge isn't to hold for long, at least not in the direction ye're hopin'!"

Drizzt nodded again and wasn't about to argue with the perceptive dwarf's reasoning. He had teased Artemis Entreri with the promise of his jeweled dagger, but delays would likely turn intrigue into anger.

An angry Artemis Entreri was not among the goals of Drizzt Do'Urden. "Today," he heard himself telling Amber before he even considered the promise. "We'll head out today."

He would forego his planned visit with Arunika, he decided then, for with Guenhwyvar back at his side, he did not need to seek her out. But he could not as easily turn away from the intriguing mystery they had discovered southeast of the city. He pictured the destroyed goblin encampment once more, the marks on one throat Dahlia had attributed to a vampire, the carnage at the tent he believed a trademark of another type of foe. Dahlia had insisted that they go back out in pursuit of the goblin killer, her eagerness for the hunt only increasing as the night had deepened.

The elf woman entered the common room then, her expression revealing that she had not appreciated waking up alone in her bed.

"When the others come down, find me in the square outside the market and we'll set a rendezvous point north of the city," Drizzt instructed the dwarf. He grabbed a couple of morningfeast buns from the tray set out and met Dahlia before she had crossed half the room.

"Be quick," Drizzt said to her. "The merchants are unfolding their wares, and we might find our best bargain if we are first to the kiosks."

Dahlia looked at him curiously.

"Our time grows short," Drizzt explained. "Let's find your vampire."

Dahlia stood staring at Drizzt with hands on hips. He understood her confusion, for on their return trip to the city the previous night, when she had concocted the idea of purchasing some magical assistance to seek out a vampire, Drizzt had openly doubted her, had even ridiculed her a bit.

Drizzt merely returned her doubting look with a nod, tossed her a small pouch of coins, and headed out of the inn.

Within the hour, Andahar the unicorn thundered along the eastern road out of Neverwinter, heading into the rising sun, easily bearing Drizzt and Dahlia.

At Dahlia's bidding, Drizzt slowed the pace a bit. He glanced back at the woman, and at the curious, softly-glowing wand she pointed off at the forest to their right.

"There," she said, nudging the wand toward the trees.

"So you trust in the merchant's words and believe that wand?"

"I paid good gold for it."

"Foolishly," Drizzt muttered under his breath, but merely to lighten the mood. It had been his coin, after all.

He turned Andahar aside and began trotting off across the small field leading to the tree line. The wand, so the merchant had explained, was imbued with a dweomer to detect undead creatures, of which there had been no shortage of late in this area, since Sylora had created the vile Dread Ring.

Drizzt pulled Andahar to a stop and swung around to regard Dahlia directly, though she hardly seemed to note his glance, so intent was she upon the wand.

"Why is this suddenly so important to you?" Drizzt asked.

A startled Dahlia looked up at him. She paused for a few heartbeats before responding, "You think that letting a vampire run free is the valiant act of a good citizen?"

"The forest is full of danger, with or without a vampire."

"So Drizzt Do'Urden wishes to leave such a stone unturned?" Dahlia quipped. "And here I was under the impression that you were a hero."

Drizzt put on a smirk, and was glad that Dahlia was verbally jousting in such a playful manner. There were times when Dahlia hinted that there could be much more between them, times when Drizzt dared hope that he could mold these new companions into a band worthy of his memories.

Dahlia's expression changed abruptly.

"Indulge me," Dahlia pleaded, in all seriousness.

"You think it's your old companion?"

"Dor'crae?" Dahlia blurted, and her surprise was genuine, Drizzt could tell. "Hardly. I destroyed him, utterly and gladly! Don't you remember?"

Drizzt did remember, of course. Dahlia had battled Dor'crae, the dying dwarves beside them. She had driven him from the antechamber, already mortally wounded, only to fly under the deluge of the water elementals re-entering the primordial pit in Gauntlgrym. Under the assault of the rushing, magical waters, the vampire had seemingly been obliterated.

So it wasn't the thought of Dor'crae driving Dahlia, he then understood, and he suspected another angle to Dahlia's desire to see this through. Perhaps she believed that this Effron creature, her son, was behind the attack.

He found that he couldn't follow his own thoughts down that road, however, given the reminder of Dor'crae's last moments—for indeed, how could Drizzt ever forget that awful moment when he had come across the pit and into the antechamber to find his friends dead or dying beside Gauntlgrym's all-important lever?

"Then it cannot be him, and we should . . ." Drizzt started to say, but his eyes widened as he considered the scene at the lever immediately following the demise of Dor'crae. He recalled Bruenor's last words to him, sweet and sad and forever echoing in his mind, of Bruenor fast dying, the light leaving his gray eyes, and of Thibbledorf Pwent . . .

Thibbledorf Pwent.

Drizzt thought of the torn tent in the goblin camp, the recognizable carnage. Vampire or battlerager, he and Dahlia had debated.

All of those nagging thoughts coalesced, and Drizzt had his answer. He was right in his guess, and so was Dahlia.

Without another word, he turned around and urged Andahar forward.

"Thank you," she whispered in his ear, but she needn't have, for if he had been alone, Drizzt would have taken this very same course.

They slowed when they entered the tree line, Drizzt picking his way carefully through the trees and tangled branches. They had barely entered the thicket when Dahlia's wand glowed brighter and a wisp of blue-gray fog reached out from it, wafting into the forest before them.

"Well, that is interesting," Drizzt remarked.

"Follow it," Dahlia instructed.

The foggy coil continued to reach out before them like a rope, guiding their way through the trees. They came past a stand of oaks, and near what they thought to be a boulder.

Andahar pulled up suddenly and snorted, and Drizzt gasped in alarm, for it was no rock before them, but a large and strange beast, a blended concoction of magic run afoul.

Part bear. Part fowl.

"So we go north," Afafrenfere remarked. "You know this place?"

Artemis Entreri tossed his full sack over the back of the saddle and leaped astride his nightmare. "Only an hour's ride up the road," he explained.

"Aye, and me friend here can run like no other," Ambergris said. "But with me short legs, I'm thinkin' I best be riding."

Entreri nodded, then merely walked his mount away and said over his shoulder, "A pity you've got no horse then, or pig."

Ambergris put her hands on her hips and stared up at the man. "It'll be takin' us longer to get there, then," she said.

"No, it will take you longer," Entreri corrected, and he kicked his mount into movement and leaped away, charging out Neverwinter's northern gate.

Brother Afafrenfere snorted and chuckled helplessly.

"Aye," Ambergris agreed. "If I had a better road afore me, I'd be walkin' away."

"Better than . . . what?" the monk asked. "Do we even know what adventure Drizzt might have planned for us?"

"We need to be keepin' him close," Ambergris explained. "Dahlia, and aye, that one, too," she said, nodding toward the now-distant Entreri. "If Lord Draygo or Cavus Dun comes a'huntin', I'll be wantin' the blades o' them three between me and the shades."

Afafrenfere considered her words for a few moments, then nodded and started toward the northern gate.

"Don't ye outrun me," the dwarf warned. "Or I'll put a spell on ye and leave ye held and helpless in the forest."

The reminder of the unexpected assault in the bowels of Gauntlgrym had Afafrenfere turning around, glowering at the dwarf. "That worked once," he replied, "but not again. Never again."

Ambergris laughed heartily as she came up beside him. "Best spell what e'er found ye, boy," she said. "For now ye've got a finer life ahead o' ye! A life of adventure, don't ye doubt. A life o' battle."

"Aye, and probably a life of battling my own companions," he said dryly, and Ambergris laughed all the harder.

***

That beast, an owlbear, didn't rise up to meet them, and Drizzt calmed quickly, recognizing that it was quite dead.

"Well now," Dahlia said, sliding down from the unicorn's back to stand beside the slain behemoth. And it was a behemoth, as large as a great brown bear, but with the head and powerful beak of an owl atop those powerful ursine shoulders.

"Indeed," Drizzt agreed as he slid down.

Dahlia bent low beside the beast, ruffling the fur—the bloody fur—around its neck. "I expect that we've found our vampire's most recent kill."

"A vampire killed an owlbear?" Drizzt asked skeptically and he, too, bent low and began inspecting the corpse, but not its neck.

"So you admit that it was a vampire?" As she asked, Dahlia used both hands to pull the beast's thick fur aside, to reveal the canine puncture wounds.

"So it would seem," Drizzt replied. "And yet—" He put his shoulder to the owlbear and nudged it over just a bit, then similarly parted the fur, to reveal a larger hole, a much deeper puncture. "I know this wound as well."

"Do tell."

"A helmet spike," Drizzt could hardly get the words out. He thought again of the grisly scene beside the lever, thought of Pwent.

"Perhaps a vampire and a battlerager are working together?"

"A dwarf allied with a vampire?" Drizzt asked doubtfully. He had another explanation, but one he wasn't ready to share.

"Athrogate traveled beside Dor'crae."

"Athrogate is a mercenary," Drizzt said, shaking his head. This wasn't just any battlerager he was considering. "Battleragers are loyal soldiers, not mercenaries."

Dahlia stood and pointed her wand toward the forest once more. The mist reappeared and snaked away through the trees.

"Well, let's find out what's going on, then," Dahlia said.

Drizzt dismissed Andahar and they moved into the forest on foot. For many hours they searched fruitlessly, Dahlia expending charge after charge of her wand. Many times, Drizzt put his hand to his belt pouch, but he knew that he shouldn't bring in Guen, not for another day at least.

"If we wait until nightfall, perhaps the vampire will find us," Dahlia remarked later on, and only then did Drizzt realize that the sun had already passed its zenith and was moving lower in the west. He considered Dahlia's words and the thought did not sit well with him. Guenhwyvar would be with them in the morning, and she would find their prey.

So intrigued had Drizzt been by the possibilities swirling before him that he had forgotten one other detail of the day's plans. He looked to the north, where their three companions waited, at his request. Artemis Entreri would not be pleased.

"Where to now?" Dahlia asked.

Drizzt turned back to the west. They were too far out, having passed into reaches of the forest that neither of them knew. "Back to Neverwinter," the drow decided.

"You would leave Entreri and the others out alone in the forest with a vampire about?"

"If we're not at their camp by twilight, they'll return to the city," Drizzt said absently. He could not focus on the others. This hunt, so suddenly, was more important. "Vampire. . . ." Dahlia said again, ominously.

"We will find it tomorrow."

"You indulge me," Dahlia remarked. "I like that."

Drizzt didn't bother to explain his own interests, particularly when Dahlia moved closer, wearing an impish grin.

"Vampire," she said again with a wide smile, her eyes sparkling.

Drizzt considered that grin, and wanted to share in her mirth at that moment, but found it impossible, for he was too troubled by the possibilities.

Dahlia moved right in front of him and casually draped her arms around his shoulders, putting her face very close to his. "No argument this time?" she asked quietly.

Drizzt managed a chuckle.

"Vampire," she said and her smile turned in a lewd direction. She shifted to the side and lunged for his throat, biting him playfully on the neck.

"Still no argument?" she asked and she bit him again, a bit harder.

"You are hoping for a vampire, I can see," Drizzt replied, and it was hard for him to keep his thoughts straight at that particular moment. It was the first time they had touched, other than riding, since they'd left the darkness of Gauntlgrym. "I would hate to disavow you of your wishes."

Dahlia moved back to stare him in the eye. "Hoping?"

"Hoping to be one, then," Drizzt said, "apparently."

Dahlia, laughing, hugged him close. She brought her lips to his ear and kissed him softly, then asked, "Have you forgiven me?"

Drizzt pushed her back to arms' length and studied her face. He couldn't deny his attraction to her, particularly when she wore her hair in this softer style, and with the war woad barely visible.

"I had nothing to forgive."

"My kiss with Entreri?" Dahlia asked. "Your jealousy?"

"It was the sword, playing on my insecurities, pressing my imagination to dark places."

"Are you sure that's all it was?" she asked, and she reached over and brushed Drizzt's long white hair from in front of his face. "Perhaps the sword was only exploiting that which it saw within you."

Drizzt was shaking his head before she had ever finished. "There's nothing to forgive," he repeated.

He almost added, "Have you forgiven yourself?" but he wisely held that thought, not wanting to open anew the wound inflicted by the appearance of the young and twisted warlock.

"Let's go to Neverwinter," Drizzt said, but now Dahlia was shaking her head.

"Not yet," she explained, and she led him to a mossy bed.

Dahlia tapped Drizzt on the arm and when he looked up from his bowl of stew, nodded toward the tavern door.

Drizzt was not surprised to see the three enter, nor was he caught off guard by Artemis Entreri's dour expression. When the assassin noticed him, he led the other two straight through the crowd to the table.

"Winter fast approaches," Entreri said, pulling up a chair across from Drizzt.

"The night is cold," he added when Drizzt didn't respond.

"Good, then, that you decided to return to the city," the drow replied casually.

"Oh, grand," Afafrenfere remarked to Ambergris off to the side. "I will so enjoy watching these two beat each other to death."

The dwarf snorted.

Drizzt, seeming unbothered by it all, went back to his stew, or tried to until Entreri's hand snapped across the table and grabbed him roughly by the wrist.

The drow lifted his gaze slowly to regard the man.

"I don't appreciate being left in a cold forest," Entreri said evenly.

"We got lost," Drizzt replied.

"How could you get lost?" Entreri asked. "You were the one who named the place of rendezvous."

"Our road took us to the east, to unfamiliar ground," Dahlia interjected.

"What road?" asked Entreri, still staring at Drizzt.

Drizzt sat back in his chair as Entreri let go of his wrist. The drow glanced to the side and motioned to the other two to take a seat. He wondered where he should take this. He was pretty certain now who and what Dahlia and he were hunting. The question was: Did he want Artemis Entreri along on that hunt? The encounter, should it happen, was going to be difficult enough to control as it was, and how much more difficult would it become with the unpredictable and merciless Artemis Entreri in the mix?

"What is your plan, drow?" Entreri asked.

All four of the others, even Dahlia, looked to him for exactly that answer, and it was a good question.

"You escorted me to the bowels of Gauntlgrym to be rid of that cursed sword," Entreri said. "For that, I owe you."

Entreri looked to Dahlia, pointedly so. "Or *owed* you," he clarified. "But no more. I waited where you asked, and you did not arrive."

"A great sacrifice," Dahlia said sarcastically.

Afafrenfere giggled and Ambergris snorted.

Entreri turned his gaze from Dahlia to the other two before settling back on Drizzt.

"You owed me nothing," Drizzt answered that look. "Not before and not now."

"Hardly true," said Dahlia.

"To be rid of Herzgo Alegni, to be rid of Charon's Claw"—he paused and looked directly at Dahlia"—to be rid of Sylora Salm—all of these things were good and right. I would have undertaken them had I been alone and the opportunity had come before me."

"Drizzt the hero," Entreri muttered.

The drow shrugged, unwilling to engage the assassin on that level.

Artemis Entreri stared at him a few moments longer, then placed both his hands on the table and pushed himself to his feet. "We do not part as enemies, Drizzt Do'Urden, and that is no small thing," he said. "Well met and farewell."

With a last glance at Dahlia, he turned and walked out of the tavern.

"And where is that leaving us?" Brother Afafrenfere asked Ambergris.

The dwarf looked at Drizzt for an answer. "Which road are ye thinking to be more excitin'?" she asked. "Yer own or Entreri's? For meself, I'm itching for a fight or ten."

"Ten, and ten more after that," Afafrenfere added eagerly.

Drizzt had no answer, and when they looked instead to Dahlia, the elf woman could only shrug.

Drizzt, too, looked at Dahlia, her crestfallen expression stabbing deep into his heart. Not a stab of jealousy, however, and he found that curious.

"Well we're not to solve it here, then," Ambergris declared, and she too leaped up from her seat. "And me belly's grumblin' to be sure!" At the sound of a crashing plate, she looked over to the bar where a band of ruffians began jostling for position.

"House covers the bets," the bartender announced.

"Oh, but I'm startin' to like this Neverwinter place," Ambergris said. "Come along, me friend," she added to Afafrenfere. "Let's go earn a few coins."

She turned to Drizzt and Dahlia and offered an exaggerated wink. "Don't look like much, does he?" she asked, indicating her rather small and scrawny companion. "But bare-fisted, ain't many to be standin' long against him!"

She gave a great laugh.

"We'll be about, if ye find a road worth walkin'!" she said. She glanced back at the bar, where two large men were stripping down to the waist to begin their battle, and where others passed coins and shouted their odds and bets.

"Ye might just find us in the most expensive rooms to be found in the city," Ambergris offered and started away, Afafrenfere in tow. As they left, Drizzt and Dahlia heard the dwarf remark softly to her monk companion, "Now don't ye drop any o' them too quick. Keep the next one hopin' that he can beat ye, that we might be playin' it out for all it's worth."

Dahlia's chuckle turned Drizzt back to her.

"We seem to attract interesting companions," he said.

"Amusing, at least." She immediately sobered after the remark, and gave Drizzt a serious look. "What is our road?"

"Right now? To find our vampire, is it not?"

"Battlerager, you mean."

"That, too."

"And then?"

Drizzt wore a pensive look as he sincerely tried to sort out that very thing.

"Find an answer quickly or we're to lose three companions," Dahlia remarked. "Or two more, for it seems that one is already gone."

Drizzt considered that, but shook his head. The allure of the jeweled dagger would keep Entreri beside him, he believed, for at least a bit longer. Despite Entreri's parting words and obvious anger, Drizzt knew that he could get the man on the road beside him, as long as they started that journey soon.

"You wish to keep them by our side?" Drizzt asked, nodding toward the monk and dwarf.

"The world is full of danger," she replied. She looked past him, then, to a commotion beginning to brew, and she nodded for him to turn around.

There stood Afafrenfere, stripped to the waist, his wily form seeming puny indeed against the giant of a man he faced.

The hulking fighter took a lumbering swing, which the monk easily ducked, and Afafrenfere quietly jabbed the man in the ribs as he did so. A second wild hook by the large man missed badly, and the crowd howled with laughter.

The third punch, though, caught Afafrenfere on the side of the jaw and he went flying to the floor, and the crowd howled again.

"It hardly touched him," Dahlia remarked, and with respect in her voice indicating that she had recognized the monk's feint. Drizzt had seen it as well. Afafrenfere had turned with the blow perfectly, always just ahead of it enough so that it couldn't do any real damage.

The monk got up to his feet, appearing shaky, but as the hulking man fell over him, Afafrenfere found a perfectly balanced stance and tore off a series of sudden and vicious strikes at the man's midsection—again, subtly, in close, and few noticed that the big man leaning over him was too tight with pain to offer any real response.

Afafrenfere slipped out of the hold to the side and struck repeatedly, his open hands slapping against the man's ribs.

"He's pulling his strikes," Drizzt remarked.

"Now don't ye drop any o' them too quick," Dahlia said in a near-perfect Ambergris impression. She ended abruptly, though, and winced, and so did Drizzt, when the big man spun around with a left hook that seemed to come all the way from his ankles, a wild and powerful swing that might have ripped Afafrenfere's head from his shoulders had it actually struck.

But the monk ducked, again so easily, and the fist sailed over him to crash into one of the tavern's support columns so forcefully that the whole of the building shuddered.

And how the big man swooned as he pulled in his broken hand, his eyes crossing, his knees wobbling, and it seemed like he was doing all he could manage to prevent himself from vomiting.

Afafrenfere slipped around to the side of him with great speed, bent low, and spun a circuit on the ball of his right foot. He grasped the bar, planting himself firmly as his lifted left foot set against the large man's back, giving him full balance and brace as he kicked out. He launched the man through the air to crash face first into a table, sending plates and glasses and splintering wood flying, and patrons dancing aside.

The crowd cheered wildly, and even more so when the big man tried to rise and simply fell back to the floor, clutching his smashed hand as he slipped in and out of consciousness.

Jingling coins and sputtered curses, wild cheers and calls for more, filled the air as the tavern took on an even greater festive atmosphere.

And amidst it all, Drizzt and Dahlia focused on Ambergris, pulling forth her holy symbol as she moved to the fallen pugilist. "I'll be fixin' yer hand for ye," she said, and added, "for a few coins."

"Brilliant," Drizzt muttered helplessly, and behind him, Dahlia laughed again.

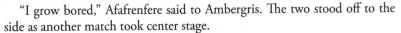

"I grow bored," Afafrenfere said to Ambergris. The two stood off to the side as another match took center stage.

"Bah, not to worry," said the dwarf. "After that last one, I ain't to get anyone to challenge yerself anyway."

As she spoke, a burly man in the current brawl hoisted his opponent up over his head and threw him across the room, to smash down among the chairs and tables.

"More coins for a healer," Ambergris whispered. She started away, but stopped abruptly, considering the victor, who stood with his large arms upraised, roaring and prancing about.

"Might that that one'll want a try at ye," the dwarf said to the monk.

"He is a lumbering fool," Afafrenfere replied.

"Aye, but a proud one."

The monk shrugged.

Soon after Ambergris had cast a healing spell upon the latest loser, Afafrenfere squared up against the large man, who seemed to have a bit of ogre blood, so tall and wide was he.

Of course, that only made him a bigger target.

He came on brazenly, swiping his thick arms across one after the other, while Afafrenfere ducked back, then under, then off to the side.

The cheers began to quiet, shouts of complaint arising as many twists and turns resulted in not a blow being landed.

Afafrenfere kept glancing at Ambergris, who held a bag of coins, for which she could find no takers.

The big man came at him, hands open, and Afafrenfere did not dodge then, but stepped forward and punched the man in the face.

The move cost him dearly, though, as the big man grabbed him around the neck with both hands and lifted him off the ground. Afafrenfere kicked out at him, but so long were the man's arms that the monk couldn't get any solid hits.

He glanced over again at Ambergris, who was arguing with several patrons who were demanding that she honor her offer and place her bets.

The dwarf convincingly argued—too convincingly and for far too long, Afafrenfere thought, as the big man choked him and jerked him side to side like a doll. Finally, Ambergris relented and handed over the coins.

She noted the monk's glance her way and tossed him a wink.

Afafrenfere grabbed the big man's thumbs and held on tight then kicked out at him with both feet but pulled them back in close before they connected. He used the momentum to go right over, lifting his legs above him and thus breaking free of the hold.

He landed back a stride or so, but the big man kept up in pursuit, as Afafrenfere had hoped, and grabbed again at the monk's throat. Before the behemoth could come close and hoist Afafrenfere from the floor again, however, the monk grabbed at his hands, hooked his thumbs under the big man's thumbs and folded his legs under him, dropping straight to the floor.

The big man lurched forward, but before he realized what was happening, the monk landed in a kneeling position and used the momentum of that drop to drive his hands down and over with sudden and brutal force, bending the big man's thumbs back over the large hands.

The dull thud of the monk's knees hitting the floor fast became the sharp crack of finger bones breaking.

The big man made a strange sound, half growl, half howl, and pulled his hands away. Up came the furious monk, leaping forward to strike a quick left and right into the man's face. And up came the broken hands and Afafrenfere came on even harder, letting fly a tremendous right into the man's gut. He staggered back to crash into the back and lurched over, arms crossed over his belly.

Afafrenfere's left hook cracked him across the face, whipping his head to the side. He brought his hands to block, and the monk's tremendous right-handed uppercut hit him in the gut with enough force to lift him off the ground.

Down went the big man's hands and across came Afafrenfere's left hook, again snapping his opponent's head to the side. Up went the man's hands defensively and another uppercut lifted him from his feet.

The devastating cycle repeated a third time, which left the big man out on his feet, his arms just hanging there helplessly. Still angry about the choke hold, Afafrenfere leaned right against the big man and his right hand pumped repeatedly, each blow hoisting the brute from the floor and dropping him back in place.

"Enough!" came a cry from the crowd.

"Aye, ye're to kill him! Enough!" shouted another.

Brother Afafrenfere turned around and put up his hands unthreateningly. He stared into a score of amazed expressions, many shaking their heads in disbelief.

The monk looked at Ambergris and gave a helpless shrug and a crooked grin, and the dwarf, recognizing the intent behind that look, shook her head and grimaced.

Just as Afafrenfere spun a sudden circuit up on his the balls of his feet, coming around with great speed and force, a spinning left hook that chopped the side of the big man's jaw and sent him flipping and flopping over and down, to land heavily flat on his back on the wooden floor.

The whole room seemed to stand in place and time, cheers and jeers and shouts becoming a sudden frozen silence, all eyes locked on this shocking, wiry man with his thunderous hands.

The big man groaned and shifted, showing that he wasn't dead at least, breaking the spell, and several patrons near to Ambergris began shoving the dwarf and yelling. Afafrenfere moved quickly to her side.

"What magic, dwarf?" one man asked.

"None," answered a woman from behind, unexpectedly, and the crowd parted and turned to see a red-haired woman well known in Neverwinter.

Arunika moved up to the dwarf and monk and scrutinized Afafrenfere carefully. She took him by the wrist, and when he didn't object, she turned his arm over, revealing a tattoo of a yellow rose inside his forearm.

She gave a knowing laugh.

"No magic," she said to those others around. "A fair win, though I'd not be betting on this one's opponents."

"Ah, ye gamed us, ye wretched little dwarf!" a particularly dirty patron grumbled.

"Ah, so's yer sister," Ambergris yelled right back at him. "Ye weren't for givin' me a bet, and then yer boy looked to be a winner and ye called me on me coin!"

"Ye set it up that way!" the patron declared.

"I set it up to get the life choked out o' me friend?"

"He's looking alive to me!"

"Aye, but if we're to be agreeing with what ye're sayin', then yer champion there ain't much o' nothin'! Think about it, ye dolt!" As she built momentum, Ambergris moved very near the man and poked her thick finger right in his face, driving him back before her. "Yerself's arguing that I let me boy get himself choked half to death knowin' that he could then break out and pound yer boy to the floor. Says nothing good about yer boy, and I'll be sure to tell him o' yer confidence and praise"—she looked over at the man lying flat out on the floor "—soon as he's waking up."

That had the aggressive man back on his heels.

"Pay her," Arunika told the patrons. "Coin won fairly. And if you're to bet, then you're to pay your losses."

Much grumbling ensued, but Ambergris and Afafrenfere walked out of the tavern with several small bags of gold.

"We won't be winning anymore that way," Afafrenfere remarked. "We should have stopped after two."

"Bah! They'll bet again. Can't help themselves, the dolts."

"They will bet on me, so where is your win?"

"Ye might be right," Ambergris said, and she grinned wickedly and winked at him. "Unless ye're thinkin' ye can take a pair o' them."

Afafrenfere started to respond, but just sighed instead. More likely, he knew, Ambergris would put him in a match against three opponents.

"There is your seer," Dahlia remarked to Drizzt.

The drow reflexively put a hand to his belt pouch, but he moved it back immediately. He didn't need Arunika, for Guen was back beside him.

But then another idea came to him, and he smiled at Dahlia and waved to Arunika to join him.

"You look well," the red-haired woman remarked when she came over and took a seat beside the two.

"He found his panther," Dahlia explained. "And now we seek—" Drizzt put his hand on her forearm, cutting her short, something Arunika surely noticed.

"Barrabus—Artemis Entreri, is here," Drizzt said. "He is in the third private room upstairs. Would you go to him for me? I will pay."

Dahlia's eyes widened and she turned to stare at Drizzt, her expression full of surprise and anger.

"I am no whore," Arunika replied with a laugh.

"No," Drizzt replied with a laugh of his own, "not like that. Entreri has agreed to accompany us to the north, but now has fostered second thoughts. His best course is to the north, I insist, and I would like you to confirm that for him."

"On your word?" the woman asked skeptically.

"Use your powers then," Drizzt bade her. "I know where to find something he wishes returned to him."

"The sword?"

"Is destroyed," Dahlia interjected.

"Ah," said Arunika, and she seemed impressed.

"This is something different, but no less important," Drizzt assured her.

Arunika stared at him for a while, and whispered some words—a spell, he realized—under her breath.

"An item, or an epiphany?" the seer asked slyly.

"Yes," Drizzt answered.

Arunika started to rise and Drizzt reached for his coin purse. But the woman deferred and promised, "I will go to him."

***

"What do you want?" Artemis Entreri asked from behind the cracked door. He was stripped to the waist—and Arunika made certain that he noted her appreciative stare at his muscled torso.

"Barrabus," she replied.

"That is not my name—never again my name."

"Artemis, then," she said. "Speak with me. We're great players amidst a sea of peasants. We shouldn't be strangers, or enemies."

Her words were weighted with more than a little magical suggestion, but she needn't have bothered. For most males, and Entreri proved no exception, the magically disarming and enticing affect of her spell-enhanced appearance sufficed. Entreri stepped back and opened the door, and Arunika happily entered his den.

"It's good that you've returned," she said, taking a seat on his ruffled bedding and demurely crossing her legs. It occurred to her that she should abandon Drizzt's request and convince Entreri to remain in Neverwinter. Could she make him an informant, perhaps, another great cog in the network she'd fostered? She knew the exploits of Barrabus the Gray, after all, and he was a man of no small danger and power.

Too much danger, she decided not long into her conversation with Entreri, not long after looking into his cold eyes. Yes, she did remember Barrabus the Gray, and had always understood that he was one of the few mortals she had ever met capable of defeating her.

Still, that didn't mean he couldn't be useful to her, and in a number of ways.

Despite her protests earlier, the redhead did engage in a bit of overpowering seduction, to indulge herself as much as to please Entreri. She didn't leave his room until the sky was beginning to lighten with the dawn, and she left Entreri quite exhausted, indeed fast asleep.

She had shown him great pleasure, and he had reciprocated. An added bonus, the succubus thought, for the purpose of her seduction had not been her own pleasure. Not this night, though it had come as an added bonus, surely! No, in the midst of their entwining, Arunika had placed an enchantment upon this dangerous assassin, a dweomer of clairvoyance. And when they were done, collapsed in each other's arms, the red-haired succubus, a whispering demon, had lived up to the reputation of her kind, offering quiet encouragement into Entreri's ear, assuring him that his best road forward lay beside Drizzt and Dahlia.

Her reputation as a seer wasn't wholly unearned, after all, and now Artemis Entreri, marked by the dweomer of Arunika, would spy for her.

CHAPTER 4

MY FRIEND THE VAMPIRE

THE CHANGE IN PERSPECTIVE WAS QUITE DISORIENTING FOR DRAYGO Quick. First he was standing in his room, watching the panther turn to mist, then he was traveling the ether, swirling and spinning, his sensibilities secretly carried along with Guenhwyvar.

Soon he was beside the drow ranger and Dahlia on Toril, but low to the ground, stalking. He could hear the pair but he couldn't turn to regard them. Not having command over the cat's muscles, but rather just seeing, hearing, smelling, and feeling through her created a strange, out-of-body, and more importantly, out-of-control, experience for the old warlock.

An altered reality, actually, for the panther's eyes did not view the world as a human would. Everything seemed elongated, with distances more clearly defined. The crystal clarity led to a dizzying, almost magnifying effect on the grasses and branches and fallen leaves, as if a hundred mirrors had taken the sunlight and magnified it many times over to completely alter the color of the world.

Sounds filled Draygo Quick's mind—some were soft, like the call of a distant bird, then became suddenly loud as the panther turned her ears. In that turn, other sounds were muted. It seemed to Draygo that the cat could lock her hearing directionally, this way or that, amplifying regions of sound almost to the exclusion of other areas.

She was moving then, swiftly, in pursuit of something, and the ground and low brush sped by so wildly that Draygo reflexively closed his own eyes to try to block it out. But he could not close Guenhwyvar's eyes and so his actions had no effect. He almost broke the connection, but then Guenhwyvar's prey suddenly came into view.

Humans and tieflings—Ashmadai zealots—scrambled in alarm, gathering up their war scepters, shoving each other aside.

A blinding flash ripped the air above him, and an Ashmadai man went flying away.

Then the warlock felt as if he were flying, too, as Guenhwyvar leaped. He saw a woman dive aside, another turn and shriek, and he flew past them both, crashing hard against the chest of a burly tiefling warrior. Draygo Quick felt the impact as that warrior tried to bang his scepter against the panther's flank, but more keenly, Draygo Quick tasted the sweat and flesh as Guenhwyvar bit down. His vision failed him. The cat had closed her eyes, but he heard, keenly, the tearing of flesh and the crunch of bone, and the smell—oh the smell!—overwhelmed him. Coppery and warm.

The scent of gushing blood.

He felt as if he were flying again, and his vision returned suddenly. He saw the drow spinning by, scimitars humming through the air. Dahlia vaulted past and he heard a grunt and a groan and the slapping of her staff against the skull of a woman. The panther crashed into another man, tackling him to the ground, breaking branches and flattening the brush. As soon as they landed, Guenhwyvar spun around and sprang away. Draygo Quick didn't even realize that he was pawing and clawing the air reflexively to mimic the feeling of Guenhwyvar's claws ripping the flesh from the man.

Back into the sprint they went, an Ashmadai spinning down before them. A scimitar flashed out, right before Draygo Quick's vision, and he shouted and threw his arms across his face, trying desperately to retreat from the overwhelming sights, sounds, and smells.

He felt as if he were falling, falling, into a vast and dark hole.

". . . it led us here because there was something here." Drizzt's voice reached out to him, drawing him from the darkness and back into the senses of the panther. "Something powerful . . ."

The last word faded away as Guenhwyvar turned her ears to focus on a distant shout. Had some of the Ashmadai band escaped?

". . . working with the vampire?" Dahlia asked.

The cat sprang away, running up the side of a tree, and all Draygo Quick could catch of Drizzt's response was, ". . . it's much worse than that."

Oh, go back, you idiot cat! the warlock's mind screamed futilely.

The elf and the drow continued to talk below, but the panther focused off into the distance, and Draygo Quick heard the breathing of a fleeing Ashmadai warrior more keenly than he heard their voices. His thoughts pleaded with Guenhwyvar, but of course, the panther could not hear them.

The panther jumped down from the tree, and Draygo Quick cried out in horror to see the ground rushing up at him. The sheer shock broke his connection with Guenhwyvar, but as his consciousness returned to his room in the Shadowfell, he heard the voice of Drizzt saying, "What do we know of the fate of Valindra Shadowmantle?"

"Lord Draygo?" Effron asked quietly, moving into the old warlock's private chambers. He glanced all around. The place seemed quite empty. By all accounts, though, Draygo Quick was in here. The old warlock had summoned him, even.

He moved slowly and cautiously, always as if walking on tiles of blown glass when around this most dangerous and vindictive wretch. Effron had not leaped with joy when Draygo Quick's messenger had arrived with the summons.

He passed the side room, where Guenhwyvar was kept, and resisted entering it, for fear that he would be discovered and accused of trying to steal the panther yet again.

"Lord Draygo?" he repeated as he entered the main chamber.

Still empty. Effron again turned to the side room. He summoned his courage and moved to the door, gently turning the handle and shouting out, louder now, "Lord Draygo!"

He froze in place when he looked into the chamber, for there sat Draygo Quick, on the floor! What was left of the old man's scraggly hair stuck out at curious angles, and he stared at Effron vacantly. Always before had Draygo Quick seemed composed and proper, his hair kempt, his clothing, be it robes or a smart vest and breeches, always neat and straight.

Draygo Quick stared at him for many heartbeats, and only then seemed to register his presence.

"Ah, Effron, good that you have come," he said at last, and he began pulling himself up from the floor.

Effron dashed over to help him to his feet.

The withered old warlock ran his hands over his head to smooth his meager hair, and he flashed a yellow-toothed smile.

"Quite a ride, boy," he explained.

Effron didn't understand. He looked around the room, to the cage. Its bars were not glowing, and no panther stalked within.

"I have been to Toril," Draygo Quick explained. "Through the senses of the great panther."

Effron stared at him, not quite catching on.

"I am bound to the creature, by the blessing of a deceived druid," the withered old warlock explained. "And so I can see through her, hear through

61

her, smell through her, and even feel through her. It's quite an exhilarating ride, I assure you!" He laughed, but sobered quickly, his face turning serious. "Never have I experienced a kill like that before. The smell . . . it was . . . personal." He looked up at Effron. "And beautiful."

"Master?"

Draygo Quick shook his head, almost as if to dismiss a trance. "No matter," he said. "Not now, at least, though I do intend to explore this more."

"Yes, Master," Effron said and his gaze went back to the empty cage. "And what is my role?"

"Your role?"

"I was told you wished to see me, at once."

Draygo Quick seemed quite flustered for a few heartbeats—something Effron had never witnessed before. He couldn't help but glance back at the empty cage, trying to fathom what wondrous or terrifying experience had befallen Draygo Quick.

"Oh that, yes," the warlock said after he had composed himself. "You wish a chance to redeem yourself, and so I offer you one. I had intended one direction, but now, very recently indeed"—he glanced at the cage and grinned "—some other information has come to me. What do you know of this Valindra Shadowmantle creature?"

"The lich?" Effron asked. "I have watched her from afar. She is quite insane, and doubly dangerous."

"Go and spy on her again. For me this time," Draygo Quick informed him. "I would know her movements and intent, and if she poses any serious threat to the region of Neverwinter."

"Master?" Effron was less than enthused, and his voice revealed that fact clearly.

"Go, go," Draygo told him, and he waved his leathery hands at the young warlock. "Learn what you may and return with a full accounting. And let me warn you again, my impetuous young protégé, beware your dealings with Dahlia and her companions—particularly with her companions. Dahlia is inconsequential at this time."

Effron's face grew very tight.

"To you, perhaps not," Draygo Quick offered. "But your needs and desires are not paramount here, and indeed pale beside the larger issue that is, quite likely, Drizzt Do'Urden. So I warn you, and there will be no debate or disobedience, stay away from them."

Effron didn't blink for many heartbeats.

"Do this, and when the time is right I will help you find your revenge," the old warlock promised.

That had to be good enough, for there really wasn't any choice left to Effron. He had to admit, to himself at least, that without some help, there was little he could do against the likes of Dahlia, Drizzt Do'Urden, and Barrabus the Gray, any one of whom would prove a formidable foe.

"Valindra Shadowmantle," he replied quietly. "Of course."

Effron hadn't even left the room fully before Draygo Quick settled once more on the floor, closed his eyes, and measured his own breathing to calm himself and prepare for a return trip into the senses of the panther. At long last, his wits clear and strong once again, he summoned the connection.

An image formed in his mind, surprisingly clear given the darkness. Night had fallen—had it been that long?—and Draygo Quick found himself off-balance in the senses of Guenhwyvar again. The panther's eyes caught what little light there was around and magnified it many times over, giving the tree branches a strange, shadowy appearance. Stark, contrasting, colorless lines demarked the edges of the twigs waving in the night breeze.

He could hear the heartbeats of his two companions, clearly and distinctly. How curious, then, when Guenhwyvar turned her head to reveal not just Dahlia and Drizzt, but a third companion as well, a grubby-looking dwarf dressed in ridged armor and with a helmet spike half again as tall as he!

This was the one without the heartbeat, Draygo Quick understood, and given the previous conversation, he knew why. This could get interesting, and important, he thought.

"Go home, Guen," Drizzt said then . . . and all became a mist of gray fog and swirling vapors.

Back in his room, Draygo Quick cursed his misfortune. Dahlia and the drow had found an old friend, it seemed, a dwarf turned vampire. Draygo wanted to see how that might play out. If Drizzt Do'Urden aligned himself with a vampire, even a former friend turned to darkness, that might be a powerful clue regarding which goddess would name this particular drow as a chosen disciple. Would Mielikki, the goddess of nature, accept such an unnatural creature?

And wouldn't Lady Lolth love such a union?

Draygo Quick could only sigh and remind himself to be patient. Guenhwyvar was back in her cage.

But Drizzt would call her again.

"I'll be wantin' to eat," Thibbledorf Pwent dourly remarked. After Drizzt and Dahlia had found him in the forest, he had returned to his lair, a cave in the hills. "And it might be that this time I won't find any goblins."

"You won't," Drizzt insisted, or begged, actually, though he had tried to mask that desperation from Dahlia, and particularly from Pwent. Unsuccessfully, he knew when he regarded the elf woman.

"No?" the dwarf answered. "Ye don't know that, elf." He walked toward the mouth of the cave and plopped himself down on the floor. He seemed even more dispirited than Drizzt. "I died. Should still be dead. Might be that I'll just sit right here, wait for the sun."

Drizzt didn't doubt his resolve. This was Pwent, after all.

Beyond the dwarf, the air began to brighten a bit as the pre-dawn glow lit up the east.

"That might be best," Dahlia said, walking past him and out into the open air. She added flippantly, "There is little chance of you feasting on some poor child when you are but dust."

"When you're dust," Drizzt silently mouthed, and he couldn't help but grimace as he watched Dahlia walk away. She didn't understand the loss here, or the indignation. That the proud and loyal battlerager should be reduced to this wretched fate was almost more than Drizzt could bear.

And Dahlia didn't seem to care in the least. Indeed, her emphasis on that last word, "dust," had Drizzt shifting uncomfortably from foot to foot. He walked over to his friend and put a hand on Pwent's sturdy shoulder.

"There must be a way," he said.

"Nah, but there ain't," said Pwent.

"There is no turning back the curse of vampirism," Dahlia said, rather coldly. "I have known such creatures, for they abound in Thay. Many tried—oh, how they tried!—to return to the light. The mightiest of the Red Wizards and the most powerful priests sought these answers. But alas, there is no return."

Drizzt stared at her coldly, but the elf woman merely shrugged.

The drow wondered what he might do. This was Pwent, loyal Pwent. Thibbledorf Pwent, who had led Stokely Silverstream and his boys from Icewind Dale to help in the fight in Gauntlgrym. Thibbledorf Pwent, who had carried Bruenor across the primordial pit and helped his beloved king pull the lever to trap the fiery beast back in its hole.

Thibbledorf Pwent, the hero.

Thibbledorf Pwent, the vampire.

Drizzt looked inside his own heart—what would he do if he had been so afflicted? He couldn't deny the dwarf's logic. Pwent was a vampire, and a vampire would feast. The smell of blood would surely overrule any moral code, for that was the way of it. There was no avoiding that truth of the curse, and there was, alas, no cure to the affliction.

"That's how you'd end it, my friend?" he asked quietly. "You choose to burn?"

"I died with me king, in Gauntlgrym. I'm just lettin' meself go back to him."

"There is nothing I can say?" Drizzt asked.

"Me king," the dwarf answered. "He'll be waitin' for me at Moradin's side, and I ain't done nothing yet that'd make Moradin turn me away! But I will. I'm knowin' that I will if I don't end this now."

Drizzt tried to focus on the words, but a disconcerting thought had crossed his mind at Pwent's mention of his king.

"Bruenor will not . . . rise?" the drow asked, his voice hesitant. He could hardly bear to look at Pwent, his old friend, in this wretched state, but to see Bruenor Battlehammer, his dearest friend for more than a century, similarly afflicted, would be more than his heart could bear, he was sure.

"No, elf." Pwent assured him. "He's set in his grave, where ye put him. Killed natural and for good and all, and dyin' the hero. Unlike meself."

"None question the heroics of Thibbledorf Pwent, in the fight for Gauntlgrym and in a hundred before that," Drizzt said. "Your legend is wide and grand, your legacy secure."

Pwent nodded and grunted in thanks and didn't speak the obvious: that his legacy would remain secure only if he turned away from his current course. And there was only one way to accomplish that.

He put his thick hand atop Drizzt's and repeated, "Ah, me king."

"So be it," Drizzt said, and he had trouble getting those words out of his mouth.

Dahlia called to him. "Let's get moving. I want to get back to Neverwinter, and soon!"

"Farewell, my friend," Drizzt said, and he walked out of the cave. "Sit in feast and hoist a mug beside King Bruenor in Dwarfhome."

"To Clan Battlehammer and to yerself, too, elf," Pwent answered, and it did Drizzt's heart a bit of good to hear the serenity in his voice, as if he had truly come to terms with this, understanding it as his best, or only, choice. Still, Drizzt's heart could not have been heavier as he walked out of that cave.

He paused outside and turned back to regard the dark opening, though Pwent was now out of sight. He should stay and witness this, he thought. He owed that much to this shield dwarf who had given so much to him and to Bruenor over the decades. Pwent had been as much a hero in the last fight

65

in Gauntlgrym as any of them, and now Drizzt would just walk away and let him be burned to ashes by the rising sun?

"Come along," Dahlia bade him, and he shot her an angry look indeed.

"You can't do anything for him," Dahlia explained, walking over to take Drizzt's hand. "He makes the right choice, morally. You would disagree with that? If so, then go and enlist him to our side. A vampire is a powerful companion, I know."

Drizzt studied her, not quite understanding her real intent, and not quite able to discount her words or the possibility of taking Thibbledorf Pwent along. Didn't he owe his old friend that much at least?

"But he will eat," Dahlia added. "And if he can find no food other than goblinkin, he will feast on the neck of an elf, or a human. There is no other possibility. He cannot resist the hunger—if he could, you would find great and powerful communities of vampires, and what king might resist them or their temptations of immortality?"

"You know this?"

"I have much experience with these creatures," Dahlia explained. "Thay is littered with them."

Drizzt glanced back at the cave opening.

"There is nothing you can do for him," Dahlia whispered, and when Drizzt turned back to regard her, he found true sympathy in her blue eyes, for him and for Pwent, and he was glad of that. "There is nothing anyone can do for him, except the dwarf himself. He can end his torment, as he has decided, before the curse further eats his mind and drives him into the darkness. I have seen this: young vampires, newly undead, destroying themselves before the affliction could fully take hold."

Drizzt took a deep breath, but did not turn from the cave, even leaned toward it as if thinking of returning.

"Let him have this moment," Dahlia whispered. "He will die again as a hero, for few so afflicted could ever so resist the dark temptations, as he now intends."

Drizzt nodded, and knew that he had to be satisfied with that, that he had to take the small victory and hold it close. In his mind, he drew a parallel between Pwent and Artemis Entreri, as he considered Dahlia's claim that Pwent would indeed feast upon an elf or human or some other goodly person. That was his nature now, and it was a powerful, irresistible demand.

So what of Entreri? The man had killed many. Would he kill more, and not only those deserving, or not only in the service of the greater good?

Aye, that was always the question, Drizzt recognized. And it was always his hope that Entreri would find his way around that vicious nature.

How ironic that Thibbledorf Pwent had to sacrifice himself, without hope, while Entreri continued to draw breath. How tragic that the insurmountable danger was Pwent's to bear, while hope could remain for Artemis Entreri.

Indeed, that reality proved to be a bitter pill.

CHAPTER 5

PURPOSE

A T DRIZZT'S INSISTENCE, THE FIVE COMPANIONS LEFT NEVERWINTER EARLY the next morning. Though he had not slept at all the night before, Drizzt was determined to be on his way. Many times did he glance to the east, to the forest where he had found the cursed Thibbledorf Pwent, and many times did that sad reality throw him back in time, to the fall of Pwent and Bruenor.

He kept shaking the darkness away, and moved with purpose now, leading the five companions up the coastline before the onslaught of winter, which came early and hit hard, burying the land around the forest in deep snows and bringing sheets of dangerous ice all along the northern Sword Coast. Many times during their short journey Dahlia asked Drizzt what he was planning, and many times Entreri inquired about his dagger, but the drow remained quiet and wore a calm and contented grin.

"Port Llast?" Entreri asked when their destination became obvious, for they turned onto a trail that led down from the rocky cliffs to the quiet seaside town. Once a thriving quarry and port city, Port Llast hardly resembled anything that could be called a village any longer.

"Ye slurring yer words for a reason?" Ambergris asked.

"Not a slur," said Drizzt. "That is the town's name. Port Llast. Two Ls."

"Similar to the Hells," muttered the ever-sarcastic Entreri.

"I'm not knowin' the place," the dwarf replied, and Afafrenfere shrugged in accord.

"A thriving city, a century ago," Drizzt explained. "These cliffs provided many of the stones for the greatest buildings of Waterdeep, Luskan, and Neverwinter, and towns all along the Sword Coast."

"And what happened?" Ambergris asked, glancing around. "Looks like good stone to me, and can ye ever really run short o' the stuff?"

"Orcs . . . bandits . . ." Drizzt explained.

"Luskan," Entreri put in, and Drizzt winced reflexively, though he was fairly certain that Entreri had no idea of Drizzt's role in the catastrophe that had taken place in the City of Sails, which was just a few days' ride farther up the coast.

"Port Llast was overrun and worn down," Drizzt explained. "It went from a city of nearly twenty thousand to just a few hundred, and in short order."

"Still substantial, then," said Afafrenfere. "A few hundred, and that in a port city?"

"That was before the Spellplague," Entreri said. He looked at Drizzt and added, "Tell them of our paradise destination."

"Land rose up out there," Drizzt said, pointing to the west, to the open sea. "Some effect of the Spellplague, it is rumored, though whatever the cause, the land is surely there. This new island changed the tides, which ruined the harbor and finished off any remaining hopes for the city."

"Finished?" asked the dwarf.

"We circumvented this place several times," Dahlia said, confused. "There are people there still."

"Some, but not many," Drizzt explained.

"It's Umberlee's town," Entreri said, referring to an evil sea goddess with a reputation of sending in horrid sea monster minions to wreak havoc along the coasts of Faerûn.

"And still, the people hold on and fight back," Drizzt countered.

"Noble," said Afafrenfere.

"Stubborn," said Ambergris.

"Stupid," Entreri insisted, with such clarity and confidence that he drew the looks of the other four. "Hold on to what? They've no harbor, they've no quarry. All they've got are memories of a time lost, and one that's not coming back."

"There's honor in defendin' yer home," Ambergris argued.

Entreri laughed at her. "Without hope?" he said. "How many villagers remain, drow? Three hundred? Two? And less each year, as some give up and move away and others are slain by the devils of Umberlee, or the orcs and bandits that dominate this region. They've no chance of defending their home. They've nothing of value to lure new settlers, and no reinforcements for their diminishing ranks."

Dahlia wore a knowing smirk as she looked at Drizzt. "They have us, apparently."

Entreri stared hard at Drizzt, and asked incredulously, "Truly?"

"Let's see what we might learn of the place," Drizzt answered. "The winter will be no more dangerous for us here than anywhere else."

70

Entreri shook his head, more in abject disbelief than in resignation, but said no more. His look at Drizzt spoke volumes, though, mostly in reminding Drizzt that Entreri had only come along for the sake of retrieving his prized dagger.

The trail wove down through high walls of dark stone. Several carved plateaus showed the ruins of old catapults, all trained on the harbor far below. After a myriad of angled hairpin turns down the steep decline, the five companions came at last to the city's southern gate, to find it closed and well-guarded.

"Halt and hail!" a soldier called down from the rampart. "And what a strange band of deckhands to be knocking at our door. A drow elf in front and a motley crew behind." The man shook his head and called back. Another pair of soldiers joined him at the wall, their eyes going wide.

And not surprisingly, for not only was a drow leading the party, but he sat astride a unicorn, and with a man behind him astride a nightmare of the lower planes!

"Not a sight ye'd see every day, eh?" Ambergris called up at them.

"Well met," Drizzt said. "And pray tell, does Port Llast still name Dovos Dothwintyl as First Captain?"

"You know him, then?" the guard replied.

"Not so well. Better did I know Haeromos Dothwintyl, in days long past, when I sailed with Deudermont and *Sea Sprite*."

That had the three speaking amongst themselves, and when they turned back, a second guard, a woman, called down, "Who would you be, dark elf? A fellow by the name of Drizzt, perhaps?"

"At your service," Drizzt said, and he bowed a bit, constrained as he was upon Andahar's back.

"Passing through?" she asked. Drizzt noted a bit of an edge to her voice, and he understood, for when Captain Deudermont had overstepped the bounds of reason and tried to tame wicked Luskan, the resulting revolution had put evil men in charge of the City of Sails and that in turn had cast a long shadow over the struggling town of Port Llast. Drizzt had been part of Deudermont's failure, so went the common lore, and the fact that he had tried to turn the captain from his dangerous ambitions long before the catastrophic events wasn't widely known.

Drizzt had been through Port Llast a couple of times over the last decades, but had not found a particularly warm welcome there since the debacle in Luskan. More often, he avoided the city in his travels north and south.

"We hope to winter in your fair town," he replied.

Two of the guards disappeared, the third turning around, apparently to join in a conversation the companions couldn't make out from below. Before they ever got a verbal reply, the gates creaked open.

"Well met to you, then," the guard who had been third up on the wall said with a nod as they passed by. "There's an inn, Stonecutter's Solace, under the shadow of the east cliffs. You'll find good accommodation there, would be my guess. Be smart, and stay east, and go nowhere near the docks."

Drizzt nodded and slid down from his seat, then dismissed Andahar. The guard's eyes widened as the powerful unicorn leaped away and seemed to diminish to half its size. A second stride halved it again, and again a third and fourth time, where Andahar simply vanished into nothingness.

"You've been to Neverwinter of late?" the guard asked, trying to appear calm, though he was obviously awestricken. "How does she fare?"

"Growing strong," Drizzt replied. "The immediate and greatest threats to the city have been driven off."

The man nodded and seemed quite pleased by that news, and Drizzt understood the reaction well. Port Llast needed a strong and secure Neverwinter to help keep the pirates of Luskan away, and perhaps to bolster them in their continuing tribulations against the creatures of Umberlee's ocean domain. The City of Sails would have little trouble in overwhelming this once thriving, but now nearly abandoned city, and Drizzt was keenly reminded of that when he looked to the sheltered harbor, where but a dozen or so small ships bobbed in the tides, and several of that meager fleet hardly appeared seaworthy. Catapults set on the eastern cliffs overlooking the city, still operational and manned, were a more imposing sight. But slinging a stone at a moving ship was no easy task. If the high captains of Luskan came calling, Port Llast would almost surely fall with barely a whimper.

"Doesn't seem a friendly place," Afafrenfere remarked as the five wound their way down the road past the dilapidated stone houses and shops. Indeed, most of the shutters were pulled tight, and others banged closed as the unusual troupe passed.

"These are troubled lands of wild things," Drizzt replied. "The citizens are cautious, and for good reason."

"I expect that simply by walking in here, we have doubled their defenses," Dahlia quipped.

"I expect that you underestimate the strength of settlers," Artemis Entreri unexpectedly put in, and the other four turned to regard him, still astride his nightmare. "They survive here, and that alone is no small thing."

"Well said," Drizzt remarked, and started off once more. "This will be a fine place to spend the winter."

"Why?" the assassin asked, and when Drizzt stopped and turned back, he added, "Do you ever plan to tell us?"

"Tonight," Drizzt promised, and on he went.

The road forked, but the left way was blocked by a stone wall manned by a trio of guards. That road led to the lower reaches of the city, the harbor and coast, and scanning around, the five could see that many new walls had been erected, virtually cutting the city in half, east and west. The right-hand fork led almost directly east, toward the cliffs and the higher sections of the city, and even from this distance, the companions could easily spot their destination, a newly constructed central building, free of moss and of stones not yet weathered to dark gray.

The common room at Stonecutter's Solace was wide and deep and well-attended, with several hearths burning brightly and dozens of townsfolk sitting about the circular tables that filled the floor before a grand bar. A half wall behind it revealed the bustling kitchen.

"I might be gettin' used to this place," Ambergris offered at the promising sight. She sauntered by the nearest table, flashing a smile at the trio sitting there, a man and two dwarves, all three with faces weathered under a seaside sun, hands calloused by digging stones and arms thick with muscles.

"Well met," Ambergris said to them.

"Aye, lassie, and sit with us, why don't ye?" one of the dwarves replied.

Ambergris skidded to a stop, looked back to her four companions, winked, and then did just that.

"No fighting," Drizzt remarked to Afafrenfere as they walked past the table. "I'll not have us thrown from this inn or this bar."

"Never my choice," the monk replied. "Ambergris always wants her coins jiggling as she walks, you see."

"I see and I saw, and I'll have none of it now," Drizzt answered. "We have important work to do here."

"Perhaps you'll tell us sometime soon," Afafrenfere replied rather harshly, and he moved toward the bar.

Drizzt stopped and turned to Dahlia. "Stay with him," he bade her quietly, glancing back at the distracted dwarf. "Get to know our monk companion. I need to understand his demeanor and loyalty."

"He can fight," Dahlia remarked.

"But does he know *when* to fight, and against whom?"

"He'll do what the dwarf tells him," Entreri said.

Drizzt glanced over at the table, where Ambergris was putting back shots of potent liquor with her three new friends.

"You think you know her?" Entreri remarked. "You're putting Bruenor's face on her. Take care with that."

"Artemis Entreri warning me about those I choose to walk beside," Drizzt muttered. "The world has gone mad."

73

Dahlia laughed at that as she skipped away, following Afafrenfere to the bar. Drizzt and Entreri, meanwhile, found an empty table in the corner opposite the door.

"This is a doomed town," the assassin said as soon as they took their seats. "Why are we wasting our time here?" He considered those words for just a heartbeat before changing them subtly. "Why are you wasting my time here?"

"Not doomed," Drizzt replied. "Not unless we give up on it."

"And you haven't," Entreri surmised.

Drizzt shrugged. "There is a chance for us to do good here," he explained, and he stopped abruptly when a serving girl came over to offer drinks.

"Do good here?" Entreri echoed doubtfully when she had gone.

"The people of Port Llast deserve the chance," Drizzt said. "They have held on against all odds."

"Because they are stupid," Entreri interrupted. "I thought we had already settled on this."

"Spare me your sour jokes," Drizzt replied. "I am being serious here. You have lived a . . . questionable life. Does that not itch at your conscience?"

"Now you pretend to lecture me?"

Drizzt looked at him earnestly and shook his head. "I'm asking. Honestly."

The serving girl, a young and pretty brunette of no more than fifteen years, returned with their drinks, set them down, and scampered away to the call from another table.

"Sounds like you're lecturing," Entreri replied after a long swallow of Baldur's Gate Red Ale.

"Then I apologize, and again, I ask, do you feel no regret?"

"None."

The two stared at each other for a long while, and Drizzt didn't believe the answer but found little room for debate in Entreri's steadfast tone. "Have you ever done anything for someone simply because it was the right thing to do?" he asked. "Need there always be a reward for you at the end of the task?"

Entreri just stared at him and took another drink.

"Have you ever tried it?"

"I came north with you because you promised me my dagger."

"In time," Drizzt said dismissively. "But for now, I would know, have you?"

"Do you have a point to make?"

"We have a chance to do some good here, for many people," Drizzt explained. "There is a level of satisfaction in that exercise I doubt you've ever known."

Entreri scoffed at him and stared incredulously. "Is this how you heal your wounds?" he asked. When Drizzt looked at him in puzzlement, he continued, "If you can reform me, then you need not feel so guilty about letting me escape your blades in the past, yes? You could have killed me on more than one occasion, but didn't, and now you question that mercy. How many innocents died because you hadn't the courage to strike me down?"

"No," Drizzt said quietly, shaking his head.

"Or is it something else?" Entreri asked, clearly enjoying this conversation. "I once met a paladin king—in his dungeon, actually, where I was his guest. Oh, how he loathed me, because he saw in me a dark reflection of his own heart. Is that it? Are you afraid that we two are not so different?"

Drizzt considered that for a moment, then returned Entreri's confident look with one of his own. "I hope that we are not."

Entreri's expression quickly changed. "And so you must redeem me so that you can feel your own life justified?" Little certainty rang out in his tone.

"No," Drizzt answered. "Our paths have crossed so many times. I don't call you a friend—"

"Nor I, you."

Drizzt nodded. "But a companion . . . of circumstance, perhaps, but a companion nonetheless. Let me lead you down this road. Consider it a chance to see the world through a different perspective. What do you have to lose?"

Entreri's expression hardened. "You promised me my dagger."

"And you will get it, or at least, I will show you where it is."

"If I indulge you here?" he asked with a sarcastic edge.

Drizzt took a deep breath and tried to let the assassin's stubborn ripostes fall off his shoulders. "Whether you indulge me or not. I didn't offer you a bargain, but merely suggested a road."

"Then why would I help you?"

Drizzt was about to argue, but he caught something, in the background of Entreri's callous question, that clued him in to the truth of this discussion. He smiled knowingly at his old nemesis.

Entreri drained his mug and banged it on the table, signaling for another.

"You're paying," he informed the drow.

"You'll owe me, then," said Drizzt.

"What? A few silver coins?"

"Not for the ale," Drizzt answered.

Entreri tried to look as if this whole conversation had bored him and annoyed him, and perhaps there was some truth in that. But Drizzt couldn't contain his grin, for he knew, too, that he had intrigued his old nemesis.

That grin disappeared a moment later, though, as the common room's main door banged open and a group of citizens burst in. A woman and a male elf flanked a man, and indeed held him up, his arms across their shoulders, his head lolling about uncontrollably.

"Help here!" the woman cried. "Fetch a priest!"

They came in nearly sideways to fit through the door. When they straightened out, the problem was clear for Drizzt and everyone else to see. The man's shirt was torn and soaked in blood, a line of wounds stretching from hip to ribs.

"Get 'im here!" Ambergris yelled, as others ran for the door, one heading out and crying for a cleric. Ambergris swept her table clear of drinks, mugs splashing to the floor, and the three with her jumped back and started to protest until they saw the dwarf pull forth her holy symbol and lift her broad hands in supplication, whispering the name of Dumathoin as she did.

Drizzt, Entreri, Dahlia, and Afafrenfere all got to the table about the same time as the wounded man's companions laid him down atop it. The monk, quite familiar with the dwarf's work, rushed beside Ambergris and bent low, holding the wounded man still.

All about them, questions filled the air, along with shouts of "Sea devils!" and curses at the wicked god Umberlee. In the midst of that turmoil, Drizzt pulled the elf aside. He followed after a short hesitation, surely confused by the sight of a drow in Port Llast.

"How did this happen?" Drizzt asked.

"As they are claiming," the elf replied, and he continued to look at Drizzt suspiciously.

"I am no enemy," Drizzt assured him. "I'm Drizzt Do'Urden, friend of—"

He didn't have to finish, for the name sparked recognition in the elf, revealed his welcoming smile and nod. "I'm Dorwyllan of Baldur's Gate," he said.

"Well met."

"Sea devils," Dorwyllan explained. "Sahuagin, the scourge of Port Llast."

Drizzt knew the name, and the monster, for he had battled the evil fishmen on several occasions during his years riding *Sea Sprite* with Captain Deudermont. He glanced at the wounded man—Afafrenfere had pulled his torn shirt aside and others had splashed water on it to clear the excess blood. The drow saw the wounds clearly now: three deep punctures, as if a trio of javelins had hit him in a straight line. He could well imagine the trident, a preferred weapon of the sahuagin, that had stabbed the poor fellow.

"Where?"

Others were asking the same question.

"The northern boat house," Dorwyllan answered.

"And so it begins," Dahlia mumbled at his side.

The elf looked at her and started as he came to fully appreciate this female elf standing before him, her beauty and that curious pattern of bluish dots that adorned her face.

"Good fortune that we arrived this day," Drizzt said.

"Bah, but this sight's more days than it ain't!" one of the dwarves who had been sitting with Ambergris explained. "Sea devils thrice a tenday, or it ain't Port Llast, don't ye know?"

Many began filing out of Stonecutter's Solace then, and shouts for a posse filled the air outside the tavern.

Drizzt looked to Dahlia and Entreri and the three moved to follow, but Dorwyllan grabbed Drizzt by the arm. "No need," he explained when Drizzt looked back at him. "The sea devils have fled to their watery sanctuary, no doubt, for they know that we got over the wall in our retreat. The folk will go down in a great show of force, lining the docks, lobbing rocks into the dark waters, just to let the creatures know that Port Llast remains vigilant. And the sahuagin will hear the splashes above, safe in their watery homes and ready to return. It has become almost a sad game."

"Then why were you three down there alone?"

"They are not often ashore in the daytime," Dorwyllan replied.

"But at night?" Artemis Entreri asked from the side before Drizzt could get the question out.

"They slither from the tide," Dorwyllan answered. "They near the wall and throw taunts and stones and spears. They are testing us, looking for a moment of weakness that they might raid the upper city and feast on man-flesh. And each day, we send down patrols." He nodded at the woman and wounded man with whom he had entered the inn. "The sea devils are building defenses in preparation for the coming battle. We go down each day and try to find these barricades and tear them down."

"But at night?" Drizzt asked leadingly.

"We avoid the docks at night," Dorwyllan answered. "We man the wall, heavily, but we don't cross beyond it. We don't have enough folk with the ability to see in the dark, and carrying a torch makes one a fine target."

"Then I assume the sea devils come ashore at night, each night."

Dorwyllan nodded. Drizzt grinned and glanced over at Entreri, who wore a grim expression, understanding exactly where this might be leading.

"Are you almost done with your work, Amber?" Drizzt asked.

"Aye, and he'll live, but not to be drinkin' for a bit or he's suren to leak," the dwarf answered as she wiped her bloody hands.

"Get your own drinking done early," Drizzt advised. "Tonight, we work."

He took a step away, but again Dorwyllan held him by the arm, turning him back. "They will be out in force," he warned.

"I'm counting on it," Drizzt replied.

Drizzt gathered the five soon after, and limited their drinking, though they were soon to enjoy a grand meal, it seemed, as the proprietor of the

Stonecutter's Solace wanted to repay Ambergris for her fine healing work on his wounded friend.

"You have enough magic left to help us through a difficult night?" Drizzt asked the dwarf.

"Got plenty. What'd'ye got in mind, elf? And it better be good if ye're thinking to keep the ale from me lips."

"The darkness won't bother you?" Drizzt asked Entreri.

"Long ago, I was given the gift of darkvision."

"By Jarlaxle," Drizzt said, for he recalled that fact from long ago.

"Don't mention his name," the assassin said.

"So only Afafrenfere will be hindered by the night," Drizzt reasoned.

The monk snorted as if the reasoning was preposterous.

"Won't be," Ambergris explained. "That one's trained to fight blind, and been living in the Shadowfell for years. Not quite a full shade yet, but he got close enough, don't ye doubt. Yer night's a shining beacon aside the Shadowfell day."

"Perfect," Drizzt said.

"We're going over the wall," Dahlia reasoned. "You've made some deal to save this town."

"We're going over the wall because it's the right thing to do," Drizzt corrected. "We're going to strike hard at those sahuagin, and maybe convince them to stay away long enough for Port Llast to rally."

"Sea devils are formidable foes," Ambergris solemnly warned.

"So are we." As he made the declaration, Drizzt looked to Entreri, whom he thought would be the most likely to reject the plan. But the assassin seemed quite at ease, leaning back in his chair with his arms crossed over his chest. He offered no objections.

"We'll let the moon come up," Drizzt explained.

"Not much of one this night," said Dahlia.

"I'm thinkin' that'll help us," said the dwarf.

Drizzt nodded and said no more, as the staff of the Stonecutter's Solace came over in a line, each bearing a tray piled with fine morsels. And it was food all the more precious because it had been collected under duress, Drizzt and the others realized. The trays were full of fish and clams, seaweed salad and huge red lobsters, which had once been considered the greatest delicacy of the Sword Coast North. Few in Luskan trapped them now, and of course, any venture to the seaside in and around Port Llast was fraught with danger.

"We get down to the sea for our fishing," said the proprietor, a tall and thin man who walked with legs set in a permanent bow, and a face so leathery it looked like it could be cut from his head and used for armor. "One day soon, I'm serving sea devil, and here's hoping the foul things taste better than they behave!"

That brought a round of "huzzah" from all about the tavern, and it reached a second crescendo when the man who had taken the trident propped himself up on his elbows and joined in with relish.

"Huzzah for Amber Gristle O'Maul," they cheered.

"Of the Adbar O'Mauls!" the three who had been sitting with her before the disturbance added.

"A fine meal," Ambergris said and belched a short while later.

"Last meals usually are," Entreri said.

Drizzt and the others looked sourly at the man.

"What?" he said innocently, looking up, and holding a lobster claw in each hand.

"Ye always so full o' hope?" the dwarf asked.

"I don't fear for myself," Entreri explained innocently. "I know I can outrun you, dwarf. And that one," he added, pointing a claw at Drizzt, "is sure to stay behind, valiantly fighting to the bitter end so that his companions can escape."

Afafrenfere and Ambergris both turned curiously to Drizzt at that statement, and Entreri added, "Why else would I remain beside the fool?"

Drizzt couldn't even begin to answer, so stupefied was he to think that the levity of Artemis Entreri would help to settle his nerves before a dangerous endeavor.

***

They crept through the dark avenues of the lower city, moving with precision from structure to structure and staying mostly along the city's southern reaches, under the shadows of the same high rock walls they had traversed when first coming down to Port Llast.

Entreri, Dahlia, and Drizzt did the "frog-hopping," as Ambergris called it, taking turns in the point position, scouting and securing, then motioning for the next in line to hop past. Afafrenfere remained with the dwarf, always settling into position beside the trailing member of the frog-hopping trio.

Drizzt came to the northwestern corner of a low stone building and peered around. He crouched at the end of one long and fairly straight street, stretching far into the heart of the lower city. Just east of his position, back to his right and barely a block away, loomed the wall, where torches burned at regularly-spaced intervals. To his left, at about the same distance, this section of the city fell away steeply to the rocky coast.

The drow glanced back to Entreri, the next in line, and instead of signaling him to move past, motioned instead for him to join Drizzt at the spot. Almost as soon as he arrived, the assassin nodded, seeing the same potential Drizzt had noted in this particular location.

Drizzt pointed to Entreri, held up two fingers, and motioned to the southeastern corner of the building where they crouched, and the parallel road beyond. Then he held up two fingers again and pointed to the building opposite this one to the west, across the street.

Entreri slipped back the way he had come and collected the others. He and Dahlia went to the east of Drizzt, the dwarf and monk settling in at the road parallel and west.

There the five crouched in the shadows and waited, but not for long. A cry from the city's dividing wall alerted them.

Drizzt looked to Entreri and Dahlia, who were nearest that wall, and the assassin glanced back at him and pointed to the north and nodded. With that, Drizzt eased an arrow onto Taulmaril's string and moved around the corner of the building, crouching low in the shadows against the structure.

To the east, Dahlia whistled, the sound of a night bird. To the west, Afafrenfere answered, as they had previously planned.

At the first sign of motion down the avenue, Drizzt drew back and held firm, Taulmaril leveled. He saw some forms moving about for cover in the shadows of a building far down the road, and heard the crash as stones flew at them from the city wall. Still he held his shot, wanting to be sure.

A humanoid form moved back from the pack, into the center of the road and hoisted a javelin to throw.

Humanoid, but no human, Drizzt could discern clearly even from this distance in the dark night. At least as tall as a man, and with a small, spiny ridge running from the top of its head down its back, it moved with jerking, reptilian motions.

The creature hurled the javelin as Drizzt let fly his arrow, the silver flash streaking down the street and bringing forth a myriad of flickering images and shadows as it sped.

The creature staggered back several steps under the weight of the blow, and half-turned to look back Drizzt's way. It continued turning around, though, circling lower and lower with each movement, finally collapsing into the street.

Other forms scrambled and Drizzt sent off a line of arrows, not at anything in particular, but mostly to hold the attention of the creatures.

He saw a pair dart across the street, rolling to the safety of a building on the other side. He heard curious squeals, high-pitched and filled with sharp whistles that faded off into discordant hissing sounds.

More arrows flew off, Drizzt sweeping Taulmaril right to left across the street and back again.

He caught sight, just for a heartbeat, of one sea devil on the rooftops, leaping from building to building to his left, working its way toward him. A moment later, he spotted it again, once more just for a heartbeat.

Long enough.

In the silvery brilliance of Taulmaril's arrow, he noted the creature's surprised and horrified expression right before it went flying away with such force that Drizzt noted its webbed feet as it tumbled head over heels.

There were more of them up there, he guessed, and likely some coming along the buildings on his side of the street as well.

He rolled out from his position to the middle of the road and began spraying shots down the lane once more, demanding attention. He didn't follow the trajectory of the shots, didn't bother to aim at anything specific, and kept glancing up, right and left, ready for the inevitable melee.

As soon as they noted the flash of Drizzt's first arrow, Entreri and Dahlia moved off quickly. They rushed around the first building and into the narrow alleyway beyond, then out and about the second, as well, and so on down the line.

After several such jaunts, Entreri started out again, but Dahlia grabbed him and held him in place. For she had noted the drow's shot across the way, the arrow flying up to the roof to take out the sea devil.

Dahlia motioned upward with her thumb, and even as she and Entreri glanced up, a sea devil passed right over them, leaping to the roof of the building they had just passed.

Dahlia planted her staff and Entreri spun around and crouched, setting his hands to help her in her leap. Up she went, inverting at the top of the eight-foot pole, throwing herself over the lip of the roof. She landed crouched, almost on her belly and facing back into the alleyway, but wasted no time in whirling around and bringing Kozah's Needle to bear with a great sweep across that sent a sea devil staggering.

Up leaped Dahlia, thrusting repeatedly to keep that sahuagin and a second at bay, buying time.

Up came Entreri, climbing the wall with ease, and coming over the roof's lip with sudden ferocity. He charged past Dahlia, past the tips of the two tridents matching stabs with her. Inside that reach, the assassin halted and spun to the right. The sea devil on that side tried to bite him as he came in close, but it changed its mind, or Entreri changed it, as a dagger jabbed up under the creature's chin, through its lower jaw and into its upper. Never letting go, Entreri rolled around to the side and behind his foe, and tore free his blade as his sword came around to slash the creature across the back, cutting it down.

The second sahuagin stayed with Dahlia, who stumbled as it pressed its attack. Sensing a kill, the sahuagin bore in with the trident, which Dahlia side-stepped with ease.

The sea devil wasn't as nimble when the elf countered, Kozah's Needle thrusting into its upper chest and stopping short its advance. Dahlia retracted and struck again, driving it back a step, then struck third time, in the throat, and the creature staggered and continued to backstep.

The fourth strike launched it from the roof, flying down to the street to land hard on its back.

"More," Entreri called, and led Dahlia's gaze to the next rooftop in line.

Dahlia broke her staff in half, then into flails, and she and Entreri sprinted at the incoming threat. They leaped the next alleyway side-by-side, landing in a run and charging into the coming monsters.

Dahlia turned sidelong, avoiding a thrust, and her right hand slapped across, her spinning weapon wrapping the handle of a trident. She pulled it back and up, continuing forward under the lifting weapon and snapped her second flail out hard into the sahuagin's face. The creature wobbled, clearly dazed, and Dahlia turned, bent at the waist, and rolled into it, still tugging with her wrapping flail.

The creature bit at the back of her neck, but Dahlia continued to bear in, pulling the sea devil right over her. It let go of the trident as it tumbled, and Dahlia sent the weapon flying with a snap of her wrist. As the creature tried to turn and rise, she hit it again with her other flail, a heavy blow to its forehead. Stubbornly it stood, just in time for Dahlia to leap into a flying double-kick and send it, too, soaring from the roof.

She landed and bounced back to her feet to meet the charge of another sea devil, this one without a weapon, but hardly unarmed, clawed hands rending the air as it came at her.

Her flails went into a blur before her, slapping at those hands, and banging together repeatedly, as well, building a charge of energy.

Beside her, Entreri battled a second creature, and Dahlia managed to glance his way and flash a smile—which disappeared when she looked behind him, to realize that he had already cut down two others.

Now it was a competition, and one Dahlia planned to win!

Ambergris bumped into Afafrenfere, who had stopped his movement along the western wall of a building halfway down the street. The dwarf almost said something, but wisely held her tongue.

The monk had his left hand up to a boarded window, the tips of his fingers barely touching the wood, almost as if he sensed vibrations within. His eyes were closed and he seemed frozen in place.

Except for his right hand, which slowly lifted up before his breast, fingers bent like an eagle's claws.

Or a snake's fangs, Ambergris understood as Afafrenfere struck, his hand snapping out with the speed of a viper, smashing through the wooden boards and against the side of the skull of the sea devil within. The monk managed to grab on to the sahuagin's piscine ridge as he retracted, pulling the creature's head through the hole. Afafrenfere turned as he did this, his left arm going up high, and with the sahuagin's neck planted on the splintered edge of the broken wood, the monk drove his elbow down hard, like the falling blade of a guillotine.

The creature made a strange watery gurgling sound to accompany the sharp crack of its neck bone.

Ambergris rushed past the monk at the sound of stirring within the building, timing her arrival and sweeping two-handed strike of Skullbreaker, her four-foot mace, perfectly as the next sea devil burst out the cottage's back door. The sahuagin went flying to the side at the end of that powerful stroke and pitched down to the ground, sitting on the cobblestones.

It rose tentatively, lurching and with one arm hanging, and apparently wanted no more of the dwarf, for it turned and ran off.

But a second leaped out of the door onto the distracted dwarf, clawing and biting and bearing her down to the ground under it.

The dwarf's mace flew from her grip. She struggled and twisted, freeing up one hand enough to pin the sea devil's arm in tight. But still, the claws on that hand dug painfully into her upper arm.

And worse, the sahuagin managed to get in line, its face hovering right above Ambergris's. With a hiss, the sea devil opened wide its maw, showing lines of sharpened teeth.

Wide, too, went the dwarf's brown eyes, and she spat in defiance, right into that opened maw.

More a statement than a defense.

Drizzt noted a sea devil flying from the roof down the street to his right side, but he couldn't bring Taulmaril to bear to finish the creature. One appeared immediately above him to the left, arm lifted and ready to throw a javelin.

The drow let fly and fell back, his arrow taking the sahuagin in the chest and lifting it into the air. The creature's aim was not as good, or perhaps too good, for the javelin drove into the ground and stuck there, right where Drizzt had been crouching.

Drizzt had won that duel, but another sea devil took that one's place, and the drow heard, too, another behind him, on the roof to the right. He planted his foot and dug in his heel, turning around. Two strides and a dive sent him behind the cover of the north wall of that left-hand building, and up close so that the sea devil on the roof would have to lean right over to get a throw at him.

It did, foolishly, and Taulmaril's arrow blew right through its skull.

As that one fell, so too did another descend from that roof, leaping down at Drizzt, and two came down from the roof across the way as well, both holding javelins.

Out flashed Drizzt's scimitars as in flew the missiles. Drizzt spun to his left, away from the building, dodging one cleanly and lifting Twinkle just in time to deflect the second, though not enough to lift it cleanly past him.

⁂

"Go!" Artemis Entreri shouted, and Dahlia snapped her left-hand flail out at her opponent, driving the sea devil back. As she retracted, she dropped her left foot back and rotated around and out to her right, as Entreri cut before her.

She came up in front of the assassin's opponent, and the sahuagin was still watching Entreri. Her flail caved in its skull at the same time Entreri's sword cut the throat out of her previous opponent.

On they ran, side by side. Entreri went down, spinning left and to the ground, his sword coming across to bat aside a flying javelin.

Down Dahlia went, too, spinning right and to the ground at the same instant. She reconstituted her flails into solid four foot poles as she did so, and joined those into the eight-foot-long staff as she and Entreri ran on for the edge of the building.

Too late, though, they both knew as they approached, for a pair of sea devils on the next roof in line were already at the ledge, tridents lowered to block their progress.

Artemis Entreri skidded to a stop as he neared the ledge, his hand going to his belt.

Dahlia came up beside him but didn't slow, planting the end of her long staff and vaulting out, flying for the creature. The sea devil realigned its trident appropriately and seemed sure to skewer the elf woman, but at the last moment, Dahlia threw her legs up higher, tightened her torso muscles, and pressed out with her considerable strength, lifting her higher into the air. She flew past the rising trident, clearing the scaly humanoid, and turned as she went so that she landed facing back the way she had come. She pulled her staff in close and swept it in line just in time to block the slicing trident as it whipped around.

She glanced at the other sea devil, but it had no interest in her. It clutched at its belly, and at Entreri's embedded buckle-knife. Still it managed to keep its trident waving out before it, fending off the assassin's attempts to cross over from the other roof.

Dahlia parried the thrusting trident of her opponent, trying to figure out how to break free of her combat and clear the way for her companion to join her. She glanced at Entreri, to see him slapping futilely at the long weapon with his sword, though he could barely reach it and had no chance of knocking it free, or even aside enough for him to leap across.

Dahlia was about to yell out exactly that to him, but held her tongue as she came to understand that Entreri's whole play was naught but a ruse, his waving sword demanding the sahuagin's attention. Lurching and hissing, the sea devil followed the sword's movements with its trident, and remained completely oblivious as Entreri threw his dagger into its face.

The sea devil staggered back a couple of steps. The dagger hadn't flipped around properly to dig in and had merely bounced off the sahuagin's forehead, but still had the creature surprised and off-balance. By the time it recovered and re-focused, Entreri stood on the roof before it and a fine sword dived for its chest.

It tried to turn, it tried to parry.

But all it could do was grunt as the weapon struck home.

Entreri pressed it in all the way to the hilt, moving up close so that the dying creature couldn't begin to bring its long trident to bear.

Dahlia's opponent squealed an awful sound and angled its trident to jab at Entreri, but the elf was having nothing of that. She countered with a heavy barrage of thrusts and chops, always just ahead of the trident as the sea devil tried to recover and fight back to even footing with her.

Finally the frustrated creature simply threw its trident at her, which she easily dodged, then threw itself at Dahlia, biting at her and raking with its claws.

Or trying to, for the elf warrior hit it several times, Kozah's Needle punching hard and repeatedly, and on the last strike, Dahlia released the staff's lightning energy, the blast hurling the sea devil backward, flinging it from the roof with enough force to send it crashing into the wall of the other building.

Dahlia looked at Entreri, who swung around and flung the impaled sahuagin from his blade so that it, too, would fall dead into the alleyway, his free hand quietly retrieving his belt knife from its belly as it departed.

"Four," he announced, going for his dagger, which lay on the roof.

Dahlia growled at him and started off.

Started, but didn't get far, as a stone clipped her across the temple and drove her down to her knees, dazed.

Entreri stared, bewildered, then looked north toward the wall and figured out the sudden turn of events, for the air filled with flying stones, a barrage of missiles from the townsfolk who couldn't distinguish a sea devil from an ally in the darkness!

<hr />

The sahuagin bit down at her, and Ambergris snapped her head up to meet its attack, her forehead slamming the sea devil's upper jaw. She got gashed badly as the dazed creature retracted, but she accepted the pain for the gain she had made.

Then Afafrenfere's foot flashed in, kicking the stunned sea devil in the side of its jaw. Ambergris saw at once that the monk wouldn't be her savior here, though, as he leaped away to meet another sahuagin coming out of the cottage.

As the sea devil atop the dwarf lifted up a bit to regroup and collect its spinning thoughts, Ambergris managed to tuck her legs up under her. She kicked out, straight upward, and tugged the monster's arms as she did, lifting it right up and over her. Her powerful legs drove hard and the strong dwarf lifted her butt right from the ground, rolling up to her shoulder blades, and launching the sea devil right over so that it landed hard on its back.

Ambergris arched her back and snapped the muscles of her upper back, throwing herself right to her feet. She swung around immediately, and realizing that her mace was too far away, pulled her small round shield off her back and leaped at the fallen creature. She took up her small shield in both hands and drove its edge down with all of her considerable strength against the prone sea devil's neck.

The creature's legs lifted from the ground under the force of the blow, then began to twitch as the sahuagin thrashed about, gulping for air that would not come.

Ambergris glanced over her shoulder to watch her companion in action. He had a sea devil on its knees before him, helpless against a barrage of punches that snapped its head left and right.

"Behind ye!" the dwarf yelled, seeing yet another enemy, trident leading, coming out of the door. She needn't have bothered, for the battle-skilled monk was quite aware of the creature, obviously, and was even goading it to charge by appearing so distracted.

Afafrenfere rolled backward as the trident prodded for him, going right behind and around the thrusting tip. He grabbed the long pole with his left hand, and down chopped his right, a powerful blow that snapped the trident's handle cleanly. Afafrenfere wasted no time in bringing his left hand sweeping across, flipping up the trident's pointy end as he did to throw it into the sea devil's face.

The monk jumped up in the air behind that missile, snap-kicking the sea devil in the face. He landed and spun on the ball of his foot, leaping again into a circle kick that slammed the sahuagin's chest and sent it flying backward to slam against the cottage wall.

The monk dropped to one knee, grabbed the fallen trident half, and came up in a full spin, facing the sea devil with the missile lifted up high behind his ear.

Afafrenfere's hand snapped forward, the broken trident whipping into the sahuagin's chest. It grabbed at the handle, but Afafrenfere was there as well, tearing the three-headed trident free of the scaly creature then thrusting it again, angling up to put it into the sea devil's throat. He tore it free again, and thrust it back into the chest, poking three new holes above the three from the throw.

He gave a short cry with each movement, his energy enhanced by the sharp calls of his order, his chi focused like the tip of a spear.

Or the tip of a trident.

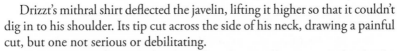

Drizzt's mithral shirt deflected the javelin, lifting it higher so that it couldn't dig in to his shoulder. Its tip cut across the side of his neck, drawing a painful cut, but one not serious or debilitating.

And not as painful as the hit from the other missile, Drizzt realized as he turned with the blow to see that the previous javelin had driven deep into the thigh of the creature that had leaped down from the roof beside him. Still that stubborn sea devil came on, limping badly, the javelin hanging from its leg.

Drizzt darted at it, kicking out at the javelin. The creature lurched in pain and the drow raced past, slashing with Twinkle. The stubborn creature tried to turn to keep up, but Drizzt skidded to a stop and spun on it directly, his twin blades battering the sahuagin before it began to formulate some defensive posture.

The drow had to jump back as the other two bore down on him, and still, amazingly, the stubborn, wounded sea devil came at him. A dozen deep wounds dripped blood about its arms and torso. The javelin hung more awkwardly from its leg. Drizzt's kick had widened the wound. But with that pole flapping, trailing several lines of blood, still the sea devil pursued.

Drizzt ran away from it, circling wide to charge in at the other two, meeting their pursuit with a fierce blur of movement, spinning and slashing, sliding down low and turning to cut at their legs, leaping up high and similarly spinning and slashing. To an unskilled onlooker, it would have seemed pure chaos, but to a seasoned warrior, every turn, every dip and rise, every slash and stab by the drow ranger would chime as harmonious as the notes of a sweet and perfect melody. Each move led to the next, logically, in balance and with power. Each strike, whether a straight thrust or a wide slash, found its mark.

And every angled retraction of those blades defeated a sahuagin's raking claw, or a kick, or a sudden rush. It went on for only a matter of a few heartbeats, but when Drizzt darted and rolled away from that frenzied melee, he left both of the sea devils staggering and bleeding and disoriented, giving him plenty of time to dive down and retrieve his bow.

He rolled around back to his feet, turning and setting an arrow as he rose.

The nearest sahuagin flew away in a flash of lightning.

The second stood straight, piscine eyes going wide.

Drizzt blew it to the ground, its skull exploding under the weight of the shot.

That left the third, still limping for him, impaled javelin waving, blood streaming. Drizzt put up another arrow and leveled the bow with plenty of time to spare. He stared down the length of that missile at the creature, looking for some sign of fear, some recognition that it was about to die, some understanding that it could not hope to get near to him.

He saw nothing but determination and hatred.

He almost pitied the thing.

Almost.

He blew the sea devil away.

"Rest are runnin' for the sea," Ambergris reported, the dwarf and monk hustling back around the building across the way from Drizzt. "We might get ye a couple more shots if we're hurryin'."

"Let them run," Drizzt answered. "We'll come back tomorrow after sunset, and the next night. Sting them and sting them. They'll grow weary of this and we'll help the folk reclaim Port Llast to the sea."

"Heroes," another voice chimed in sarcastically, and the three turned to the street to see Entreri and Dahlia moving toward them, the elf woman barely upright and leaning heavily on the assassin, who showed wounds of his own, including an eye swollen enough so that the others could see its disfigurement even in the starlight.

Drizzt ran to Dahlia and took her from Entreri's side, and immediately noted that her hair was sticky and matted with blood.

"Amber!" Drizzt called, easing Dahlia down.

"Looks like yerself might be using a spell or two o' mine, as well," the dwarf remarked, kneeling beside Dahlia, but considering the line of blood on Drizzt neck.

When Drizzt regarded the dwarf, her forehead bloody and gashed, he realized that she might be saying the same of herself.

"We should retreat to the higher reaches beyond the wall," Afafrenfere offered. "The sahuagin might return in force and formation."

"Yes, let's," Entreri offered. "I have a few words to offer those grenadiers." His tone had all eyes looking his way.

"Be warned," Entreri grimly added, "we might be on the road soon after."

CHAPTER 6

THE BATTLE OF PORT LLAST

THE CHEERING FOLLOWED THE FIVE COMPANIONS ALL THE WAY BACK TO Stonecutter's Solace, and even inside the tavern, where their table was visited repeatedly by proud Port Llast villagers, clapping their backs and promising that their gold would never be good in the seaside town.

"They've been starved for such a night as we have given them," Drizzt remarked in one of the few moments when the five found themselves alone. "And starved for a bit of hope. For too long, this town has been in retreat, the minions of Umberlee in advance."

"Bah, but won't it go right back to that?" Ambergris asked.

"Only if we allow it," Afafrenfere interjected before Drizzt could, and the drow nodded and smiled at the monk in agreement and appreciation.

Others came over to them then, each bearing a fistful of foamy, spilling mugs, and the conversation widened to swallow the many notes of "huzzah" being thrown their way. The dwarf took it all in with a gap-toothed smile, enjoying the accolades, but not as much as she enjoyed the ale.

Afafrenfere, too, reveled in the glory, though he wouldn't partake of alcohol, pushing the mugs placed in front of him to the dwarf, which of course only made Ambergris all the happier.

Truly, Drizzt enjoyed watching his companions' reaction to the celebration more than the joy of the townsfolk, which he found satisfying, and the libations, of which he would only modestly partake. It did his heart good to watch Ambergris, who reminded him of so many old friends he had known in his decades in Mithral Hall, and Afafrenfere, who appeared to be validating the dwarf's belief in the goodly bent of his disposition. What warmed Drizzt most of all, though, was the reaction, the sincere smile, of Dahlia. She deserved that smile, he thought.

The journey to Gauntlgrym had battered this woman. Even attaining her most desired victory in killing Herzgo Alegni had taken more from her than it had given, Drizzt knew. On the road to Gauntlgrym, before they had known that Alegni had survived the fight at the winged bridge, Entreri had posited that perhaps the expectation of revenge had sated Dahlia's unrelenting anger better than the realization of that revenge. The way Entreri had explained it to Drizzt was that a person could always pretend that some future event would solve many more problems than the realization of such an event could ever bring.

Drizzt winced slightly as he watched the young elf woman now, and weighed that image against the sight of Dahlia mercilessly pounding dead Herzgo Alegni's head with her wildly-spinning flails. The tears, the horror, the unrelenting anger . . . no, not anger, for that word hardly sufficed to describe the emotions pouring forth from the outraged Dahlia.

Drizzt had come to understand that rage, of course, for Dahlia had painted for him a very dark scene indeed. Herzgo Alegni had murdered her mother, and that after he had raped her, though she was barely more than a child at the time.

And now, in addition to the complicated emotions swirling within Dahlia due to her exacting revenge, there came a second rub, an even deeper, or at least, an even more confusing and conflicting issue: that of the twisted tiefling warlock, Dahlia's son. What turmoil must be coursing within that deceivingly delicate frame, Drizzt wondered? What questions, unanswerable, and what deep regrets?

Drizzt could only imagine. He could equate nothing in his past to the storm swirling within Dahlia. While he had faced his own trials and trauma, even the betrayals of his own family seemed to pale compared to that which this young elf had faced—and indeed, that only reminded Drizzt that she was barely the age he had been when he had left House Do'Urden to serve his time in Melee-Magthere.

He wanted to empathize, to understand and to offer some advice and comfort, but he knew that any words he might say would surely sound hollow.

He couldn't truly understand.

Which had him turning his head toward someone who, apparently, could. Bound by trauma, Artemis Entreri and Dahlia had found comfort in each other. That much seemed undeniable to Drizzt. He understood now their quiet words, and what a fool he felt himself to be given his irrational jealousy and anger. True, the wicked Charon's Claw had magnified his response, and had prodded him incessantly with images of the two entwined in passion, but still it felt to Drizzt as if, blinded by his own needs and pride, he had failed an important test in his relationship with Dahlia.

And where he had failed, this man Entreri had succeeded.

He watched the assassin now, sitting calmly, accepting the drinks, and even pats on the back, but with a distant, detached expression.

Drizzt leaned over and whispered to Entreri when he found a break in the stream of congratulations, "You must admit some satisfaction in what we have done this night, in the good we have wrought."

Artemis Entreri looked back at him as though he were the offspring of an ettin. "Actually," he corrected, "the way I see it, we helped them and they threw rocks at us."

"They didn't know it was you on the roof," Drizzt argued.

"Still hurts."

But even Entreri's unrelenting sarcasm couldn't dull the night for Drizzt. He had led his companions to this place hoping for exactly this situation and outcome. No, that description didn't fit, the drow thought, for this night exceeded his wildest hopes for their venture to Port Llast.

And it was only the beginning, Drizzt Do'Urden vowed, lifting a mug in toast to Artemis Entreri.

The assassin didn't respond, but Ambergris did, heartily, and Dahlia joined in, and even Afafrenfere put aside his aversion to alcohol and lifted a mug.

"Only the beginning," Drizzt mouthed silently between foamy lips.

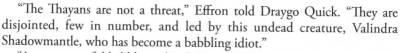

"The Thayans are not a threat," Effron told Draygo Quick. "They are disjointed, few in number, and led by this undead creature, Valindra Shadowmantle, who has become a babbling idiot."

"A very powerful babbling idiot," Draygo Quick reminded. He sat in his chair, striking a pensive pose, with his fingertips touching and tapping before him, and a superior expression etched on his weathered old face, as if he were looking at this from on high, and with an understanding that his minions on the ground far below him couldn't quite comprehend.

At least, that was how Effron viewed it.

The twisted young tiefling tried to keep a tight hold on his emotions here. He knew that he was already on shaky ground with Lord Draygo and didn't want to complicate that potential morass with an outburst.

But he truly wanted to scream. He had gone to Neverwinter Wood and had observed the Thayans, whose numbers had been reduced to disorganized pockets of Ashmadai zealots. These were independent bands now, clearly lost, with no coordination from higher powers, particularly not Valindra, who roosted in the same treelike tower Sylora had taken, but seemed incapable of spouting anything other than gibberish.

When Draygo Quick had given him this assignment, he had thought it an important mission, but soon into his scouring of Neverwinter Wood, Effron had come to wonder if the withered old wretch had simply moved him to the side of the more important matters.

"You appear as if you believe your words should comfort me," Draygo Quick said.

"The Thayans are no threat," Effron replied as if the logic should surely follow.

"Valindra Shadowmantle is undeniably powerful and dangerous."

"She's an idiot."

"Which makes her doubly dangerous."

"She will never recover the faculties to organize the scattered remnants of the Thayan force into a spear aimed at Neverwinter, nor even as a capable hedge against any advances we might again make into Neverwinter Wood."

"I care nothing for either at this time."

Effron started to reflexively argue, but held his tongue and instead digested Draygo Quick's words and let them sink in as he tried to follow the old Shadovar's reasoning. Why would Draygo Quick say such a thing in the context of Thayan power? Or more specifically, in the context of the relative volatility and danger presented by Valindra Shadowmantle? If he didn't care about returning to Neverwinter Wood or in trying to regain the city, then why would Valindra and the other Thayans matter at all?

"I don't believe that Szass Tam will deign to return to the region," Effron said. "The Dread Ring seems quite dead, actually, and bereft of any real power. Given the painstaking care needed to create such a ring, or recreate one, it would hardly seem to be worth the trouble, or the risk. The people of Neverwinter know of the Thayans now, and will battle them fiercely."

"I have no reason to believe that Szass Tam will turn toward Neverwinter anytime soon," Draygo Quick replied. "He might, or more likely one of his upstart and ambitious minions might, but it doesn't matter."

Effron wound up right back where he'd started, and he again had to fight back his building frustration. He almost asked Draygo Quick what the problem might be, given all that the warlock had just said, but he understood that to be an admission of failure, an admission that Draygo Quick was thinking at a higher level here than he was, and that, of course, Effron could not allow.

So he stood there staring at the old Shadovar for a long while, putting all the pieces together in logical order and weighing each tidbit Draygo Quick had offered in concert with the manner in which the secretive warlock had offered them.

And then he understood.

"You fear that Valindra Shadowmantle will threaten Drizzt and Dahlia . . . no, just Drizzt," he said. "This is all about the rogue drow. None of the rest of it matters to you."

"Very good," Draygo Quick congratulated. "Perhaps you are finally listening to me."

"She won't go after Drizzt, and if she did, he and his companions would obliterate her," Effron said.

"You do not know that. Either point."

"But I do!" Effron insisted. "Valindra sits in her tower, muttering the name of Arklem Greeth over and over again, like a litany against an encroaching sanity rather than an attempt to maintain it. And now she's added a second name, that of Dor'crae, to that mix. Half the time she spouts the two intertwined into gibberish." He threw up his arms and dramatically tilted his head back and proclaimed, "Ark-crae Lem-Dor-Greeth!" in ridiculous fashion.

"I doubt that she's lucid enough to recall that she can cast spells, let alone actually recite the words to one," he finished.

"Then you will gladly go and kill her," Draygo Quick replied.

Effron tried to stop the blood from draining from his face, but unsuccessfully, he knew. For all his ridiculous dramatics, he knew in his heart that Draygo Quick's estimation of Valindra Shadowmantle's formidability was likely much closer to the truth than his own. She was a lich, after all.

"Is that what you command?" he asked somberly.

Draygo Quick chortled at him, and Effron understood, yet again, that the withered old wretch had garnered the upper hand.

"If she remains in Neverwinter Wood, pay her little heed, other than to confirm that which you have told me," Draygo Quick ordered. "Our true targets have moved along from there, it seems, and so perhaps Valindra will forget all about them."

The first part of that last sentence had Effron's ears perking up. "Moved on?" he asked under his breath.

"Worry not about that," Draygo instructed. "Trust that I am watching them."

Effron's face tightened, and he winced when he realized that Draygo Quick had noted the nervousness in his tone.

"What do you command of me, Lord Draygo?" he asked.

"Go back to your studies. I will inform you when you are needed."

Effron rooted himself to the floor, resisting the unacceptable order, but having no real power to contradict or countermand it. A few heartbeats passed and Draygo Quick looked at him curiously.

"I wish to return to Toril," he blurted, and he knew that he sounded desperate and pathetic.

Draygo Quick smiled.

Effron shifted uncomfortably. He was at the old warlock's mercy. He had just admitted as much.

"Not to spy on Valindra any longer, I would presume," Draygo Quick remarked.

"I will help you scout out Drizzt Do'Urden."

"You will strike out and be destroyed—"

"No!" Effron emphatically interrupted. "I will not. Not without your express permission."

"Why should I trust you? Why should I allow you this?"

Effron merely shrugged, and such a curious and pathetic movement it seemed with his twisted form and his dead arm flopping uselessly behind his back. He had no answer, of course, and so he was surprised when Draygo Quick agreed.

"Go to Toril, then," the old warlock said. "Check on Valindra and confirm your suspicions and expectations—and know that I will not be merciful toward you should she cause me trouble! Be thorough and not anxious. This is important!"

"Yes, Master."

"Then scout the city as you safely can. Drizzt and his companions may still be using that as their base, but if not, then follow in their footsteps. Find them, but watch them from afar. Learn of the people around them. I would have a complete recounting of their environ: the towns, the militia, everyone and everything that they name as allies and everyone and everything they name as enemies."

"Yes, Master!" Effron said, trying futilely to keep the excitement out of his voice.

"And learn for me most of all, to which goddess does Drizzt Do'Urden pray?"

"Mielikki, one would presume."

Draygo Quick stared at him hard, and he backed away a step.

"And discern as well, if you can, which goddess answers his call."

"Master?"

Draygo Quick just sat there, unblinking, as if there were nothing left to discuss.

With a curt bow, Effron spun around and rushed from the room to prepare his pack for the journey back to Toril. He didn't immediately leave Draygo Quick's tower, however, for though he hoped to follow his master's commands—for of course he was terrified at angering Draygo Quick again—he realized that this particular group had deflected, diffused, and defeated any and every plan or trap that he, his father, and Draygo Quick had set for them.

Effron intended to be prepared, more so than perhaps Lord Draygo would understand.

He waited for an opportune moment then slipped back into Draygo Quick's private quarters. He knew the rooms quite well, having served as direct understudy to the man for close to a decade. He moved to the far side of the room first, to a large oak wainscoting decorated by a marvelous relief of a grand hunt, with shadow mastiffs leading Shadovar hunters in pursuit of a fleeing elk.

Effron hooked his fingers behind the elk's antlers and pushed down, and the wainscoting slid aside, revealing a pigeonhole message box behind it, thirty rows across by twenty rows top to bottom, enough cubbies for six hundred separate scroll tubes. Most were filled.

Effron knew the filing system, since he had implemented it. In the very middle, and in mediocre scroll tubes, were the greatest spells. He slid one out, glanced at it, and replaced it—one after another, until he found the dweomers he desired. With trembling fingers, he opened the scroll tube and slid the parchment out, not daring to even unroll it. This spell was far beyond him, he knew, for without the scroll he couldn't even attempt to cast it. And even with the scroll, it would be a desperate move.

But these were desperate times.

Effron tucked the spell under his arm, replaced the cap on the tube, and slid it back into its cubby. He closed the wainscoting by pressing the wheel of one of the pursuing hunter chariots and moved to the side to a bin of empty scroll tubes to protect the stolen spell.

The young tiefling took a deep breath and assured himself that Draygo Quick would not likely even come to this secret cabinet, let alone miss this particular scroll. It had been in Draygo Quick's possession for longer than Effron had been alive, after all, and the old warlock rarely found need of such spells here in the Shadowfell. Effron swallowed hard again at that thought, for might Draygo Quick depart for Toril sometime soon? And if so, and if to catch Drizzt Do'Urden, might he not want a second copy, a scroll, of this very spell?

Effron tucked the scroll tube into his robes, determined to take the risk.

The next part would be trickier, he knew, for he would be procuring something much more obvious. Draygo Quick might notice this item missing, of course, but in that case, Effron decided that he could justify borrowing it as a necessary protection.

The cage holding Guenhwyvar was not the only such implement Draygo Quick possessed, though surely it was the most elaborate. Guenhwyvar's cage, after all, not only had to shrink and hold the cat, but had to prevent her from returning to her Astral home.

These other jails were not nearly as elaborate, and indeed, appeared as no more than simple jars behind the closed doors of another cabinet.

Effron opened those doors and waved his hand to part the perpetual magical mist that kept the contents of the cabinet intact and in a state of stasis. Beyond the mist, Effron glanced upon Draygo Quick's menagerie, and it was not one that would make a little girl dreaming of puppies and kittens jealous. More likely, such a collection would make any child of any race flee in terror, or tumble to the ground, paralyzed in the deepest pits of fear.

For none of the creatures in those many jars were alive. True to Draygo Quick's necromantic leanings, these were dead things, or rather, undead things, in various stages of decay, and with a couple of magical constructs, golems, as well. Effron removed the newest jar and marveled at the tiny umber hulk within. Draygo Quick had taken this corpse from the streets of Neverwinter only recently.

Just a few moments removed from the cabinet, the tiny umber hulk stirred and unsteadily stood up, seeming to regard Effron. It was tiny only because of the jar, and if he dumped the zombie out, it would quickly regain its twelve-foot stature.

Yes, he might need such a shock trooper against these formidable enemies. He slid the jar into his pouch.

He hadn't come here for that one, however, but for another, for a creature he had created on Draygo Quick's command, using an ancient *Manual of Golems* his master had provided. This had been one of Effron's greatest tests, and greatest achievements. It, perhaps more than anything else—except his heritage—had gained him great stature within the ranks of Lord Draygo's underlings.

He removed the jar from the cabinet. Inside was a snake skeleton no longer than Effron's middle finger. It stirred and coiled, then lifted up and began to sway, a dance that had Effron forgetting himself for a moment even though the golem was within a jar and reduced to a fraction of its actual length, which was more than twice the height of a tall human man.

Effron looked more closely at it, marveling at his long-ago handiwork. The golem, a necrophidius, had a head fashioned from a human skull, but with a serpent's fangs.

"My death worm," Effron whispered, using the more common name for such a creation. "Are you ready to hunt?"

Afafrenfere watched curiously as his sidekick danced and melodically chanted, waving a censer that filtered an aromatic smoke throughout their room at Stonecutter's Solace. Ambergris had bought the room rather than renting it, though at a bargain price, given the good feelings toward the companions after their victory against the sea devils.

"What are you doing?" the monk asked, but the dwarf just kept up her dance and chant and didn't answer.

Afafrenfere crossed his arms over his chest and sighed heavily.

A long while later, the dwarf finally stopped. She looked around and smiled, clearly pleased with herself.

"Well?" the monk prompted.

Ambergris winked at him. "Me sanctuary now," she answered. "The place I'm callin' home."

"You intend to reside here?"

"We're staying through the winter," the dwarf answered with apparent confidence.

"And then?"

Ambergris shrugged as if it didn't matter.

"Seems a foolish exercise, then," Afafrenfere remarked, and he started out of the room for their breakfast.

Ambergris merely smiled and did not bother to explain. What she knew that Afafrenfere did not was the significance of the word "sanctuary." When she had set out to the Shadowfell as a spy for Citadel Adbar, Ambergris had been given a special brooch, one containing a single enchantment, a dweomer that would recall her to the designated sanctuary in the blink of an eye.

She followed Afafrenfere out of the room—almost, for she stopped at the door and turned back to regard the remnants of the incense filtering around the corners of the sanctuary. Only then did the significance of this action come clear to her. Her previous sanctuary was in Citadel Adbar, in the home of her birth, and never before had she given a thought to changing the location.

But now it had seemed a perfectly obvious choice.

Ambergris wore a sincere smile. She had found a new sanctuary because she had found a new home, and had found a new home, so unexpectedly, because she had found, in effect, a new family.

She had done it with hardly a thought, and simply in an attempt to be pragmatic about her current situation. But now, looking back at the room, the dwarf understood well the deeper implications, the subconscious hopes and emotions that had taken her to this dramatic action. She closed the door and followed Afafrenfere to the common room with a decided spring in her step.

The days became a month and the winter snows began to fall, and still the companions remained in Port Llast. They went out from the defensive wall often to seek out sahuagin, and each encounter proved quicker than the previous as the sea devils learned that the sooner they fled from this powerful band, the fewer losses they would suffer.

The more important work, though, went on behind Port Llast's impromptu wall. For what Drizzt and his four companions had brought to the beleaguered villagers most of all was a sense of hope, and in that new light, Dorwyllan and the people of the town regrouped and rearranged their forces into efficient attack patrols. Drizzt and the others trained them, and often one or more of the companions accompanied the townsfolk on their ventures to the more dangerous reaches.

They took great care in those endeavors; never was a patrol beyond the wall without a line of support all the way back to the settlement.

For too long, the night in Port Llast had belonged to the sea devils, but all who knew the dark elves understood differently. In Port Llast now, the night belonged to the drow, and more importantly, to his willing followers.

"Winning the battles is just the first step," Drizzt explained to the townsfolk at one gathering of all three hundred. "Winning and holding ground will be more difficult."

"Beyond the wall, near impossible," one voice came back at him.

"Then move the wall," Artemis Entreri offered.

Drizzt looked the assassin over carefully. Little had changed in their relationship in the passing tendays. Entreri remained dour and cynical and ready to criticize anything and everything Drizzt tried to do here. Despite that outward hard armor, though, the man's actions spoke louder. He hadn't left Port Llast for a more accommodating city, though Neverwinter was an easy ride away on his nightmare mount, and he went out to fight without hesitation, if not without complaint. Perhaps Artemis Entreri was actually coming to enjoy this new role he had found.

But he was also constantly nagging Drizzt about retrieving his dagger, and Entreri held that practical gain up as the sole reason for his compliance. Whether Drizzt believed that or not, whether there was some other reason for Entreri's assistance that went beyond any tangible gain, seemed irrelevant, in fact, since the road to Luskan and a man named Beniago had been promised, and in the near future.

By the second month, the second wall was well under construction. They started along the cliffs in the north, building out almost halfway from the current wall to the sea. At first the task perplexed them: How might they build a wall and leave it to the sea devils when they retreated back behind the first each night?

Ambergris provided the answer, by designing a portable wall section that could be angled out from the first wall to the end of the unfinished second wall each night. And so, as the stonecutters and masons worked on the second wall, another crew created access doors along the corresponding sections of the first wall behind it, and a third crew finished the box by securing the portable wall Ambergris had designed from the first to the new end of the second wall.

The unfinished second wall was manned by guards each night, with easy support coming from the town proper if necessary, and easy retreat routes available to them.

That second wall stretched more than halfway across the north-south breadth of the city by the time the sea devils mounted a coordinated assault against it.

But Drizzt Do'Urden was out among the sahuagin that night, though they didn't know it, and the warning got back to the townsfolk in plenty of time, so when the sea devils came on, they were met by the whole of the Port Llast garrison, standing shoulder to shoulder.

A hundred torches flew out from the wall, lighting the night, and half a dozen priests and a like number of wizards, all coordinated by Ambergris, turned that darkness into daylight with a barrage of magical illumination.

Armed with rocks and javelins, spears and bows, the militia's heavy volleys drove the sea devils back.

At the same time, a sizable force led by Entreri, Dahlia, and Afafrenfere, slipped down along the southern reaches of the city and swung back in at the flank of the marauders. Their coordination shattered by the barrage of missiles from the wall, the minions of Umberlee were caught unprepared, and the early phases of the battle became wholly one-sided, with the townsfolk slaughtering sea devils by the dozen.

Drizzt watched the battle unfolding from a rooftop several blocks away. At first it seemed a sure rout. Sahuagin seemed more interested in getting away than anything else.

But then they unexpectedly regrouped, and went back in at Entreri's force, seeming eager for a pitched battle.

Drizzt grimaced at the thought. The folk of Port Llast could ill afford any substantial losses here. The drow moved from roof to roof, trying to find the source of this renewed coordination. He kept Taulmaril in hand, but did not join in, unwilling to surrender his scouting position for the sake of a few kills.

He moved down toward the sea, very aware of the fact that he was beyond any hope of reinforcement should he be discovered.

But it was night, the time of the drow.

At last he came upon the source of sahuagin determination, a sea devil of extraordinary size standing on the docks and calling out orders—both to runners moving back and forth between the docks and the lead forces and to other sea devils, calling them from the sea to join in.

Drizzt crouched low and softly called to Guenhwyvar, and the panther soon appeared. Drizzt started to recite her duties, but he paused and couldn't help but forget the events around him for a few moments. Guen appeared haggard, her breathing shallow and uneven. Her muscled flanks hung low, her fur had lost its luster.

Would that Drizzt could have taken her to a lighted room to better inspect her then!

But he could not, he told himself. The sooner he completed his task, the sooner he could send Guen home for some much-needed rest. He bade the panther to stay by him and stand as his guardian. And his focus again became absolute, by necessity. He moved to another roof, and saw a better vantage point on yet another roof ahead. To get there, though, required him to leap far out, and crossing over a narrow street teeming with sea devils as he did.

It would be a difficult jump, and an almost impossible one without being noted.

Drizzt reached into his heritage, to the sensations of the deep Underdark that still vibrated within his drow form. He summoned a globe of magical darkness that hovered above that street, covering most of the open area through which he must leap.

But how difficult that jump now appeared! He would have to spring into blackness and cross over the street to the farther roof and somehow touch down safely.

He relayed his plan to Guenhwyvar. The sound of heavy fighting behind him, back up by the wall, reminded him that every heartbeat of delay might mean another villager cut down.

Off he ran, to the edge of the roof, where he sprang up and into the magical darkness, flying as far as he could. Logically, he knew that he could make this leap, but jumping blind as he was had his heart thumping with excitement and fear.

He came out of the globe just as he touched down, and without seeing the roof before connecting with it, he landed awkwardly, and it was all he could do not to cry out as he fell into a roll to absorb the shock of the landing. Guenhwyvar came out beside him and above him, easily soaring through the globe and with enough flight left from her powerful leap to give her time to gracefully and silently touch down.

Drizzt collected his thoughts and shook off his minor bruises and scrapes, rushing to the northwest corner of the wall, the closest point to the sahuagin leader.

The creature continued its commands, oblivious to the assassin perched barely twenty strides away.

Drizzt leveled his bow and held his breath to keep his hands perfectly steady. He glanced at Guen and winked, a signal to her that they would soon be in for some excitement. Again, he drew a bead.

Off flew the first lightning arrow, blasting into the sahuagin's scaly torso. Off flew the second, blowing a second hole right beside the first, and off flew the third, taking the creature right in the face. It curled and coiled, its serpentine body winding down to the cobblestones.

Drizzt sprinted back to the center of the roof, then to the southern edge, where he dropped down to the street just ahead of a volley of sea devil javelins. He and Guenhwyvar continued to move, but toward the sea, away from those sea devils now giving chase. The few they encountered met the fire of Taulmaril and the leaping attacks of Guenhwyvar, and the thunderous retorts of arrows, the calls and cries of sea devils and the roars of Guenhwyvar were complimented by a single whistle, blown through a unicorn head pendant.

Moments later, Drizzt, upon Andahar, charged out to the south and cut back to the east, galloping along the cobblestoned streets, a mob of sea devils giving chase.

"Be gone, Guen!" Drizzt ordered, and he put his head down low against Andahar's strong neck, trusting good fortune and speed to keep the flying javelins from finding him.

The first ally he came upon in his flight was Dahlia herself, poised behind the corner of a building. Across from her crouched Afafrenfere, and behind both stood lines of townsfolk.

The sea devils continued to give chase, continued to focus on their elusive drow prey, and so they were surprised indeed when the waiting forces fell over them.

So began the true battle of that dark night, the pitched battle for the center of Port Llast. It was over in short order, though to all involved, those horrible moments passed all too slowly, to be sure.

The voice of the leader of the sahuagin battle group had been silenced and their reinforcements fell thin. And the whole of the citizenry of Port Llast were out to meet them.

Victory.

A tenday later, the second wall was complete, stretching across the city, and Port Llast had reclaimed double the land of its previous haven. Though their losses had been minor in that vicious battle, and indeed, through the work of Ambergris and the other priests, less than a handful of citizens had been killed, and though scores of sahuagin bodies lined the streets, this expansion brought with it a new dilemma.

"We will be stretched more thinly now, with more land to defend," Dorwyllan said at the gathering of the town's leaders immediately following the wall's completion.

"The winter will help," another offered. "The corners of the harbor are icing over."

"The sea devils will seek deeper water in the cold," said a third.

A few months' respite, possibly," Dorwyllan said. "But they will come on relentlessly in the spring. We haven't the bodies to hold this farther wall against that assault, I fear."

But to this, too, Drizzt Do'Urden had an answer. He nodded to Dorwyllan and promised, "You will."

CHAPTER 7

DROW WEBS

"Y OU DON'T LIKE WHAT YOU SEE?" THE DROW SAID TO HIS DWARF COMPANION.
The sturdy dwarf, his black beard wrapped into two dung-tipped braids down the front of his muscled chest, his powerful morningstars strapped diagonally across his back with their adamantine heads bouncing at the ends of their chains around his shoulders, had to take a deep breath and stroke his hairy face. He couldn't quite find his voice. Athrogate didn't hate the dark elves the way most Delzoun dwarves would—his closest friend in the world was one, after all, and standing right beside him. And indeed, Athrogate was now a formal member of Bregan D'aerthe, a mercenary band from the dark elf city of Menzoberranzan—the clerics of that almost exclusively drow organization had nursed him back to health after his near-fatal fall in Gauntlgrym.

Still, the dwarf couldn't quite find his voice to respond, given the sights around him. The battle-hardened dwarf had been close to death before in his long, long life, but never in the manner he had found in this dark place, and never against an enemy so completely overpowering. He had fallen over the rim of the primordial pit, plummeting for the fiery maw of the preternatural and unstoppable beast. Good luck alone had landed him on a ledge, and his companion, Jarlaxle, had saved him, pushing him to the back of a cubby and summoning water elementals to ward off the biting flames of the primordial. Even still, Athrogate had nearly died and had known pain beyond anything he had ever imagined, his burned skin slipping off his bones.

And more than anything else, brave and mighty Athrogate had felt . . . insignificant and helpless. These were not emotions that sat well with the proud dwarf.

Now they were in Gauntlgrym again, descending a great spiral stairway to the lower levels of the complex, a stairway that had recently been repaired, and by craftsmen with a different and more delicate style than the original dwarven work.

They knew what they would find in the ancient complex, for they had been sent here—Jarlaxle had been sent here—by Kimmuriel Oblodra, the acting head of Bregan D'aerthe, executing an order from a much more powerful entity, the matron mother of Menzoberranzan's ruling House.

"Well?" Jarlaxle prodded as they continued down, crossing from the newer drow work to the remnants of the original dwarven stair. "Speak honestly. I'll take no offense, I promise."

Athrogate was almost always blunt, and particularly so concerning issues of dwarven importance, and certainly the disposition of Gauntlgrym fit that description. But the dwarf could only grunt and shake his hairy head as images of his fall to the ledge and memories of profound agony filled his thoughts.

And now his emotions were even more roiled. He didn't like these developments. Not at all. The aura and aroma of this drow settlement seemed an absolute desecration of Gauntlgrym. It didn't confound him on a logical level. It made perfect sense, after all. Why wouldn't the drow, or some other race, come back to this place and try to rebuild it?

And better the drow than goblins, he tried to tell himself.

But in his gut, the notion of a drow city growing amidst the ruins of the most ancient dwarven homeland seemed like a tragic loss, or a great theft, for and from his people—even though his people had long-ago rejected him and the dark elves had taken him in.

Jarlaxle patted him on the shoulder, and when he looked up, the drow winked at him with his one eye that wasn't covered by that strange magical eyepatch, signaling that he truly understood the turmoil swirling within Athrogate.

"You would do well to keep your doubts well-hidden," Jarlaxle quietly advised as they moved lower on the stair, low enough now to see that a group of drow astride subterranean lizards awaited them on the floor below. "House Xorlarrin is here, whether you or I or anyone else likes it or not, and if they perceive your distaste as a threat, they will deal with it in their particularly efficient and permanent fashion."

"Bah, but ain't that what I got Bregan D'aerthe backing me for?" Athrogate replied.

"Do you see the one astride the largest lizard, with the glowing shield on his arm?" Jarlaxle asked, motioning his chin toward the floor. Following that movement, Athrogate easily discerned the indicated drow.

"He is a Baenre," Jarlaxle explained. "A very well-loved and important Baenre."

"The First House?"

"If House Baenre objects to your attitude, Bregan D'aerthe cannot help you. In truth, we would deliver you to Matron Mother Quenthel as quickly as possible to avoid any complicity in your idiocy."

Athrogate smiled widely at the threat for he knew that Jarlaxle would do no such thing. Kimmuriel would, of course, and so would the rest of the Bregan D'aerthe crew. But Jarlaxle wouldn't, and indeed, Jarlaxle admitted as much implicitly when he returned the dwarf's knowing smile.

"At last, Jarlaxle," greeted the drow astride the great lizard. "It has been far too long since last I saw you."

"Were I to know your name, I am sure I would return the compliment," Jarlaxle replied with a gracious bow.

The rider, Tiago Baenre, bristled and glanced to his companions, left and right, an older weapons master Jarlaxle knew as Jearth Baenre, and a younger Xorlarrin wizard. Jarlaxle actually knew the Baenre, of course, and by name, for this was a name often spoken of late, in no small part because of the shield Tiago wore and the sword he carried on his hip, both wondrous new creations of old magic. Jarlaxle tried hard not to gawk when looking at that round shield now, for it appeared to be a truly remarkable item. It was nearly translucent, as if made of ice, and with diamond sparkles within. Despite his feigned indifference, Jarlaxle couldn't help but look more closely, for within that glassteel were lines, connecting in a definite pattern. For all intents and purposes, it looked as if a brilliantly symmetrical spider web had been trapped within the ice.

Magnificent, Jarlaxle thought but did not say. It hardly mattered, though. His expression had revealed his feelings, he realized, when he tore his gaze away and looked at Tiago to find the young warrior brimming with pride.

"You have curious taste in companions," Tiago said, noting Athrogate.

"Aye, but I can handle the smell," the dwarf quipped.

Tiago's eyes flared with anger. Jarlaxle wanted to silence his friend. He also wanted to laugh out loud. Neither seemed possible at that moment.

"I am Tiago Baenre," the young warrior proclaimed. "Grandnephew of Matron Mother Quenthel and Grandson of Weapons Master Dantrag."

"I knew him well," Jarlaxle replied.

"You understand why we requested this meeting with Kimmuriel," said the spellspinner, and the mere fact that he had dared to speak without being bade so by Tiago Baenre tipped Jarlaxle off to his identity. This was young Ravel Xorlarrin then, the mage credited with leading the expedition to Gauntlgrym.

The spellspinner whom Jarlaxle's brother Gromph had coerced into "discovering" Gauntlgrym with information Gromph had garnered from the skull gem Jarlaxle had given him.

"We have many enterprises on the surface now, and this new . . . settlement is a likely way station between those enterprises and Menzoberranzan," Jarlaxle replied. "Bregan D'aerthe would have reached out to you in any case."

"Would have?" Tiago asked slyly. "Or already have?"

"Well, I am here now," Jarlaxle replied, not understanding the cryptic reference.

"What about the trio from Bregan D'aerthe who were here previously? Just a few tendays ago, when first we ventured to Gauntlgrym?"

Jarlaxle held up his hands as if he had no idea what they might be talking about, and in truth, he did not. "I was asked to come and greet you, and so here I am."

"There were three here earlier who claimed to be of Bregan D'aerthe, including one *darthiir* who named herself your mistress," Ravel said, using the drow word for surface elves.

"Truly?" Jarlaxle tapped a finger to his lips. "Was she lovely?"

"Darthiir!" Tiago scolded. "That is disgusting."

Jarlaxle laughed aloud. "Not the word I would use, but for a parochial sort who has rarely traveled outside of Menzoberranzan, such might be the belief."

"Spare me your condescension," said Tiago.

"Condescension?" Jarlaxle echoed with feigned innocence. "More relief than condescension. With so many of my kin sharing your expressed viewpoint regarding any who are not drow, there are more delicacies for me to enjoy."

"She was with a drow, and a human, a small and gray-skinned man," Ravel interjected, trying to keep the discussion on track.

"A human who came to Menzoberranzan beside you long ago, so claimed Berellip Xorlarrin," Jearth put in.

Jarlaxle tried to hide his surprise, but unsuccessfully, he feared, and even if he had managed to do so, Athrogate gasped beside him.

"So you do know this human," Tiago remarked.

"If it is who you say, he should be long dead," said Jarlaxle. "Did you garner his name, any of their names?" he asked, though he thought he already knew the answer. But how Artemis Entreri, if it was indeed the assassin, came to be with Drizzt and Dahlia once more was quite beyond his understanding.

"Masoj Oblodra," Tiago replied.

"Oblodra?"

"The drow," the young Baenre clarified. "Kin to Kimmuriel, I expect. That was the name he used, at least."

The way he said it revealed as much as the words themselves, Jarlaxle knew. Masoj, after all, had been the mage from whom Drizzt had taken Guenhwyvar many decades before, though Masoj was surely no Oblodran. He knew now, beyond any doubt that these fools had run up against Drizzt without even realizing it.

Tiago's dead grandfather, dead by Drizzt's hand, surely was somewhere in the Demonweb Pits, groaning in frustration!

"We did not care enough to ask the names of the other two," Tiago added.

"Were they or were they not of Bregan D'aerthe?" Ravel asked pointedly.

"Who can say?" Jarlaxle bluffed, and he used a bit of magic from his eyepatch to carry some weight behind the words. "We have many independent agents moving along the Sword Coast. It is possible that one or another—"

"You would know if it was your consort, as was claimed, would you not?" Tiago asked, the sharp edge of his voice showing that he believed Jarlaxle to be cornered.

"One of how many dozen?" the sly mercenary shot right back. "As I told you, the fact that so many of my brethren are too foolish to appreciate physical beauty widens my garden of lovelies. Indeed, there are many in this area who could make that claim!"

Athrogate snorted.

"Where are these three of whom you speak?" Jarlaxle asked.

"Long gone," said Jearth, "as are the Netherese they battled."

"Then it is a discussion for another day," Jarlaxle decided. "My time is short, and if these three are of no consequence—"

"They killed a Xorlarrin noble," Tiago interrupted.

Jarlaxle nodded and spent a moment digesting the implications. "Then I will inform Kimmuriel and we will put all efforts into determining who they are and if there is any actual connection to our humble organization." He bowed again, and in the movement, cast a private glance at Athrogate to warn the dwarf that their business here had just grown very serious.

"Are we to discuss our preliminary business arrangements here, among this small group?" Jarlaxle asked.

"It would be premature to formalize anything," said the spellspinner. "But let us show you our efforts, and perhaps there are services and items Bregan D'aerthe can supply to us that will foster those later arrangements. Materials, for example, and formulas." He looked right at Athrogate as he finished, "We have the Forge."

"Lead on," Jarlaxle bade, and he and Athrogate stepped forward.

"Not him," Tiago insisted, pointing to the dwarf.

"He works for me."

"Not him." There was no room for debate in Tiago's tone, and Jarlaxle was surprised that the brash young warrior was so openly challenging him. Given that, it wasn't an argument Jarlaxle thought prudent to have, and besides, he knew that he could facilitate his own escape if necessary, but wouldn't likely be able to help Athrogate get safely away. He turned to the dwarf and whispered, "Up above," and Athrogate nodded his agreement and understanding. At the top of the ladder, Jarlaxle had enacted an enchantment from his wide-brimmed, hugely-plumed hat to create an extra-dimensional room as a safe haven.

Jarlaxle summoned his nightmare and rode off with the three lizard-riders, and Athrogate was fast indeed up the long stairwell to the safety of that secret room. Athrogate never shied from a fight, but these were, after all, dark elves.

"That is an amazing shield," Jarlaxle remarked some time later, when he and Tiago were in the forge room, looking down the line of craftsmen working the glowing ovens. His eye roamed to the spider hilt of the sword at his hip as he added, "Recently forged?"

Tiago laughed. "It was the second item created by the re-fired great forge of this complex."

"The sword being the first," Jarlaxle stated.

Tiago drew the blade and held it up for Jarlaxle to see. It was crafted of the same glassteel substance as the shield, and similarly flecked with sparkling diamonds, with its black spider web quillan and spider-shaped handle.

"Gol'fanin's work," Jarlaxle said, and that recognition obviously startled the young Baenre warrior.

"An old friend," Jarlaxle explained. "Is he around?"

"He is, but resting, I expect. I will pass along your well-wishes."

Tiago was hedging, Jarlaxle knew, afraid that if he brought the two together, Jarlaxle would gain some upper hand over him in his relationship with that most important blacksmith.

"House Xorlarrin will go to war with Bregan D'aerthe, then?" Jarlaxle asked bluntly, and Tiago's eyes popped open wide. "If it is found that these three were associated with Kimmuriel's band, I mean. Since they killed a noble—or is that merely suspicion?"

That last part was no minor quibble. Drow killing drow was an acceptable practice in Menzoberranzan, as long as no definitive evidence revealed the killer.

"Brack'thal Xorlarrin," Tiago explained.

Jarlaxle knew the mage. "Interesting. I had thought him driven mad by the Spellplague."

"Son of Zeerith and elderboy of the House," Tiago said.

"And you have definitive proof of this crime?"

"Does it matter? This is not Menzoberranzan, and in this place, the Xorlarrins are free to make the rules. You would do well to learn the truth of these three and deliver them to us posthaste."

A wry grin spread across Jarlaxle's face, an amused look that he was all too willing to share with Tiago.

"You truly believe that?" he asked.

Tiago remained stone-faced.

"Your great-aunt Quenthel would be as amused as I am by your thinly veiled threat, no doubt."

"As amused as she would be to learn that Jarlaxle of Bregan D'aerthe associates with the heretic Drizzt Do'Urden, who fought against her family in the battle that killed her beloved matron mother? The heretic Drizzt Do'Urden who killed her brother, my grandfather Dantrag, the greatest weapons master Menzoberranzan has ever known?"

Jarlaxle almost pointed out that, if such was the case, then Drizzt should not have prevailed in that duel with Dantrag, but he wisely held silent.

"You make bold claims, young Master Baenre," he said.

"The three claimed to be of Bregan D'aerthe."

"That only means that they were clever, not that they were telling the truth," Jarlaxle replied. "But wait, are you saying that among the trio was the rogue Do'Urden?"

Tiago stared at him hard, and Jarlaxle recognized that this one was no fool.

"Interesting," Jarlaxle added, feigning surprise. "The rogue Do'Urden is still alive?"

"And of Bregan D'aerthe," Tiago said dryly.

"A clever lie."

"So you say, and so you would have to say. The human with the drow once accompanied you to Menzoberranzan," Tiago argued.

"Long before you were born, if it even is the same human."

"Berellip Xorlarrin attested to it. Would you doubt a priestess of the Spider Queen?"

That, too, brought some laughter from Jarlaxle. When in his life had he not doubted those priestesses?

"That would make him a very, very old human," Jarlaxle said. "And I assure you, I have not seen this man of whom you speak in half a century or more. Nor is he a member of Bregan D'aerthe. Nor is Drizzt Do'Urden a member—if that is your suspicion regarding the drow's true identity—nor has he ever been. Nor would he ever desire to be, as you would understand if you knew anything at all about the heart of Drizzt Do'Urden."

Tiago eyed him with clear suspicion. "I will ask such of Drizzt Do'Urden himself," Tiago remarked, "right before I kill him."

He meant it, Jarlaxle knew from looking at him. This one was brash, and brimming with confidence, and apparently very well armed and armored, even beyond what one might expect from a Baenre. Jarlaxle made a mental note to look more deeply into the growing reputation of this Tiago Baenre—and of Ravel Xorlarrin, he silently added when he noted the spellspinner coming his way.

From his recent visits to Menzoberranzan, Jarlaxle knew that those two were among the most prominent of the new generation of the city. Gromph had spoken highly of Tiago, and had hinted that Tiago would likely soon supplant Andzrel as weapons master of the First House. Through his eyepatch, Jarlaxle had detected quite a bit of magic on Tiago, and the overwhelming glow from that shield and sword went a long way toward confirming Gromph's suspicions, for truly Andzrel would not be pleased to find Tiago wielding such wondrous items, and truly, Matron Mother Quenthel would not have allowed Gol'fanin to craft this paired sword and shield for Tiago if she meant to keep him behind Andzrel in the house hierarchy.

Of course, if Tiago went after Drizzt, as he had declared, whatever his arms and armaments, then Andzrel would likely have a long and quiet reign in his position as weapons master, with no living heir apparent.

Jarlaxle managed a slight smile at that notion, but only a slight one, for there was something unsettling about this young one—and his allies, Jarlaxle thought, when Ravel, equally confident and brash, joined them.

He was Jarlaxle, long-time leader of Bregan D'aerthe, feared and respected throughout Menzoberranzan for centuries. That respect was not so apparent in the expressions and words of these two. Was he becoming old and irrelevant?

Were these two rising? Was this their hour?

Would Drizzt be quick enough this time against the descendant of Dantrag?

***

"Ye thinkin' o' tellin' me?" Athrogate asked, long after he and Jarlaxle had left Gauntlgrym. The two were upon their mounts, Jarlaxle on his hell horse and Athrogate astride his hell boar.

"I'm sure I have no idea what you're talking about."

"Ye been full o' glum since ye came back from them drow."

"They are not a pleasant group."

"More than that," Athrogate said. "Ye ain't even told me about the fired forges!"

Jarlaxle slowed his mount and considered his dwarf companion. "Truly it is a wondrous place and already creating extraordinary weapons."

"For damned drow elfs!" Athrogate said. He spat upon the ground, drawing a wide-eyed expression from Jarlaxle. "Not yerself. Them other ones."

"Indeed."

"It's Entreri, ain't it?"

"Might be, given their description."

"Nah, I'm meanin' that it's Entreri what's got ye all glummed up. Ye ain't thought much on him in a lot o' years, but now it's in yer face again."

"I did what I had to do, for his sake as well as our own."

"So ye keep tellin' yerself, for fifty years now."

"You disagree?"

"Nah, not me place in doing that. I weren't there, but I'm knowin' what ye was facin', both from them Netheril dogs and from yer own kin and kind." He nodded ahead to the side of the road, where a darker patch of shadow loomed, a familiar drow standing beside it. "And speakin' o' yer kin and kind . . ."

The two dismissed their magical mounts and walked over to join Kimmuriel. They didn't have to deliver any report, of course, for Kimmuriel had been in on the trip to Gauntlgrym, telepathically linked with Jarlaxle throughout his meeting with the Xorlarrins and their entourage.

"Their progress has been considerable and laudable," Kimmuriel started the conversation. "Matron Mother Quenthel was wise in allowing the Xorlarrins to make this journey. The bowels of Gauntlgrym will prove valuable and profitable to us all, I am sure."

"It remains preliminary," Jarlaxle replied. "Many know of the place now, so it is likely that the Xorlarrins will find trials yet to come."

"Aye, not many dwarfs thinking to let the durned drow have Gauntlgrym for their own," Athrogate put in, and both dark elves glanced at him, Jarlaxle's amusement clear on his face, Kimmuriel's not so much.

"There will be a lot of dead dwarves then," Kimmuriel said dryly, and he turned back to Jarlaxle, visually dismissing the foolish dwarf. "This settlement will validate our surface concerns."

"It will surely allow us greater access to the drow marketplace, since it is an easier journey by far than Menzoberranzan," Jarlaxle agreed. "A pity that we have so abandoned the nearer points."

"Luskan," Kimmuriel said, and with clear annoyance, for he and Jarlaxle had argued quite vehemently over the disposition of the City of Sails. Jarlaxle had wanted Bregan D'aerthe to remain significant among the high captains who ruled the city, but Kimmuriel, his sights set elsewhere, had overruled him.

"Come now, my cerebral friend," Jarlaxle said. "You see the value of Luskan now, more clearly. You can deny that truth, but not with any conviction. We need to go back there in force, and become again the quiet power behind the high captains. I would be happy to lead that effort."

"Yes," Kimmuriel agreed, and Jarlaxle tipped his hat, grinning until Kimmuriel added, "and no."

"You presume much." Jarlaxle didn't hide his anger.

"Shall I remind you of the terms of our partnership?" Kimmuriel was quick to reply.

"Bregan D'aerthe is not yours alone."

Kimmuriel bowed in deference to Jarlaxle, and that action muted much of Jarlaxle's building anger. Jarlaxle and Kimmuriel shared the leadership of Bregan D'aerthe, but for the sake of the band, Kimmuriel could assume control whenever Jarlaxle's other interests—notably, the many friends, including a fair number of *iblith*, or non-drow, he kept on the surface—conflicted with what, in Kimmuriel's judgment, was best for the mercenary band. Ever logical and driven by the purest pragmatism, Kimmuriel would never use this agreement beyond its intended scope.

Kimmuriel had witnessed the exchange with Tiago and the others in the bowels of Gauntlgrym, and so he understood the true desire behind Jarlaxle's gracious offer to lead Bregan D'aerthe back to the City of Sails, and so, indeed, Kimmuriel's invoking of their agreement was entirely proper regarding the interests of Bregan D'aerthe. Jarlaxle had done well in selecting this brilliant lieutenant to serve in his stead.

Too well, perhaps.

"We have possibilities with a collection of Netherese lords in Shade Enclave," Kimmuriel said. "They are quite interested in facilitating an underground trade network."

"Shade Enclave?" Jarlaxle muttered. He had never been to the place, in what had been the desert of Anauroch before the Spellplague and the great upheavals that had so changed the land.

"You would be the perfect facilitator," Kimmuriel said. "In your efforts against the primordial, you delivered a great blow to the minions of Thay, as these lords are aware. They will be pleased to meet you and begin the negotiations."

"What of Luskan?"

"I will deal with Luskan."

"You should speak with the Baenres."

"I already have."

They will lose their prized young weapons master, Jarlaxle's fingers flashed.

I will see to it, came Kimmuriel's cryptic response.

Jarlaxle did well to hide his frustration with this drow who always seemed one step ahead of everyone else—at least he thought he had hidden it until he realized that he hadn't enacted the psychic shields afforded by his eyepatch and Kimmuriel was probably fully reading his mind.

"Shade Enclave, then," Jarlaxle said.

Kimmuriel stepped into the shadows and was gone.

"Where's this place?" Athrogate asked. "Me bum's already starting to hurt."

"Oh, it will hurt from riding," Jarlaxle replied, still staring at the now-diminishing shadows. "A thousand miles to the east."

"Right in the empire, then."

"The heart of the Empire of Netheril," Jarlaxle explained.

They summoned their mounts, nightmare and hell boar, and started away.

They rode easily, as usual, at a steady and consistent pace, trotting more than galloping though neither of their summoned mounts would tire.

"Ye think it really was him?" Athrogate asked as the sun lowered in the sky behind them.

"Who?"

"Ah, but don't ye play clever with me," the dwarf demanded. "I'm knowin' ye too well for that."

"Then it might be time for me to kill you."

"Too well for that joke to be anything more than a joke, too," said the dwarf. "So do ye think it really was Artemis Entreri?"

"I don't know," Jarlaxle admitted. "He should be long dead, but even in those last years, it seemed to me that he wasn't aging as a normal human might. He certainly wasn't losing his edge in battle, at least."

"Shade stuff?" Athrogate asked. "Ye think his dagger sucked a bit o' long life into him when he sticked a shade?"

"That was the reasoning," Jarlaxle agreed, but then added, "Was."

Athrogate looked up at him curiously. "So what're ye thinkin' now?"

Jarlaxle shrugged. "It could be the dagger, but with any of the life-stealing it performs and not that from a shade necessarily. Perhaps such a draw of an enemy's life energy—any enemy—adds to one's vitality and lifespan."

Athrogate, who had been cursed with long life as part of a long-ago punishment, snorted at the horror.

"Or, more likely, Artemis Entreri is long dead, and no more than dust and bones," Jarlaxle added.

"That Tiago fellow thought it was him."

"Tiago Baenre isn't old enough to know of Entreri's visit to Menzoberranzan."

"But ye said his sister—"

"Perhaps," Jarlaxle interrupted, and that uncharacteristic interjection alone clued both of them in to how intriguing and unsettling this possibility was to the drow mercenary.

Jarlaxle gave a frustrated sigh and shook his head vigorously. "No matter," he said, unconvincingly. "More likely, Drizzt and Dahlia have found a companion, whomever it might be, and Drizzt fed him that story to save them all when they were taken by the Xorlarrins."

"Nah, that's not Drizzt's way," Athrogate came back, and the response surprised Jarlaxle—until he looked down at his companion to witness Athrogate's smile. The dwarf was prodding him, trying to draw him out.

"Drizzt ain't one to weave a net o' lies in advance," Athrogate added. "That's yer own way, not his."

"Which is why I thrive while he merely survives," Jarlaxle quipped. "I am sure that he and Dahlia will find a place soon enough. He always does."

"Oh no ye don't," said Athrogate.

"I am sure that I do not know what you are talking about."

"I'm talking about Entreri, and ye're knowin' it full well. That one's ghost's been following yerself for half-a-hunnerd years."

Jarlaxle scoffed at that notion. "I have buried closer friends, and many lovers."

"Aye, but how many needed buryin' because o' yer own actions?" Athrogate said.

There it was, spoken openly, and Jarlaxle suppressed his initial response to lash out at the dwarf. Athrogate was right, he knew. Jarlaxle had betrayed Entreri to the Netherese many years before, when the empire had come in force for the sword, Charon's Claw. It wasn't often in his long life that Jarlaxle had been trapped without recourse, but the Netherese had done it, and before physically surrounding the pair, the powerful lords of Netheril had appealed to greater powers in Jarlaxle's own circle of potential allies, to Kimmuriel and Matron Mother Quenthel.

Indeed, the snares of Netheril had been complete.

And so their offer had been accepted.

Jarlaxle said no more for a long while, letting his thoughts slip back to Baldur's Gate, the city where the final play had occurred. In exchange for his freedom, Jarlaxle had facilitated the takedown of Artemis Entreri, and indeed had even trapped the man in one of his extra-dimensional pockets for the Netherese. Both Entreri and Jarlaxle would have surely died otherwise, Jarlaxle told himself—then and now and a thousand times in between. And he had only chosen the route of betrayal because he had expected to quickly launch a rescue of Entreri, though likely one without retrieving the sword, of course, soon after his flight from Baldur's Gate.

But that rescue attempt had never occurred, and indeed, many years passed before Jarlaxle had ever learned of the conspiracy working against him. Kimmuriel and the Baenres, for Jarlaxle's own sake, had worked in concert to break down Jarlaxle's magical defenses and thus allow the psionicist to invade Jarlaxle's mind and alter the details of the Baldur's Gate betrayal. As far as Jarlaxle could recall, just a few short hours after he had abandoned Entreri to the Netherese, that scenario had never happened, the actual events replaced by the suggestion of a betrayal by Entreri against Jarlaxle. Thus, by the time Jarlaxle had even sorted out the truth and remembered that Entreri had been taken as a prisoner of the Netherese, it was too late for Jarlaxle to do anything about it.

By that point, Matron Mother Quenthel had made it quite clear to the outraged Jarlaxle that he needed to forget the whole ordeal.

Pragmatism told him to honor her demands, for what would have been the gain of Jarlaxle attempting any such rescue, or even looking into the disposition of Artemis Entreri by that point, anyway? Even if Entreri had somehow managed to survive the initial capture and early imprisonment, he would have likely died of old age by then.

Unless . . .

"So now I find meself hopin' that ye think o' me as high as ye thought of Entreri," Athrogate said, drawing him from his contemplations.

"What?" a surprised Jarlaxle said, looking again to his bearded companion.

"He's still with ye," Athrogate explained. "After all these tens o' years. I'm thinkin' that few others'd get more than a passing thought from Jarlaxle, even if ye came to think that one ye thought dead weren't."

"I am intrigued, is all."

Athrogate's roaring laughter mocked him.

Jarlaxle's face grew tight and he looked straight ahead, urging his nightmare on at a slightly swifter pace.

"Aye, get done with our business so ye can find Drizzt and his companions, eh?"

Jarlaxle pulled up hard on the reins, halting his steed, and turned to glower at the dwarf. Athrogate had indeed struck a nerve with Jarlaxle. He knew there was little he could do to change the past, but for some reason, it was important for him to set the record straight with Artemis Entreri.

"Why do ye care, elf?" Athrogate asked him.

"I do not know," came Jarlaxle's honest response.

CHAPTER 8

THE ARRANGED MARRIAGE

E FFRON DIDN'T MUCH LIKE THE SNOW, AND THE SWORD COAST WAS SEEING more than its share of the wintry precipitation as the turn to the Year of the Six-armed Elf neared. He had returned to check in on the progress or retreat of the Thayans, as his master had demanded. Lord Draygo had told him to be thorough and not anxious, and the old warlock's insistence that this mission was important had resonated with Effron, all the more so because he knew that showing his loyalty to Draygo Quick and his competence in carrying out these demands would likely be rewarded.

For all of his desperation to pay back Dahlia, Effron understood that he couldn't manage any such thing alone. She was surrounded by powerful allies, and he would need a powerful response. The resources and personal power of Lord Draygo Quick would more than suffice.

So Effron had faithfully gone into Neverwinter Wood once again, and had thoroughly scouted and spied upon the remnants of the Thayan force, particularly the lich known as Valindra Shadowmantle. The Ashmadai were scattered and leaderless, posing no threat at all to the city or to any of Draygo Quick's ambitions in this area, if he held any. It didn't take Effron very long to realize that his previous report to Lord Draygo had been correct, for he saw nothing of Valindra Shadowmantle to indicate anything other than sheer insanity. The lich wandered out from her tree-like tower on occasion and meandered through the forest paths calling for Arklem Greeth or Dor'crae, and rarely speaking either name correctly and without some insane stutter, wailing and keening, and occasionally throwing a bolt of purplish-black necromantic energy at a tree or a bird for no reason whatsoever.

Effron figured that she would be caught by the citizen garrison of Neverwinter soon enough and properly dispatched.

He turned his eyes away from Valindra and the Thayans then, but lurked around the forest. Now he looked toward Neverwinter. Every time he noted activity near the city gates, he peered closely and anxiously, as if he expected Dahlia to walk into view. And what would he do if that came to pass, he had to ask himself?

Would he hold to his promise to Draygo Quick of restraint and patience?

He told himself that he would, that he had to be careful with his father Herzgo Alegni gone. More than once, though, he wondered if he was lying to himself.

On the morning he had determined to be his last day near the city, Effron walked a perimeter outside the wall, finding empty regions by which he could travel deeper into the place with his wraith form and other various methods of magical invisibility.

By late morning, he had covered most of the perimeter, and had ventured into the city four separate times, and with still a lot of wall yet to scout. He almost quit and simply took to the north road, growing convinced that Dahlia had indeed departed, as Lord Draygo had hinted.

"I would never have thought you foolish enough to return here, unless it was at the head of an army," a voice whispered from behind him barely a few heartbeats after he had convinced himself to continue his last look around.

Effron froze in place, plotting spell combinations and contingencies, either to get away or to strike out hard, for he knew that voice, and more importantly, he knew the diabolical truth behind it.

"Come now, young tiefling, we need not be enemies," the red-haired woman said.

"Yet I remember your presence in the ranks of my enemies in the square near the bridge that day," Effron reminded her.

"Well, I didn't say I would let you conquer my city," the woman replied. "Have you returned with such intentions? If so, please do tell that I might be done with you now."

"You underestimate my skills."

"You know the truth of mine," she replied.

Effron spun around to regard her. She seemed so plain and calm, nondescript, even. She exuded motherhood at that moment, and it occurred to Effron that he wished he had been blessed with such a mother. Warm and comforting, someone to hold him close and tell him that everything would turn out well . . .

The twisted warlock laughed at himself and shook that notion away. This was Arunika. Arunika was a devil, a succubus from the Nine Hells, wearing the mantle of a simple and gentle red-haired woman with a slightly freckled face. An ordinary citizen of Neverwinter, just going about her daily chores as any good human might.

"You are hunting Barrabus and that sword," Arunika remarked.

It occurred to Effron that perhaps she didn't know everything after all.

"What do you know of him?" Effron asked. "And of his companions?" he quickly added, trying not to sound too obvious.

"Why would I tell you?"

Effron ran his good hand between his horns and scratched at his purple hair. It was a good question, he had to admit.

"I have information you will wish to hear," Effron offered a few moments later.

"Do tell."

"Well, that is the whole point, isn't it?"

Arunika laughed at him. "I've already established that I know that you know."

"Not that, devil."

"I should kill you for torturing my imp," Arunika remarked. "Not for the sake of the imp, of course, but because of the breach of protocol. Invidoo is my property, and so I demand recompense. Tell me your secret, twisted warlock."

"I will," Effron promised. "And you tell me of Barrabus."

"I owe you nothing."

"But what harm in telling me? Surely you don't hold any loyalty to Barrabus the Gray, and certainly not to his companion, this drow ranger. Indeed, should Drizzt learn the truth of Arunika, he would chase you from the land."

Her expression revealed her unpleasant surprise at that thinly veiled threat. "Then I should make sure I destroy anyone else who might betray that secret. Is that your point?"

Now Effron laughed, but it was an uncomfortable ploy.

"I would not tell him . . . anything," the twisted warlock said. "Nor Barrabus and the other, Dahlia. You witnessed the fight on the bridge when Herzgo Alegni was driven from this land. Effron is no friend to those three, I assure you. But I have mentioned the truth of Arunika to others among my Netherese brethren, including several lords who would not take well your threats against me. Beware, succubus, else you tempt the wrath of Netheril."

Arunika stared at him hard, and yet, even in that look, there remained something so very appealing about this creature.

"But there is no need for any of this," Effron insisted. "We are not enemies, or should not be. Netheril will not return to Neverwinter. We have no reason to care, with the Thayan threat destroyed."

"Netheril was here before there was a Thayan threat to Neverwinter," Arunika reminded him.

"True enough," Effron admitted. "Our work was in the forest, and indeed, we may return to that place, but with no designs on ruling the city. It is not our place. It brings unwanted attention. So there, that is my secret, offered in friendship."

"And offered before you exacted your demand."

"All I ask is for you to guide me along the proper road to find Barrabus and his companions," Effron replied. "And why would you not? Should they return to Neverwinter, they'll not befriend Arunika, and should they ever determine the truth of your identity, they will seek to destroy you. So what do I ask of you that will not benefit you?"

Arunika laughed again. "I do so enjoy the play of mortals," she said. "With their foolish impatience as they scramble to make a legacy that will not last, no matter how many they kill."

Effron started to respond to that confusing statement, but Arunika waved him to silence.

"There is a band of highwaymen along the road just a few days north of here. If you make yourself conspicuous enough, they will likely find you."

"Would that be a good thing?" he asked after considering Arunika's words, and considering why she might have spoken them.

Arunika smiled sweetly—too sweetly. "Find the highwaymen and you will learn much of Barrabus and his friends," she said.

Effron thought of going back to the Shadowfell and letting Draygo Quick guide him to a more advantageous location back on Toril, but part of his mission, likely the most important part, was to learn the lay of the land around their prey.

So off he went. He had enough supplies for a tenday, at least. He had gone through almost half of those supplies before he came upon another person, a score of miles and more north of Neverwinter.

"Halt and be counted," the woman demanded, stepping out into the snow-covered trail before him, two large men at her side.

"If you are a guard, pray tell from what town?" Effron replied innocently. Arunika's words echoed in his thoughts. "I am not familiar with this region."

"If you were, you wouldn't be foolish enough to be traveling the roads alone," the woman replied with a rather sinister grin. She nodded to the thugs flanking her and both began a steady advance.

Effron didn't flinch, and even smiled, which had the two men, both much larger than he, glancing at each other.

"Then the only question that remains," the small warlock remarked, "is whether I should sting you and chase you away, or simply kill you and be done with it." He shrugged and let his useless arm swing weirdly behind him, using it to further press the idea that he wasn't the least bit intimidated.

An arrow whipped out of the trees to the side of the road, speeding straight for the warlock, but Effron was, of course, magically defended against such attacks and his shield of magical energy deflected the arrow enough so that it whipped just a hair's breadth from his face—and had he not instinctively turned aside, the missile would have likely taken a bit of his nose with it.

"The latter, I think," he calmly stated.

"Port Llast has little to offer," Dorwyllan told Drizzt and the others when he found them gearing up for the road.

"Ye're here," Ambergris replied dryly.

"Why thank you, good dwarf," the grinning elf said with an exaggerated bow.

"Not what I'm meanin'!" Ambergris insisted, but she couldn't keep the toothy smile wholly off her face against Dorwyllan's clever retort.

The elf tossed her a wink. "I am here out of loyalty to these people who have stood so fiercely for their homes and their place in the world. I have lived here for many decades. My friendships go back generations to some of the families of Port Llast. A sorry friend I would be indeed if I were to now desert them."

"Perhaps that is what makes Port Llast attractive then," said Drizzt. "A sense of loyalty and friendship and common cause. Community is no small thing."

Dorwyllan grew serious as he explained, "It will take more than that to displace others that they might come to join in this community, don't you think? The quarry, the reason for the founding of the city in the first place, is not nearly as rich now, with most of the valuable stones and metals already taken. It can supply some trade, likely, but not enough to support any sizable city.

"The tides no longer favor Port Llast," he went on, and he nodded out to the west, to the sea. "The changes after the Spellplague have greatly reduced Port Llast's position as a vibrant seaport, and with Neverwinter rebuilding and Luskan to the north, I do not see the advantage of trying to strengthen the port in any significant way."

"Perhaps you should campaign to be chosen as mayor of the town," Afafrenfere remarked sarcastically. "Your words have convinced me to stay."

"Grim truth, spoken among those who have earned the truth," Dorwyllan replied. "There is trade and some profit to be found in the sea, if we can drive off the minions of Umberlee. Plentiful food, and some considered delicacies, and rightly so. But Neverwinter and Luskan and Waterdeep can all claim the same, so I am at a loss to understand what might lure enough people to Port Llast to secure our land and attempt to return the city to any sort of prosperity."

"For those who already have community, I would agree," said Drizzt.

"If you are speaking of your troupe here, then know that—" Dorwyllan started to reply, but Dahlia cut him short.

"Stuyles," she said, figuring it all out. "You're talking about farmer Stuyles. And Meg, the woman on the farm outside of Luskan. And the fool butcher who almost cut off my foot!"

"He was trying to save you," Drizzt quietly reminded her.

"Might be tasty," Ambergris added lightheartedly, and Afafrenfere giggled. Dorwyllan wore a perplexed expression.

"The castoffs," Drizzt explained to the elf. "Those who farmed the regions outside of Luskan, and under the protection of Luskan before the City of Sails fell to disrepair."

"That was a century ago," Dorwyllan said.

"The rot was longer in spreading from Luskan's walls," Drizzt said. "The farms became less important to the pirates, and so Luskan grew more likely to send forth raiders than a protective militia. But some of the folk outside the city remain in their ancient homes, though they are sorely pressed, and with nowhere else to go."

"And some are on the roads around your own village," Dahlia added.

Drizzt glared at her, but that only made Dahlia grin.

"On the roads?" Dorwyllan asked, and his tone showed Drizzt that he had not missed the silent exchange between Drizzt and Dahlia. "Refugees? There are no refugees. Or do you mean highwaymen?"

"Given what you're asking, they deserve the truth," Dahlia stated before Drizzt could formulate an appropriately diplomatic response. Again he cast a glance her way, trying to look more disappointed this time.

"They live in the wilderness," Drizzt explained. "They are not bad sorts, but surely desperate ones, former farmers, former craftsmen, cast to the wilds by the entrenched powers of the Sword Coast. Luskan used to protect these communities, but now the high captains view them with indifference at best, or even as enemies, and to these desperate folk, the high captains are regarded no more highly than orc bosses."

"I cannot disagree with that assessment," Dorwyllan remarked.

"Then you understand?"

"Highwaymen? I would shoot them dead if I encountered them on the road with little consequences of guilt."

"So I thought of myself," Drizzt said dryly. "And yet, when I had the chance to punish them, I did not, and when I did not, I came to understand the deeper truth behind this particular group of desperate folk."

"They could have gone to Neverwinter, you understand?" Dorwyllan said. "The settlers of that town seek additional citizens almost as desperately as we do here in Port Llast."

"The Shadovar were there, with the Thayans lurking around the forest."

"Now you are merely making excuses."

Drizzt nodded solemnly. "They are in need of a home, and you are in need of citizens. Capable citizens, which these folk have proven themselves to be by the mere fact that they and their families have survived the wilds of the Sword Coast without the benefits of walls and garrisons. Do I go to them, or not?"

"I don't speak for Port Llast."

"Don't play such semantic games with me."

Dorwyllan let his gaze drift to the right, overlooking the still mostly empty city, the new wall, and the threatening sea beyond.

"I will say nothing of this conversation," the elf quietly remarked.

When Drizzt glanced at Dahlia this time, he was the one wearing the smile.

"Need I remind you that the last time we dealt with Farmer Stuyles, we wound up in a desperate battle in the forest against a legion devil and its minions?" Dahlia asked when Dorwyllan had departed.

"Ah, but that's not soundin' good," Ambergris remarked.

Entreri snickered, drawing Drizzt's gaze, and when he had it, the assassin pointedly shook his head and looked away.

"Stuyles and the others knew nothing about Hadencourt's true identity," Drizzt argued.

"You have to believe that, don't you?" said Dahlia, and she snorted derisively.

The drow's smile was no more, even though he believed his claims. These two, ever cynical, would not allow him to hold fast to hope. In their cynical view of the world, he was a foolish idealist, unable to face the harsh realities of life in the shadowy Realms.

It occurred to Drizzt that they could be right, of course. In fact, hadn't that been the very weight he had been dragging along like a heavy chain around his ankles for years now, back far before Bruenor's death, even?

"No," he heard himself replying to Dahlia. He stood up from his seat, painted a determined expression on his face, and spoke clearly and loudly and with all confidence. "I say that because I know it to be almost certainly true."

"Because the world is full of good people?"

Drizzt nodded. "Most," he answered. "And forcing them into untenable choices is no way to measure morality. Stuyles and his band do not hunger for blood, but for food."

"Unless there are more devils among them," Dahlia interrupted. "Have you considered that possibility?"

"No," Drizzt replied, but it wasn't so much an admission as a denial of the entire premise.

Dahlia moved as if to respond, but chortled and looked to Entreri instead, and Drizzt, too, found himself turning to regard the assassin.

Entreri looked away from Dahlia and returned that look to Drizzt, and he nodded his support to Drizzt, albeit slightly.

⁂

"I could have killed you all," Effron pointed out to the four battered and reeling highwaymen. "Be reasonable."

"Ye put spiders under me skin!" said one man, the archer who had nearly killed Effron with the first shot.

Effron looked at him and grinned wickedly. "Are you sure you got them all out? Or are others even now laying their eggs?"

The man's eyes widened in horror and he began scratching and rubbing his skin raw, as much as possible given the bindings Effron had placed upon all four, tying them together, back-to-back. The man's frantic shuffling had his companion to either side shoving back with annoyance, to Effron's great amusement.

"Not funny," the woman insisted, wisps of black smoke still wafting from her clothing.

"You attacked me," Effron replied. "Does that not matter? Am I to apologize for not allowing you to murder me?"

"We weren't meaning to murder anyone!" the woman insisted.

Effron nodded at the frantic, whining archer. "His first shot would have slain me had I not come prepared with magical defenses."

"He's not so good a shot, then," said one of the larger thugs.

"Just supposed to scare you," the woman said.

"You would do well, then, to hire better archers. For this fool has surely doomed you." Effron paused there and walked around to directly face the woman, who seemed the leader of the band, striking a pensive pose with the index finger of his good hand against his pursed lips. "Unless—" he teased.

"What do you want?" the woman demanded. "You already have our gear and our few coins."

"Which I will happily give back," the twisted warlock explained, "if you let me join your band."

"Join?"

"Is that too difficult a concept for you to grasp?"

"You want to join in with us?"

Effron sighed profoundly.

"Why?"

"Why?" Effron echoed, then realized that he was acting much like the fool sitting before him. "I am without companionship in a land I do not know. I have no home and it is winter. I could have killed each of you—I still can do so, and quite easily—but to what gain? None to you, obviously, and merely a pleasurable diversion for me. Practically speaking, I am much better off with companions who know the lay of the land."

"You're a half-devil Shadovar, and a magic-user," said the thug.

"Do you doubt my potential value?"

"But why?" asked the woman. "Surely you've got better opportunities before you."

Effron laughed. "I don't even know where I am. So take me in. You will find that my skills will help you with your little roadside endeavors, at the least."

The woman started to answer, but bit back the response and looked past Effron, cueing him in to the new arrivals before one of them even spoke.

"It is not her call to make," said a man's voice.

Effron turned around to see a group moving into position all about, forming a semicircle around him and the captives.

"Ah, so you have friends," he said to the woman.

"They're going to kill ye to death!" the archer insisted.

Effron turned to him, grinned, and said, "The spiders will still be in there."

The man whimpered and went back to his frantic scratching and jostling.

"You move away from them, then, and we'll hear you out," said the newcomer, a middle-aged man of considerable girth and a ruddy and grizzled appearance, stubbles of white and gray beard roughening up his heavily-jowled face.

Effron looked at the group and snorted, as if they hardly mattered to the equation.

"If you move aside from them, I guarantee your safety here," the man said.

"Do you think that matters?" Effron replied. "I assure you that I'm not in any danger, whether I walk away from them or slay them where they sit."

The man stared hard at him.

"But I'll not slay them, of course! I did not come here to make enemies, but to find a place, for I fear that I have none. I admit it, I am an outlaw, banished from the Shadowfell because I do not much enjoy the workings of the Empire of Netheril," he improvised, taking an educated guess that the Empire of Netheril wasn't much appreciated by this band of highwaymen. "Had I remained, they would have probably killed me, or thrown me into a dungeon, and I found neither option appealing." He looked over at the four prisoners. "Would you have me then?" he asked of the newcomers. "You heard my request of your companions. Do I not deserve at least a trial for the mercy I have shown this group? I would have been well within my rights by the law of this or any other land to slay them on the road and continue on my way, after all. They attacked me, not the other way around. And yet, look, they live."

"Just kill him!" the thrashing archer said.

Effron laughed. "Next time, aim better!" he answered the man. "Either kill your foe or, if it is your intent to miss, then actually miss, that I might have seen your shot as a warning and not a lethal attack. And do quit scratching. There are no more spiders."

The poor man didn't know which way to turn, so it seemed, and still he squirmed and still he whimpered.

The grizzled leader and his companions conferred privately for a moment, then he came forward to Effron, his hand extended. "Stuyles, at your service," he said. "You can put up your tent with us for the winter, at least. A sorry band of ne'er-do-wells we'd be to throw out one wandering the roads alone."

Effron took the man's hand and gave a weak shake. He started to offer his name, but bit it back. Only for a moment, though, as he realized that he had nothing to lose by offering his real name, since his unique appearance alone would surely scream out his identity to anyone learning of him.

"Farmer Stuyles!" Drizzt called every few strides. He rode down the path upon Andahar, the unicorn's magical bell barding singing gaily and bringing some brightness to the overcast sky, clouds heavy with snow. Beside him rode Entreri, astride his nightmare. The assassin hadn't said much in the two days since they'd left Port Llast, but neither had he complained, and to Drizzt, that alone spoke volumes. Entreri's silent nod to him back in the city had been an affirmation of Drizzt's plan.

Directly behind the pair rambled a wagon, borrowed from Port Llast and pulled by a pair of strong mules. Ambergris drove with Afafrenfere sitting beside her and Dahlia half sat, half stood on a pile of sacks full of seafood. They had come bearing gifts, but even in the cold weather, Drizzt feared that the food wouldn't stay fresh long enough to be of use to anyone.

"Farmer Stuyles!" Drizzt yelled again. "Are you about, man? I come bearing—"

"Ye best be holdin' right there!" a low, rumbling voice called back to him.

Drizzt and Entreri pulled up and Ambergris stopped the wagon.

"These your friends?" Entreri quietly asked.

Drizzt shrugged.

"Leave the wagon and your pretty mounts and start walkin' back the way ye come," the voice roared.

"I expect not, then," said Entreri.

Drizzt held up his hand for the others to be quiet and he shifted in his seat, this way and that, trying to catch a glimpse of the would-be robber.

"We have come in search of Farmer Stuyles and his band of highwaymen," Drizzt called. "Come as friends and not enemies. Come with gifts of food and good ale, and not to be stolen, but to be given."

"Well give 'em, then, and yer pretty horses too, and get yerself gone!"

"That won't happen," Drizzt assured the speaker, and he had determined by then that the ruffian was settled in a low rut to the right side of the trail, obscured by a small stand of aspen. "I wish to speak with Stuyles. Tell him that Drizzt Do'Urden has returned."

"Well enough, then," came a voice from behind the wagon, and all five turned to see a trio of highwaymen step out of the brush and onto the road. Two held bows, but they were not drawn, and the third, between them, sheathed his sword and approached with a wide smile.

"Last chance to walk away, elf!" boomed the voice up ahead.

"Enough, Skinny!" called the swordsman behind the wagon. "These are friends, you fool!" He walked around the wagon, nodded to Dahlia with obvious recognition as he passed, and moved up beside Drizzt's mount.

The drow dismounted, remembering the man from the campfire months before, when he had told his stories to Stuyles's crew in exchange for some food, shelter, and companionship.

"Well met, again," the man said, extending his hand.

Drizzt took the hand, but wore a perplexed and apologetic expression. "I do not remem—"

"Don't know that I ever offered it," the man interrupted. "Kale Denrigs at your service."

"Skinny?" they heard Entreri ask, and they turned as one to regard him, then followed his gaze along the road, where half a dozen others had convened, including, it seemed, the previous speaker, a man of gigantic height and girth, indeed one who more resembled a hill giant than a man.

"Half-ogre," Kale explained. "But a good enough sort."

That brought a laugh from Ambergris on the wagon.

"Is Stuyles about?" Drizzt asked.

"Not far."

"We come bearing food and other supplies, and with news to benefit your band."

"Recompense for Hadencourt?" Kale Denrigs asked, and he assumed a clever look.

"You should be paying us for Hadencourt," Dahlia called from the wagon.

"What's a Hadencourt?" Afafrenfere asked.

"Nah, who," Ambergris corrected.

"Both," said Dahlia. "Hadencourt the legion devil, harbored by Farmer Stuyles's band."

"Wonderful," Entreri muttered.

"The what?" Kale asked.

"Legion devil," Drizzt repeated. "He came after us in the forest, and he brought friends from the Nine Hells to make his case."

"And they're all back in the Nine Hells where they belong," Dahlia said.

"Hadencourt? *Our* Hadencourt, a legion devil? How can you—?"

"It was a painful realization, I assure you," Drizzt said dryly. "If there are any remaining associates of his among your ranks . . ."

"None," Kale Denrigs replied without hesitation, and the man truly seemed shaken by the revelations.

"Take us to Stuyles," Drizzt bade the man. "I must speak with him, and quickly." He glanced up at the sky, where thick clouds were gathering.

Kale looked at him skeptically. "A tough road with the wagon, I fear."

"Then leave it here. My friends will stay with it and await my return."

Still with doubt clear on his face, Kale glanced at the mound of sacks in the back of the wagon, then started to motion to his team.

"Leave those as well," Drizzt remarked.

"Have you baited us, then?"

"Let me speak with Stuyles," Drizzt said. "Either way, the supplies will be yours, but you need not take them now."

"Explain."

But Drizzt had heard enough. He shook his head and told Kale to take him to Stuyles again.

Kale bade his band to remain with the wagon as well, and they gladly agreed when Ambergris broke out the ale and offered up drinks all around. With just him and Drizzt, the travel was quick, but over difficult terrain, and Drizzt understood the truth of the claim that it would have been no easy task to take the wagon, or even just the supplies, along.

Soon enough, though, they arrived in a wide campground of scores of tents—Stuyles's band had grown in the months since Drizzt had last seen them—and Drizzt and Farmer Stuyles shared another warm handshake. With many coming out to view this strange visitor, Drizzt motioned back at the tent from which Stuyles had emerged.

They left many wide eyes behind as they entered. Among the onlookers stood a young tiefling warlock, his shoulders twisted from a fall off a cliff when he was but a babe.

Kale Denrigs, a lieutenant of the band, joined the pair inside, and explained the situation with Hadencourt to a wide-eyed Stuyles.

"A demon?" Stuyles asked incredulously.

"Devil," Drizzt corrected. "It is my belief that he was a scout for Sylora Salm."

"The Thayan in Neverwinter Wood?"

"She is dead, her forces scattered, her Dread Ring diminished."

"By your hand?"

Drizzt nodded.

"I expect that Hadencourt was looking for me and for Dahlia, at the behest of Sylora. Among the Thayans were the Ashmadai, devil-worshiping zealots."

"We've had some unpleasant dealings with them," Kale said.

"They'll not be much trouble to you now," Drizzt assured him.

"Then you come with good news and with supplies," said Kale, and at the mention of supplies, Stuyles looked at Drizzt curiously.

"Supplies only if you decline my offer," Drizzt said cryptically, a wry grin on his face.

"That seems a strange proposal," said Kale, but Stuyles, obviously recognizing that Drizzt had something much more important in mind, held up his hand to cut the man short, and nodded for Drizzt to continue.

And so the drow laid it out before an incredulous Stuyles and Kale Denrigs, explaining the situation in Port Llast, a settlement in need of hearty settlers, and made his offer.

"It will be a home," he said.

"Hardly a haven, though," said Kale.

"I'll not lie to you," Drizzt replied. "The minions of Umberlee are stubborn and fierce. You will see battle, but take heart, for you will fight beside worthy comrades."

"Including yourself?" asked Stuyles.

Drizzt nodded. "For the time being, at least. Myself and my friends. We have already done battle beside the folk of Port Llast, and have driven the sahuagin—the sea devils—to the sea, though we hold little doubt that they will return. Winter has brought a respite, perhaps, but the citizens of Port Llast must remain ever vigilant."

"Truly, this is a memorable tenday," Kale Denrigs said. When Drizzt regarded him, he added, "Full of memorable visitors."

Drizzt didn't think much of that remark, until Kale looked to Stuyles and completed the thought, adding, "Among the companions our friend Drizzt left at his wagon were three who also showed some hints of the Shadowfell."

Drizzt eyed the man with interest.

"The gray man on the strange steed," Kale quickly explained, and he held up his hands unthreateningly as if to indicate that he had meant no insult. "And the dwarf and man on the wagon. Not Shadovar, certainly, but tinged with the shadowstuff."

"You've a keen eye," said Drizzt.

"For shades, yes indeed, and with good reason," answered a clearly relieved Kale. "I've fought my share—"

"What did you mean when you said 'also'?"

Kale looked to Stuyles.

"We found a shade, a tiefling no less, along the road just a few days ago," Stuyles explained. "A formidable creature, though he certainly doesn't appear as such. Some . . . associates of mine waylai—err, encountered him along the road, but he soon gained the upper hand. He claimed himself an orphan of society, and so became the least expected member of our band since Skinny the half-ogre and his kin found their way to us not long after you had gone."

"Devils, ogres, tiefling Shadovar," Drizzt remarked. "You should take care the company you keep." He was trying to figure a way to garner more information about this newcomer, when Stuyles volunteered all that Drizzt needed to hear.

"It is good that you didn't have Effron along with you this day," Stuyles said to Kale. "The encounter along the road might have gone much differently, and much more dangerously!"

He said it with a lighthearted flair, and was smiling quite widely, until he looked at the grim-faced drow.

"Effron the warlock," Drizzt said. "Take care with that one, I beg. For your own sake."

"You know him?"

"Take me to him."

Stuyles started to talk again, to question the drow's sudden change in demeanor, no doubt, but he swallowed hard and bade Kale to find the twisted warlock.

"What do you know?" Stuyles asked Drizzt when they were alone.

"I know that Effron Alegni is a troubled and angry young warlock. He carries a great burden upon his broken shoulders."

"Will they accept him in Port Llast, then, should we accept your generous offer?"

Drizzt shook his head. "It will not likely get to that point."

He moved to the tent flap and pulled it open, peering out. He didn't want to get caught by surprise in an enclosed place against the likes of Effron. He noted immediately, though, that Kale stood perplexed, hands on hips, with many others around him, all shaking their heads and some pointing off into the woods.

"He saw my approach and likely fled," Drizzt said, turning back to Stuyles.

"You and he are avowed enemies, then?"

Drizzt shook his head. "It is far more complicated than that, and trust me when I say that I would love nothing more than to find reconciliation with Effron, for myself and for—" he almost mentioned Dahlia, but decided not to go that far down the road.

He just blew a sigh instead. "It is a good offer for you and your band," he said. "You will find community there, and a better way."

"Some might think we're doing well as it is," Stuyles said.

"You live in tents in the snowy forest in the Sword Coast winter. Surely the houses of—" He paused as Stuyles held up his hand.

"It is not as easy as that, I fear," he explained. "For myself, the offer is tempting, but not all in my band are likely to be welcomed openly by the folk of—well, of any town. Some have found us because they quite simply have nowhere else left to go."

"They do now."

"You offer amnesty? Just like that?"

"Yes," Drizzt said evenly. He wasn't about to let this idea fall apart when he seemed so close to actually making a difference here. "A clean handshake, with no call to divulge any unseemly history." He paused on that for a moment and looked Stuyles directly in the eye. "So long as you can vouch for them, in that they will cause no mayhem in Port Llast. I'll not insert more danger into the lives of those goodly folk."

Farmer Stuyles thought on it for a few moments, as Kale entered the tent.

"I can," he said, motioning for Kale to hold his news for the moment. "For almost all, at least. One or two might need some questioning, but I will leave that to you."

Drizzt nodded, and both he and Stuyles looked to Kale.

"Gone," the man informed them. "It would seem that Effron has flown away. I have sent out scouts."

"Recall them," Drizzt said. "He is likely back in the Shadowfell. And I would ask of both of you, as a friend, please mention nothing of Effron to my companions."

"Not even Lady Dahlia?" Stuyles asked.

"Especially not Lady Dahlia," said Drizzt.

A single wagon had departed Port Llast a couple days earlier, but nearly a score now rumbled down the last road to the town, though most of those had been stolen along the road over the previous months. Stuyles's band had done quite well, for there was no shortage of people in the region left behind by the designs of the high captains of Luskan, forgotten by the lords of Waterdeep, and expelled from the turmoil of Neverwinter. The band of highwaymen numbered well over a hundred, for they had joined with another similar group of civilization's refugees.

It hadn't taken much convincing from Stuyles, for almost all had readily accepted Drizzt's invitation: the promise of a new life, and true homes once more, as they had known in better times.

At the head of the caravan rode Farmer Stuyles, driving a wagon beside Drizzt and Andahar. They took their time along the last stretch of road, the long descent between the cliffs to the city's guarded gate, and by the time they arrived, word had spread before them and much of the town was waiting to greet them.

Dorwyllan came out from the gate to stand before Drizzt and Stuyles.

"Refugees," Drizzt explained. "Folk abandoned by the shrinking spheres of civilization."

"Highwaymen," Dorwyllan replied with a grin.

Farmer Stuyles turned a concerned glance at Drizzt.

"*Former* highwaymen," Drizzt corrected.

"Port Llast citizens, then," the elf agreed, and his smile widened as he extended his hand to Farmer Stuyles. "Throw wide the gates!" Dorwyllan cried, looking back over his shoulder. "And tell the minions of Umberlee that they'll find no ground within Port Llast uncontested!"

A great cheer went up inside the wall, and following that rose an answering cheer among the weather-beaten and beleaguered folk of Stuyles's renegade band.

"There'll be more to join us," Stuyles explained to the elf. "Coming from all parts."

"The farmlands outside of Luskan, mostly," Drizzt explained to the nodding Dorwyllan.

"I've sent runners," Stuyles explained.

"We've many empty homes, and a plentiful harvest to be culled from the sea," Dorwyllan replied. "Welcome."

Drizzt had always suspected it, but now it was confirmed, that "welcome" was his favorite word in the Common Tongue, and a word, he understood, with no equivalent in the language of the drow.

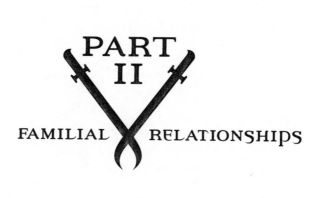

PART II

FAMILIAL RELATIONSHIPS

Freedom. I talk about this concept often, and so often, in retrospect, do I come to realize that I am confused about the meaning of the word. Confused or self-deluded.

"I am alone now, I am free!" I proclaimed when Bruenor lay cold under the stones of his cairn in Gauntlgrym.

And so I believed those words, because I did not understand that buried within my confusion over the battling shadows and sunlight of the new world around me, I was in fact heavily shackled by my own unanswered emotions. I was free to be miserable, perhaps, but in looking back upon those first steps out of Gauntlgrym, that would seem the extent of it.

I came to suspect this hidden truth, and so I pressed northward to Port Llast.

I came to hope that I was correct in my assessment and my plans when that mission neared completion, and we set out from Port Llast.

But for all my hopes and suspicions, it wasn't until the caravan led by me and Farmer Stuyles approached the gate of Port Llast that I came to fully realize the truth of that quiet irritation that had driven me along. I asked myself which road I would choose, but that question was wholly irrelevant.

For the road that I find before me determines my actions and not the other way around.

Had I not gone to Port Llast to try to help, had I not remembered the plight of Farmer Stuyles and so many others, then I would have been abandoning that which is so clear in my heart. There is no greater shackle than self-deception. A man who denies his heart, either through fear of personal consequence—whether regarding physical jeopardy, or self-doubt, or simply of being ostracized—is not free. To go against your values and tenets, against that which you know is right and true, creates a prison stronger than adamantine bars and thick stone walls. Every instance of putting expediency above the cries of conscience throws another heavy chain out behind, an anchor to drag forevermore.

Perhaps I wasn't wrong when I proclaimed my freedom after the last of my companions had departed this world, but I was surely only part of the way there. Now I am without obligation to anyone but myself, but that obligation to follow that which is in my heart is the most important one of all.

So now I say again, I am free, and say it with conviction, because now I accept and embrace again that which is in my heart, and understand those tenets to be the truest guidepost along this road. The world may be shadowed in various shades of gray, but the concept of right and wrong is not so subtle for me, and has never been. And when that concept collides against the stated law, then the stated law be damned.

Never have I walked more purposefully than in my journey to find and retrieve Farmer Stuyles and his band. Never have fewer doubts slowed my steps.

It was the right thing to do.

My road presented this opportunity before me, and what a fraud I would have been to turn my back on these demands of my heart.

I knew all of that as I descended beside Stuyles along the road to Port Llast's welcoming gate. The expressions from the wall, and those among the caravan, all confirmed to me that this seemingly simple solution for the problems of both these peoples was the correct, the just, and the best answer.

The road had brought me here. My heart had shown me the footsteps of Drizzt Do'Urden along that road. In following that conscience-dictated trail, I can claim now, with confidence, that I am free.

How amazing to me that an early confirmation of my trail came not in the cheers of the citizens of Port Llast, nor from the relief I noted so commonly among Stuyles's refugee band that they would at last be finding a place to call a home, but in the slight nod and approving look of Artemis Entreri!

He understood my scheme, and when Dahlia publicly denounced it, he offered his quiet support—I know not why—with but a look and a nod.

I would be a liar if I insisted that I wasn't thrilled to have Artemis Entreri along with me for this journey. Is he a redeemed man? Unlikely. And I remain wary of him, to be sure. But in this one instance, he showed to me that there is indeed something more there within his broken and scarred heart. He'll never admit his own thrill at finding this solution, of course, no more than he returned from our first foray against the sahuagin with a satisfied grin upon his ever-dour face.

But that nod told me something.

And that something makes this choice of mine—nay, makes *these choices* of mine—for I coerced Entreri into coming north with me in the first place, as I accepted his offer of help against Herzgo Alegni previously, and even trusted his guidance through the sewers of Neverwinter—all the more important and supportive of that which I now know to be true.

I am choosing correctly because I am following my conscience above all else, because my fears cannot sway me any longer.

Thus, I am free.

Equally important, I am content, because my faith has returned that the great cycle of civilization inexorably moves the races of Faerûn toward a better destination. Ever will there be obstacles—the Spellplague, the fall of Luskan to pirates, the advent of the Empire of Netheril, the cataclysm that leveled Neverwinter—but the bigger tale is one of trudging forward, of grudging resolve and determination, of heroes small and large. Press on, soldier on, and the world grows tamer and freer and more comfortable for more people.

This is the faith that guides my steps.

Where before I saw uncertainty and walked with hesitancy, now I see opportunity and adventure. The world is broken—can I fix it all?

I know not, but I expect that trying to do so will be the grandest adventure of all.

—Drizzt Do'Urden

CHAPTER 9

COMPETING SELF-INTERESTS

WITH THE SUN HIGH IN THE SKY, DORWYLLAN WATCHED THE LONG procession winding down the road below his perch on the side of a steep hill. Ramshackle carts pulled by haggard donkeys and painfully thin horses and cows bobbed by on uneven, wobbly wheels.

More women than men drove those carts, and more elderly folk than young—except for the *very* young. Children raced around from cart to cart, wagon to wagon, playing fanciful games of great imagined adventures. Looking at the sullen faces of the drivers, Dorwyllan understood that their parents desperately hoped that any such adventures remained imagined.

They answered the call of good farmer Stuyles, and several of his agents were among the caravan ranks. Winter was letting go finally, the roads clearing, and Stuyles had sent wagons north to the farmlands outside of Luskan, spreading the word for the folk to join in the tenday-long journey to Port Llast, to a new home.

And indeed, Port Llast was thriving, compared to the previous autumn. With the help of Drizzt and his friends, and the reinforcements from the band of highwaymen, the citizens had reclaimed the city all the way to the sea, and a new wall was nearly complete, one battered more by the high tide than by any sahuagin activity. The catapults along the cliff faces had been repaired and were well-manned . . . or well half-ogred, as the case might be. And best of all, a dozen boats were now seaworthy once more, and a plentiful harvest was to be found within the harbor, within the protection offered by the grenadiers on the wall.

Just a couple of months before, Dorwyllan had explained to Drizzt that he had remained in the dying town of Port Llast merely out of loyalty to the stubborn and stoic townsfolk, and his answer had clearly shown his sincere belief that the town was in her last days. But now the recollection of that answer, of those doubts, almost embarrassed the elf.

And here before him came new citizens, and the bustle of children playing would once again fill the lanes of Port Llast, and truly that was a sound Dorwyllan had never expected would return to the battle-scarred, blood-stained city.

"If they get there," the elf reminded himself, and scolded himself as he turned his attention back to the winding road north of the procession. They had many days before them, but none would be more dangerous than these first steps, Dorwyllan feared. He put his hand over his eyes and squinted to the north, imagining the uneven skyline of Luskan. The high captains of that city had abandoned these people, it was true, but Dorwyllan doubted that those same high captains would tolerate reciprocal treatment.

The elf let the procession get beyond his position, rolling down to the south, then took up his bow and moved out to the north, scouting the road.

Before the sun had fallen halfway to the horizon, he had his bow out and leveled at a group of four riders, Luskar garrison, trotting their horses easily to the south.

Dorwyllan chewed his lip, unsure. Did they know of the quiet exodus? If so, had they sent word back to the north?

He put up his bow when another group of riders approached, galloping down from the north. They met and exchanged some words, and the elf understood when the combined group, now ten strong, moved off swiftly to the south.

Dorwyllan shadowed them, running along the high ground, a straighter path than the winding road.

When the sun dipped below the western horizon, the winter's twilight settled deep, and several campfires appeared far to the south. Dorwyllan doubted that the riders on the road below could see those, as they, too, paused and lit torches of their own.

Dorwyllan put his horn to his lips and blew a long and mournful note.

A few heartbeats later, that call was answered from the south.

The elf looked to the road, where the Luskar patrol milled around, some pointing up in his general direction. He wasn't overly worried, though, for these seafaring deck-swabbers would never find him in the forest night.

Nor did they care to try, apparently, and Dorwyllan took that as a hopeful sign that the pirate fools had no idea that the horn exchange had been a warning to the caravan of their approach, that one note had spoken of less than ten soldiers, and that the people of the caravan would be quite ready for their arrival.

"Ever has that one drawn much attention," Gromph remarked with obvious amusement.

"He is not hard to find," Kimmuriel replied.

"You have Jarlaxle continually seeking him out."

Kimmuriel nodded, conceding the point. "But you speak with Jarlaxle nearly as often as I do." The psionicist had almost referred to Jarlaxle as "your brother," but had wisely redirected. "I have often wondered why the archmage doesn't simply go find the renegade and be done with him, once and for all. Surely Drizzt Do'Urden would prove of little trouble to one of your magical prowess."

"Surely."

"Then why?"

"Why hasn't Bregan D'aerthe?" Gromph replied. "Would not the grand trophy of Drizzt Do'Urden's head elevate your standing, and your prices?"

"Jarlaxle," Kimmuriel replied without hesitation. "He long ago determined that Drizzt was not our concern, and forbade any of us from seeking him out for the purposes of collecting a trophy."

"And why do you suppose that is?"

"Personal friendship, likely," Kimmuriel replied. "Ever has that been Jarlaxle's prime weakness."

"More than that," Gromph remarked.

"Then why not you for this mission? You could find him and be rid of him."

"To what end?"

"The trophy."

"I am Archmage of Menzoberranzan, and have been so for longer than you have been alive. I have all the riches, all the power, all the luxuries, all the time, and all the freedom any male in Menzoberranzan could ever expect. What gain would the death of Drizzt afford me?"

"He has killed members of your family."

"So have I."

Kimmuriel was not a mirthful sort, of course, but he almost broke out in laughter at the manner in which Gromph responded, so matter-of-factly, so evenly, that such events seemed a foregone conclusion, which of course they were among the great Houses of Menzoberranzan.

"Are you fond of him?" the psionicist asked.

"I do not know him and do not wish to."

"Then of his legacy?" Kimmuriel pressed. "I am quite certain that Jarlaxle admires this warrior from House Do'Urden for his escape from the clawing priestesses of Menzoberranzan."

"Then Jarlaxle is a fool who should keep his feelings well-hidden," Gromph replied—and warned, not so subtly pointing out to Kimmuriel that he was going down a dangerous road here. "Queen Lolth desires chaos, and so Drizzt serves Lolth's purpose, if not Lolth herself."

Kimmuriel found himself surprised that Gromph had so openly admitted that which had been whispered throughout the First House since the fall of Matron Mother Baenre to the axe of Drizzt's dwarf friend a century and more ago. He understood then that he wasn't going to get any further with Gromph along this line of probing, and he knew better than to keep pressing a drow as powerful as the Archmage of Menzoberranzan.

"Matron Mother Quenthel Baenre will not be so casual regarding Drizzt Do'Urden when her favored grand-nephew is returned to her on a slab," Kimmuriel said instead, bringing the conversation back to where it had started: with Tiago's revelations about, and his desire to hunt, Drizzt Do'Urden.

"Do not underestimate that one," said Gromph.

"Neither," Kimmuriel reminded. "But while I am unconvinced of the capabilities of Tiago Baenre's announced entourage, these two Xorlarrin waifs Saribel and Ravel, I can assure you that Drizzt has surrounded himself with formidable allies."

"Tiago is young and eager," Gromph replied. "He will likely alter his course soon enough."

"The trail is hot," Kimmuriel said.

"Then make it cold," Gromph replied, exactly the words the psionicist had wanted to hear.

Kimmuriel had quietly sought a large agreement with some Netherese lords, and Jarlaxle had already sent word back from Shade Enclave that these particular lords, led by one named Parise Ulfbinder, had inquired of Drizzt and were showing a rather curious interest in the rogue. Jarlaxle had offered no insight into the matter, and Kimmuriel couldn't sort it out, either, particularly regarding whether or not they saw Drizzt Do'Urden as an enemy or an ally.

Caution and good sense told Kimmuriel that a confrontation now between Tiago and Drizzt might not be good for business, however it might end.

Now he had Gromph's blessing to do what he thought best, insulating him and Bregan D'aerthe from the potential wrath of the First House.

"Bah, but we didn't kill the dogs, and that's got to matter for something," Ambergris said when the wagons unloaded their cargoes, refugees, and ten prisoners back in Port Llast a few days later.

Drizzt and the others, including the leaders of Port Llast and Farmer Stuyles, looked on with trepidation.

"We cannot let them go," Dorwyllan remarked. "They will run right to the high captains with news of our renewal."

"Nay, but we won't!" one of the captured Luskar insisted.

"Nor can we keep them against their will," said Drizzt. "They have done nothing against us."

"They attacked the caravan, or meant to," Ambergris reminded him. "We'd've been justified by law in killin' them out on the road, and not an honest magister'd argue!"

Drizzt had to nod at that, but he calmly put in, "But you didn't, and that is a good thing," to try to squelch some of the more impassioned shouts bubbling up around him.

"Still could," Ambergris replied, but with a smile, a growl at the prisoners who stood together near a wagon, and a wink back at Drizzt.

He shook his head to cut her short. She wasn't helping.

"Luskan knows anyway," Artemis Entreri put in, and his contribution surprised those who knew him well. "Just let the fools go, or put them on a boat and float them out to feed the sea devils. It matters not at all."

Whispers arguing both points rose up from the growing crowd.

"Keep them," Drizzt spoke over those, demanding the attention of all. "Keep them safe and keep them well. These are not our enemies. Artemis and I will go to Luskan."

"And I," Dahlia remarked.

"You two alone, then, and leave me out of it," a surprised and annoyed Entreri muttered.

"Not so," Drizzt corrected him. "You and I have business there anyway."

That surprised Entreri, and he returned a suspicious look.

Drizzt put a hand to his right hip, the same location where Artemis Entreri used to wear his jeweled dagger, and nodded.

"Lead on," said the assassin.

"I have anticipated this day," Drizzt said to Dorwyllan and a few others near to him. "I have contacts in Luskan. Artemis Entreri is correct. They know something is happening here in the south, though perhaps remain ignorant that it is Port Llast and not just Neverwinter that is growing strong once more. They understand that those farmers departed the fields around Luskan in an exodus to the south and they will learn the truth soon enough. You might well see Luskar sails outside your harbor any day now."

"They'll not cross the wall into the city as enemies," Dorwyllan decreed.

"Not at first, with a ship or two. But if it comes to blows. . . ." Drizzt left that thought hanging in the open. All in attendance understood that mighty Luskan could crush Port Llast with little effort if the City of Sails so desired.

"I will go and serve as emissary."

"And if that fails?" asked Dovos Dothwintyl, the city's current lord, but one who had been all but invisible through the reclamation efforts.

"Then perhaps we all go to Neverwinter, and seek the suffrage of Jelvus Grinch, who I am confident will welcome us warmly."

Some of the group began to grumble about that—hadn't they held on to their town through all these years, after all?

Dorwyllan calmed them. "It had to come to a climax," he said in a matter-of-fact, yet soothing voice. "Our stalemate with the sea devils was a slow death. Our victory over them grants us Port Llast returned or full retreat. If Drizzt is not successful in Luskan, we shall appeal to Neverwinter and Waterdeep for protection against Luskan."

"Let's hope that won't be necessary," Drizzt said, and he nodded and started away, motioning for Entreri to follow. In truth, Drizzt didn't think it would come to blows. He had made inroads into the ascendant Ship Kurth, after all.

Dahlia moved off with Drizzt and Entreri, but the drow blocked her. "We have two mounts, and must ride with all speed to beat any armada Luskan might launch at Port Llast. And I need you here."

"I will ride with you, hardly slowing mighty Andahar," she argued.

But Drizzt shook his head and would not be swayed. "I would have all of Luskan agreeing to leave us in peace, *including Ship Rethnor,*" he said bluntly, emphasizing those last three words to remind Dahlia that she had more than a little history, and not all of it favorable, with the powers of Luskan.

Dahlia narrowed her eyes, her face a mask of contempt and a warning to Drizzt that this, and his other inattentiveness of late, was not strengthening their relationship.

Surprisingly to Drizzt, that didn't bother him profoundly. Indeed, hardly at all.

No matter how hard he tried, Beniago couldn't look quite as uncomfortable as grizzled old Advisor Klutarch, shifting from foot to foot. They were, after all, in a cellar in Luskan surrounded by a handful of drow mercenaries.

"Thus we return," Kimmuriel said. "We have renewed interest in the area, to the benefit of Ship Kurth and the others."

"And ye've met with the others, then?" Klutarch asked.

"Need I?" Kimmuriel replied.

Klutarch looked surprised, but Beniago, of course, knew the truth of it.

"Well, they're—" Klutarch started.

"Irrelevant," Beniago finished for him. "Our good friend Kimmuriel here has just informed us that Bregan D'aerthe's return to Luskan will signal the ascent of Ship Kurth above the others. The other high captains will agree, or their successors will."

It took a moment for Klutarch to digest that, judging by his expression, but when he caught on to the implications behind the confident statement, his face brightened, albeit briefly.

Briefly, for clearly implied in Beniago's words loomed a similar threat against House Kurth.

"We should go to High Captain Kurth," Klutarch said.

"You go," Kimmuriel answered, and he turned to stare at Beniago, who cleared his throat and waved Klutarch away.

"There is more, then?" Beniago asked when he was alone with the dark elves.

"You grow comfortable in your light skin, I see," Kimmuriel replied.

With a chuckle, Beniago reached up and pulled off his earring, dispelling the illusion, and he stood before Kimmuriel in his true drow form.

"Kurth will agree," Kimmuriel stated more than asked.

"He is stubborn and headstrong, but ultimately pragmatic," Beniago answered anyway.

"If he doesn't, are you ready to assume the mantle of high captain?"

Beniago wasn't thrilled at that prospect, but said, "As you command, of course."

"Let us hope it doesn't come to that."

"Then there is more," Beniago reasoned

"Your cousin, Tiago Baenre, has settled in with the Xorlarrins in the ruins of Gauntlgrym," Kimmuriel explained. "Their expedition appears to be going along splendidly."

"Thus, Bregan D'aerthe's renewed interest in the region."

"Of course, but there is a potential problem. Your cousin Tiago has taken an interest with a rogue from Menzoberranzan known to be wandering the region."

Beniago sighed, understanding the implications all too well. "Drizzt Do'Urden will kill him, and Quenthel will go to war over it."

"And war, in this case, is not good for business," said Kimmuriel.

"What would you have me do?"

"Get Drizzt out of the way."

Beniago looked at his leader with incredulity, and not a small amount of terror. Drizzt would prove formidable enough by himself, of course, as Beniago knew from personal experience, and even more so given the characters with whom he had surrounded himself, and even if Beniago—Beniago *Baenre*—could somehow find a way to dispatch the rogue, Jarlaxle had made it quite clear to all of them that such an event would trigger harsh retribution. No drow, particularly no drow of Bregan D'aerthe, cared to cross Jarlaxle.

"Not to kill him, you fool," Kimmuriel remarked, and Beniago breathed a sigh of relief.

"Be clever," Kimmuriel explained. "Find a way to keep Drizzt and Tiago apart, for the foreseeable future at least."

"You could go to Tiago."

"We have," said Kimmuriel. "Jarlaxle himself spoke with him."

"And he is as stubborn, prideful, and headstrong as ever," Beniago presumed. Kimmuriel didn't bother responding, so Beniago asked, "Where is Drizzt?"

"In Port Llast."

That perked up Beniago, for Port Llast was becoming the focus of the discussion about Luskan over the last few days. The situation had just become more complicated, he feared, but when he got past that initial reaction, he saw as well a glimmer of hope.

He was a lieutenant of Bregan D'aerthe, he reminded himself, and though with many peers, he was outranked only by Kimmuriel, Jarlaxle, and the independent Valas Hune in the organization's hierarchy. Luskan was his post, and Luskan was about to become very, very important to the organization once more.

This was Beniago's chance to elevate himself above the many other lieutenants. He wasn't about to let his miserable cousin Tiago, whose father had betrayed Beniago and had him driven from the Baenre ranks to the waiting arms of Bregan D'aerthe in the first place, spoil it.

"Make Kurth agree," Beniago bade Kimmuriel. "I can better serve our interests from my current position. Instruct Kurth to grant me leeway in negotiating the disposition of Port Llast."

"You're already plotting your course," Kimmuriel said, and Beniago bowed at the compliment from this most intelligent and pragmatic drow.

"Problem?" Artemis Entreri asked Drizzt that night, the pair already a third of the way to Luskan despite their late start.

Drizzt rolled the figurine of the black panther over in his hands. "I don't know."

"You haven't been calling her lately."

"I haven't seen the need."

Entreri tapped him on the shoulder and forced him to look up, straight into the assassin's doubting expression. "We've been in a dozen fights since you felled the sea devil on the docks."

"I was often behind the wall, using a bow," Drizzt replied.

"And often not."

Drizzt sighed and nodded, unable to escape the accusation.

"The cat looks haggard," Entreri said before he could. "Her skin hangs low, as if with exhaustion."

"You've noticed."

Entreri shrugged. "Call her."

Drizzt looked back at the figurine and thought it over for a short while, then softly called out for Guenhwyvar. A few moments later, the gray mist arose and formed into the panther, who stood right before the seated drow.

"She pants," Entreri observed.

Drizzt put a hand out to stroke the cat, and to feel the slackness of her skin, as if her muscles beneath had grown old. He had seen her like this before, but usually after she had spent many hours by his side, battling trolls or the like.

"You see it?" he asked.

"Do such magical creatures age?"

Drizzt had no answer. "Ever before when Guenhwyvar has been so exhausted, a day in her Astral home would rejuvenate her. I fear that the fight with Herzgo Alegni, when she was lost to me, has harmed her."

"Or maybe she's not properly returning to her Astral home," Entreri offered.

Drizzt snapped his head around to regard the assassin.

"Still, she looks a bit better than she did when last she was at your side, so perhaps it will pass."

Drizzt wasn't sure of that, but as he had no need of Guenhwyvar at that time, he gave her a hug and quickly dismissed her. Remembering Entreri was watching, he felt a bit embarrassed, but to his great surprise the man offered no judgment—no negative one, at least. Drizzt filed that in the back of his mind and thought again of shadow gates and his suspicions of where Guenhwyvar had been lost to him. He wondered if he might soon be visiting the Shadowfell after all.

"Do you think Port Llast will thrive once more?" Drizzt asked a short while later.

"Do you think I care?"

Drizzt laughed and resisted the urge to blurt out "Yes!" He would allow Entreri his perpetual disaffection, for whatever purpose that might serve the man.

"So when we retrieve your dagger, you will sail out of Luskan and give no further thought to me, or Port Llast."

"I give no thought to you now."

Drizzt laughed again and let it go, fully confident that Artemis Entreri would be riding beside him on the return journey to Port Llast.

If they got that far, he reminded himself when he considered the task before him. He knew where Entreri's dagger was, so he believed, but he wasn't about to kill the only man who might broker the deal he needed for the sake of Port Llast in order to retrieve that dire blade!

Thanks to their enchanted mounts, they reached Luskan the next night, and neither found any problem in secretly climbing over the wall. Drizzt knew that Beniago would be more than willing to meet with him. He got his bearings and led Entreri through the city's alleyways.

"I don't know you," Beniago remarked a short while later, having turned down the alleyway to the appointed spot where he expected to meet Drizzt, only to find a small man leaning easily on the wall of the alleyway, appearing rather bored.

"That dagger you carry on your hip is mine," the small man replied. "And I would have it back."

"I have carried this for many years."

"Where did you get it?"

"That's not important."

"It is to me."

"I hardly remember."

Entreri kept his distance, but narrowed his eyes to let this man Beniago clearly see his building anger. "I will have it back."

"I cannot give it to you."

"Your corpse will not hold it so tightly, and if it does so, then I will merely chop off your fingers."

Beniago laughed, but betrayed a bit of concern with his posture and movements.

"He really will kill you," came a voice from above, and Beniago froze, and slowly looked up to see Drizzt Do'Urden sitting comfortably along a narrow ledge along the building to his left, legs outstretched before him, fingers locked behind his head as he rested against the structure's chimney.

"I have seen you fight, and witnessed this man, Artemis Entreri, in combat many times," Drizzt went on. "You will hold your ground against him for a short while—perhaps longer because he knows to beware your dagger. But soon enough he will overwhelm you, and you'll feel the killing blow before you ever see it coming."

"You betrayed me," Beniago said. "You lured me out here to an ambush!"

"Not so. Only so if you make it so."

"And I suppose your panther prowls nearby in case I try to flee."

"You know the way I prepare a battlefield," Drizzt replied and dropped down easily from his perch, landing lightly in the alleyway just a few strides from Beniago. "But I did not lure you out here for any ambush, or indeed for any fight. It wasn't until we saw you coming that my companion recognized your dagger as the one he carried many years ago." The statement was true enough, though Drizzt left out the part that he and Entreri had known of the item, and indeed that was why he brought Entreri along.

"I've grown quite fond of it," Beniago replied.

"More than you are fond of breathing?" Entreri asked.

"It's not worth it," Drizzt said to the tall, red-headed man. "Artemis Entreri's claim to the dagger is as legitimate as his ability to take it from you, should you choose that course."

Beniago looked from Drizzt to Entreri, then back to the drow. "I am a businessman," he said.

"I counted on that."

"Then what do you offer," Beniago asked, and he looked to Entreri and remarked, before Entreri could, "in addition to my life?"

"That which you once asked of me," said Drizzt. "I, and Dahlia, and my friend Entreri here, can serve House Kurth quite valuably, from afar. We are in a position now to give High Captain Kurth a tremendous advantage over his peers."

"Pray tell," Beniago prompted.

"We come as emissaries of Port Llast."

Beniago appeared greatly surprised at that. "Port Llast? It is a name I am hearing more often in the last few tendays."

"And you will hear more of it in the future, I assure you," said Drizzt. "The populace grows in number and in strength. They are reclaiming their city from the minions of Umberlee, and indeed have brought their city limits to water's edge once more."

"It is a rival city to Luskan's designs."

"No more," said Drizzt. "The tides will not favor Port Llast. She will not rise as a trading port, but from her cold waters comes a bountiful harvest of shellfish and other delicacies, and fine rocks from her quarry. There is nothing in Port Llast to threaten Luskan, but plenty of opportunity for one wise enough to see far ahead."

"That would be Ship Kurth," Beniago said.

"That would be your choice," said Drizzt. "And you would have the eyes you once claimed to want. My eyes, Dahlia's eyes."

"Why? You don't seem like the type who would throw in with Ship Kurth, as you made clear in our last encounter."

"I'm not, but is one crew better than another here in Luskan? I don't intend to fight for you, nor to provide you anything you might use against undeserving innocents. But I expect that I can stay within my moral boundaries and still be of use to a . . . businessman."

"Persuasive," Beniago admitted. "And so I would be a fool not to take that bargain. I assume that in exchange for this arrangement, Ship Kurth should not accede to any coordinated attacks on Port Llast from Luskan."

"Correct, and if you change your mind, understand that Port Llast is much better defended, and with far more capable hands, than her small size would indicate."

Beniago laughed at that unveiled threat.

"Then we are agreed?" Drizzt asked.

"I have to speak with my high captain, but it seems reasonable."

"And the dagger?" Drizzt asked

"And your life?" Entreri interjected.

"The deal is separate, I think," said Beniago, "now that I understand that you won't let your friend attack me. Without me, your tie to Ship Kurth is greatly diminished, of course, and since my associates know that I came out to find you at your request, if I turn up dead or missing they will be more likely to initiate an action against Port Llast, don't you think?"

"I'm growing bored," Entreri warned, but Drizzt held up his hand to keep the dangerous man at bay.

"We have prisoners from Luskan who assaulted a caravan bearing refugees to Port Llast," he told Beniago. "They are unharmed, and are being treated well. We want no war with Luskan. They are from at least three of the other Ships, as well as one man from your own."

"And you will give them to me," said Beniago, and Drizzt nodded.

"Their rescue, by you, will buy you good will and capital, I expect."

Beniago considered it for a few moments, then nodded. "It's a good start. But I need something else, and you are just the drow to do it. I have a ship of goods sailing for Baldur's Gate as soon as winter fully breaks—perhaps four tendays. She will be well-armed and manned, a crack crew, but I would have some of my own mercenaries aboard her for extra protection of certain . . . interests I have on the boat."

"You ask me to run guard on a merchant ship?" Drizzt asked incredulously.

"She will see no trouble on the seas."

"Then why—?"

"There are things aboard I would have doubly protected, perhaps from other mercenaries aboard. But again, you will likely find no trouble. None in Luskan would move against Drizzt Do'Urden without more support than they might find on a small boat."

"Ship Rethnor might disagree with that assessment, particularly if Dahlia accompanies me."

"There will be no Rethnor agents aboard. I promise that much."

"My dagger?" asked an impatient Entreri.

"It is a valuable dagger," said Beniago. "I hate to part with it."

"You have no choice," said Entreri, and he started forward.

"Drizzt?" Beniago asked.

"Deal," said the drow.

Beniago drew out the jeweled dagger, flipped it over, and handed it out hilt first to Entreri.

"Do I ride with you back to Port Llast to retrieve the prisoners?" Beniago asked.

"You haven't a steed that can pace us," Drizzt replied. "You, or your emissaries, ride out in two days. Our wagon with the prisoners should meet you on the road about halfway to the city."

Drizzt glanced at Entreri, who stood holding his jeweled dagger before him, staring at it, his expression filled as much with confusion as relief at having it back in his hand. Drizzt understood that; surely feeling the weight of the jeweled dagger again was evoking in Artemis Entreri a flood of memories, some good, many not so good.

The two were back on the road soon after, riding hard to the south on their untiring mounts. Artemis Entreri didn't utter a word all the way back to Port Llast.

And Drizzt didn't press him.

CHAPTER 10

THE TIP OF SEA SPRITE'S MAST

MINNOW *SKIPPER* GLIDED OUT OF LUSKAN'S HARBOR, TURNING ABOUT Closeguard Isle to slip out into the strong spring currents. Standing at her prow, holding the guide rope, Drizzt watched the familiar sights drift past, for this was the skyline he had viewed for years and years on end in his younger days. All that was missing was the strange, treelike structure of the Hosttower of the Arcane, with its seemingly organic, spreading limbs.

Drizzt wasn't pleased with any view of Luskan now, though. He had never been overly fond of the harsh and often lawless place, particularly since the fall of Captain Deudermont, but for several years, he had called this port home. That had all been shattered, of course, but somehow, out here on the water, that most unpleasant memory, Deudermont's death to Kensidan the Crow of Ship Rethnor, seemed to fade to a distant blur. Drizzt's thoughts cascaded back beyond those darkest days to the years when he and Catti-brie had sailed with Deudermont aboard *Sea Sprite* out of this very harbor.

A smile spread on the drow's face as he remembered the thrill of the chase as *Sea Sprite* hunted down a pirate. He would stand ready on her deck, scimitars in hand, Catti-brie beside him with Taulmaril the Heartseeker, ready to rake the pirate's deck and set the stage for Drizzt and Guenhwyvar to lead the boarding charge.

The drow closed his eyes and let the wind and the brine rush about him, slowly turning his head this way and that to catch the thicker scents and better feel the heavier salty gusts. On one such movement, he opened his eyes briefly, enough to see the tip of the mast of an old wreck that had been driven up against the rocks in the south harbor.

Sea Sprite.

It was her mainmast, Drizzt knew, trailing down under the dark waters to the shattered hull of the destroyed ship. That any sizable portion of the schooner remained at all intact in the rough waters around Luskan was a testament to her wondrous design and workmanship, but that hardly comforted Drizzt as he stood at the rail, looking at the lost glory of Captain Deudermont.

And Robillard, he recalled, the crusty ship's wizard, a mage of considerable power and possessed of a tongue as sharp as his frequent lightning bolts. Robillard long served as Deudermont's trump card at sea, for no wizard was more adept at splitting the beams of an enemy ship right at the waterline, or at filling sails with wind to speed *Sea Sprite* along.

Robillard would likely be long dead now, Drizzt knew, and he wondered if the man had left this world in a blaze of fireballs and the hail of ice storms, slicking the deck of a pirate ship. That thought brought a grin back to Drizzt, as he remembered when Robillard had used that very tactic on one pirate vessel in heavy seas. How the pirate archers had pitched and tumbled, and nearly half the crew had slid into the open ocean, making for an easy catch.

He thought of *Thrice Lucky* then, young Maimun's ship.

"Young Maimun?" Drizzt whispered aloud, for surely that one, too, was long gone from this world. He had taken up Deudermont's mantle as the greatest pirate hunter of the Sword Coast, Drizzt had heard, after the fall of Luskan to the five high captains, and for years afterward, Drizzt had often heard the name *Thrice Lucky* whispered in taverns up and down the Sword Coast, most often in gratitude and with raised mugs from those abiding the law, and accompanied by curses from those who walked a less seemly road.

Drizzt locked his gaze on *Sea Sprite*'s mast, showing in the low wake clearly whenever the waves rolled past.

He gave a solemn nod to the proud vessel, to the noble crew and captain who had taken her so far for so long. It was a good memory, he decided. Good times with good friends doing good deeds.

And the excitement, always that, with a pirate sail on every horizon, it seemed, and a crew ever ready and eager to take up the chase.

"The finest ship to ever sail the Sword Coast," Drizzt remarked when Dahlia walked up beside him, to find him still staring at the mast.

"Not any more, it would seem," she said flippantly.

"Aye, a long tale, and one worth telling," Drizzt replied. "And no better place to tell it than on a ship's deck on the open waters, under the stars and with the lull of the ocean nodding truth to every word."

Dahlia draped her arms around Drizzt and he tensed up for just a moment, then forced himself to relax. Somehow that touch didn't seem right to him. Not out here. Not on these same waters he had so often sailed with Catti-brie.

"We've no private cabin, but we can find a private place," the elf woman whispered into his ear. "Do you think the ocean will nod about that?"

Drizzt didn't answer, other than to offer a chuckle, a half-hearted one, and he understood that Dahlia had recognized it as such when she unwrapped her arms and stepped back from him. He turned to her, trying to find some way to soothe that unintentional sting, but he diverted it instead, seeing their three other companions moving to join them.

"I'm not for knowin' how these bowleggers take to this pitchin' and rollin' days on end," Ambergris grumbled. She planted her feet wide and square, but even then the slightest pitches of *Minnow Skipper* had her stumbling side-to-side. That just made her dig her heels in harder, but to little positive effect.

"You take the sea's roll with your belly," Afafrenfere explained to her, and he tapped his hard abdomen.

"Ah, shut up afore I spray me breakfast all about ye," said the dwarf.

"You will get used to the motion of the sea," Drizzt promised. "And when we put in to port, you'll find your legs unsteady once more."

That brought a laugh from Afafrenfere, and from the dwarf, but Dahlia just stared at Drizzt, seeming more than a little wounded by his rebuff, and Artemis Entreri looked as dour as ever as he walked past Drizzt to the rail.

"That one's been sailin' afore," Ambergris muttered, shaking her head at Entreri's smooth gait, for he didn't miss a stride even when *Minnow Skipper* pitched unexpectedly under the roll of one heavier wave.

"Often, yes?" Drizzt asked, turning to face the man.

"Too often," said Entreri.

"Then you know Baldur's Gate?"

"Every street."

"Good," said Drizzt. "I know not how long we'll dock there, but you'll be our guide."

Entreri turned to look at him, to offer him a smirk. "Just long enough for Luskan to destroy Port Llast, I would expect. So not long at all."

That had the other four crowding in closer.

"What'd ye know?" Ambergris asked.

"It merely occurs to me that Beniago conveniently arranged to get the five best fighters out of Port Llast all at the same time," Entreri mused.

"Ooo," Ambergris groaned, apparently having not thought of that before.

But Drizzt had. "Beniago asked only that I go in the deal for your dagger," he said. "He could not have foreseen that I would bring you four along with me."

"But he knows now," said Entreri.

Drizzt snorted the uncomfortable thought away. "Luskan's high captains cannot agree on which dock to use for a visiting lord without a street battle to settle it," he said. "They couldn't muster any sizeable force and march or sail on Port Llast in the few tendays we will be away. Nor would they begin to understand the level of power within the city any time soon, with or without us there."

Entreri looked at him and chuckled softly, his expression practically screaming the word "simpleton." But he said nothing and walked away, back to the hatch and into the hold.

"For my benefit alone," Drizzt said to the remaining three, shaking his head dismissively at the departing man. He believed the truth of his hypothesis. Ever was Artemis Entreri trying to throw doubts into Drizzt; indeed, he seemed to derive some strange pleasure from doing so.

Drizzt turned back to the sea, gave a last glance at *Sea Sprite*'s mast, then turned his gaze out to the wide-spreading waters before him. He closed his eyes and took a deep breath, inhaling the briny smell and letting it take him back to better days and—he tried unsuccessfully to exclude Dahlia from the thought as it formed—to better company.

"Who is on that boat?" Effron demanded of the dockworker. The tiefling warlock had arrived on the docks in time to watch *Minnow Skipper* glide out past Closeguard Isle. He had heard the rumors of some late arrivals to the ship's crew, and now, from the docks of Luskan, it was becoming very clear that he had missed his prey by a matter of moments.

So from an alleyway, he had assaulted and captured one of the men who had thrown out *Minnow Skipper*'s lines.

"I don't know you, Master!" the terrified dockworker replied.

"You tell me now, or I will put spiders under your skin!"

"Master!"

Effron shook the fool roughly with his good arm, his eyes, one red, one blue, flaring with outrage.

"K-Kurth's ship," the man stammered. "Under Ship Kurth's flag."

"And who was on it?"

"Twenty-three crew," the man replied.

"Tell me of the guards! The drow!"

"Just one," said the man. "Drizzt. And a dwarf and two men and a woman, an elf woman."

"Her name!"

"Dahlia," the man replied. "Dahlia who killed High Captain Rethnor, and Ship Rethnor's all up and angry about her coming through Luskan under Kurth's protection."

He continued to stammer on about the politics around it, but Effron was hardly listening at that point, staring out at the diminishing sails, watching his hated mother sail far, far from him.

"Where are they bound?" he asked, but quietly now, his moment of outrage pushed aside.

"Baldur's Gate."

"And where is that?"

"Down the coast," the man said, and Effron scowled at him for the obvious, vague answer.

"Down past Waterdeep. Couple, few hundred miles."

Effron let him go and he tumbled to the ground, and lay there, his arms up defensively in front of him.

The tiefling warlock paid him no heed. Trying to suppress his anger, Effron reminded himself that he was unable to confront Dahlia anyway, under pain of reprisal from Draygo Quick. He had ways to travel quickly, and Baldur's Gate was not too far.

He left the alleyway, then left Luskan all together, trying not to worry that *Minnow Skipper* would sink with all hands lost. Dahlia could not be lost to him in this manner. The Sword Coast was rumored to be a dangerous place for any ship to sail, but surely one under the flag of Ship Kurth would be afforded some distance by most pirates.

By the time he was back in the Shadowfell, Effron was shaking those fears away more easily. Not only would the flag of Ship Kurth help, he realized, but having Drizzt, Dahlia, and Artemis Entreri aboard was also a pretty good indicator that *Minnow Skipper* would get to her destination safely.

Dahlia remained with Drizzt long after Afafrenfere and Ambergris had gone belowdecks in search of rum and dance, and long did the drow stand there at the prow, staring at the dark waters opening wide before him. He didn't look back any longer, for there was no point, as Luskan was long out of sight, and the view behind resembled that before them.

After a while, Dahlia moved up right beside him, and Drizzt draped his arm around her waist and pulled her close. He felt almost hypocritical as he did, though, for it occurred to him that he was only doing so because of the unsettling feelings he had been entertaining in the last hour. He could not continue to compare Dahlia to his beloved wife if he wanted to maintain any feelings beyond friendship for this elf.

Minnow Skipper was not *Sea Sprite,* and Dahlia was not Catti-brie, and to Drizzt, those comparisons seemed a fitting analogy. But he pulled her tight against his side now, more for his benefit than for hers.

Because he was afraid.

He was afraid of continuing with her, knowing, and now admitting, the truth in his heart, and he was afraid of ending his relationship with her because he did not wish to walk his road alone.

"I've grown unused to you touching me," Dahlia said after a few moments.

"We've been busy," Drizzt answered. "Momentous events."

Dahlia scoffed, clearly seeing right through his dodge. "Such victories we have known often led to carnal pleasures," she remarked.

Drizzt had no answer—none that he wished to openly express, actually— other than to pull her even tighter against him.

"Entreri will leave us in Baldur's Gate." Drizzt was surprised that she chose that particular moment to change the subject.

He looked at her carefully, but couldn't read her expression.

"He's been making that threat since Neverwinter," Drizzt replied.

"He has his dagger now."

"The dagger was an excuse, and never the reason he didn't leave."

"What do you know?" Dahlia turned, releasing herself from Drizzt's arm.

"Artemis Entreri is free again, but fears the chains of his memories," Drizzt replied. "He doesn't wish to become what he once was, and the only way for him to avoid that fate is to remain with us—with me, actually. He will find this excuse or that to justify his actions, for he would never give me credit or adulation, but he won't leave us."

"In Baldur's Gate," Dahlia said.

"Or back in Luskan, or back in Port Llast thereafter."

"You sound confident."

"I am," Drizzt assured her.

"About all of your companions? Then you are a fool," she said, and with a little smirk that Drizzt couldn't quite comprehend, Dahlia walked away.

Drizzt turned back to the sea, and instead of letting himself fall back into his long-past adventures with Catti-brie and Captain Deudermont, he thought of his recent history, of the last wintry months. Dahlia's remarks were true enough: rarely did he touch her any longer, or engage her in any but the most banal conversations. They were moving apart, and it was all Drizzt's doing, subconsciously perhaps, but inexorably.

The thought alarmed Drizzt, and for a brief moment, he blamed Entreri. Entreri's empathy for and understanding of Dahlia's trauma and deep emotional scar had forced Drizzt aside.

The idea couldn't hold, and only a few heartbeats later, Drizzt was laughing at himself. True enough, Entreri had come between them, or at least, his empathy for Dahlia had, but only because it had revealed to Drizzt the shallowness of his relationship with this elf warrior he really didn't even know.

Drizzt couldn't see where this might lead. He tried to follow the thread to a logical conclusion, but soon enough, he was aboard *Sea Sprite* again in his mind, Catti-brie beside him, Guenhwyvar curled on the deck before them, the wind in their faces, the adventure in his heart and soul.

His hand went reflexively to his belt pouch, and he couldn't resist the calling of his heart. Soon he had Guenhwyvar beside him, looking haggard perhaps, but seeming content to be with him, indeed, resting heavily against him.

And her presence brought Drizzt cascading back more fully to his days aboard *Sea Sprite,* and he was happy.

Artemis Entreri had been assigned a small hammock along the starboard hold of *Minnow Skipper,* but he didn't return there after leaving Drizzt and the others at the forward rail.

Something bothered him regarding this whole arrangement. Entreri wasn't overly familiar with the ways of Luskan any longer, but he couldn't imagine that things had changed so dramatically since the earlier days of the reign of the five high captains. This ship sailed under the flag of Ship Kurth, which was still a dominant force among the leadership of the city, given the strength evident around Kurth's residence on Closeguard Isle, and given the mere fact that Beniago had been able to make such a deal with Drizzt concerning Port Llast.

So why did *Minnow Skipper* need such extra and extraordinary guards?

Perhaps this was all a power play by Beniago and Ship Kurth, getting Drizzt and Dahlia to prove their allegiance by sending them on such a trivial task as this. Or perhaps, Entreri feared, it was something more, much more, and much more sinister.

Was there a terrible danger lurking in the dark waters? The sahuagin, perhaps? Had the sea devils abandoned their assaults on Port Llast to wage war on the merchant vessels instead?

Or was this, as he had hinted—for no better reason than to bother Drizzt— truly a diversionary tactic to strip Port Llast of her most powerful denizens in preparation for an assault on the town by the powers of Luskan?

That possibility didn't bother him very much, but what troubled him most of all was not knowing. Artemis Entreri had survived the streets of Calimport as a child and had thrived as an adult because of knowledge, because his instinctual understanding of people combined with his ever-present scouting and information gathering had allowed him a great advantage, which he never relinquished.

He felt as if he had allowed Drizzt to surrender that advantage now, because of the drow's desire to cut his deal. So Entreri did not return to his bunk, and in fact, was not even in the hold at all, though he had initially gone down there to deflect any attention from the busy crew. Then he had quietly slipped back up, moved along a pre-ordained course, and with a quick glance, had eased his way into the captain's quarters aft of the main deck, passing through the feeble lock with hardly a thought.

The hanging nets and plethora of trophies and other decorations made it easy enough for the skilled assassin to fully conceal himself.

Then he waited, with the patience that had so marked his successes in Calimport and beyond, knowing that the captain would remain out on the deck until they were long clear of Luskan and the many rocks along the coastline.

He had barely settled into position when the cabin door opened and the first mate, not the captain, entered. The man—if it was a human, for he seemed to have a bit of orc blood in him—fit the part of the old seadog perfectly, with a scraggly beard gone more gray than its previous black, a face that reminded Entreri of the cracked and deeply lined tundra of the Bloodstone Lands during the dry summer tendays, and spindly legs so bowed that he could slide onto a short horse from behind without ever lifting a leg. One of his eyes was dead, a wide-open orb grayed over by a thick film. Even his demeanor spoke of a sailor who had seen too many waves and cheap whores, for he grumbled and cursed under his breath with every step as he moved to the desk.

"Take 'em on. They'll be guardin' ye," he mumbled in a voice meant to mock someone Entreri did not know. "Aye, and be guardin' us from what, will they? From the angry dock boys o' Baldur's Gate? Useless bit o' dirt walkers, the whole lot o' 'em, and if that dwarf's not ready for bedding, then know that I'm to be throwing the she-dog o'erboard!"

He ruffled through some papers messily, searching for a particular chart, Entreri could see, then he rolled it, tucked it under his arm, and shambled back the way he'd come. He almost made the door before Captain Andray Cannavara entered, pushing it closed behind him.

"You were heard on the deck, Mister Sikkal," Captain Cannavara said, trying to sound regal, and trying to look the part, too, and being successful at neither attempt. He wore a tailed waistcoat, as was the fashion, and a great plumed tri-cornered cap—one taken from another man, obviously, for it hardly fit his enormous head, particularly given his enormously bushy mop of hair. He had cut the hat on one side in an attempt to slide it down farther, but alas, such an act had also taken the integrity from the hat's band, and so with every movement he made, the hat climbed back up to sit far too high, ridiculously high, upon his dirty hair.

"Do you mean to wound the morale of my crew before we have even left the harbor, man?" he said. "If so, do tell before we are too far out for you to swim back to the docks."

The salty first mate lowered his eyes and respectfully answered, "Me pardon, Captain."

"Your last pardon, Mister Sikkal."

"Aye, Captain, but I isn't saying any what th'others ain't thinkin'," he replied and he dared to look up. "Five land dogs."

"Five formidable warriors."

"Aye, but no friend o' Luskan is Drizzit Dudden, not matterin' what Captain Kurth's sayin'!"

"The water is cold," Cannavara replied somberly, and threateningly.

"Me pardon again, then, or still me first pardon stretched longer."

The captain turned and pushed the door to make sure it was properly closed, then motioned Sikkal to follow him to his desk.

"I care for this no more than you do," he quietly explained—quietly, but of course, Artemis Entreri was in perfect position, wrapped around a beam above the net above the desk, to hear every word.

"I was, we were, given no choice in the matter," he went on. "Beniago's orders were clear, and I'm hardly to go against that one!"

"What's his tie to these dogs?" asked Sikkal. "The little man's carryin' his poker!"

The captain shook his head. "More a tie to the dark elf, I expect. Beniago is doing as he was instructed to do, as I expect that High Captain Kurth is doing as he was instructed to do."

"Kurth? Instructed?" Sikkal started to reply, but then his face brightened as he said, "Them damned drow're back."

"So I would guess."

Up above them, Artemis Entreri clutched at the beam and fought very hard against growling at the surprising news. Were they speaking of Jarlaxle? It had to be, or of Bregan D'aerthe, at least. So suddenly, everything changed from Entreri's perspective, for so suddenly, he wasn't so sure that this was about Drizzt at all. Surely Jarlaxle's band had an interest in Drizzt, but wouldn't their greater interest be in him, in Entreri? If they knew that he had broken free of Herzgo Alegni, then Jarlaxle and that wretched Kimmuriel surely understood that they were not safe.

Jarlaxle! The name screamed through Entreri's thoughts. He recalled the last look the drow had thrown him, one of sadness perhaps, or at least resignation—but behind any such emotions lay Jarlaxle's greatest feeling, Entreri knew: relief. For as Entreri lay there, caught in a net, surrounded by enemies, Jarlaxle had found freedom, walking through the ranks of the Netherese with hardly a care.

Entreri forced the memories to the back of his mind and reminded himself to pay attention.

"Bah, but it's only a couple tendays or so to Baldur's Gate, as we'll find a favorable tide," muttered Sikkal, but the captain was shaking his head with every word.

"We're swinging wide," Captain Cannavara replied, and he motioned to the chart he had sent the man to retrieve. "Wide to Baldur's Gate and wider back to Luskan, for we'll be ordered to Memnon once we're in port."

His eyes went even wider as he echoed incredulously, "Memnon?"

"We'll be surprised by the order, of course, but to Memnon we'll sail, and perhaps all the way to Calimport beyond that."

"What're ye talkin' about? What goods've we got for them places?"

"It is not about goods, Mister Sikkal."

"It's about them five!"

"Aye, and we're to keep them out of Luskan for the whole of the summer and to the last northern run before the winter."

"What . . . ?" Sikkal started to ask.

"I do not care to argue with Beniago, and care less so to take up any complaints with Kimmuriel's band. This is their demand—I do not know why."

Sikkal groaned, but the captain laughed and patted him on the shoulder.

"Easy work!" the captain explained. "We'll find the whole season on the waves where we belong, and should we encounter any foolish enough to disrespect the flag of Ship Kurth, be they pirates or minions of Umberlee, or even a warship from the lords of Waterdeep, then know that we've got grand protection, by sword or by parlay, in the five we have taken aboard."

"Aye, but they're not to be doin' any work, are they?"

"You could probably convince Drizzt Do'Urden to pull his share. He is quite familiar with the sea, after all."

"Aye, sailin' with that cursed Deudermont!" Sikkal spat upon the floor.

"However he came by it."

"Might be that he'll have a bit of an accident, then."

The captain stared at him sternly, and Entreri took comfort in that response. "We left with five, we return with five—alive unless unforeseen circumstances, and circumstances not of our own making, befall us. You would risk the wrath of the drow, brave Mister Sikkal, but know that if you do, my own wrath will put you in a shark's belly long before *Minnow Skipper* ever docks in Luskan again."

The man, looking down at the floor again, nodded. At the captain's bidding, he unrolled the chart on the desk and the two plotted their run to Baldur's Gate. Up above, Artemis Entreri watched it all, thoroughly intrigued. He feared that they were being set up, delayed on their return to Luskan until Jarlaxle and Kimmuriel could arrange a proper greeting for them at the docks.

But he assuaged those fears with the reminder that Jarlaxle was not an enemy of Drizzt Do'Urden, and anything involving him surely went deeper than any fears or grudges the drow might have with a relatively minor player like Artemis Entreri.

He didn't manage to get out of the captain's quarters until the sun was low in the sky, giving him many hours to contemplate all that he had learned. He decided against sharing the information with the others.

If an ambush by Bregan D'aerthe was awaiting them in Luskan, then he surely wouldn't be around to watch it, but if something else . . . perhaps he could get a chance to repay Jarlaxle's treachery, and that, of course, would be worth the risk. He kept putting his hand to the hilt of his jeweled dagger whenever he thought of Jarlaxle, imagining the sweetness of stealing that one's black soul.

CHAPTER 11

DARK ROOM, DARK SECRET

EFFRON PACED THE VAST DOCKS OF BALDUR'S GATE AS HE HAD EVERY morning for more than a month now. He found himself at a loss—the boat should have been in to port soon after his arrival. Every day he came down here; every day he asked every dockhand he could find who would take a few moments to speak with him.

Nothing.

No word of *Minnow Skipper,* and looking out at the vast, dark water rolling before him this rainy day, it was not hard for Effron to imagine that the boat had been lost to this inhospitable environ known as the Sword Coast. In fact, this particularly dreary morning, the warlock was certain of it.

The ocean had taken her, and all aboard, likely, or some sea devils or a great shark or whale or kraken even, had splintered her hull and pulled her under to feast on the crew.

If he was right, then his mother was dead, and his purpose in life had run into an abrupt end.

Or maybe his mood was a result of the weather and not some reasonable conclusion. The air felt heavy this day, though spring fast raced toward summer.

Effron dismissed that superficial notion. The weather might not be helping, but this was not nearly as abrupt an ending as it seemed. This morning came as a logical conclusion of his building dread. For two tendays now, Effron had been fighting a nagging feeling that they were gone, swallowed by the sea, and that his perspective on life—on his own life—was about to dramatically shift.

He had wanted her dead. He had wanted to kill her.

Now he was an orphan. Now his dream had been realized, but the taste, so suddenly, seemed not so sweet.

"Damn you," he whispered under his breath as he paced the massive quayside of this impressive port city. Those were the only words he spoke, not even bothering to inquire of the dockhands if any had seen or heard a whisper of *Minnow Skipper*'s approach.

There was no point.

And perhaps, he feared, there was no point to much of anything, any more than asking empty questions of dockhands in Baldur's Gate.

He walked slowly, his dead arm a pendulum behind his back. The moisture around his eyes was more than the drizzle of the heavy and humid day.

For so many years, he had tried to prove himself to his father. He could never become the warrior Herzgo Alegni would have preferred, obviously, with his shoulder and arm useless and a dozen other less obvious or garish infirmities wreaking his fragile form. But still he had tried, every day and in every plausible way. Was there a warlock in the Shadowfell of his power anywhere near his age? He had overheard comments that not even Draygo Quick had been as advanced as Effron was now until he had passed his fortieth birthday, though Effron was barely half that age.

He had lived his life with daring and discipline, and even the lords of Netheril had taken note of him at times.

Had any of that made Herzgo Alegni proud?

Effron honestly didn't know. If so, his brutish tiefling father had never revealed it, and even on those few occasions when a word or glance from Herzgo Alegni might have been taken as fatherly pride, hard experience had taught Effron to view them more as manipulation than anything else, as if the self-absorbed Herzgo Alegni was boosting Effron's morale because he wanted to get something more out of him.

Effron considered the possibility that he had no deeper feelings for Herzgo than he had for Dahlia.

Ah, Dahlia. For Effron, she was the rub, the ultimate pain, the desperate question, the ever-nagging doubt.

She had thrown him from a cliff.

His mother had rejected him, utterly, and had thrown him from a cliff.

How could she do that?

How he hated her!

How he desired to murder her!

How he needed her.

He could not wrap his thoughts comfortably around the emotions assailing him from every direction that dreary day. Now, on these docks this morning, he accepted the reality that she was gone, and the waves coming at him from opposite directions rolled and rose, crested and collided in the middle of his consciousness.

"Ha!" came a cry as he walked past one pair of older men, one with a mop, the other wearing a pair of hand gaffs for unloading sacks of grain.

"I told ye today'd be the day the ugly one didn't ask!" continued the gaff-armed gaffer, and he let loose a squeal of laughter.

"Are you mocking me?" the dour Effron asked.

"Nah, devil-boy, he's just laughing at his own prognostication," the man with the swab replied. "He said yerself wouldn't ask about *Minnow Skipper* today."

"And pray tell how he would know that?"

"Because today's the day word's come in," said the gaffer, and he laughed again, though it sounded more like a cackling cough. "She's out there, north and west. Tide's bad and wind's wrong, but her sails might dot the horizon before sun's to setting. Either way, she'll slide in tomorrow."

Effron tried to hold steady, but he knew that he was shaking, for he could feel the increasing movement of his dead arm. "How do you know? Tell me. Tell me!"

The other fellow lifted his mop and pointed it at a boat that had just come in, obviously, for her crew was still at work and hadn't come ashore. "They seen her trailing these last three days. Flying Kurth's flag. Luskan boat, that one there, and they're knowing *Minnow Skipper.*"

Effron looked blankly at the other boat, but inside, his mind cascaded along avenues thought lost. Dahlia. Likely aboard, and almost surely alive.

Dahlia, who had the answers to the questions Effron most feared and most needed to hear.

Only then did it occur to him that his impatience, which had brought him to the docks these last days, might now dearly cost him.

"Listen to me," he said intently to the pair. "There's coin in this for you. Gold coin."

"Keep talking," said the man with the mop.

"I would know who comes off that boat," Effron explained. "And I would not have them know that I have asked."

"Gold coin?" asked the gaffer.

"Gold coins," Effron assured him. "More coins than the fingers of both your hands and both his hands.

"Look for a dark elf, and a female elf beside him," Effron explained.

"Female drow?"

"No, just the male."

"Lots of elves about. How're we to know it's her?"

"You'll know," Effron promised, his gaze inexorably drifting back to the empty waters to the northwest, as if expecting the sails to appear at any moment. "You'll know."

"He said three days," Drizzt said, referring to the time they would spend in Baldur's Gate. Walking beside him, Dahlia turned back to regard Entreri, just a few steps behind, wondering if that time frame applied to him.

Entreri had been surprisingly chipper after the initial sail out of Luskan, and had accepted the ridiculously roundabout route and incessant delays at sea with less complaining than any of the band of five, and most of the crew as well. And now he was smiling. He lifted one hand toward Dahlia and waggled three fingers to emphasize the drow's point, though whether he was reinforcing that remark or mocking her because it applied to her and not to him, she couldn't tell.

Dahlia realized that she desperately wanted Artemis Entreri aboard for that return journey, and it flashed in her mind that if he wasn't going back, neither would she.

"Three days?" Ambergris said, she and Afafrenfere walking immediately behind the assassin. "Ah, well, get to it, then. Three days for drinking and twining . . . here's hoping Baldur's Gate got some handsome dwarves wanderin' about!"

She squealed in laughter, and Afafrenfere helplessly shook his head.

"Hehe, I'm thinkin' the rockin' boat's got me legs a bit bowed!" Ambergris added and she squealed again.

"Well, who's for knowing what's to crawl off of Luskan's docks?" a voice to the side said, turning Dahlia's attention forward once more, and across Drizzt to a pair of dockhands, one middle-aged and one well past his prime—and in a life spent at sea, judging from his appearance and the way he carried himself.

Drizzt stopped, as Dahlia did beside him, and looked the two over.

"Ah, but not yerself, drow," the older man said. He looked past Drizzt to Dahlia and winked.

The other man leaned his mop up against his shoulder, lifted both hands, waggled his fingers, and said, "More gold coins than fingers."

Dahlia didn't quite know what to make of them, and didn't really care. She started off again, pulling Drizzt beside her.

"I do believe he just propositioned you," Entreri said from behind them when they were far down the dock.

"Then I should go back and kiss him," Dahlia replied, and all four of her companions looked at her incredulously. "Then take his coins, cave in his skull, and drop him into the sea."

She kept walking, breezily, as if the thought might be half joke, but then again, might not. And these companions, having seen the elf warrior in action, didn't doubt either possibility. Certainly Drizzt showed as much when he gave her a less-than-accepting stare.

Dahlia had seen that look far too much from the drow of late, she realized.

When they got into the city, they split up, Dahlia and Drizzt moving for the finer inns, Ambergris pulling Afafrenfere toward the many seedy taverns just off the docks, and Entreri, with a casual salute, moving away on his own. For many steps, Dahlia watched the man, trying to get a feeling for which section of Baldur's Gate attracted him the most. The city was fairly well divided along clear demarcations: wealthy merchants, artisans, and the poor. Dahlia figured Entreri would seek out the middle levels, but near to the wilder regions not far from the wharves. His direction seemed to confirm as much.

"Shall we rent one room or two?" Dahlia asked Drizzt, and he turned on her sharply in obvious surprise. "Or perhaps just bunks in a common dormitory, so that we can pretend we're still aboard ship?"

Drizzt's stare turned incredulous.

"It will allow you the excuse you seem to need."

Drizzt stopped and turned to face her directly.

Dahlia took a deep breath and said, "You haven't touched me in tendays, in months even."

"That's not true."

"Isn't it? Other than our first day at sea."

Drizzt swallowed hard and looked around. "Not here," he said, and he took Dahlia's arm and headed to the nearest inn, where he purchased the very best room available.

As soon as he had closed the door, Drizzt went at Dahlia aggressively.

She took some satisfaction in that, but still found herself pushing him away. At first, she didn't quite know why, but it soon dawned on her that Drizzt was making this advance more out of obligation than desire—or if desire, then physical desire and not emotional.

While Dahlia could understand and appreciate it, she wasn't much interested in conceding to it.

"Why?" she asked into his confused expression—confused, but not wounded, she recognized—and if he was disappointed, he was doing a good job in hiding that fact, too.

"What do you mean?" he asked.

Dahlia pulled away from him with a snort, even turned away because she didn't want to look at him at that moment. "You're trying to mollify me."

"You just said—"

She turned around, facing him with her arms crossed over her chest, one foot tapping.

Now it was Drizzt's turn to sigh. He walked to a chair set against the far wall, like a bar fighter moving to his corner between combat rounds. He pulled the chair around and straddled it, his elbows atop the chair back.

"Have I ever told you about Innovindil?" he asked. "An elf I once knew?"

Dahlia changed neither her stance nor her expression.

"A friend I knew a century ago," Drizzt explained. "She was older than you, older than me. She came to me in a time of turmoil, with orcs ravaging the countryside and pressing the kingdom of my dearest friend—a friend I thought dead, along with all the others, including—"

"Catti-brie," Dahlia remarked, for Drizzt had told her of his wife. "So you lost her and filled your days with an elf companion."

Drizzt shook his head. "I thought I had lost her, lost all of them, but no, this was before that time."

"Is there a point to your story?"

Drizzt sighed again. "Not an easy one to get to," he admitted. "You're barely into your fourth decade of life, but Innovindil's lessons were an explanation of a life witnessing the birth and death of centuries."

"Then why would I care?"

"Because it will explain . . . me," Drizzt blurted. "My actions, or inactions."

"Must everything become such an important act to you?" Dahlia said.

Drizzt chuckled. "You're not the first to say such a thing to me."

"Then perhaps you should listen."

"I tried to," the drow said, and he motioned to the spot before the bed where he had pursued Dahlia.

"Months," she replied dourly.

"Innovindil told me to live my life in shorter expanses, in human terms, then to start over from there. Particularly, she said, if I meant to befriend, even to fall in love, with the lesser-living races."

"She told you to get past your grief."

"I suppose you could phrase it like that."

"I just did. And so here we are—has it been a century now since you lost this human woman?—and you don't seem to be taking her advice." She noted Drizzt's wince at the way she had pronounced human, clearly marking the word as an insult, and that, she thought, was telling. "And this is the same advice you intend to give to me?" She chortled again. "Shouldn't you learn to abide by it first?"

"I'm trying!" he retorted, and sharply, much more so than Dahlia had expected. Well, she thought, at least she had gotten some emotion out of the fool.

"Is my lesson over?" she asked with equal sharpness.

"Perhaps mine has just begun," Drizzt said with clear lament. "This is more complicated than you understand. When you are older—"

"Drizzt Do'Urden," she interrupted, coming forward with a finger poking his way, "hear me well. You have known seven years for my every one, but in so many ways, I am older than you, likely more than you will ever be. In matters of"—she paused and glanced around, looking for the right word, and wound up just motioning dramatically for the room's bed "—I am more experienced and more rational."

"Your ear studs speak differently," he said quietly.

"I may have demons to chase, but at least I don't make love to ghosts," she replied, and she stormed to the door, slamming it hard behind her.

She fingered the black diamond stud in her right ear, the last stud in that lobe, and realized that she might soon find her mortal battle with the drow she had just left behind.

That was why she had chosen him, after all. Finally, mercifully, at long last, Dahlia had found a lover who would almost surely defeat her, who would give her peace.

Strangely, though, Dahlia felt little comfort in that notion. Drizzt had pulled away from her. Drizzt was rejecting her, without even meaning to. When he told her that he didn't want to hurt her, he spoke sincerely, she knew.

But still . . .

Dahlia's striking blue eyes were moist when she left the inn, and more than one tear had streaked her delicate cheeks.

Dahlia walked into the tavern with a sour look on her face, not expecting to find her prey, since she had already visited several of these establishments in this area of Baldur's Gate. Truly the city overwhelmed the elf's sensibilities. She had been to Luskan several times, of course, and had grown up in the cities of Thay, and had even visited mighty Waterdeep on one occasion, but now that she was exploring Baldur's Gate, the energy and commotion of the place overwhelmed her.

She certainly had no idea of just how many taverns and inns and assorted emporiums, often with apartments up above, would line every street. When she and Drizzt had broken away from the others, Dahlia had never imagined that locating Artemis Entreri would prove so trying an ordeal.

So she entered the tavern expecting nothing, her hopes sinking to emptiness.

The crowd parted before her, a coincidental shift in two separate groups of merchant sailors offered her a wider view of the place, and there he was, sitting alone at a small table in the far corner of the room.

Dahlia hesitated—he hadn't seen her, she believed—and she considered her course. There would be no turning back now, she reminded herself.

She strode across the room. One man popped up in front of her, offered a wicked smile and a hungry expression, but she eased him aside with her walking stick, and when he resisted, she froze him with a look so cold that the blood drained from his face.

No one else intercepted her.

Entreri took note of her and leaned back in his chair.

"Imagine my surprise at seeing you here," she said, taking the seat across from him.

"Yes, imagine. Where's Drizzt?"

"I do not know, and I do not care."

Entreri gave a little laugh. "After a month at sea? And with more months at sea before us? I would have expected you two to . . . catch up."

"More months at sea before *us?*" Dahlia scoffed.

Entreri looked at her as if he didn't understand.

"You said that Baldur's Gate would be your last stop," Dahlia reminded him, "that you would not be returning to Luskan with *Minnow Skipper.*"

Entreri shrugged as if it didn't matter. He lifted his glass and took a deep swallow.

"So you are continuing on with us to Luskan?"

"I didn't say that."

Dahlia sighed at the man's ever-cryptic offerings. She glanced around, irritated almost as much as she had been when she left Drizzt back in the room. "Where is that barmaid?"

Entreri laughed, drawing her gaze back to him.

"No server," he explained, and motioned over to Dahlia's right. "Bar's over there."

"Well, go buy me some feywine."

"Unlikely."

Dahlia started to glare at him, but let it go and rushed from her seat, pushing impatiently through the talking patrons. One started to protest, even to threaten her, but he looked past her—to Entreri, she realized—and he bit his words short and fell far back. Indeed, Entreri knew this city well, and it, apparently, knew him.

Soon after, Dahlia returned to the table with two full bottles of feywine and a pair of glasses.

"Planning a late night?" Entreri asked.

"Let's play a game."

"Let's not. Go play with Drizzt."

"Are you afraid?"

"Of what?"

"Of losing to me?"

"Of losing what?"

"Your superior attitude, perhaps."

Entreri laughed at her as she poured them both drinks. She lifted her glass in toast, and the assassin reluctantly followed suit and tapped the goblets together. He took just a sip, though, and Dahlia realized that she had put him on his guard, which was most decidedly not what she had in mind.

"We could play for coins," she said.

"I have few. And I don't care to seek work ashore."

"For items, then?"

Entreri looked her over. "I might fancy that strange weapon you carry."

"And I would fancy your dagger."

Entreri shook his head and crossed his arms over his chest. "Not for any odds you might offer, Dahlia. I lost this once, but not again."

"Not that dagger," she said with a mischievous look and a sparkle in her eye.

Entreri's expression did not soften—quite the opposite.

"Go back to Drizzt," he said evenly.

Dahlia realized that she had pushed him too far. Was it a code of honor, she wondered? Was he afraid of Drizzt? That seemed far-fetched to her. Was Entreri, perhaps, really more of a friend to Drizzt than either of them cared to admit?

"I need to talk," she said, trying a different tact.

"Go talk to Drizzt."

Dahlia shook her head. "He doesn't understand."

"Then tell him."

Dahlia sighed and slumped at the man's barrage of short, closed answers. "He knows, but he doesn't understand," she said, letting more emotion into her voice. "How can he? How could anyone who has not lived through the darkness?"

Entreri seemed to have run out of snappy answers. He just sat there, arms still crossed, though he did mutter, "Menzoberranzan?" in answer to Dahlia's assertion.

Dahlia lifted her glass in a toast again, and to her surprise, he actually responded in kind. He took a deeper draw of the wine, so much so that she lifted the bottle and refilled both their glasses.

Her subtle reminder of their shared trauma had touched him somewhere deep inside, she knew.

"Have you ever found love?" she asked, and her tone reflected more sadness than anger.

"I don't know," he replied.

"The truth!" Dahlia spouted, coming forward. She slipped out of her chair to take a seat in one right beside Entreri. "The truth," she said again more quietly. "You don't know because you cannot be sure, because you are not sure what the word even means."

"Do you love Drizzt?" he asked.

The question surprised her, and she blurted out, "No" before she really even considered it.

Because Dahlia wasn't here to consider such things. They didn't matter. Dahlia was here to begin a string of events that would lead to the place she truly wished to be. And Artemis Entreri would carry her to that place like a fine steed.

"It is a matter of convenience," she explained.

Entreri's smile widened at that, and he drained his glass again, and this time refilled it of his own accord. "Does Drizzt know that?" he asked while pouring.

"If I spent my days worrying about what that one knows or does not know about love, I would think of nothing else, I am sure. But it hardly concerns me. He cannot understand the truth of who I am, or of the place from where I came, so how deep might any love run with him."

She shifted closer to Entreri, put her face near to his and bade him, "Tell me about your early years."

He resisted, but his arms were no longer crossed.

Dahlia would be patient. She could see the truth: The man was wracked by memories he had never shared, and his warrior's stubbornness hadn't put those dark days as far behind him as he would have liked.

Dahlia saw him as vulnerable, and because of her own background, and because she had long seen the truth about herself, she knew how to wrestle free that vulnerability and take advantage of it.

"Do you know why I wear such baubles on my ears?" she asked. Entreri looked at her curiously, studying her diamonds, the many clear ones on her left ear, the single black diamond stud on her right.

"Former lovers," she said, tapping her left ear.

"Current on your right," Entreri said, and he chuckled. "Black diamond for a drow, I see."

"I hope it doesn't look awkward when I move it to my left lobe with the others," she said.

Entreri laughed at her.

She poured more wine.

"Will you listen to my tale?" Dahlia whispered.

"I think I know most of it."

Dahlia looked around. "Not here," she said. "I cannot." She slid her chair back and stood up, drained her drink in one gulp, then similarly drained Entreri's. She collected the bottles and glasses and looked at the man plaintively.

"I need to tell it," she said. "In full. I have never done that. I fear I'll not be free until I do."

She looked across the room to the stairs leading to the rooms above, then back at Entreri, who, to her pleasant surprise, was rising from his seat. He stopped at the bar on their way, and collected two more bottles of the wine.

Dahlia had been caught by her own net, she realized once they'd arrived in his room, and realized, too, that she didn't care. So she told him all of it, of her trip that morning long ago to the river to fetch some water, of returning to her clan's small village to find it full of Shadovar.

With tears in her eyes, she told him of the rape, of watching her mother's murder.

They drank and they talked, and she began to pry at Entreri, and Entreri began to talk. He told Dahlia of his own mother's betrayal, of being sold as a slave and taken to Calimport—and he nearly spat as he spoke that city's name. He started to tell of his rise on the streets, but suddenly he stopped, and he looked at her with a puzzled expression.

She swallowed hard.

"Tell me about those other diamonds," Entreri said. "The ones in your left ear."

"About those other lovers, you mean," Dahlia said, and she let a hint of wickedness slip into her tone. But any hopes that Entreri was looking for a voyeuristic thrill were quickly dashed by the stern-faced assassin.

"Which one represents Herzgo Alegni?" Entreri asked.

Dahlia tried unsuccessfully to keep the startled look off her face. Why would he say such a thing? Particularly now?

"I notice that you did not move any upon Alegni's death," Entreri said, and Dahlia realized that a long while had passed while she had chewed over Entreri's previous comment. "You didn't remove any, or shift any from one ear to the other. Why is that?"

"You do not wish to hear," Dahlia replied.

"Should I be jealous? Or afraid?"

"You do not seem to me to be the jealous type."

Entreri grinned back at her, a look that made her think that he knew a lot more about her macabre game with the diamond studs than he was letting on.

"Herzgo Alegni was my rapist, never a lover," she said evenly, and Entreri nodded and didn't seem intimidated by her threatening tone, and seemed rather as if he'd expected that very answer and was glad of it.

"And when will you move the black diamond?"

Dahlia stared at him sternly, but didn't reply.

"The old swordsman's rule, yes?" Entreri teased, and he took a drink, lifting a full glass with his right hand and draining it. He wiped his mouth with his left sleeve and said, "Dispatch with your right hand, dispose with your left."

Again Dahlia sat silent, digesting the assassin's cutting insights. Of course, none of the diamonds represented the beast Alegni, but it was also true that all of them represented Herzgo Alegni. Those diamonds, this whole game, had been put in place because of him, after all. Taking her lovers was because of him, murdering her lovers was because of him, and because those lovers were not strong enough to win the necessary fight and end her own pain.

And thus all of them served to satiate the woman, all of those lovers, one by one, getting Alegni's just reward . . .

But what about Drizzt, then, she wondered?

They drank some more, and Dahlia made sure to get very close to Entreri as they sat on his bed, and made sure to turn just so, that she could afford him some tantalizing views of her blouse, unbuttoned low. And she made sure to touch him just so, to comfort him at first, then to tantalize him.

And she realized that she was indeed having that very effect.

"You deny it, but you love Drizzt," Entreri said unexpectedly, throwing her back, but just a bit.

"I am not with Drizzt," she protested.

"Because you love him, and he has pushed you away. Dahlia cannot accept that, can she?"

"Do you really want to talk about Drizzt?" she said, determined not to get sidetracked.

"Or are you, perhaps, jealous of him?" Entreri posed. "Jealousy, or simple admiration?"

Dahlia sat back and stared at him incredulously.

"Because he was stronger than you," Entreri explained. "Because of his choices. I can assure you, from first-hand experience, that Drizzt's homeland of Menzoberranzan is as bad as anything you have ever known—even the violation by Alegni."

"I do not think you can make such a claim." Dahlia tried hard not to get angry.

"A vile place. Horrid in every regard."

"And worse than anything I have known?"

Entreri paused for a moment and seemed to be considering the question deeply, but then he nodded. "Or at least as bad. And Drizzt grew up there, betrayed always by his family.

"As bad?" Dahlia said and she pointedly snorted. "Do you speak of my feelings for Drizzt? Jealousy? Admiration? Or of your own?"

"No, it really is love for you, I think," Entreri said, dodging. "I don't blame you. Drizzt survived. Drizzt has thrived, where you have not."

"Where *we* have not," Dahlia insisted.

Entreri had no answer.

They drank some more, and their talk turned to their current situation, but Dahlia would hear no further discussion regarding Drizzt, and indeed, when Entreri tried to bring up the subject of the drow, Dahlia fell over him, burying his words in a passionate, hungry kiss.

And though she had intended to feign exactly this to reach her more important goal, that goal was nowhere in Dahlia's mind, and her hunger wasn't faked.

She grabbed at his shirt and began unbuttoning it. He tried to protest, but half-heartedly, his objections no match for the feelings Dahlia stirred in him.

Down the hallway a bit, a door cracked open, and a shadowy face peeked into the corridor, watching Entreri's rented room.

The sounds from within made clear what was happening behind that door, and it brought a scowl to the face of the watcher.

Effron Alegni resisted his initial urge to charge into that other room and unload a barrage of devastating magic on the couple. He reminded himself of Draygo Quick's warning, then pointedly reminded himself that Draygo's cautions had been regarding Drizzt, not these two.

So he could go in there and slay them in their distraction . . .

But he didn't.

Effron closed the door, put his back to it, and took a deep and steadying breath.

The slanted rays of morning slipped in through the dirty window, and fell upon fair Dahlia as she slept.

Artemis Entreri watched her.

He considered his next moves. He hadn't used the pronoun "us," hadn't included himself in the group that would sail out of Baldur's Gate on *Minnow Skipper* by accident, for he intended to do exactly that. The boat was going on to Memnon, after all, though Drizzt, Dahlia, and the others didn't know it, and the closer Entreri could get to Calimport, the better, so he figured.

But why?

What was in Calimport for him, after all? Dwahvel was long dead—he had no more friends there than anywhere else in this miserable world.

In truth, he had no friends at all.

He looked at Dahlia.

And he wondered.

CHAPTER 12

THE DESPERATE CHILD

EFFRON WAS IN A FOUL MOOD AS HE MOVED TO BALDUR'S GATE'S DOCKS that next morning, in no small part because of his disgust with his mother and her bed-hopping. And with Artemis Entreri —Barrabus the Gray, no less—a man Effron had come to profoundly dislike in the time they had fought together under the command of Herzgo Alegni.

The man who had leaped in and foiled Effron's best attempt to catch Dahlia, and had cost the young tiefling greatly in both coin and reputation by stifling Cavus Dun's ambush.

He kept repeating Draygo Quick's orders as a reminder of the clear boundaries the dangerous Netherese lord had enacted around him. But every recital came with a sneer.

He moved down to the docks and found his informants. As always, it seemed, they appeared to be busy, both swabbing with mops this day, and it didn't take Effron long to recognize that they weren't actually accomplishing anything, again, as always with these two.

The old gaffer nudged his partner when he noted Effron's approach.

"When?" Effron asked, moving up, and having no intention of remaining out there in the open for any length of time. After these two had reported to him on the disposition of Drizzt and Dahlia, he had tasked them with a simple question, and so he wanted a simple answer.

But both men wore wide smiles, hinting at something more.

"A tenday before she's out, we're hearing," said the younger man.

"Was supposed to be but three, but her Captain Cannavara delayed her," added the older.

Effron nodded and tossed a small pouch to the man, but both the old gaffer and his partner kept grinning slyly.

"What more do you know?" Effron asked.

"Ah, but that's worth gold to ye," said the old gaffer. "More than the first ye give us."

"Ah, then to you, it's probably worth continuing to breathe," Effron replied without the slightest hesitation, for he was in no mood for any nonsense from these two fools this day. He narrowed his eyes into a glare and with a low and even tone slowly repeated, "What more do you know?"

The gaffer started a wheezing laugh, but his partner swallowed hard and patted him to silence, staring at Effron all the while—staring and obviously understanding that there was nothing overstated in the dangerous young tiefling's threat.

"They're not back for Luskan," the middle-aged swabby replied.

"Who? *Minnow Skipper*?" Effron asked.

"Aye, Memnon's her next port of call, and then Calimport beyond that, if the season's not too late. Won't be putting in to Luskan until the first winter winds're blowing hard from the Spine o' the World."

The news knocked Effron back a step, his thoughts spinning. "How do you know this?" he managed to ask.

"We got friends on the boat. Course we do," said the old gaffer. "On all the boats." He continued on to explain that he knew *Minnow Skipper*'s first mate and had crewed with the man many times over the years. He had asked about working his way back to Luskan, and was told of the upcoming southern journey.

Effron was hardly listening, knocked fully off-balance by the surprising turn. Memnon? Calimport? He wasn't even sure exactly where those places might be, but the one thing that certainly had come through to him was that once *Minnow Skipper* put out of Baldur's Gate, his trail to Dahlia might fast grow very cold.

He absently reached into his pouch and grabbed a handful of coins, some gold, some silver, and handed them over without even counting them, then stumbled back along the wharves and into the city proper.

He thought again of Draygo Quick's warning regarding this band, but the orders didn't resonate. Not then, not with his mother on the verge of slipping away, perhaps forever.

He had wondered if it would come to this, of course. He slipped his hand inside his robes and felt the scroll tube he had stolen from Draygo Quick.

Dare he?

***

He was going to lose them. That unsettling notion walked beside Effron throughout the next few days, and drove him to pay acute attention to every detail of the movements of the companions, particularly, of course, of Dahlia. To that end, the warlock spent nearly as much time in his wraith-like form, hiding in crevices of cracked mortar and along the separations in the wooden walls of this inn or that.

Dahlia was spending her nights with Drizzt again, but there was a level of unmistakable tension in their room when they were together. They shared a bed, but were hardly entwined, sexually or otherwise. She hadn't told him about her encounter with Entreri, obviously, and Effron mused on more than one occasion that he might play that particular card if he got into trouble with the drow ranger.

From what little he knew of the drow, he couldn't imagine Drizzt Do'Urden forgiving such a transgression.

He reminded himself that bringing any harm to Drizzt might not be a wise choice, given Draygo Quick's insistence, and that divulging his information might well put the drow into a mortal battle against Dahlia and Entreri.

Dahlia wasn't often in the drow's room otherwise, returning late every night, and leaving early in the day. Drizzt, on the other hand, spent most of his days in the inn, if not the room itself. Dark elves were not a common sight in Baldur's Gate, after all, and so Effron could well understand Drizzt's reluctance to wander around.

It wasn't hard for him to guess where Dahlia was going each morning, and he followed her movements closely, movements that almost always put her back near Artemis Entreri.

Curiously, he didn't note her retreating to Entreri's room again, as on that first night. Usually they sat together at the table that Entreri had taken as his own in the common room (even ejecting, with a few well-chosen words, anyone who might be there whenever he arrived), huddled over a bottle of Feywine.

On one such occasion, the second night after he had learned of *Minnow Skipper's* intended roundabout voyage, Effron took a great chance, casting his wraithform enchantment and melting into the inn's wall, then traveling the seams in the wood very near to Entreri's table to eavesdrop on the pair.

They said little as the night passed, and Effron realized that he couldn't stay much longer, that his enchantment would wear away. With a mental sigh, he started off, but just then he heard Dahlia whisper to Entreri, "You can't imagine the pain."

"I thought I could," he replied. "Isn't that why you're here?"

"I think it's different," she replied. "The violation—"

"Don't begin to suggest that," the man said, each word sounding sharp-edged.

"The pregnancy, I mean," Dahlia clarified.

There was something about the timbre of her voice that had Effron off his guard. The Dahlia he knew was brash and angry, and even with Drizzt there was always a hunger in her voice, crude and abrasive. But not now. Now there was a deep sobriety, though she had drained a bottle and more of Feywine, and a profound sense of humility ran about the edges of her tone.

And of course, the word "pregnancy" had Effron riveted.

"Every day reminded me," Dahlia said. "Every day, knowing that he would return to me, probably to kill me now that I had done my part to bear him a child."

She was certainly talking about Herzgo Alegni, Effron thought.

Entreri lifted his glass and tipped it slightly to show his deference.

"I hated it and hated him," Dahlia spat. "And hated the baby most of all."

"Murderously so," Entreri remarked, and Dahlia winced, and Effron, though he could only barely see her from his wooden perch, thought he noted a bit of moisture in her eyes, and indeed, a tear rolled down Dahlia's cheek.

"No," she said, then quickly admitted, "Yes," and the tremor in her voice rang clearly. "And I did it, or thought I had."

"The only regret that I have ever known is that I regret when I regret," Entreri said, rather callously, Effron thought. "You cannot change what has happened."

"But you can move forward to make amends."

Entreri scoffed at that remark.

"Isn't that what you're doing right now?" Dahlia accused. "Isn't that why you traveled to Port Llast with us?"

"I wanted my dagger back."

"No," Dahlia said, shaking her head and now smiling, and now, too, that the conversation had shifted back to Entreri's issues, Effron had to take his leave. He slipped out of the building into the alleyway and returned to his corporeal form, then immediately fell back against the building, needing the support of the solid wall to keep him upright.

He tried to make sense of the conversation he had overheard, but the mere fact that it was a reference to him, and to that murderous act, had him overwhelmed, and only added to his already mounting sense of desperation.

He needed to hear that conversation again, but not between Dahlia and someone else. He needed to hear her admit her crime to him, openly, so that he could pay her back violently.

But she was going to sail away, for months, and on a journey that might well drop her at any port along the way, particularly considering the explosion he foresaw between Dahlia and Drizzt. Drizzt would return to Baldur's Gate, unless Dahlia and Entreri killed him, but Dahlia and Entreri might not. There was nothing for them in the north, any more than elsewhere, for they were clearly not possessed of Drizzt's sense of duty regarding Port Llast.

He was going to lose her, perhaps never to regain the trail.

And he was so close!

And so it was decided for him, then and there. He rushed down to the docks, a purse of gold in his hand. Then, his task complete, he hustled for a particular alleyway, a dead end corridor he had meticulously scouted along the route Dahlia would surely take on her return to Drizzt.

There were a few people on the main boulevard despite the late hour. Effron grew nervous watching them, and began stepping from foot to foot. Would they intervene and stifle his well-laid plans? What was he doing here? Even if he got away, Draygo Quick would be waiting for him on the other end of his shadowstep, and the old wretch would not be amused.

He almost abandoned his plans. Almost, but then he told himself that it was now or perhaps never, and then, before he could argue in the other direction, she appeared at the end of the lane.

She walked past the street lamps, seeming distracted—likely, she had just come from Artemis Entreri's bed, Effron surmised, and that unsettling notion only made him hate her even more.

Effron fought hard to get out of his own thoughts. He had almost missed the cue, he realized. He had timed this perfectly, count by count, step by step, and if he wanted to catch one as dangerous as Dahlia, he had to be perfect.

He counted the street lamps, then again, measuring her pace, holding himself back until the very moment she reached the appointed spot. Then he held his steps in proper cadence, and didn't run into her path as his heart screamed at him to do.

He crossed to the far side of the main avenue, directly in line with Dahlia's sight, at just the right time.

She was close enough to see him, but not close enough to catch him.

Dahlia's eyes went wide, and she staggered a bit, clearly overwhelmed.

Effron purposely did not look directly at her, and shifted past, into the alleyway. He broke into a run, suppressing his fears that she would not follow, refusing to allow the doubting words into his mind: Had he so shocked her with his presence that she might just run off?

The end of the alley turned to the right, around the back of one building. From that corner, he peeked back toward the street, and his heart leaped when Dahlia, walking cautiously, turning into the alleyway. With the backlighting of the street lamps, he could see her, but she couldn't see him. He knew that fact from his meticulous scouting, but despite his intellectual confidence, his emotions almost broke him again.

Effron mentally scolded himself and began his quiet spellcasting. With a last glance toward Dahlia, who was now several strides into the alleyway, he released his dweomers, his three dimensional form becoming that of a wraith once more.

He walked into the seams of the stone building—he had wraith-walked this route many, many times, determining it exactly—and slithered along the course of the alleyway, passing Dahlia, who did not notice. Now beyond her, nearer the street, he waited, and that was the hardest part of all!

Dahlia reached the corner and peered around, now in a low crouch, weapon in hand. Yes, weapon in hand, Effron thought, for she meant to do that which she had failed to do on the day of his birth.

Effron slid out from the wall and resumed his normal form. He wanted to shout out at Dahlia, but couldn't actually find his voice in that moment. He took out a jar and dumped its contents on the cobblestones. The tiny undead umber hulk began stomping toward its prey even before the miniaturization dweomer had worn away, like a large bug skittering down the alley. Just a few tiny strides from Effron, it began to grow, and its footsteps began to resound with a thunderous report.

Dahlia leaped around, her eyes going wide, to Effron's satisfaction.

The umber hulk charged in, fully grown now, twice a man's height and thrice a man's girth, with huge clacking mandibles snapping at the air, and waving menacingly giant hooked hands that could dig through stone, let alone tender flesh.

With trembling fingers, Effron brought forth the scroll tube. Dare he try? Or should he just kill her and be done with it?

A lumbering swing of his pet never got near to hitting the quick elf, and she countered with a solid stab of her long staff right between the mandibles—and retracted the weapon far too quickly for those hooked weapons to snap shut on it.

This was not an umber hulk, Effron reminded himself. It was a zombie, gigantic and imposing, but not nearly as clever, quick, or overpowering as it had been in life.

And Dahlia, apparently, was already figuring that out. She struck and struck again with her powerful weapon, and another lumbering swing from the behemoth missed badly. The beast ducked low to snap at her, only to have her smash it several times atop the head. Effron could see her confidence growing. She had started with her long staff, no doubt to keep the powerful creature somewhat at bay, but now, obviously confident that this monster wouldn't get close to hitting her, she broke Kozah's Needle down to the twin flails and went into a spinning dance, using every step in the tight alleyway to buy her enough room to strike and retreat.

For many heartbeats, Effron just watched the magnificence of this elf woman at her craft. She actually leaped to stand atop the monster's thick arm on one low swing, rattled off a barrage of strikes with her weapons, and back-flipped away before the umber hulk zombie could respond.

The young warlock heard his breath coming in gasps, and the shock of that, the shock of realizing that he was wasting time, that his moment was slipping quickly away, jolted him into action. He popped the end off the tube and slid out and unrolled the spell, and immediately fell into casting. The dweomer was far beyond his understanding, of course, and the probability was that he would waste the scroll to no effect, or worse, destroy himself in the futile attempt.

But Effron didn't let those doubts deter him, focusing instead on the situation before him, fast deteriorating.

He was losing her!

Again, Dahlia would get away, or would get to him and be rid of him, as she had tried once before.

Anger drove him. Outrage drove him. He began the incantation, every symbol on the scroll crystallizing before him, every syllable he spoke a distinct denial that Dahlia would again escape him.

He lost himself in that focus. Nothing mattered except the next word, the proper cadence, of the dweomer. Nothing else could matter, or all would be lost.

He was halfway through, but he didn't know it.

Down the alleyway, Dahlia scored a solid hit and heightened it with a tremendous blast of lightning energy form Kozah's Needle that threw the behemoth backward, to tumble to its back, but Effron didn't know it.

He pressed on. He got to the last line, the critical release, and as he spoke the last word, he peered over the top of the scroll.

There stood Dahlia, staring back at him, staring back at her broken son, her arms limp at her sides, her jaw hanging open, her face a mask of shock, as if she couldn't bear to look at him.

A metal plate appeared in the air and swung down to slam against the woman. A second appeared on the other side, knocking her back the way she had come. A third and a fourth showed, all swinging as if on a puppet master's string. Dahlia tried to block, but they were too heavy and tossed her about with ease. She tried to dodge away, but there were too many, and the magic too coordinated.

And they were moving closer together, barely swinging now, surrounding her fully, encasing her.

Closing like a coffin.

Effron called his umber hulk back and put the jar on the ground in its path. As it neared, the magic pulled it, instructed it, and shrunk it.

As he scooped that caged pet up, Effron produced the other. The powerful dweomer, the Tartarean Tomb, now locked its plates around Dahlia, pressing in tight, holding her fast, despite her ferocious struggling. Even this great spell wouldn't cage this fine warrior for long, Effron understood, and had understood during his careful planning, and now his final piece, the death worm, slithered into position.

The tomb was not complete, the elf woman's feet and lower legs showing beneath the bottom edge of the metal plates, and the necrophidius coiled around one of those legs and climbed up into the tomb with Dahlia.

How she screamed!

In horror at first, and then in pain as the death worm bit into her.

She kept screaming, kept thrashing.

"Just succumb," Effron begged her in a whisper, for to his surprise, these cries of pain and terror no longer rang sweetly in his ears.

"Just fall, damn you!" he shouted out against them, and as if on cue, the screaming stopped.

Effron froze, barely able to catch his breath. The paralyzing bite of the necrophidius had finally taken hold, he realized.

The coffin swayed and fell over.

Effron whispered a command to his pet, telling it to stay in place, and to bite again if the woman stirred.

"Now?" Effron heard behind him.

"Fetch her," he instructed his two dockhand henchmen without turning back to regard them. They ran past him, blankets in hand. "And take care!" he called after them. "Else I will surely obliterate you!"

He walked to the street to the waiting cart his henchmen had brought up to the entrance to the alleyway. Some people were watching, but none approached, for in a place like Baldur's Gate, a person who stuck his nose in where it didn't belong most often had that nose ripped off.

The gaffer and his comrade half-carried, half-dragged the metal coffin from the alley, and got it up on the cart with great effort, even dropping it once to the street.

They rushed up onto the driver's bench and urged the mule along.

Effron went off the other way, not wanting to call attention to the cargo. He was several blocks away, circling around toward the docks and the empty boat, in whose hold he would claim his catch, before the weight of what he had done truly struck him.

He had her.

He had the woman who had thrown him from the cliff.

He had her.

He had the mother who had rejected him, and left him to a life of broken misery.

He had her!

CHAPTER 13

THE PATIENCE OF A MONK

WELL THEN FIND HER," CAPTAIN CANNAVARA SAID TO ENTRERI.

"Aye, or we'll be leavin' ye here, and won't that be better for us?" added Mister Sikkal. He stood at Cannavara's side, bobbing up and down on his bowed legs so that his head bounced stupidly. How Artemis Entreri wanted to put his recovered dagger to good use at that moment!

"I only came to tell you that we cannot find her," Entreri remarked, addressing the captain directly, but throwing one warning glance at Sikkal as he did to keep the fool's mouth shut. "Not to be lectured by either of you."

"Then you four will be aboard when we sail?" the captain asked.

"No," Entreri replied without the slightest hesitation—and he was surprised at his own certainty, though as he considered it, he couldn't deny the truth. He would not leave Dahlia behind, would not leave Baldur's Gate until he learned what had happened to her.

"*Minnow Skipper* sails on the morning tide," Cannavara declared.

"Then you will explain to Beniago and High Captain Kurth why my friends and I returned to Luskan before you. You are on to Memnon, are you not?"

The expression on Cannavara's face, and on Sikkal's as well, spoke volumes to Entreri before either had uttered a word—if either had been able to speak at that moment. As far as Cannavara knew, clearly, they had told no one of their course change, and from Sikkal's point of view, likely he had done some whispering that might get him thrown to the sharks.

"You think you know all the strands of the web," the assassin quietly said. "That is a dangerous belief when dealing with . . . my associates."

His tone left little doubt in the two men as to whom he might be referring. Bregan D'aerthe or Ship Kurth, the two men facing him obviously assumed, given the blood then draining from their respective faces.

Entreri used that moment to pull back his cloak and put a hand to the hilt of his fabulous dagger. Cannavara let out a little gasp at that, obviously recognizing it and remembering for the first time where he had seen that particular blade before.

With a dismissive snort, Artemis Entreri turned and walked back down the gangplank.

By the time he stepped onto the wharf, he had put the two men out of his thoughts, focusing again on the missing Dahlia. Half the night and half the day now, and not a sign of her.

This was more than petulance, he knew.

He was afraid.

Ambergris and Afafrenfere walked the wharf slowly, taking their time on their way to *Minnow Skipper*. Drizzt and Entreri moved separately through the various neighborhoods of the city, checking every inn and tavern, and every alley, but the dwarf had resisted Afafrenfere's calls to separate and cover more ground.

"I got me an idea," she announced to her partner, with one of her exaggerated winks, and she led him directly to these docks, where more than a score of ships were moored, some out on the water, others pulled up tight against the wharves.

"You think she's on one of these boats?" Afafrenfere asked when Ambergris's destination became apparent.

"She ain't been out through any o' Baldur's Gate's gates, from what them sentries're saying."

"Dahlia could have easily gotten past them unnoticed."

"Aye, but to what end?" Ambergris asked. "Long roads to walk alone, and why would she, when there's better ways to be long gone from Baldur's Gate, eh?"

"So you think she left of her own accord?"

Ambergris stopped and turned to face him, hands on hips. "Well, say it out loud, then," she remarked when Afafrenfere made no move as if to answer her look.

"I think she was kidnapped, or murdered," the monk said.

"Things ain't been so good between herself and Drizzt," Ambergris said, an observation she and Afafrenfere had noted for the last few days, and even before that, out on the seas.

"She wouldn't leave like that," Afafrenfere argued, shaking his head. "Not that one. Lady Dahlia does not run from a fight."

"Even from a lover's quarrel?"

That gave Afafrenfere pause, but only for a moment before he shook his head. He didn't know Dahlia all that well, but in the months he'd spent with her, he believed that he had a fairly solid understanding of the elf's motivations.

"I'm only arguin' with ye because I'm fearing that ye're right," Ambergris admitted.

"Then why have you led me to the docks?"

"If ye was to kidnap someone, to sell to slavers or to force to serve yerself, would ye be wanting to keep her in Baldur's Gate with us friends o' hers walking about?"

"And if you murdered her, what better place to dump the body?" Afafrenfere came right back.

"Aye, and let's hope it's not that."

Afafrenfere wholeheartedly agreed with that sentiment. He hadn't known much camaraderie in his life, other than his long relationship with Parbid. He hadn't thought it possible when first they had left Gauntlgrym, when he had walked out of that complex under great duress and in the company of those who had killed his dear companion, but Afafrenfere had come to think of these four, even the drow who had slain Parbid, as more than mere companions. He enjoyed fighting beside them—to deny it would be a terrible lie.

As he walked with his dwarf friend along those docks, he thought of a starry night far out at sea on *Minnow Skipper*. Unable to sleep, Afafrenfere had gone up to the deck. Drizzt was up there, distracted, standing at the prow and staring off at the sea and sky.

Afafrenfere had moved up, quietly as was his nature, but before he addressed Drizzt, he realized that the drow was already engaged in a quiet conversation—with himself.

Drizzt, this most curious drow rogue, was talking to himself, was using the serenity of the nighttime sea to sort through his thoughts and fears. And judging from his tone, the drow had already gone far around with his current subject and had found his answer, his words clearly reinforcing that which was in his heart.

"So now I say again, I am free, and say it with conviction," Drizzt had declared to no one but himself. "Because I accept that which is in my heart, and understand those tenets to be the truest guidepost along this road. The world may be shadowed in various shades of gray, but the concept of right and wrong is not so subtle for me, and has never been. And when that concept collides against the stated law, then the stated law be damned."

Drizzt had continued, but Afafrenfere had moved away, shocked, and not by the words, but by the exercise itself. Afafrenfere had learned similar techniques at the Monastery of the Yellow Rose. He had learned to fall deeply into meditation, an empty state, and then to subtly shift that bottomless trance, to use that ultimate peace, into a quiet personal conversation to sort out his innermost turmoil. Not with spoken words, but certainly in a similar soliloquy to that which Drizzt was doing at the front of that boat on that dark night.

That dark night had proven enlightening, for the monk had realized that this experience with these companions was very different than that which he had known in Cavus Dun. He had nothing as intense here as his relationship with Parbid, certainly, but there was another matter that he could not deny: unlike Ratsis, Bol, and the others of Cavus Dun—indeed, unlike Parbid, though Afafrenfere was afraid to admit that to himself—these companions would not leave him behind. Even Entreri, the surliest and most violent of the bunch, would not abandon him should they find themselves in a difficult place.

Ambergris's elbow drew the monk from his contemplations.

"Remember them two?" the dwarf asked, barely moving her lips and so quietly that no one else could hear.

Without being obvious about studying the pair, Afafrenfere tried to place them.

"When we was first off the boat," Ambergris prodded, and then he did indeed remember.

And Afafrenfere also noted that the pair, an old gaffer and a middle-aged man, watched him and the dwarf with more than a passing curiosity yet again. He made a mental note of them, and looked at *Minnow Skipper* tied up not so far aside.

"Yerself thinking what I'm thinkin'?" the dwarf asked.

"I believe I am," Afafrenfere whispered back, then in a louder voice, added, "And now I am without coin. I hope that Captain Cannavara will give me work until we put to sea once more."

The monk and the dwarf then boarded *Minnow Skipper,* and Afafrenfere didn't even bother to ask the captain for any pay, but just remained on the boat, grabbing a mop and trying to look busy, when Ambergris headed back to rendezvous with Drizzt and Entreri.

Simple patience stood as among the greatest lessons Afafrenfere had learned in his years at the Monastery of the Yellow Rose, and he put that training to use now.

He would get to know the movements of these two dockhands, given all the interest they seemed to be showing in him and his friends.

After many frustrating hours of scouring the taverns of Baldur's Gate, Drizzt headed across town to meet up with Artemis Entreri at the inn where the assassin was staying.

His mixed feelings chased him along every step.

Drizzt had an inkling of where Dahlia had been before she disappeared, and indeed, of where Dahlia spent most of her time apart from him.

He didn't know how far her relationship with Entreri had progressed. He had known for a long time that there was something between them, of course, an idea that the sentient sword Charon's Claw had seized upon to turn Drizzt's suspicions to a murderous rage against the assassin back in Gauntlgrym. Even when Drizzt had realized the sword's intrusions, and had thus brushed them aside, he couldn't deny that Claw had found a hold on him because of some very real jealousy that had been stirring in his thoughts.

Dahlia had spent a lot of time with Entreri along the journey from Luskan; oftentimes, Drizzt had seen her working the lines of a sail right beside the man, and always the two were engaged in conversation.

There might well be a spark there between them, one that went beyond their shared understanding of each other's deep emotional scars.

Drizzt would be a liar indeed if he claimed that the thought of Dahlia in a tryst with Entreri didn't bother him.

Curiously, though, even though he considered the possibility of his own cuckolding, such matters seemed trivial to him. Something had happened to Dahlia, and he doubted that she had run off of her own accord. Surely she would have confronted him and told him, or at least, he realized, she would have told Entreri.

And wasn't it curious, Drizzt thought, that he wasn't suspicious of Entreri at all in this mystery? Entreri had been the last of the group to see her, and the man was, after all—or had been, at least—a ruthless killer. And yet, Drizzt was certain that he hadn't done anything to harm Dahlia, or even that he wasn't hiding anything about Dahlia's disappearance at all.

That notion slowed Drizzt's steps, as he had to pause to truly consider his feelings here, his gut instinct.

There were so many dark alleyways he might allow his imagination to float along, notions of Entreri getting rid of Dahlia because the assassin feared Drizzt's reaction to him taking Dahlia as a lover, perhaps. Or Dahlia, in her visit, discovering something nefarious about the assassin, and threatening to reveal him. It was all too easy to understand how a relationship with Artemis Entreri could go very bad, very fast, and yet, Drizzt knew that he was right in his feelings of Entreri's innocence.

As he moved toward Entreri's inn, Drizzt could hardly believe how little he cared about Dahlia's relationship with Entreri, whatever it might be. Not now, at least. Now, all that mattered to him was finding out what had happened to her.

When this was settled, however it turned out, he would have a long time in sorting through this morass of confusing emotions.

Entreri looked up briefly when Drizzt entered the crowded tavern, but quickly went back to his drink.

He was having a hard time looking the drow in the eye.

"Nothing," Drizzt said, moving up to the table and sitting opposite the man—in the exact seat Dahlia had taken on that first night in port when she had come to him, Entreri realized.

"I have been in every tavern in Baldur's Gate," Drizzt went on. "None have seen her."

"Or none admit to seeing her," Entreri remarked.

"Would she have left us without notice, on her own?"

Entreri wanted to say, "Left you, perhaps," but he bit it back. And when he thought about it, he realized, to his surprise, that he didn't really want to say something like that to Drizzt. He had cuckolded the drow, and though this ranger had long been his bitterest enemy, Artemis Entreri was not proud of that fact.

He had not made love to Dahlia out of any ill-regard to Drizzt, or out of any regard to Drizzt at all.

And that was why he was so bothered, because that reality was the basis of his pain. He had been with Dahlia because of how Dahlia had touched him, how she made him feel, how she understood so much about him due to her own experiences, their parallel history.

He had been with Dahlia because of his feelings for Dahlia, and now, with her gone, perhaps lost to him, the assassin was being forced into emotions so foreign to him.

Artemis Entreri had been down this road once before, with a woman named Calihye, and to a horrible end. Artemis Entreri had vowed to never again walk such a road of vulnerability. He would depend upon himself and no one else, a rock and island against these unwanted emotions.

And yet, here he was, miserable and worried and fearing that Dahlia had been taken from him.

"Where do we turn?" Drizzt asked.

And here Entreri was, discussing her with Drizzt Do'Urden, her other lover. He looked up at the drow, and answered, "How would I know?"

"You know her as well as I do," Drizzt admitted. "Better, likely."

Entreri winced at the words, expecting a barrage of curses to immediately follow, and looked down to his drink once more, lifting it and draining it without making eye contact with his counterpart.

"Well?" Drizzt prompted.

There was no judgment in the drow's tone. None at all that Entreri could detect. He placed his glass down and slowly looked up to return Drizzt's gaze.

"Dahlia is a profoundly troubled woman," he said.

Drizzt nodded.

"Complicated," Entreri went on. "The violations inflicted upon her wounded her in ways you cannot—" He stopped there, not wanting to twist a dagger into Drizzt.

But Drizzt answered, "I know," and he let it go at that.

He knew other things as well, Entreri realized, or at least, Drizzt suspected, and yet Drizzt was putting that all behind him at this dangerous time. Drizzt tiptoed around the obvious issue, unwilling to confront Entreri openly.

Because he cared about Dahlia, Entreri understood, and that realization stung him all the more in his guilt.

"Effron," Entreri said, and Drizzt perked up.

"He is the only one I can imagine," Entreri explained. "His hatred for Dahlia, if it can even be called hatred, permeates his every thought."

"We are a long way from Port Llast," Drizzt said, "and took a roundabout path to get here."

"That young tiefling is not without resources," Entreri replied. "Even Herzgo Alegni showed him great deference, and Herzgo Alegni hated him profoundly."

"Herzgo Alegni was his father," Drizzt reminded him.

"It mattered not," Entreri explained. "Or perhaps that was the focus of the hatred. Effron came to us in Neverwinter at the request of a Netherese lord. I had many dealings with these lords in my time as Alegni's slave. Do not ever underestimate them."

"You believe this Netherese lord helped Effron get to Dahlia?" Drizzt asked.

"I fear it," Entreri admitted, and he was being quite honest at that moment, "for if that is the case, then Dahlia is lost to us forever."

Drizzt slumped back at that, and he and Entreri stared at each other for many heartbeats. But again, and again to Entreri's surprise, the drow did not broach that most delicate subject.

"I need another drink," Entreri said, standing, for what he really needed was to take a break from this unrelenting pressure. The idea that Dahlia was forever lost to him gnawed at his sensibilities in a way that he simply could not process.

"Get a drink for me," Drizzt surprised him by saying when Entreri turned for the bar. "A large one."

Entreri turned back to him and snickered, seeing the hyperbole for what it was. Still, he returned with a pair of drinks and the bottle of rum, even though he realized that he'd be drinking most of that bottle himself.

From before dawn until after sunset, Brother Afafrenfere scrubbed the deck of *Minnow Skipper,* or worked the lines, or patched with tar, or performed whatever other chore he could fashion, or Mister Sikkal assigned him, so long as that work did not move him belowdecks. He wasn't there to actually work, after all.

"Get yerself down under and help Cribbins with the patching," Sikkal ordered him late one afternoon.

"Down under?"

"Bottom hold," Sikkal explained. "We be taking a bit o' water, and I'm not for that. So get yerself down there and get yerself to work!"

Afafrenfere looked around, noting several other crewmen sitting here or there on the open deck, done with their work, if any of them had even been assigned any this day. *Minnow Skipper* was stocked and seaworthy and only sitting here because of the missing Dahlia, though no one aboard seemed to know that Dahlia was missing, or cared to admit to it, anyway.

"I do not think I will go and do that," Afafrenfere replied.

" 'Ere, what did ye say?" Sikkal demanded.

"Send another," the monk replied.

"If we was at sea, I could have yerself thrown to the sharks for that answer, boy!"

"If we were at sea, you could try," the monk replied calmly. He wasn't looking at Sikkal as he spoke, though. The two dock hands had appeared on the wharf, the old gaffer with a sack over his shoulder. Afafrenfere had seen this play before, the previous twilight.

Sikkal rambled on and on about something, but Afafrenfere was no longer listening. The two old dockhands revealed their nervousness as they moved along the wharf, glancing this way and that with every step. Just like the night before.

Afafrenfere let his gaze shift far to the side, to an old scow, appearing far less than seaworthy, that was strapped up tight to the farthest dock. These two would make their way to that one, the monk believed, for the night before they had gone aboard, carrying a similar sack. Afafrenfere had watched the boat for a long while, but had never seen the pair depart, nor had they gone out the previous morning. The monk hadn't thought much of it at the time, since many of the dockhands in Baldur's Gate, as in every port, used the moored boats as personal inns. But earlier this day, Afafrenfere had noted the pair gazing that way more than once, and had expected they would arrive on the docks around dinnertime, bound for the scow.

And why, after all, had they obviously slipped off the boat in the middle of the night?

"Hey!" Mister Sikkal shouted and he grabbed Afafrenfere's arm.

The monk slowly swiveled his head, first glancing at the other members of the crew, all looking on with more than a passing interest now, then turning down to eye Sikkal's dirty hand, and then, finally, settling his gaze on Sikkal himself, looking the man straight in the eye with a glare that was more promise than threat.

Sikkal couldn't hold that stare, or the arm, and he backed off, but only momentarily, for he seemed to gain a bit of courage when he broke free of Afafrenfere's glare and considered the crew around him.

"Get below," he ordered Afafrenfere.

In a low voice, so that only Sikkal could hear, Afafrenfere spelled it out more clearly. "Only if that is where I am asked to move your corpse."

"Captain's to hear of this!" Sikkal cried, but Afafrenfere wasn't looking at him anymore, turning again to the wharves, and to the dockhands, and just in time to see them toss their sack onto the distant scow and slither aboard.

Sikkal rushed off for Cannavara's cabin, but he hadn't gone three steps before the monk leaped over *Minnow Skipper*'s rail to land lightly on the dock.

Sikkal called after him, and Afafrenfere resolved to rush back to the ship and crush the idiot's windpipe if he persisted in raising a ruckus.

But Sikkal didn't, and the monk moved in fits and starts, slipping along the wharves from barrel to crate, carefully picking his stealthy way to the old scow. Near to the boat, he nestled behind a stack of kegs and listened intently.

He heard some murmuring, but nothing definitive. He couldn't make out any actual words, for the waves lapped loudly against the wharf's supporting posts and broke with a watery crash just a few steps from his position.

Patience, Afafrenfere told himself, and he waited for twilight to deepen.

With practiced stealth, Brother Afafrenfere slipped onto the deck of the scow and into the shadows beside the main cabin. He heard the pair of dock hands within, laughing and wheezing, and he thought then, to his great disappointment, that this boat was nothing more than their nightly retreat. He remained anyway, for he had to be certain. He didn't know if these two had been involved in Dahlia's disappearance, but Ambergris's hunch had resonated with him, and watching them for the last couple of days had done nothing to dissuade Afafrenfere from believing these two to be a nefarious pair, and with something to hide, though whatever it might be, he could not be sure.

The monk moved quietly around the deck, looking for clues. Everything seemed unremarkable . . . until he noted a meager light between the deck boards, lamplight coming from the hold and not the cabin.

Growing up in the Bloodstone Lands, Afafrenfere wasn't versed in ship design, but he had been on a couple of boats similar to this one, and he didn't think there was any way for the dockhands to get belowdecks from the cabin. He slipped back to the cabin, and heard the pair still inside, with the younger seadog grumbling about the smell of the older one's pipe weed.

Across from the door to that cabin, right in the open on the deck, sat the bulkhead. It wouldn't be easy to get there unseen, the monk realized, but he started that way, belly-crawling.

"Get out on the deck, then, ye stinky fool!" he heard from inside the cabin.

Alarmed, the monk stood and leaped as the cabin door swung open and the old gaffer came forth.

Puffing his pipe, and indeed the stench was terrible, the wheezing old seadog moved right under Afafrenfere, who had wrapped himself like a snake around the crossbeam of the mainmast. The cabin door was still open, creaking as it swung gently with the rocking boat. Afafrenfere caught glimpses of the other swabby inside, moving around, preparing a meal, it seemed.

The old gaffer moved to the rail, looking out to sea.

Afafrenfere slithered along the crossbeam, again right above him. With a quick glance to the other, to ensure that he was distracted, the monk dropped down behind his prey, his right forearm tucking tightly against the gaffer's throat, his left hand coming across behind the man's head, grabbing a handful of hair and an ear, and pressing the man forward, tightening the choke. In a matter of a few heartbeats, the gaffer went limp in Afafrenfere's strong grasp, and the monk eased the unconscious fool down to the deck.

Afafrenfere didn't even pause at the cabin door, bursting in quickly, violently, and similarly locking the other man into the incapacitating hold. Soon after, the two were seated in the cabin, tied and gagged back to back, as the monk moved quietly to the entry to the lower hold.

Flat on his belly, Afafrenfere peered through the cracks in the old bulkhead. He did well to stifle his gasp when he did, for there Dahlia was, bound and gagged in a chair across the way. And there sat Effron, off to the side in a chair and staring at her.

Dahlia couldn't look the tiefling in the eye, Afafrenfere realized. He tried to remember all that he knew of this dangerous young warlock. So he took his time here—besides, he wanted to know what this was all about. What was really going on between Effron and Dahlia? Why had he taken her, and given that, why was he still here on Toril? He could shadowstep with her back to the Shadowfell, Afafrenfere knew.

There was much more to this story, and Afafrenfere wanted to know it.

So he waited as the night deepened around him. Judging from the location of the moon, it was past midnight before Effron finally stirred.

The young tiefling moved over to Dahlia and pulled down her gag.

"They are all sleeping now, of course," Effron said. "No one will hear you if you scream out—"

"I won't scream out," Dahlia replied, and still she did not look at him.

"I could make you."

Dahlia didn't even lift her eyes. Where was the firebrand Afafrenfere had come to know? If Drizzt or Entreri, or anyone else, had spoken to her like that in Port Llast, bound or not, she would have spat in his face.

"Do you know how much I hate you?" Effron asked.

"You should," Dahlia replied in barely a whisper, and with true humility, it seemed.

"Then why?" the young warlock demanded, his voice rising and trembling. "If the memory hurts you as much as you claim, then why?"

"You couldn't understand."

"Try!"

"Because you looked like him!" Dahlia shouted back, now, at last, raising her teary eyes to look at Effron. "You looked like him, and when I looked upon you, all I saw was him!"

"Herzgo Alegni?"

"Don't speak his name!"

"He was my father!" Effron retorted. "Herzgo Alegni was my father. And at least he cared enough to bother to raise me! At least he didn't throw me off a cliff!"

Again Afafrenfere had to work hard to suppress a gasp, for it seemed clear to him that Effron wasn't talking figuratively here.

"You wanted me dead!" he yelled in Dahlia's face, and she was weeping openly now.

"I wanted him dead," she corrected, her voice breaking with every syllable. "And I couldn't kill him! I was a child, don't you understand? Just a little orphaned elf hiding in the forest with the few of my clan who had survived the murderous raid. And he was coming back for you."

Effron sputtered several indecipherable syllables. "Then why didn't you just let him take me?" he demanded.

"He would have killed me."

"Most mothers would die for their children. A real mother would have died—"

"He would have violated me again, more likely," Dahlia said, and she wasn't looking at Effron any longer, and her tone made it seem to Afafrenfere as if she were speaking more to herself than to him at that point, trying to sort through her own painful recollections. "He would have filled me with another child, that I could serve him like a brood mare, like chattel.

"And you," she said, now looking up at him, and seeming to find some measure of strength once more. "You would have been taught to hate me in any case."

"No."

"Yes!" Dahlia snapped back. "He would have trained you from your youngest days. He would have made you just like him, ready to go forth and murder and rape—"

"No!" Effron said and he slapped Dahlia across the face, but then fell back a step, seeming as wounded as she, and she melted into sobs once more.

Afafrenfere had seen enough. He slithered back from the hold and climbed a guide rope, setting himself into position.

He played this through in his thoughts repeatedly, recalling all that he knew of Effron, recognizing the tiefling's deadly arsenal.

He heard another slap from below.

Afafrenfere leaped down, double-kicking below as he descended on the bulkhead, his weight, momentum and powerful kicks exploding the old wood beneath him. He landed in the hold in perfect balance and sprang immediately for the surprised Effron, diving into a forward roll.

Dahlia screamed, Effron threw his good arm up defensively, and Afafrenfere came up to his feet with a barrage of blows. The warlock had magical defenses in place, of course, but still the monk's relentless barrage got through, slamming Effron about the face once and again.

Effron fell back and Afafrenfere pursued, kicking, punching, launching a full-out offensive volley to keep the warlock off balance, to keep him from casting a spell. His best chance, he knew, was to simply overwhelm the young tiefling, to bury him before the dangerous Effron ever found his balance.

A sharp left jab sped past the warlock's uplifted arm, snapping his head back. A right cross followed, but much of its weight was blocked, inadvertently, by the rising arm of the staggering Effron. It hardly mattered, though, for Afafrenfere threw the right simply to half-turn Effron and open a hole in his defenses, and to get Afafrenfere's own right foot forward. Now came the real attack, a sweeping left hook that flew around the warlock's uplifted arm and cracked him across the side of the jaw, snapping his head to the side.

Afafrenfere spun a tight circuit, lifting his trailing right leg up high, nearly clipping the beams of the low hold's ceiling, and he brought that leg down and across, chopping the warlock across the collarbone, dropping him to his knees.

The monk didn't dare relent, understanding that a single spell from Effron could quickly reverse his fortunes. For some reason, though, Effron didn't seem to be fighting back. Perhaps it had been the speed and brutality of the attack, but there seemed something more to Afafrenfere, some deeper resignation.

If he had paused to consider that, Afafrenfere would have sorted it out, of course: the tiefling had been as overwhelmed by the confrontation with his mother as was Dahlia.

Afafrenfere wasn't about to take the chance that such apparent surrender would hold. He waded in, slapping away the meager attempt to block, then backhanded Effron in the forehead, driving the tiefling's head back, opening a clear strike at the exposed neck. In the same movement, Afafrenfere set himself powerfully and lifted his right hand up behind him, fingers locked claw-like for the killing blow.

Effron couldn't stop it.

Effron didn't appear as if he wanted to stop it.

CHAPTER
14

SHADOWS OF TRUTH

THE GENTLE CURVATURE OF THE WATERY HORIZON GREETED EVERY VIEW from *Minnow Skipper*'s crow's nest. Three days out of Baldur's Gate, the ship found fair winds and following seas, and no land in sight and none wanted.

None that Drizzt wanted, at least. He sat far above the deck, losing himself in the rolling waters, letting them take him gently into his own thoughts.

He wanted to help Dahlia. He wanted to comfort her, to guide her through these days, but in truth, he had no idea what to say that would make any difference to the emotionally battered woman, particularly not with Effron tied to a chair in a sectioned-off part of the hold.

Dahlia seemed a different person to Drizzt after Afafrenfere's gallant rescue, and Effron seemed a different enemy. Neither showed much sign of life, the young warlock not offering anything in terms of resistance, the elf warrior not offering much of anything at all. Dahlia's capture by her son and their long meetings had drained both of all energy, it seemed.

Drizzt figured that if pirates boarded *Minnow Skipper*, both would simply surrender without lifting a hand to fight, and he could well imagine the shrug either might offer on the last steps off the plank.

That notion had the drow glancing down at the deck. Dahlia was there among the crew, by the starboard rail, ostensibly stitching a torn sail, though at the rate she was going, a finger's length tear might occupy her for the rest of the journey to Memnon.

Drizzt's gaze drifted farther aft, to the open bulkhead, where Ambergris had just appeared. The dwarf reached back and bent low, grabbing hold on Effron and helping him up into the open air, with Afafrenfere closely following.

Amidships, Dahlia glanced back to look at the young tiefling, but she quickly looked down and went back to her task.

Making busy work, Drizzt could see, trying to pretend that Effron wasn't on the deck, or that he wasn't on the boat at all.

But Drizzt could see even that wouldn't prove enough emotional insulation for Dahlia. She took a deep breath and closed her eyes, then gathered up her things and moved to the forward bulkhead, never looking back.

Never looking back at Effron.

"Effron," Drizzt whispered from on high, and then it hit him, the simplest answer to the questions and doubts that had been pounding him for these many days. This wasn't about the relationship he had with Dahlia, whatever that might be. This wasn't about him at all. It was about that twisted tiefling leaning over the taffrail of *Minnow Skipper.*

Drizzt couldn't begin to decipher the many emotions that must be running through Effron and Dahlia, wrenched from hidden corners of their hearts by circumstance and the abrupt turn of events. But in this moment, finally, the drow came to realize that it was all right that he couldn't understand.

Because this wasn't about him.

Drizzt hopped out from his seat, catching a handhold and wrapping his ankles around the guide rope, then half sliding, half hand-walking his way quickly to the deck. With a last glance at the bulkhead through which Dahlia had gone—and brushing away his certainty that she was belowdecks speaking with, or at least sitting with, Artemis Entreri—Drizzt moved aft along the deck.

"Hey now!" Mister Sikkal yelled at him. "Get yerself back at the lookout!"

Drizzt didn't even turn to regard the old first mate. He moved easily around the captain's quarters and to the back, where the dwarf called a greeting to him.

"Take my place at the crow's nest," he said to Afafrenfere when the monk also turned to greet him. "I won't be long."

Afafrenfere glanced at Effron, who hadn't even turned away from the sizzling foam in *Minnow Skipper*'s wake, who hadn't even shown the slightest interest in anything other than the empty dark water. With a nod, the monk moved past Drizzt.

"You can go with him," the drow said to Ambergris.

"I ain't for climbin' no durned dead tree pole!" the dwarf insisted.

"Stay at the mast's base, then."

Ambergris offered him a little grin. "Our deal with Cannavara says two're to be with this Effron boy at all times, including meself and me silencing spells."

Drizzt motioned with his head in the direction Afafrenfere had gone.

"I'll be just around the corner, then," the stubborn dwarf replied, and she walked past Drizzt and around the edge of the captain's cabin, but there plopped down noisily and made a point of beginning a song, an old dwarf ballad of deep mines, thick silver veins, and a host of goblins in need of a bit of dwarf-style relocation.

Drizzt moved up to Effron, but faced back at the captain's cabin as he leaned against the taffrail.

"Where will this go?" Drizzt asked Effron—asked his back, actually, since the tiefling was still leaning out over the taffrail, staring at the empty sea.

"Do you know or do you care?" Drizzt pressed when Effron didn't respond.

"Why do you care?" came the curt reply.

"Because I care for Dah . . . I care for your mother," Drizzt replied, deciding to go there with Effron, straight to the relationship that was obviously causing him so much pain.

The young tiefling's response came as a derisive snort, which was not quite what Drizzt had expected.

"Why would you doubt that?" Drizzt asked, still trying to remain calm and reasonable, trying honestly to coax Effron from his defensive shell. "Dahlia and I have been traveling together for many months now."

"Traveling and coupling, you mean," Effron said, still not turning around. "That is our business."

"Is it Artemis Entreri's?" the young tiefling asked, and now he did turn around, an unsettling grin spreading wickedly across his face.

Drizzt couldn't quite find the words to respond, not sure where Effron was going with this, yet afraid of where that might be.

"The night I caught Dahlia, she had just left him," Effron explained.

Drizzt shrugged and wanted nothing more than to turn this conversation back to the more important topic, that of Effron and Dahlia.

"She had just left his bed," Effron pressed, and he seemed quite pleased with himself. "She stank of him."

It took all the self-control he could muster for Drizzt not to simply reach out and push the nasty young warlock over that taffrail and be done with him. Effron's every word hit him like a dagger, and more pointedly so because he had known this truth already, though he hadn't been able to admit it to himself.

"I don't understand why you and Entreri bothered to rent two rooms," Effron continued. "You would save coin and time renting just one, don't you think, with Dahlia lying between you?"

He bit off his last word, and quite nearly a piece of his tongue, when Drizzt lost control for just the blink of an eye—long enough for Drizzt to deliver a stinging slap across Effron's face.

"Concern yourself more with your own predicament," the drow advised. "Where will this all go? How will it end?"

"Badly," Effron spat back.

"That is one choice, but only that, a choice."

"I'll see her dead."

"Then you're a fool."

"You don't know—" Effron started, but Drizzt cut him short.

"It won't free you of your burden," Drizzt calmly assured him. "Your satisfaction will prove short-lived, and ever longer will your misery grow. This I know. Whatever else, whatever other details you think yourself privy to that I am not, matter not at all. Because this I know."

Effron stared at him hard.

"Where will this all go?" Drizzt asked again, and he started off. And he knew that Ambergris has been listening to every word when she came around the corner before Drizzt had reached it.

And he knew it by the look on the dwarf's face, an expression of sympathy aimed at him.

"Ask yerself the same," the dwarf advised in a whisper as Drizzt walked by.

Up above the deck in the crow's nest, Drizzt was the first to spot land, a jutting mountain to the south east. Memnon was closer than that natural mound, Drizzt knew, though it was not yet visible, as *Minnow Skipper* neared the end of the second leg of her journey.

He called down to Captain Cannavara, who looked up at him and nodded, as if expecting the call. "So keep your eyes to the horizons for pirate sails, drow!" he yelled back. "Here's the channel they haunt!"

Drizzt nodded, but thought little of it. There were no sails to be seen, and in truth, that irked Drizzt. He scanned as the captain had asked, and he hoped to see something, and was dismayed that he did not.

Drizzt wanted a fight.

He had spent the last two tendays wanting a fight. Since his confrontation with Effron, the drow had subconsciously wrung the blood out of his knuckles on many occasions, most often whenever Artemis Entreri was in view.

He looked down at the deck now, forward, where Entreri was sitting and eating some bread. Dahlia wasn't far from him, working the lines as the pilot tried to keep the sails full of wind.

The two of them in the same frame stung him, and his imagination took him to dark places indeed. He shook it away and tried to rationalize, tried to find a distinction where Drizzt left off and Dahlia began. He didn't focus on the claim he held on the woman as much as on the notion that any such claim was preposterous.

Still, the drow found himself gnashing his teeth. The intersection of emotion and rational thought was not bordered by well-marked corners after all.

"Memnon?" Dahlia asked Captain Cannavara after Drizzt's call.

"With the morning tide," the captain replied.

Dahlia glanced over at Entreri, and with alarm. It wasn't just the notion of him leaving, as he had hinted, but more the coming conclusion to the situation with Effron. One way or another, something had to be resolved. Dahlia had hardly seen her son, willingly relinquishing control of him to Afafrenfere and Ambergris, though she doubted that much attention was even needed, given Effron's obvious distress. The young warlock appeared as broken inside as out, now, and showed no signs of trying to lash out, or escape. Indeed, Ambergris had assured them all that Effron could have gotten away on several occasions, for he knew how to shadowstep. If he tried to execute such a maneuver to return to the Shadowfell, only immediate and overwhelming intervention could stop him, and surely over the course of tendays, there had been many such opportunities for Effron to escape.

But now loomed Memnon, the next dock, and Cannavara had informed the crew that they would be in port for a tenday, perhaps two, as they executed some needed repairs to *Minnow Skipper*'s hull and masts.

With a heavy sigh, Dahlia started for the hold.

"Here now, girl!" Cannavara said to her. "Where do you think you're going?"

"I've something I need to do."

"Not now, you don't, unless you're thinking that you need to work that line. We're in pirate waters, the last run to Memnon, and we're not to put aside our diligence until we're fast tied to the long dock."

Dahlia turned away from the captain. "Entreri," she called, and he looked back at her over his shoulder. She nodded to her post and gave a pleading expression and shrug.

Artemis Entreri tore off another piece of bread and nodded, moving to replace her.

Dahlia turned back to Captain Cannavara, who had already turned away to move on to other business.

The elf pointedly did not look up at Drizzt as she moved to the open bulkhead of the aft hold.

"Leave," she instructed the dwarf and the monk as she descended.

"Aye, but we're too close to be takin' such a gamble as that," Ambergris warned.

Dahlia didn't blink, and didn't regard the dwarf, her eyes locked on the small figure reclining in a hammock across the way.

"Tie him, then," Ambergris instructed the monk, but before Afafrenfere took a step toward Effron, Dahlia repeated, "Leave," her tone leaving no room for debate.

The dwarf and the monk exchanged looks and shrugs, and neither seemed to care much at that time.

"Ye do what ye need do," Ambergris offered, moving up to the deck behind her monk companion.

"We are almost in port," Dahlia said when she and Effron were alone in the small aft hold.

He didn't even look her way.

"Memnon," she explained, moving to a chair beside his hammock. "An exotic city, from what I have heard. Southern and very different from—"

"Why would I care?" he interrupted, though he didn't turn to regard her.

"Look at me," she bade.

"Get out," he replied.

Dahlia moved in a rush, leaping up, grabbing Effron and yanking him so roughly that he tumbled out of his hammock to crash down to the floor. He came up at once, violence shining clearly in his distinct eyes, one tiefling red, one elf blue.

"Sit down," Dahlia commanded, motioning to a second chair.

"Jump into the sea," he replied.

Dahlia took her seat anyway, and stared up at this half-elf, half-tiefling.

"I need to tell you, and you need to listen," she said quietly.

"And then?"

Dahlia shrugged.

"And then you kill me?" Effron asked.

"No," Dahlia answered, her voice thick with resignation.

"And then I kill you?"

"Would that please you?"

"Yes."

She didn't believe him, but understood why he had to say that. "Then perhaps I will let you, or maybe I will just let you walk away."

Effron looked at her incredulously. "In Memnon?"

Dahlia shrugged as if it didn't matter and motioned again to the chair, but Effron remained standing.

It didn't matter. The elf woman took a deep breath. "For every moment since I learned who you truly were, in the bowels of Gauntlgrym, I have dreaded this," she said, hardly able to keep her voice from cracking apart.

"Dreaded? Your admission? Did we not already have this conversation, in the hold of another boat in dock at Baldur's Gate?"

"No," she said, looking down in shame. "You already have my admission. You didn't need it, because everything Herzgo Alegni has told you about that day when he first caught sight of you is no doubt true. There would be no need for him to embellish my crime." She gave a helpless snort. "I did it."

Dahlia took a deep breath, steeled herself, and looked Effron directly in the eye. "I threw you from the cliff. I denied your existence and wanted it . . . obliterated." She took another deep breath to stop herself from simply falling over and dissolving on the floor. "I denied you. I had to."

"Witch," he muttered. "Murderess."

"All true," she said. "Do you even care why?"

That comment knocked Effron off balance, it seemed, and Dahlia had expected as much. Effron hadn't killed her, hadn't even tortured her, when he had her at his mercy in the hold of the scow in Baldur's Gate. Most of all, he yelled at her, and asked her questions that had no answers.

But perhaps she had an explanation, and perhaps that was what the young warlock truly wanted.

"I was barely more than a girl," Dahlia went on. "It wasn't so long ago, but it seems like an eternity. And still I remember the day, every moment, every step—"

"The day you tried to murder me."

Dahlia shook her head and looked down. "The day Herzgo Alegni tore my body and my heart." A sob shivered her, but she would not give it credence, would not allow herself to go there. Not now.

She took another deep and steadying breath, and she determined to look him in the eye again, and was surprised when she at last glanced up to find him sitting in the chair across the way, staring back at her.

"I went to the river to fetch some water," she began. "That was my morning chore, and one I relished." She gave a helpless little laugh. "To be out in the forest alone, in the sunshine and with the birds and the small animals all around. Could an elf lass ask for more?"

Another uncomfortable laugh escaped her lips as she looked down once more.

She told her tale, and never once looked up at Effron. She told of the surprise she found waiting at her clan's small village, of the marauding Shadovar, led by Herzgo Alegni. She didn't hold back anything for Effron's sensibilities or her own as she told of Alegni's reaction to her, and fully detailed his violation, and his ultimate betrayal in the decapitation of her beloved mother.

Tears dripped from her eyes as she continued, describing the months that followed, the pain and the fear, honestly and in full, nor did she shy from the truth of that fateful day when she went to pay back Herzgo Alegni for his crimes.

"You didn't matter," she whispered. "It was not about you, even though it was in reality all about you. But I didn't see that."

"You could have run!" he shouted at her, and there was a profound shakiness to his voice.

"I know," she whispered. "But I didn't know."

"Why didn't you just leave me? Do you know the pain I have suffered?"

"You were my only weapon," Dahlia said, and that was enough, she realized, for that was all she had. Before Effron could reply, she stood up and walked for the ladder.

"You can leave us in Memnon," she told him, "and I will not stop you. You can find me and kill me if you choose. I will not resist, and I will demand of my companions that they exact no revenge upon you, whatever my torment or ultimate fate."

Looking up the ladder and not back at him, she paused and waited for a tirade that did not come.

So Dahlia left him there.

———

"Do you wish to talk about it?" Drizzt asked Dahlia that night when he came to her as she sat alone on the deck. Guenhwyvar paced wearily beside him.

Dahlia turned to Drizzt and stared at him, considering the question, trying to fathom something from the tone. There was no hostility there. He knew about her tryst with Entreri, she knew without doubt, for Ambergris had warned Entreri of Effron's revelations, and he in turn had told Dahlia.

But neither was there comprehension in Drizzt, Dahlia believed, and apparently that showed in her expression, for Drizzt then remarked, "I grew up in a dark place. Perhaps I do not understand that which you have suffered, but my own life, for longer than you have been alive, was spent among a culture that thought nothing of murder and deception."

Dahlia licked her lips, a bit off guard by this uncharacteristic display. Drizzt was reaching out to her. Despite the distance that had grown between them—a gulf that had driven her to Artemis Entreri, no less!—the drow seemed to be honestly trying here. The elf woman reached over and patted Guen and the panther curled up at her feet, gave a great, toothy yawn, and sank down to the deck.

She appreciated Drizzt's integrity, but still, there was nothing for her to say. Not then.

Drizzt reached out his arms and Dahlia accepted the invitation. She was truly grateful for the hug. She even admitted to herself that if Drizzt tried to take that hug to further intimacy, she wouldn't stop him.

But he didn't, and in a roundabout way, that seemed to Dahlia a rejection in and of itself. She moved to line up with Drizzt's face and kissed him passionately.

Or tried to, for he turned away at the last moment.

Dahlia gave a little cry and grabbed at him forcefully, trying to push herself upon him. Drizzt was too strong for that, however, and he held her there.

So she punched him and pulled back instead, and he grabbed her and hugged her close again, tighter this time, pinning her arms.

She wanted to kill him!

Nay, she wanted to, needed to, make love to him. She needed him against her and inside her. She needed to devour him, to use him as her emotional anchor, to know that he loved her as she . . .

Dahlia stopped struggling and found it hard to breathe.

After a short while, Drizzt pushed her back to arms' length, and said, "Go and see Effron again, as often as you can."

Dahlia felt her jaw drop open, and she held that pose as Drizzt turned to the mainmast. "Be gone, Guen," he said, dismissing Dahlia as surely as he was the cat, for he then scrambled up to his post—a post that had become his most customary perch, even throughout the nights.

Dahlia didn't know what to think, or what to feel. She needed Drizzt at that moment, but he had left.

She needed her lover.

Dahlia had never needed a lover.

Never!

Until now, and she needed him and he had walked away, and it was her fault. Why had she gone to Entreri that night in Baldur's Gate? Was it anger that had driven her to his bed? Or was it fear of these startling and undeniable feelings toward this rogue drow?

She felt as if she were on that cliff again, throwing Effron to the wind. She had ruined him on that fateful day, but she had invariably ruined herself as well.

Had she done the same in going to Entreri?

She watched Guenhwyvar dissolving into gray mist, into nothingness, and she saw that as an appropriate representation of her relationship with Drizzt.

"Go to Effron," Drizzt called down to her, and she felt as if he were reading her inner turmoil. "You can repair this."

Effron.

"Effron," she whispered under her breath.

Dahlia found herself terrified of even daring to hope. She wanted nothing more than to cut her own wrist and melt down onto the deck and sob until death mercifully ended this cruel torment.

But Drizzt's words kept echoing in her thoughts, denying the despair.

Eventually, the elf woman managed to turn and look over her shoulder, in the direction of the aft hatch and the small room where Effron remained.

She went there, quietly, and didn't even rouse the sleeping dwarf and monk, or Effron, who tossed and turned in his hammock with troubled dreams. She quietly set the chair near that hammock, and eventually put her hand on Effron's twisted shoulder, whispering for him to be still.

She fell asleep there, and when she woke up, she found Effron staring back at her from the hammock, but making no move to push her hand away, for it remained on his shoulder.

She tried to decipher the young warlock's expression, but found she could not. Certainly, the pain remained etched on his thin and angular features, but what she could not then see, however, was the venom that had been so clear previously.

Dahlia swallowed hard. "We put into Memnon this day," she said. "I hold to my word, if that is your choice." Her voice nearly broke apart as she finished, "I hope you will sail back out with us."

"Why?" he asked in what seemed a sincere tone.

Dahlia shrugged. She felt the tears welling in her eyes and could not deny them.

So she rose and rushed from the hold.

Minnow Skipper glided into Memnon's harbor the next morning, the crew rushing around to drop the sails and ready the lines.

"Gather the Memnon chart from my desk," Captain Cannavara instructed Drizzt. "And up to the crow's nest with you, with them in hand. She's a safe harbor, but we'll be passing shallow rocks starboard, and I've not been here in years."

Drizzt nodded and sprinted to the cabin and to the desk. The chart sat atop a pile of parchment, easily found. Drizzt scooped it up and turned to go—and nearly crashed into Artemis Entreri, who had slipped in behind him.

And he had shut the door.

Drizzt didn't know what to make of this. The assassin stood directly before him, staring at him unblinkingly. He made no move to his weapons, and didn't seem to have positioned his hands to do so.

But the hairs on the back of Drizzt's neck stood up as he looked at the stone-faced, dangerous man. Something was clearly amiss.

Entreri scrutinized him, studying him intently, but why?

"You know," Entreri finally said.

"I know?"

"If you mean to kill me, now is your moment."

Drizzt rocked back on his heels as it all came clear to him. He thought of Effron's claims, which he knew in his heart to be true.

"You're leaving us?" Drizzt asked.

That seemed to put Entreri off his guard—he even backed off half a step.

"I've decided to stay," he answered.

Drizzt gave a slight nod, and even heard himself saying, "Good," before he simply walked past Entreri and through the door to the mast, and up to his usual perch at the crow's nest, up above it all.

He unrolled the map as best he could in the wind and got his bearings, trying to focus on the critical task at hand.

But when he looked at the water, looked for the rocks, what he saw most clearly was the memory of Artemis Entreri, saying "You know."

Twelve days later, after an uneventful visit where Drizzt and the others didn't even bother renting rooms in the city but simply stayed aboard, *Minnow Skipper* put back to sea, bound for Calimport, and from there, to turn back and sail to Luskan, expecting to put in before the cold north wind sent islands of ice drifting along the Sword Coast North.

The days blended together, full of work and full of boredom. Such was life at sea. Up in the crow's nest, Drizzt longed for his days aboard *Sea Sprite*. Those were different sails, for always, it seemed, were they in pursuit of pirates, with battle looming on every horizon. Not so now, and Drizzt took note of the influence of the flag of Ship Kurth, even this far south. They encountered many vessels in and out of Calimport that the drow, having spent years surveying such boats, suspected might dabble in high-seas' theft, yet not a one made a move on *Minnow Skipper*.

He found himself disappointed. He longed for battle. His relationship with Dahlia lay in tatters. They were friendly, they shared a few evenings at the rail, talking under the stars—no, not talking, he reconsidered, for mostly they merely sat there letting the night sky swallow them into its contemplative sparkles.

On a couple of occasions, Dahlia had moved closer, and hinted at intimacy, but Drizzt had never, and would not, let that thought gain traction. He wasn't sure why, for truly he did not wish to cause her pain, and could not deny her allure.

Surprisingly to Drizzt, he realized that it wasn't the fact that Dahlia had betrayed him with Artemis Entreri. He bore her no ill will for that. Nay, it was something deeper, and something that had more to do with the philosophy of Innovindil than with Dahlia, and more, of course, to do with Drizzt.

Dahlia wasn't going to Entreri, either, he knew, but Drizzt found that such information did not comfort him, and in truth, seemed almost meaningless to him at that point. The elf woman was deeply wounded, and her focus remained Effron.

Yes, Effron, and they all knew then that Dahlia had granted him permission to leave. Yet here he was aboard *Minnow Skipper*, though no longer under constant guard in the hold. He didn't come up to the deck often, which was understandable given his years in the dim light of the Shadowfell, but no one stopped him when he tried.

Ambergris and Afafrenfere remained charged with watching him, but from afar now, for it was obvious to all of them that such intense attention was not needed.

Dahlia went to Effron every day, though whether they spoke or argued, spat at each other or simply sat together, no one other than they knew, and Drizzt did not broach the subject with Dahlia. He watched her, though, every day, as she made her way eagerly to the rear bulkhead, disappearing into the hold, and he watched her even more keenly whenever she left the young warlock, which was usually many hours later.

It seemed to Drizzt that she was finding peace.

Perhaps it was merely his own hopes for her, and his hopes for Effron, guiding his thoughts.

He prayed that he was viewing the situation honestly.

On one such occasion, the ship north of Baldur's Gate once more, and cutting a straighter and swifter line to Luskan as the season drew late, Effron and Dahlia came out of the hold together.

That alone was surely enough to draw Drizzt's attention, for he had not seen such a thing in two months of sailing. The pair moved to the side of the captain's cabin, and Dahlia signaled up to Drizzt to come down.

The drow looked around, ensuring that no sails were anywhere to be seen, then slipped down from his perch. He noted Entreri's eyes upon him, and those of Ambergris and Afafrenfere as well, as he walked across the deck to join the couple.

"In all the time I have been with you, you have not summoned your panther," Effron said.

Drizzt eyed him curiously. "Guenhwyvar is not fond of the open waters," he lied. "She growls at every pitch of the deck."

"Not once, through the whole of the season."

Drizzt swallowed hard and narrowed his eyes as he stared at the young tiefling. Effron was mistaken here, for Drizzt had called Guenhwyvar to his side several times, at night. But never for long, for the panther appeared more haggard, truly wounded now, and withering, as if her very life-force was fast fading from her corporeal form. "What do you know?" he asked.

"She resides in the Shadowfell, not in the Astral Plane," Effron said, and Drizzt's eyes opened wide, and Dahlia gasped, as did Ambergris, who was not far away.

"In the house of Lord Draygo Quick," Effron explained.

"She serves a Netherese lord?" Drizzt asked, clearly skeptical.

"No," Effron quickly said. "She serves him only when you call her to your side, for he sees through her eyes. He has watched you for many months through her eyes."

Drizzt looked at Dahlia, who could only shrug, obviously as much at a loss as was he.

"Why are you telling me this?"

"Because I know where she is," Effron said. "And I can get you to her."

PART III

INTO SHADOW

My journey from Luskan to Calimport and back again proved, at the same time, to be the least eventful and most memorable of any voyage I have known. We encountered no storms, no pirates, and no trouble with the ship whatsoever. The activities on *Minnow Skipper*'s deck were nothing beyond routine throughout the entire journey.

But on an emotional level, I watched a fascinating exchange play out over the tendays and months, from the purest hatred to the deepest guilt to a primal need for a resolution that seemed untenable in a relationship irreparable.

Or was it?

When we battled Herzgo Alegni, Dahlia believed that she was facing her demon, but that was not the case. In this journey, standing before Effron, she found her demon, and it was not the broken young tiefling, but the tear in her own heart. Effron served as merely a symbol of that, a mirror looking back at her, and at what she had done.

No less was true from Effron's perspective. He was not saddled with the guilt, perhaps, but surely he was no less brokenhearted. He had suffered the ultimate betrayal, that of a mother for her child, and had spent his lifetime never meeting the expectations and demands of his brutal father. He had grown under the shadow of Herzgo Alegni, without a buffer, without a friend. Who could survive such an ordeal unscarred?

Yet for all the turmoil, there is hope for both, I see. Capturing Effron in Baldur's Gate (and we will all be forever indebted to Brother Afafrenfere!) forced Dahlia and her son together in tight quarters and for an extended period. Neither found anywhere to hide from their respective demons; the focal point, the symbol, the mirror, stood right there, each looking back at the other.

So Dahlia was forced to battle the guilt within herself. She had to honestly face what she had done, which included reliving days she would rather leave unremembered. She remains in turmoil, but her burden has greatly lifted, for to her credit, she faced it honestly and forthrightly.

Isn't that the only way?

And greater is her release because of the generosity—or perhaps it is a need he doesn't even yet understand—of Effron. He has warmed to her and to us—he revealed to me the location of Guenhwyvar, which stands as a stark repudiation of the life he had known before his capture in Baldur's Gate. I know not whether he has forgiven Dahlia, or whether he ever will, but his animosity has cooled, to be sure, and in the face of that, Dahlia's step has lightened.

I observe as one who has spent the bulk of my days forcing honesty upon myself. When I speak quietly, alone under the stars or, in days former (and hopefully future), when I write in these very journals, there is no place for me to hide, and I want none! That is the point. I must face my failings most of all, without justification, without caveat, if ever I hope to overcome them.

I must be honest.

Strangely, I find that easier to do when I preach to an audience of one: myself. I never understood this before, and don't know if I can say that this was true in the time of my former life, the life spent beside the brutally blunt Bruenor and three other friends I dearly trusted. Indeed, as I reflect on it now, the opposite was true. I was in love with Catti-brie for years before I ever admitted it. Catti-brie knew it on our first journey to Calimport, when we sailed to rescue Regis, and her hints woke me to my own self-delusion—or was it merely obliviousness?

She woke me because I was willfully asleep, and I slumbered because I was afraid of the consequences of admitting that which was in my heart.

Did I owe her more trust than that? I think I did, and owed it to Wulfgar, too. It is that price, the price the others had to pay, which compounds my responsibility.

Certainly there are times when the truth of one's heart need not be shared, when the wound inflicted might prove worse than the cost of the deception. And so, as we see Luskan's skyline once more, I look upon Dahlia and I am torn.

Because I know now the truth of that which is in my heart. I hid it, and fought it, and buried it with every ounce of rationale I could find, because to admit it is to recognize, once more, that which I have lost, that which is not coming back.

I found Dahlia because I was alone. She is exciting, I cannot deny, and intriguing, I cannot deny, and I am the better for having traveled beside her. In our wake, given the events in Neverwinter, in Gauntlgrym, in Port Llast, and with Stuyles' band, we are leaving the world a better place than we found it. I wish to continue this journey, truly, with Dahlia and Ambergris, Afafrenfere, and even with Effron (perhaps most of all, with Effron!) and even with Artemis Entreri. I feel that I am walking a goodly road here.

But I do not love her.

I determined that I did love her because of that which burned too hotly within my loins, and even more so because of that which remained too cold within my heart. I heard again Innovindil's advice, to live my life in shorter and more intense bursts, to be reborn with each loss into a new existence with new and exciting relationships.

There may be some truth to that advice—for some of the People, all of it might be true.

But not for me (I hope and I fear). I can replace my companions, but I cannot replace those friends, and most of all, I cannot fill the hole left by the passing of Catti-brie.

Not with Dahlia.

Not with anyone?

I have avoided sharing this truth because of Dahlia's current emotional state. I believe Effron when he said that she sought Artemis Entreri's bed. It did not surprise me, but what did surprise me was how little that information bothered me.

Catti-brie is with me still, in my thoughts and in my heart. I'll not try to shield myself from her with the company of another.

Perhaps the passing of time and the turns in my road will show me the ultimate wisdom of Innovindil's words. But there is a profound difference between following your heart and trying to guide it.

And now my road is clear, in any case, and that road is to retrieve another friend most dear. I am coming for you, Guenhwyvar. I will have you by my side once more. I will walk the starry nights beside you.

Or I will die trying.

That is my pledge.

—Drizzt Do'Urden

CHAPTER 15

TO THE HUNT

ANY EYES SETTLED ON *Minnow Skipper* AS SHE RODE THE TIDE INTO Luskan's sheltered harbor.

From the balcony of Ship Kurth's command tower on Closeguard Isle, Kurth and Beniago regarded the incoming ship with very different perspectives, though High Captain Kurth didn't know it, as he didn't know that the tall and lean red-haired man standing beside him was actually a dark elf serving Bregan D'aerthe.

To High Captain Kurth, *Minnow Skipper* carried the promise of power for his ship beyond Luskan's wall. With Drizzt and Dahlia and their companions in service to Ship Kurth, he would have the inside route to trade with Port Llast, and would have greater influence than his four competitors over events in the region surrounding Luskan.

For Beniago, all of that was of secondary concern, if of concern at all. He had done as Kimmuriel had asked, but would the passage of a few months prove enough to throw Beniago's cousin Tiago off of Drizzt's trail?

Unlikely, the drow-in-disguise realized, knowing Tiago as he did. Certainly things were going to play out between Tiago and Drizzt whatever Bregan D'aerthe tried to do, but the point, Beniago knew, was to delay that inevitable confrontation as long as possible so that Bregan D'aerthe could better influence it, and better decide on the direction in which they wanted to influence it. House Xorlarrin was making great progress in Gauntlgrym, by all accounts, and what that meant to the ever-logical and pragmatic Kimmuriel most of all was opportunity.

The best course to exploit that opportunity, the fine line between the potentially dramatic conflux of interests, was, of course, the entire purpose of the mercenary and mercantile guild, Bregan D'aerthe. And it was their salvation, for in their successes, so too did they find respite from the priestesses of the Spider Queen. But in going after Drizzt, Tiago might well be going against the wishes of Matron Mother Quenthel, and against the wishes of Lady Lolth herself, and if Drizzt killed Tiago, would Quenthel hold Bregan D'aerthe responsible, since Bregan D'aerthe knew of the hunt?

At that moment, *Minnow Skipper* in clear view, Beniago was glad that these choices fell to Kimmuriel and Jarlaxle, and not upon his own shoulders.

There would be drow blood spilled over this, he knew.

And he hoped, privately, that more than a bit of it would spill from the brash young Tiago.

North of the isle and the keep of Ship Kurth, in a small and unremarkable tower set amid the rocky foothills of the Spine of the World, Huervo the Seeker paced nervously. He couldn't see *Minnow Skipper*'s approach from the balcony of his rented tower, or at least, couldn't tell one boat from another down at the docks, but he had heard reliable confirmation regarding their return.

The wizard looked around at the shelves of books in the small library. Was there an answer here that he had overlooked? Was there something more, at least, that might protect him from the impending conversation he could not avoid?

He found nothing, of course, for he had looked over these tomes a hundred times or more in the last two months.

There was nothing. He had been deceived. He had played in fire and flames had burned him.

With a heavy sigh, followed by a deep breath that brought strength back to his shaking legs, Huervo the Seeker moved to the circular stairwell and descended.

The wretched imp sat on soft pillows at the side of the room immediately below the library, lounging like some grotesque parody of a southern Pasha, and feasting on the plump fruits Huervo had purchased a couple of days earlier.

"Do you even taste them?" the wizard said with a scowl.

"Juicy," Druzil replied, and he chomped his fangs right through the skin of the melon and began to slurp noisily.

Huervo stared at him hatefully, which only made the imp laugh. For Druzil was clearly confident that the upper hand would not change here.

The imp pointed at the wizard, then motioned to the stairwell and giggled stupidly, melon juices squirting out between its jagged teeth.

How Huervo wanted to cast a spell and obliterate the wretched little creature! This was all Druzil's fault, after all. Huervo had summoned an imp, a dweomer he had cast a hundred times since his earliest days of practicing the arcane arts, back in the far south two decades earlier. He had gotten his title, the Seeker, because he had always been the most inquisitive of wizards, focusing his efforts on divination and summoning, ever seeking enchantments and answers in books, and when those tomes did not suffice, he asked for answers from the denizens of other planes. Bringing forth a minor demon or devil, or some other inter-planar traveler was nothing out of the usual for the Seeker.

But this imp had come with a plan. Huervo had subsequently—and too late—realized it had been waiting for the summons with the ingredients to facilitate that nefarious chain of events, a tease regarding greater knowledge into the subject Huervo was researching: the name of another imp who held great secrets regarding that subject, and a secret pouch full of ingredients designed to strengthen an inter-planar gate. So Huervo had eagerly summoned the other imp, and Druzil had thrown its enhancements onto the building fires of that gate, and the other imp had not been an imp at all.

There was no escape, the wizard realized. Not now, at least. Perhaps Drizzt and the drow's friends would inadvertently facilitate Huervo's freedom—they were rumored to be quite powerful, after all.

But powerful enough?

With a heavy sigh and another determined, steadying breath, Huervo went to the stairs once more, to descend to a place and a conversation he had never in his wildest nightmares envisioned.

To speak to the balor in his cellar.

The companions, now numbering six, sat around a table in a private room in a tavern in Luskan.

"You will not even experience time the same way," Effron remarked, continuing his primer on the Shadowfell for those of the group who had never ventured there. "The passage of time itself becomes more a measure of how deeply the shadows permeate your mind."

"Truly," Afafrenfere said, and he seemed shocked by the revelation, or at least, by the succinct manner in which Effron had described it. "I was there for several years, but it seemed only a few tendays!"

"Because ye was in love," Ambergris said. "And that kept ye above the Shadowfell's movements. For me 'twas th'other way. Every tenday felt akin to a year."

"You went there of your own volition," Effron said.

"I went as a spy," Ambergris corrected. "That was me punishment for gettin' caught doin' wrong."

"A criminal?" Effron said. "Do tell."

"Nah."

"The Shadowfell," the impatient Drizzt interjected, forcing the discussion back on track. He had no time for distraction. Effron knew the location of Guenhwyvar's prison—nothing else mattered to Drizzt, and he would go to this place, the Shadowfell and the castle of this Netherese lord, and he would get the cat back. It was that simple.

"I'm just trying to prepare you," Effron said.

"I'm more than ready."

"The others, then. You cannot understand the Shadowfell until you've walked her dark ways. The air itself is different, heavy, full of palpable gloom. For those unprepared, the weight of the place—"

"Open the gate," Drizzt instructed. "You said you could guide me, so do so. Whether the others come along or not is their choice, but I am going, and I am going now."

"Well, me and me monk friend ain't a'feared o' the place," Ambergris said. "Lived there for years."

Drizzt listened to the dwarf, but his eyes were on Dahlia, who stared at him with an expression that resonated with hurt, as if the mere implication that she wouldn't be accompanying him was ludicrous, and hurtful that he would ever think such a thing.

"I owe you this much at least," Artemis Entreri remarked, the shock of the words breaking the stare between the lovers, and indeed, both Drizzt and Dahlia turned to him with a bit of surprise.

Entreri merely shrugged.

Huervo the Seeker sat in the common room of that very inn, sipping his wine and trying to keep his gaze from too obviously falling upon the stairway that led up a half-flight to the back room where Drizzt and the others had gone for a private discussion.

Occasionally, the mage rose and took a roundabout path to the bar, passing beside the stairs in the hopes of catching some of the conversation. He did hear the sound of voices on those trips, but couldn't make out more than a word or two. He had heard some mention of the Shadowfell, but given the broken tiefling creature, who was obviously thick with shadowstuff, that didn't surprise him or alarm him very much.

The night slid deeper, and the gathering at the tavern began to thin, and still the door remained closed at the top of that half-stair.

Huervo took another trip to the bar. This time he heard nothing. He waited a bit beside the stair.

No sound came forth from above. The thought of returning to the tower to admit to Errtu that he had lost track of the group was not a pleasant one.

Glancing around to ensure that he had not been noticed, the wizard slipped deeper into the shadows behind the stair. He understood the risk, but weighing it against the certainty of what he would face back at the tower, he pressed on.

He completed a spell of clairaudience, aiming it behind that door, and the sounds of the tavern dimmed immediately, as surely as if Huervo was in that very room. He expected a whispered conversation, or maybe even some snoring.

He heard nothing, other than the diminishing din from beyond the room, from back down in the tavern.

Growing concerned, the wizard cast a second divination, this one clair-voyance, and as he had put his ears in the room, so too did he now place his vision. As if he physically passed through the door himself, Huervo looked upon the room.

Upon the empty room.

It wasn't possible, he thought, for there was no other door, just a window . . .

Huervo spent a moment considering that, then rushed from the tavern and moved quickly around the side, into an alleyway. He came to the back corner of the building and carefully peeked around to the back alley.

It was empty, but he saw the window in question. He moved to the base of the wall under it, perhaps ten feet below the sill, but couldn't get too close because of the clutter all around. None of it seemed disturbed. If they had come down from the window, they had done so with great care, even the dwarf.

The riddle made no sense, unless there was a secret door in the private room, perhaps. With that thought in mind, Huervo enacted another spell and levitated from the ground, carefully hand-walking his way up the wall to peek into the room. The fire burned low in the hearth, despite a well-stocked wood bin right beside the fireplace, and the candles set on the table had all been extinguished.

A secret door, then, he thought, and he meant to go back into the tavern and find a way to get into the room to investigate. He noted, though, that the window wasn't nailed—or wasn't any longer, at least, for the nails had been removed, quite recently, and lay on the inside of the sill.

Huervo hooked his fingers under the wood and gently slid it open, and from the ease of its lift, despite its obvious age, he understood that it had indeed been opened earlier, and not long ago.

But how had they left without disturbing the clutter in the alleyway below?

He started into the room, but paused, and on a hunch began to float up higher, walking the wall to the roof. He listened cautiously for a few moments, then peered over.

Nothing.

No, not nothing, he realized, for like many rooftops in Luskan, this one was a combination of angles and with only a few small flat areas, like the short expanse before him. And like most of the flat roof areas, this one was covered with small stones, and in that bed, Huervo noted footprints, where boots had recently disturbed the settled rocks.

He looked back down and all around. Had they come up here? Why? And if so, where had they gone?

He pulled himself over the edge and walked around the roof, looking for another doorway or window, or some hint of the path they had taken from here, if they had indeed come up here and moved on along the rooftops of the city.

He cast another spell, to detect any magic at play, and then he froze in place, and his heart stopped beating for a moment. For Huervo recognized this type of emanation above all others, and he knew.

Someone had been up here, within an hour's time, and had opened a magical gate.

Huervo's eyes went wide and he looked back down again, to the window, and he inspected the edge of the roof above it, and indeed found a spike angled under the end beam, from which a rope had likely been lowered.

The truth of the scene hit him hard. The drow and his friend had come up here, and from here, they had passed through a magical gate! He had lost them, cold. They could be anywhere in the world; they could be off this very plane of existence . . . he thought back to the conversation he had overheard, the one word, Shadowfell.

Huervo swallowed hard.

He floated back down the side of the building. He rushed into the tavern, and didn't bother to ask permission before sprinting up the stairs and through the door of the private room.

The proprietor charged in right behind him, a group of patrons close behind.

"Where are they?" Huervo demanded.

But the man had no answers.

They searched the inn, roof to cellar, but the strange group—drow, elf, human, dwarf, and tiefling—was nowhere to be found.

He had lost them, and to the Shadowfell. Errtu the balor would not be pleased.

CHAPTER

16

PERPETUAL GLOOM

I CAN FEEL HER," DRIZZT REMARKED, AND HE HELD THE STATUETTE BEFORE his eyes. He looked to the side, to Effron, who nodded soberly.

"Don't try to summon her," the tiefling warned, "else you will alert Lord Draygo to our designs. Even here, perhaps especially here, he will see through Guenhwyvar's eyes."

Drizzt nodded and slipped the figurine safely away.

Dahlia watched the drow's every move, recognizing the pragmatism that drove him. If it was pragmatism, she reconsidered, and not some moral code too stringent to ever let his emotions find some freedom. She had teased those emotions from him on occasion, though not recently, of course, and had lured him into places where he had allowed himself to live in the moment and to be free of whatever nagging little voice constantly held him back.

She wanted that again, she realized, and in her mind, she replayed the conversation with Artemis Entreri, where he had accused her of loving Drizzt.

Dahlia's face grew tight as she pushed that unsettling thought aside and focused again on the drow's actions and expressions. He wanted to call Guenhwyvar, she could see that. He knew there might be some chance that in this place, such a summons would break the panther free of the bonds Draygo Quick had enacted upon her.

But he wouldn't. He would be patient. Too much was at stake for the disciplined Drizzt Do'Urden to let his desperation destroy it all. That was ever his strength, Dahlia knew, and his weakness.

"How far?" he asked.

Effron looked around, shaking his head. "The problem with utilizing a gate is location, for I dared not open one anywhere near to Gloomwrought or Lord Draygo's castle. The worlds are aligned, but not perfectly." He pointed to the far horizon. "Lord Draygo's residence is outside of the city of Gloomwrought, and for that, we should be thankful. I would not walk the ways of Prince Rolan's domain with this group."

"We're not for liking being seen with yerself, either," said Ambergris, but she offered a playful wink with the retort.

"But nor can we walk the road approaching the city," Effron went on. "Not with these two." He pointed to the dwarf and the monk.

"Cavus Dun watches the road," Afafrenfere agreed, and Effron nodded.

"A powerful troupe are they, and one with a vendetta."

"Then how?" Drizzt asked.

Effron pointed farther to the south. "Roundabout, and through a swamp. There are lesser, little used roads, but travel will be difficult and dangerous."

"How long?" Dahlia pressed.

"Three days?" Effron replied hesitantly.

"We have mounts," Entreri reminded, but Effron shook his head.

"If you summon your nightmare here, you will likely lose control of the beast, and the same for the unicorn you ride. This is not the place for such toys, I warn."

"So, three days walking," said Drizzt.

Effron nodded. "That measures the actual time, but I warn you, it may seem a month to you, for you're not acclimated to the realities of the Shadowfell."

"Meself's acclimated, and it's seemin' like a month already!" Ambergris said. "By the gods, I hate this place." She looked at Afafrenfere. "To think that ye chose to be here them years," she said, shaking her head.

"Now that I have been away, I begin to agree," Afafrenfere answered, and the dwarf's eyes popped open wide.

Dahlia regarded the two, and particularly focused on their appearance. When she had first encountered them, she had thought them shades, with dark hair and gray skin, but subtly, both had shifted in that appearance, in almost the reverse manner that a farmer's skin might darken in the first tendays of spring. Still ruddy, as with most dwarves, it seemed as if a pall had been lifting from Ambergris of late, and even her hair had changed color, showing more reddish tints now. And Dahlia realized that for Afafrenfere, the reversion to something more fully human had been even more dramatic.

Dahlia only noted that now, for the change had been so gradual, but in this place of perpetual gloom, the monk appeared again much as he had when Dahlia had first seen him, and the abrupt reversion so clearly revealed the extent of the change.

"Every journey begins with a step, then," said Drizzt, and he started off in the direction Effron had indicated.

Effron caught him by the arm quickly, though. "I would have you on the flank," he explained. "And you," he added, indicating Entreri, "on the other. This place is the stuff of nightmares, and it earns its name, I assure you."

"Aye, and tell 'em why," Ambergris said, and when Effron didn't immediately respond, other than to look at the dwarf, she added, "The swamp's full o' dead things that won't stay quiet. And they're always hungry."

Dahlia, Drizzt, and Entreri looked to Effron, who could only shrug. The drow nodded and moved out to the left flank, Entreri similarly moving out to the right. Effron took up the lead, Dahlia beside him, the dwarf and monk some distance behind.

"Why are you doing this?" Dahlia asked quietly when she was alone with her son.

Effron's face grew very tight. "I don't know," he admitted.

"Is it hatred for this Lord Draygo?"

"No," Effron answered even before thinking about it. It was true enough, though. "Draygo Quick has shown me more friendship than. . . ." He let it end there, hanging in the air between them.

"Don't try to hurt him," Effron warned. "Do not insinuate me into a fight between you and Lord Draygo."

"Because you will side with him?"

"I don't know," came the answer once more.

Clearly uncomfortable, Effron pressed on faster, and Dahlia, after considering it for a moment, didn't try to keep up.

She couldn't begin to imagine the pain and confusion Effron was suffering at that time. His life's journey was twisting and turning rapidly, and not entirely, if at all, of his own volition. Dahlia considered her own life's road then, going from Szass Tam to this new horizon. She had faced a crisis in Gauntlgrym, a stark ethical and moral choice that would have broken her had she chosen differently. If she had pulled that lever to release the fire primordial and wreak devastation upon the land, then she would have succumbed wholly to the darkness that had followed her since that day Alegni had ravaged her, and more particularly since that subsequent date when she had thrown her son from the cliff. The dark wings of her own guilt would have enveloped her forever more, making her no better a creature than the loathsome Szass Tam himself.

How different her new road. But, indeed, it was now a journey of her choosing.

Could Effron say the same?

"A copper for yer thoughts," Ambergris remarked, and Dahlia realized that lost in her internal dialogue, she had slowed her pace.

"They will cost you a bag of gold, a chest of jewels and gems, and a swift journey to a place of sunlight," she replied.

"A ransom no good dwarf'd e'er pay!" Ambergris replied with a laugh.

Afafrenfere, coming up on the other side of Dahlia, joined in, but Dahlia could only manage a polite chuckle, her gaze remaining straight ahead, at the crooked back of the physically frail creature who led the way.

There was never much of a sun shining in the Shadowfell, but when night fell, the contrast seemed even more dramatic compared to the nightfall on Toril, for in the Shadowfell, sunset awakened more inhabitants than sunrise.

The six companions felt that keenly as they set their encampment amid the muddy ground and bogs. The air hung thick with the smell of decay, the stench seeming more like a tangible and living enemy than the mere result of the flora and fauna. The annoyance of stinging insects buzzed ever-presently in their ears, and the sound of their own slapping became readily apparent and nearly as annoying as the buzzing wings.

"If our campfire doesn't give us away, then the drumming will," Entreri said.

"Ye got a better idea?" Ambergris asked, punctuating her question with a resounding smack across her own face. She brought her hand out and held it up, showing a squashed bug the size of her thumbnail, and a palm full of blood. "These sucker bugs'll drain the juices right out o' ye!"

Before Entreri could respond, both he and the dwarf turned to regard Afafrenfere, who had gone into what seemed to be a wild dance.

The monk moved swiftly, as if executing a practiced training routine, and so he was, but with a few additions, they came to realize, as his turns brought sweeps and snatches instead of punches, and every ending pose brought an onslaught of well-aimed slaps about his body. He went on for many heartbeats, then turned to his audience, smiling widely, and held forth his open hands, showing the bits and pieces of dozens of insects he had plucked and crushed or swatted flat.

Metallic tapping from the other direction turned all to witness Dahlia across the way. She smiled widely as she worked her flails and looked back at Afafrenfere. "I am better suited," she explained, and she cracked her spinning flails together repeatedly, each strike causing a slight spark of lightning from the powerfully-enchanted Kozah's Needle.

"Not unless ye're squishing bugs with them hits," Ambergris replied.

"You work the *nun'chuks* well, "Afafrenfere remarked, and Dahlia looked at him curiously, not quite sure of the reference.

But no matter. Dahlia merely smiled ever more and heightened her movements, the flails spinning around her, up over her shoulder and down and around. *Click, click, click,* they went, tap-tapping with increasing intensity.

And then came the reveal, as Dahlia leaped and spun dramatically, and brought her flails spinning in for a tremendous concussion in which she released all the building energy of her magical weapon.

A great burst of lightning blasted forth, momentarily stealing the night and filling the air with such a charge that the hair of all six companions began dancing wildly. And in that burst, for those who managed to note, came a thousand little pops of insects exploding under the concussion of the charge.

"Why don't you find a horn to blow, loud and long, to announce our position?" Entreri growled at her, clearly not amused.

But the dwarf laughed and Afafrenfere clapped in approval. "Brilliant work!" he congratulated. "Where did you learn to use the *nun'chuks* in that manner?"

"Use what?" Dahlia asked, looking at her weapons.

"Nunchaku," Artemis Entreri interjected. *"Nun'chuks."*

"Flails," Dahlia replied, spinning one at the end of its cord. Entreri shrugged as if he hardly cared about a semantic distinction.

"Nun'chuks," Afafrenfere corrected. "We train in their use in the Monastery of the Yellow Rose. They distinguish from typical flails because you can move your grip from one of the joined poles to the other." He moved toward Dahlia and held out a hand. "May I?"

Dahlia looked around at her other companions, who all seemed intrigued, then held both flails out toward Afafrenfere. He took only one, however.

Dahlia stepped back and the monk launched into his disciplined routine, moving the weapon about his torso, over one shoulder and under the other, fluidly and rapidly.

With a grin, Dahlia, too, began such a dance, and the two circled, their respective weapons spinning all around in a blur. Coincidentally, both lunged forward at the same time, letting the free end fly over, and with a twist of the wrist, both put that free end up tight into a lock with their armpit at the very same moment, and stood facing each other, muscles flexed as hand pulled against the hold.

They both began to laugh, and around them, the others applauded their coordination and precision.

All except for Artemis Entreri, who leaped up and moved clearly into the light. He was not looking at Dahlia and Afafrenfere, however, but off into the darkness to the west. "We've got company," he said.

He glanced over at Drizzt, and the drow nodded, and slipped off into the darkness to the north, while Entreri moved out to the south.

"Form around me," Ambergris ordered the others and she stood before the fire, hoisting her huge mace, Skullbreaker, up onto one shoulder.

"The fire?" Dahlia asked, for surely the light marked their position.

"We'll be needin' it," Ambergris replied.

"The walking dead," Effron explained to his mother, and Afafrenfere, on the other side of the dwarf, handed the *nun'chuk* back to Dahlia and nodded his agreement with that assessment.

The passing moments seemed an eternity before they finally heard some movement out in the dark swamp, the rustle of grass and the splash of a running footfall on muddy ground.

"Ghouls," Effron remarked.

Even as he spoke, a great stench washed over them, overpowering the heavy marsh aroma.

"They've likely got a ghast or two among 'em," said the dwarf. She reached into a pouch and brought forth her holy symbol then, and held it up questioningly before her eyes. She rolled it about in her thick fingers, the silvery image of mountains flashing in the firelight with each turn.

"Will Dumathoin grant you such strength?" Afafrenfere asked, obviously understanding the dwarf's skeptical expression.

"Me god's been closer as me skin's grown lighter," Ambergris replied, but she could only shrug meekly beyond that assurance.

Artemis Entreri rushed back into the light then, startling them all. "Back to back!" he warned. "A horde of ghouls, and with wights among them!"

The four warriors formed a box around Effron as the warlock prepared his spells.

"Wrap yer hands, monk," Ambergris told her friend. "Don't want to be touching them beasties with your open skin!"

Stealth wouldn't help him much, Drizzt knew, for the undead could smell him, could sense his life-force, and no measure of hiding behind a shrub or a stone would mitigate that. He relied on speed instead, constantly moving, constantly shifting directions.

He noted the approaching hunters, a pack of hunched and emaciated creatures, once human, but now hardly resembling the form they knew in life. Bobbing and scrabbling with every step, their movements seemed that of an animal, and their faces locked in a grimace of perpetual anger, or hunger, with their jaws hanging open, showing teeth that apparently had kept growing in the grave, or perhaps it was that their gums had greatly receded.

Drizzt drew back on Taulmaril, leveling the bow at the nearest creature. He glanced around, plotting his escape route, and thinking that his best course would be to draw off as many of these ghouls as possible, to buy his friends more time.

Just before he let fly, he realized that not all of the creatures before him were the same, for among the ghoulish ranks loomed other creatures, standing more upright, appearing less driven by rage and hunger, perhaps, and more measured in their approach toward the firelight. And while the ghouls scrabbled, these few seemed more to float above the muck of the swamp.

Drizzt was not well-versed in the distinctions of undead creatures, but it seemed clear to him that this second version, less visceral and animalistic, was likely more dangerous.

He swiveled the bow around, leveled and let fly, his lightning streak stealing the night in a blinding flash of sharp and crackling energy. It struck the wight in the shoulder, the force of the blow spinning the screeching beast around, spiraling in a full circle, stumbling, before regaining its balance.

Just in time to catch the second arrow right in its emaciated and horrid face. The creature's head exploded under the weight of that blow, and it flew back and to the ground.

And Drizzt saw another wight, a larger one, an armored one, and holding a greatsword out toward him, and the ghouls, following that direction, swarmed his way.

It was time to run, but Drizzt hesitated, staring at what he thought to be the leader of this horde of monsters. He tried to discern a route to get to the armored wight, for if he could decapitate the band, the fight might fast dissolve.

But then he realized that even this impressive being was not in command of his enemies, for behind the armored wight came a crackling flash of deep blue light, just long enough to illuminate another monstrosity. Part wraith-like, the creature appeared as if someone had placed a second and third skull on the shoulders of an emaciated corpse. It carried a staff that seemed more like bone than wood in the brief instant Drizzt had glimpsed it, and it wore a crown on its central skull.

"What?" Drizzt muttered, and indeed he wondered what he and his friends were up against.

———◆———

They came in running, fearlessly, ravenous, mostly from the west, but already flanking north and south. The companions stood to face them, most of all Ambergris, who didn't hoist her huge mace, but stepped forward and presented instead her holy symbol.

"By Dumathoin's grace, be gone!" she roared, her voice clear and melodic, full of resonance and godly power, which manifested itself in a supernatural glow, a light shining from the dwarf herself.

The press of creatures immediately before Ambergris threw up their spindly arms and clawed hands defensively, a horrid communal shriek filling the air. Some fell to the ground, thrashing, and others, many others, fled, turning back the way they had come, running with all speed from the bared power of the dwarf cleric.

"Redemption!" Afafrenfere congratulated at the dwarf's side, but that was all he had time to say, for though Ambergris had improved the odds, the numbers still dramatically favored the enemy.

A ghoul leaped in, clawing with its left hand, and the monk stepped forward with his left foot and threw his forearm against the ghoul's forearm in a solid block, taking care to avoid the filthy, paralyzing claws. Predictably, the ghoul tried to bite at that blocking arm, but Afafrenfere was already into his heavy right crossing punch. He caught the ghoul on the side of its jaw, shattering the bones and snapping the undead monster's head around viciously.

The monk disengaged his arm quickly and fell back, throwing all of his weight to his trailing right leg and lifting his left and kicking out, catching the ghoul in the throat as it turned back at him, and driving it away.

At the same time, Afafrenfere snapped off a series of overhand and under-hand slaps with his right arm, rolling fast to pick off the clawing swipes of a second ghoul. He ducked low and kicked out, cracking the ghoul's knee, shattering the bones, but undead creatures felt no pain and the ghoul leaped upon him.

Afafrenfere braced and caught the monster, then stood up straight, hoisting the ghoul above his head and launching it back at the next nearest monster. As it flew out, however, the ghoul hooked its claws on the monk's upper arm, tearing Afafrenfere's skin as it went. The monk gave the slight wound no heed, already spinning and kicking at the next incoming enemy.

But he soon enough felt the numbness spreading along his arm, the infection of ghoul touch, and the images before him began to swim and float around as he felt the strength leaving his legs.

***

Across from the monk, Dahlia was better armed against such monsters. She had Kozah's Needle assembled as a staff once more, and prodded it and swept it around to keep the enemies at bay. She worked toward Entreri as she did, and he to her, and they quickly found a rhythm, with Dahlia using the long weapon and tactical bursts of its magical lightning to create a perimeter free of clawing beasts.

Entreri stayed low and unobtrusive, giving the elf warrior full reign to guide the fight. Her heritage, her elf blood, would protect her from the ghoul paralysis, at least, where his own would not. He focused on the flanks, and whenever one of the monsters slipped past a swing of Dahlia's staff, it was met full force by the assassin's sword and dagger, weaving and darting, striking home. But Entreri, too, took great care here, and reminded himself of the nature of his enemies, particularly when his shorter blade found a mark.

Entreri could not let the dagger drink, as it always desired, for the life-force it would bring forth from the undead would hardly nourish him.

Well-versed in the matter of undead creatures, Effron the warlock recognized immediately that this was no simple ghoul hunting pack. Such roving bands were common around the marshes, but too many had come forth, and with wights among them.

And with something more sinister and powerful behind them, he understood, lurking out there in the darkness, waiting for the moment to come forth in all its sinister power.

The tiefling warlock held back his most powerful spells in the early rounds of battle, throwing forth necromantic flames to sting and slow any approaches wherever his companions' defenses seemed weakest.

Soon enough, he found himself furiously casting, one fiery assault after another, black sweeps of flame reaching out almost continuously at the encroaching horde.

Ambergris had given them a chance, he understood, for if she had not been so powerful in her divine turning, if she had not shattered the center of the undead line with the word of her god, then the five, all fighting furiously now, would surely have been overwhelmed.

As it was, they were barely holding their own, and that standstill became tenuous indeed when Brother Afafrenfere slumped down to the muck, losing his battle against the ghoulish paralysis.

Drizzt came out from behind a tree in a sudden charge.

A ghoul leaped out in front of him, tongue darting wildly, claws raking, but Drizzt had noted it, and the other two, and before the wretched thing got near to hitting him, his scimitars fast descended.

Its head split cleanly in half, the ghoul fell away.

Drizzt bowled through it, threw himself down into a forward roll across the muddy ground and came up in a full sprint, his speed enhanced by his magical anklets, his scimitars working left and right ferociously as he barreled between the other two ghouls, leaving them twisting and torn in his wake.

The armored wight hoisted its greatsword to meet the charge, and worked it deftly to slow the drow's momentum. This was no simple animated corpse, but the raised remains of one who had been a formidable warrior in life, obviously.

Drizzt didn't appreciate that in the early encounter, and had to throw himself backward and to the ground to avoid a sudden heavy sweep of that four-foot blade, the air humming with its passage barely a finger's breadth from his face.

He kept his feet firmly planted as his back touched down to the ground, and every muscle in his frame tightened that he could lift himself right up. He even managed a stab with his left-hand blade before leaping back to avoid the sweeping backhand of the greatsword.

The wight advanced in a rush behind that blade.

Drizzt started out to the right, retreated a step and bent backward, then threw himself back to the left behind the next swing. Then he darted ahead, moving past the turning wight, and struck again, and a third time, as he rushed past.

But the wight was fast in pursuit, pressing Drizzt. It felt no pain. A living opponent would be clutching at its side, where ichor and maggots now poured forth from the deep gouge of Icingdeath.

Drizzt set himself again, anticipating the warrior wight's next attack, and as the greatsword started moving, so too did Drizzt.

But the muddy ground slipped out under his weight and he stumbled.

Their defensive formation shuddered and seemed to fall apart as the ghoul poison reached deep into Brother Afafrenfere.

He swooned. He would have fallen to the ground all together, but a strong dwarf hand grabbed his shoulder, Ambergris yanking him upright with one arm, sweeping Skullbreaker out before her with the other to keep her own enemies at bay. As if that wasn't enough to keep the dwarf occupied, she chanted at the same time.

Still, the dwarf's heroic efforts would not be enough, Effron realized. He waved his hand, sending a swirling line of purplish-black flames past Afafrenfere to burn and drive back the hungry ghouls.

The warlock reached more deeply and powerfully into his repertoire for his next spell, and black tentacles pushed out of the muddy ground and began snapping at the ghouls all along that side of the formation, grabbing and squeezing and burning.

He had to move fast, he knew, for the tentacles would slow them for only a short period of time.

They could not win. Not with the greater undead monstrosities out there in the darkness.

Even as that troubling thought flitted through the warlock's mind, he noticed a ghoul rise up once more, brought back to an animated state again after Dahlia had apparently destroyed it with her lightning.

A skull lord!

A skull lord lurked nearby, Effron knew, and it would raise its army repeatedly, until attrition slowed the blades and ghoulish poison broke their ranks. He had to find that particular monster and defeat it, and quickly.

But where?

Drizzt knew that he was going to get hit; there was no way to avoid it, and so he had to choose a glancing blow from the greatsword or the wight's clawing hand. With great agility, the drow set his feet and scrambled forward past the wight, inside the sweep of the sword.

He felt the icy cold claw dig into his shoulder and he threw himself forward and to the side, desperate to disengage quickly.

He got free and out of range just in time to square up against another ghoul, his spinning blades lopping off clawing fingers, then stabbing the creature under the chin and lifting it up and back. The drow fast retracted, and let the destroyed ghoul fall to the ground.

Again, just in time, as Drizzt spun around and parried the sword of the pursuing wight.

Now he was back to even footing, working furiously, trying to get in close and be done with this undead swordsman.

But this fight had already gone on too long, Drizzt feared when he noted the approach of another, the three-skulled, wraith-like monster.

He batted aside the greatsword and leaped forward to stab at the wraith, but behind it and to the side, the skull lord waved its bone staff across before it, the deep blue energy wafting forth like a living serpent, purple and black crackling flames sweeping at the warrior wight and Drizzt.

The drow leaped back and to the side, falling into another roll, and a second tumble beyond that, and sheathing his scimitars as he went.

When he came up again, he had Taulmaril in hand, already leveled, and he let fly, straight and true, the lightning arrow slamming the three-skulled creature squarely in the chest.

It staggered backward, but did not fall, and responded immediately with another, larger wave of necromantic flames, and by calling to its minions, ghoul and wight, and swarming them at the lone drow.

The silver flash of a lightning-infused arrow showed Effron the way.

"Hold fast!" he told the four fighting around him, and to Ambergris, he added, "Be ready, on my call, to reach for the power of your god once more."

Even as he addressed the dwarf, Ambergris launched an over-the-shoulder smash with her mace that evoked its name, Skullbreaker. A ghoul's head exploded under the weight of the blow, brain matter and powdered bone flying all around.

"More fun this way," she said with a laugh, and she swept two others away as they foolishly charged in behind their destroyed comrade.

Effron couldn't deny the dwarf's physical exclamation point, but he turned away from the fierce spectacle and enacted his wraith-form dweomer.

"Hold fast!" he told the four again, his voice as thin as his two-dimensional form, and he slid down into the ground and off in the direction of the flash.

He came up from the ground in the crack of an old, rotted tree, surveying the situation at hand. As he'd hoped, Drizzt had encountered the leader of the undead gang, and Effron's eyes sparkled indeed when he looked upon the skull lord's bone staff, crackling with necromantic power.

Drizzt rushed all around, diving and rolling, coming around and letting fly, one missile after another. He obviously wanted to take out the skull lord, but the immediate press of ghouls and other minions, including a warrior wight, forced him to blast back those nearest him time and time again.

And ever was he dodging as the three-skulled monster swept forth its staff, weaving sheets of crackling flames chasing Drizzt from spot to spot. Only the drow's speed and agility kept him ahead of the attacks, and then only barely.

Effron knew he couldn't keep it up for long.

The warlock slipped out of the tree and became three-dimensional, and immediately launched an insidious attack, whispering to the distant skull lord in the tongue of the nether world, pitting his willpower against that of the undead monstrosity.

The creature turned on him, three skulls hissing in unified protest, and started to wave its staff his way. But Effron stopped it with a command, exerting his will.

"Clear them!" he shouted to Drizzt, and the skilled drow was already using the distraction of the skull lord to great advantage.

Effron watched a sizzling arrow blast through the warrior wight, then a second, the missiles boring holes right through the creature, and leaving the jagged edges of the exit wounds glowing with crackling lightning.

A ghoul went flying away, then a second, and the drow swung back and drove another missile, point blank, into the warrior wight, and it staggered backward. Its head exploded under the next point blank shot, and the drow crashed through it, knocking it aside, and fell to one knee, bow leveled and readied immediately, taking a bead on the prime enemy.

"The skulls!" Effron explained.

But the bone staff wave and a ripple of necromantic fire rolled out at the young tiefling. He growled and steeled himself against the onslaught, negative energies biting at him and stinging him profoundly, and tried through chattering teeth to issue the words of his next spell.

The undead creature's right-most skull exploded in the flash of a silver arrow.

The skull lord staggered and swung back at Drizzt, just in time catch the next arrow in the chest. Still, it managed to send forth another powerful burst.

Effron found the mystic energies of the Feywild, weaving them into a white flame, and used his telepathic connection to the skull lord to insert that fire inside the undead creature's mind. Immediately the four remaining eye sockets of the now two-headed monstrosity began to glow with that white fire, and rivulets of argent fire streamed from every orifice of those skulls, lifting into the night air and framing the skull lord in a fiery halo.

Which only aided Drizzt's aim.

Arrows flew at the creature in rapid succession. A second skull exploded, the monster's crown falling to the swampy ground.

Effron shifted his magical attack, cold starlight lancing down from above to bite at the staggering creature.

"Now, Ambergris!" he managed to yell between assaults. Back at the camp, he heard the dwarf invoke again the name of Dumathoin, and now, with the countervailing force of the skull lord destroyed, to even greater effect. So powerful was the dwarf's call that several ghouls before her were reduced to dust, and even the wights could not stand in the face of her divine call.

Before Effron, the skull lord crumbled to the muck.

More explosions turned him to see Drizzt fending a group of ravenous ghouls. Only then did Effron truly see the beauty of Drizzt's dance, for the drow dropped his bow and drew his blades so quickly that Effron could barely follow the movement.

Drizzt leaped forward, double-stabbing the ghoul before him, then tore his blades out to the side, reversed momentum, and brought them scissoring across to decapitate the creature. Hardly slowing, the drow flipped his grip on the hilts and stabbed out to either side with devastating backhanded thrusts, skewering a pair of ghouls simultaneously. He retracted almost as fast as he had stabbed, and back-flipped into a fast retreat, but landed leaning forward and in a sudden rush that brought him in against the wounded ghouls for a devastating finishing barrage.

Hardly slowing, the drow leaped upon the felled warrior wight, blades pounding away, ensuring that it would not rise again.

Seeing the battle ended, the warlock rushed to claim his prizes, lifting the crown in trembling hands. He wouldn't dare wield it, or wear it, until further study, of course, but he took no such precautions with the staff, eagerly scooping it into his grasp. It was as tall as he, fashioned of three leg bones fused as one, and with a tiny humanoid skull up near its tip. The blue lightning was gone now, but the young warlock easily recovered it, finding a magical communion with the powerful item, and by the time Drizzt joined him, bluish-black flashes had begun anew, flickering from the eyes of the staff's skull-headed top.

Drizzt looked at him suspiciously.

"Magic is neither good nor evil," Effron explained in response to that curious expression. "It merely is."

Drizzt's expression didn't shift much, retaining his edge of skepticism, but he said nothing and followed Effron back to the others. The fight there had ended as well, bodies piled before the four companions. Afafrenfere was the worst off, obviously, and Ambergris tended to his wounded shoulder and bloodied hands.

"Well fought," Drizzt said.

"Better if one of us hadn't run off," Dahlia scolded, staring at him, "and another hadn't followed."

Drizzt laughed and shook his head, owing no apologies, and even Artemis Entreri chuckled at the absurdity of Dahlia's remarks.

"Were these enemies directed against us?" Entreri asked. "By Draygo Quick?"

Effron shook his head. "Such roving bands are not uncommon in the marshes around Gloomwrought," he explained. "Though this one was particularly powerful." He looked at his new weapon as he spoke, and smiled, feeling the powers contained within the bone staff.

If undead monsters came at them again the next day, he knew, more than a few of them would be fighting on his side.

246

CHAPTER
17

THE CHOSEN

A THROGATE PLOPPED HIS HAIRY FEET DOWN ON THE LARGE PILLOW BEFORE the Bedine serving girl, who immediately began pressing her thumbs into the pressure points on his wide, flat soles.

"Meself, ha! I'm thinkin' I might be gettin' used to this life," he said for the tenth time that day, which meant that he was almost halfway to his average daily usage of the remark. Being guests of a Netherese lord in Shade Enclave was not a difficult job, the dwarf and Jarlaxle had learned. A century before, this region had been a huge and inhospitable desert, but it had not been totally barren. Sparsely inhabited, indeed, but inhabited nonetheless. The Spellplague had changed all that, the great desert of Anauroch, itself a magical construct, had been transformed. And here, the Empire of Netheril had created their principle city on Toril.

For the indigenous people of Anauroch, the nomadic Bedine, the transformation had proved neither fruitful nor favorable, for they were now the servants of the Netherese, particularly in the region immediately around Shade Enclave. Along some of the farther reaches of Anauroch, Bedine tribes held fast to their old desert nomad ways, but these people had not prospered. The tribes held few alliances outside of Anauroch and they were no match for the mighty Empire of Netheril, and thus, many now served that empire as slaves, even as gladiators.

For Jarlaxle and Athrogate, their extended stay in the House of Ulfbinder had been a journey in pleasure and luxury, their every need attended by a horde of servants. For his part, the dwarf had never looked better. His beard had been trimmed just a bit, and the dung tips at the end of his beard braids had been replaced by strings of shining opals. His dirty traveling clothes and armor had been meticulously stitched and cleaned, but he wasn't wearing it much anyway, preferring the thick and soft robes Lord Parise Ulfbinder had provided.

"It will grow tedious soon enough," Jarlaxle replied to the dwarf, as he usually did when Athrogate fell into his swoon of luxury. Jarlaxle was, of course, no stranger to the finer things in life. "There is a world of adventure out there," he added.

"Bah!" Athrogate shot back, and he bit off the expression and winced as the Bedine girl found a particularly sensitive spot on his foot. "Felt pain a hunnerd times," he said when he caught his breath. "But it ain't e'er felt so good! Bwahahaha!"

Jarlaxle just laughed and sipped his wine.

"The pleasure's great, the food's so fine, don't ye make the deal, friend, take yer time!" Athrogate half-said, half-sung, ending with another great "Bwahahaha!"

Jarlaxle smiled and lifted his glass to toast the dwarf's sentiment, but he wasn't so sure that he agreed. They had been here a long time, months, on a trade mission that shouldn't have taken more than a couple of tendays at the most. Jarlaxle and Kimmuriel had spoken at length about it in an ongoing conversation, for the psionicist could initiate communication with Jarlaxle from great distances, and undetected even by a Netherese lord, and the two had come to the conclusion that something else was at play here with the Netherese, with Parise Ulfbinder and his closest cohorts at least.

But what that something might be was only beginning to shine through. In their last negotiations, Parise had spent a lot of time discussing Menzoberranzan and the customs of drow society in service to the Spider Queen. Jarlaxle had explained that Bregan D'aerthe operated outside of Menzoberranzan, and that much of the proposed trade they could facilitate with Shade Enclave would originate or terminate far from the shadows of the Underdark.

Parise had politely followed that discussion thereafter, but on more than one occasion he had tried to push it back to Menzoberranzan. Jarlaxle was too savvy and clever a negotiating adversary to miss such a façade.

"Know that I'll be distractin' ye around that table this day!" Athrogate assured him, and the dwarf winced again at the talented Bedine girl's next press. "Bwahahaha!"

Jarlaxle waved that thought away. "You stay here today."

"I'm yer second."

"Today is a formality and nothing more," Jarlaxle assured him. "Lord Ulfbinder wishes to introduce me to one of his compatriots who resides in the Shadowfell."

"Ye're going into the shadows?" Athrogate said and he sat so quickly that he nearly knocked over the poor Bedine girl.

Jarlaxle laughed and waved for him to settle back. "We will utilize a scrying device," he explained. "Nothing more."

"Ah," Athrogate said, slumping back and nodding an apology to the startled girl. "And ye're not wantin' me face in the crystal ball, I see. Fearin' I'll embarrass ye, eh? Bwahahaha! Thought that was me job!"

"If so, then know that there is no amount of treasure I could bestow upon you to properly compensate you for your efforts."

Athrogate thought about that for a few moments then let loose another, "Bwahahaha!"

Jarlaxle sighed.

"Stay here," he instructed. "And do bathe."

Athrogate sniffed at his armpit, crinkled his long nose, shrugged, and nodded.

Jarlaxle poured himself another glass of wine, working hard to keep the grin off his face. He couldn't deny it: he had grown very fond of his competent and ferocious companion. When he had thought Athrogate dead in Gauntlgrym, the notion had terrified him. Obviously, by heritage and breeding, the two could not be more disparate, but those were the things that made the passing centuries interesting for Jarlaxle.

He thought back to his time with Artemis Entreri as he sipped his next glass of fine wine. He chuckled out loud as he recalled Entreri's short tenure as King of Vaasa, a disastrous farce that had landed Entreri in the dungeons of the legendary Damarran King Gareth Dragonsbane.

He thought of the dragon sisters, and that notion had him reflexively tapping his waistcoat, and a secret slot along its side stitching where he kept the reconstituted Idalia's Flute. He had almost freed Artemis Entreri from the emotional trappings of his sordid past with that magical instrument.

Almost.

He looked over at Athrogate, the dwarf now with his hands behind his head, eyes closed, thoroughly relaxing under the press of the foot massage. Jarlaxle pictured the two of them on the open road, hunting adventure and changing the course of kingdoms, and with Artemis and Drizzt beside them.

It was not an unpleasant thought.

But for now, he was Jarlaxle of Bregan D'aerthe, and he drained his glass and went to dress for his next meeting with Lord Parise Ulfbinder.

"Your dwarf friend will not be joining us today?" Parise Ulfbinder said when Jarlaxle was announced in the Netherese lord's lavish private quarters a short while later.

"I can go and retrieve him if you so desire."

Parise laughed at the thought. "He is your foil, not mine," he willingly admitted. "Have you become so comfortable here that you no longer need your bodyguard?" He paused and looked at the drow with a coy expression. "Or has Jarlaxle ever needed a bodyguard?"

The drow removed his wide-brimmed hat and sat down in a comfortable chair.

"Or is Jarlaxle ever without a bodyguard?" Parise asked, and he moved to offer Jarlaxle a glass of brandy.

"That is the more pertinent question," Jarlaxle replied.

"And the answer?"

"Is known only to me."

Parise laughed and took a seat opposite the drow.

"Are we to peer into your crystal ball this day?" Jarlaxle asked.

Parise shook his head. "My fellow lord is . . . otherwise engaged," he said, and Jarlaxle clearly registered a measure of weight behind that word choice. Something important was going on, likely in the Shadowfell, where this other lord, Draygo Quick, resided.

"Do we have further business, then?" the drow asked. "Or is this to be a social gathering?"

"Are you so eager to leave?"

"Not at all," Jarlaxle cheerily replied, and he rested back and lifted his brandy in a toast to his host.

Parise, too, settled back. "If our bargain is approved by your compatriot Kimmuriel and by my peers, then I suspect that you and I will find many such occasions to sip brandy and simply discuss the events of the day. You have given me your assurances, after all, that you will personally see to many of the exchanges."

Jarlaxle nodded. "Perhaps we will become great friends in the years to come." The way he spoke the sentence made clear that he recognized something was going on here, in the greater scheme of things.

"Perhaps," Parise agreed, and his tone showed that he understood Jarlaxle's inflection, and didn't seem to wish to disavow Jarlaxle of his suspicions.

There was more to all of this than a trade agreement, Jarlaxle believed. That agreement had, after all, been fairly settled in the first days of Jarlaxle's visit, and most of the "concerns" and "issues" that held back the inevitable handshake had appeared to him as nothing more than delaying tactics.

Jarlaxle had seen this type of negotiating many times before, in his early years in Menzoberranzan, and almost always before a traumatic change—a House war, typically.

The Netherese lord refilled his cup and Jarlaxle's.

"Do you miss the Underdark?" he asked. "Or do you venture there often?"

"I have come to prefer the surface," Jarlaxle admitted. "Likely, it is more interesting to me because it is not as familiar as deep caverns."

"I have not been to the Shadowfell in a year," Parise admitted with an assenting nod.

"Well, you and yours have done a grand job of bringing the darkness here, after all."

That brought a chuckle.

"We did not facilitate the Spellplague," Parise said more seriously, and Jarlaxle perked up. "Nor the link between the Shadowfell and the sunlight of Toril."

Jarlaxle thought he heard an admission there, that perhaps the celestial alignments and the fall of the Weave were not as permanent or controllable as some had postulated, and he tried to put the curious remark in the context of the earlier conversation regarding the years to come.

He didn't respond, though. He let Parise's words hang in the air for a long while.

"You are not as you pretend," Parise finally said, as he moved for the third glass of brandy for both of them.

Jarlaxle looked at him curiously.

"An emissary of Bregan D'aerthe?" Parise clarified.

"Truly."

"More than that."

"How so?"

"I have been told that the band is yours to control."

"It's far more complicated than that," Jarlaxle admitted. "I abdicated my leadership a century ago to pursue other interests."

"Such as?"

Jarlaxle shrugged as if it hardly mattered.

"You are more than a servant of Kimmuriel."

"I am not a servant of Kimmuriel," Jarlaxle was quick to correct. "As I said, it is complicated." He took a sip of his drink, his one eye that was not covered by the ever-present eyepatch staring at Parise unblinkingly. "Yet I am here in service to Bregan D'aerthe."

"Why you and not Kimmuriel?"

Jarlaxle took his time digesting that question, and indeed, this entire line of questioning, for this was the first time such matters had come up so blatantly.

"Trust me when I tell you that you would prefer me as a houseguest to that one," Jarlaxle said. "He is more comfortable in a hive of illithids than in the good graces of a cultured Netherese lord."

Parise managed a laugh at that. "And your ties to Menzoberranzan go beyond your leadership of the mercenary band, yes?" he asked.

"I lived there for most of my life."

"With which House?"

"None."

"But surely you were born into a House—one of the more prominent ones, likely, given your stature in the society of that hierarchical city."

Jarlaxle tried not to reveal his growing annoyance.

"Why did you not tell me?"

"Tell you?"

"That you were a son of House Baenre."

Jarlaxle stared at him hard, and put down his glass of brandy.

"I am not without resources, of course," the Netherese lord reminded him.

"You speak of centuries past. Long past."

"But you still have the ear of Menzoberranzan's matron mother?"

Jarlaxle considered the question for a moment, then nodded.

"Your sister?"

He nodded again, and wasn't sure whether to be angry or concerned.

"Which means that the archmage of the city is your brother."

"You speak of centuries long past," Jarlaxle reiterated.

"Indeed," Parise admitted. And please do forgive my forwardness—perhaps I am treading into places uninvited."

Jarlaxle again offered his noncommittal shrug. "Is there a point to your banter?" he asked. "Beyond our blooming friendship, I mean."

Parise managed a smile at that, but it did not last, for he assumed a more serious expression and looked the drow directly in the eye. "You serve Lady Lolth?"

Jarlaxle didn't answer, other than to chuckle.

"Very well, then," Parise redirected, obviously realizing that he was stepping into unwanted territory. "You are knowledgeable in the desires of the Spider Queen, at least as would be expressed by your sister?"

"I haven't seen my sister in years, and that is not long enough, I fear," Jarlaxle replied coldly. "You overestimate my relationship with the First House of Menzoberranzan—greatly."

"Ah, but do I overestimate your ability to garner information from Menzoberranzan?" Parise asked, and Jarlaxle suddenly became more intrigued than anything else.

"Our desire to trade through the channels you have offered is genuine," Parise went on. "To our mutual benefit. But I also barter in knowledge, and in that regard, is there a better trading partner than Jarlaxle Bae—Jarlaxle of Bregan D'aerthe?" he asked, the slip of his tongue clearly intentional.

"Probably not," the drow dryly replied.

"I admit to being fascinated by the possibilities," Parise said. "You are surely no professed follower of Lady Lolth, and yet, you are tolerated by her highest-ranking mortal. Is that due to familial bonds?"

"Quenthel? Her House benefits from Bregan D'aerthe. You need look no further for the solution to your riddle than that simple pragmatism."

"And Lolth would not punish her for . . . well, for not punishing you?"

"Lolth's city benefits from Bregan D'aerthe, whatever the love between us."

"So the drow are pragmatic above all else?"

"Every society that has stood and will stand is pragmatic above all else."

Parise nodded. "Then explain Drizzt Do'Urden."

It took everything Jarlaxle could muster for him to hide his surprise at the mention of Drizzt. When he thought about it, though, it did make sense that the Netherese would have taken notice—Drizzt had played a major role in the events of Neverwinter, after all, and more than a few Netherese had died there, including a budding warlord of great repute.

He feared for a moment that Parise was going to ask him to help pay back the troublesome rogue, and in that event, Jarlaxle expected that he would be plotting the demise of Parise in short order, and finding some reason to coerce Kimmuriel into helping him facilitate that very murder.

"Drizzt Do'Urden?"

"Do not even pretend that you are ignorant of that one!" Parise huffed.

"I know him well."

"Why is he allowed to live?"

"Because he kills anyone who tries to kill him, I expect."

"No," Parise said, leaning forward now eagerly. "It is more than that."

"Do tell, as you seem to know more about it than I do."

"Lady Lolth has not demanded his death," said Parise.

Jarlaxle shrugged yet again.

"Why?" Parise pressed.

"Why?" Jarlaxle echoed. "Does he wage war upon her minions? You have never journeyed to Menzoberranzan, that much is obvious," he added with a snort. "There is more than enough intrigue there, and more than enough enemies, to keep Lolth's agents busily murdering drow without traveling to the surface to hunt for Drizzt Do'Urden."

"It is more than that!" Parise pressed again.

"Then do tell," Jarlaxle replied. He handed his empty glass across to the Netherese lord, and added, "As you refill my glass. Such fireside tales always sound better when thrown against a muddled mind."

Parise took the glass and moved for the bottle, laughing as he replied, "Jarlaxle's mind is never muddled."

The drow merely shrugged yet again.

"Where is this going?" Jarlaxle asked. "Have you a vendetta against Drizzt Do'Urden, and fear to invoke the wrath of House Baenre?"

"Surely not!" his host replied emphatically—and to his surprise, Jarlaxle found that he believed the man.

"But I'm truly intrigued by this interesting Drizzt creature, and his relationship with the drow goddess."

Jarlaxle's blank expression aptly reflected the confusion in his mind at that most curious comment.

"Do you think it possible that she favors him, secretly?" Parise asked. "She feeds on chaos, after all, and he seems to create it—or surely he once did in the city of Menzoberranzan."

Jarlaxle drained his glass in a single swallow and considered the words, and the potential implications of his forthcoming answer.

"I have heard this suggestion before, many times," he said.

"He is given deference by the priestesses," Parise suggested.

Jarlaxle offered another shrug. "In not hunting him down, in not demanding such of me and my band, then perhaps there is merit in that notion. And yes, that of course means that the goddess hasn't instructed my sister and her peers to find him and properly punish him."

He found himself nodding as he spoke, then looked Parise directly in the eye and finished, "Your thesis is quite likely correct. I have often thought it so. Drizzt would be an unwitting instrument of Lolth, to be sure, but then again, would that not be her typically cryptic way?"

The Netherese lord seemed quite pleased by that answer, and he couldn't hide the fact behind his lifted glass of brandy.

From Jarlaxle's perspective, the more important matter was whether or not such an outlandish claim would protect Drizzt from any revenge the Netherese might be planning.

CHAPTER 18

SHATTERED

THE SHADOWS SERVED AS AN ALLY, BUT NONE OF THE SIX COMPANIONS felt particularly comforted by that reality. They crouched in the colorless brush in a copse of trees, looking up at a formidable structure: a grand house with a soaring tower, surrounded by an enormous stone wall, twenty feet or more in height. The castle of Lord Draygo Quick.

Drizzt's heart sank as the time slipped past. When he had learned of Guenhwyvar's imprisonment, his course seemed clear and direct. She was there, so there he must go, and let no obstacle prevent him from bringing her to freedom once more. But now that choice had met with a harsh reality, for what were they six to do against the formidability of this castle before them? Were they to storm the place and leave a wake of death and destruction on their way to the panther?

That seemed a foolish choice, for Effron had repeatedly reminded them that Draygo Quick could likely defeat all of them singlehandedly. And within Lord Draygo's tower, the young tiefling had also warned, loomed many lesser warlocks training under the great lord, and a menagerie of dangerous pets Draygo could unleash upon them.

"Now what?" Artemis Entreri asked after so many uneasy moments had slipped past. Their trials through the swamp had been considerable, but compared to the obstacle standing before them, those seemed minor indeed. Pointedly, Entreri had asked the question mostly to Effron, and his tone showed that he was not pleased with the young warlock.

"I was asked to take you to Guenhwyvar, and so I have," Effron replied.

"Then point her out," the assassin replied coolly.

Effron lifted his hand toward the tower, angling it to point about two-thirds of the way up the seventy-foot structure.

"Is there a side door? A kitchen or servants' entrance, perhaps, or even a waste chute?" Drizzt asked, and he desperately wanted to keep the conversation on point at that time. He hadn't come this far to turn back, whatever the challenge before them, and they had known—though surely the formidability of Draygo Quick's castle had put an exclamation point to the severity of the task—that retrieving Guenhwyvar would be no easy task.

"Inside the wall," Effron replied. "But the only entrance to the grounds lies through the front gate."

"Or over the wall," said Drizzt.

"I wouldn't recommend that."

"Do tell," Entreri said sarcastically, but he seemed to back off at the end of his dour remark, for now he had drawn the scowl not only of Drizzt, but of Dahlia.

Drizzt noted the assassin's retreat, and the apparent source. Entreri hadn't come along for Drizzt's sake, he realized, but for Dahlia's.

Once again, it occurred to Drizzt that he was not bothered by this.

Whatever the reason, he was glad that Entreri and Dahlia were here.

"The walls of many of the great estates of this region were created by the same masons and sorcerers," Effron explained, his casual tone offering no satisfaction to Entreri's attempt at sarcasm. "They are heavily enchanted to prevent such access."

"Glyphs can be removed," Ambergris said, but without much conviction.

"Lord Draygo's castle is lined with gargoyles and other sentries," Effron explained. "If we go over that wall, they will awaken."

"A fight in the courtyard," Dahlia remarked.

"With a mighty warlock looking down upon us, untouchable, from his secure chambers," Effron added.

"I may be able to get through the gate," Effron said. "I'm not even certain that Lord Draygo knows that I have joined forces with you. He may think me still in his employ, and if that is the case, I will not be turned away. I know where Guenhwyvar is, and could perhaps find a way to break her connection to the magical prison, that you might retrieve her and be gone."

"It would seem a great risk," said Drizzt.

"No!" Dahlia stated at the same time, with vehemence enough to surprise all of them, including, clearly, Dahlia herself.

"Not alone," she quickly clarified, and she seemed to be improvising as she added, "Pretend we are your prisoners, then. Or take us in for an audience with Lord Draygo—yes, go to him and explain that we wish to parlay."

"He'll have nothing to say to you," Effron replied directly to her. "He will simply kill you as punishment for the death of Herzgo Alegni and the destruction of Charon's Claw—indeed, he'll hold that second crime even higher above you! And above *you,*" he added, indicating Entreri. "You two carry a high price on your heads from Cavus Dun for your betrayal, the dwarf at least," he said to Ambergris and Afafrenfere.

"So we go in as your prisoners," said Drizzt.

They discussed the plan at length, then, trying to find some fake magical prison they might fashion to create at least the plausibility of such a ruse, but they seemed to be going in circles. Draygo Quick knew well Effron's capabilities, and knew, too, those of the other five.

"You have tricked us into speaking with him, then," Drizzt offered some time later. "We have come to barter for Guenhwyvar, but you will relate to your former master that it is all a ruse you facilitated to bring us to his feet."

"Ridiculous," Artemis Entreri replied, but in a resigned tone, he finished, "but probably the best chance we're going to get."

Drizzt studied the assassin closely. The risk for Entreri was truly great, and yet he had come. Perhaps not for Drizzt's benefit, but still, he had come.

The discussion went down that road of possibility, trying to come up with some plausible explanation as to why they would simply walk into the spider's web in such a manner. Their conversation was cut short, though, and dramatically, as the front gates of Lord Draygo's grand residence banged open and a black coach rushed forth, pulled by a team of four black horses already lathered in sweat as they charged off down the road.

"Lord Draygo," Effron breathed, watching the coach depart.

"His coach?" Dahlia asked.

"Him," Effron assured them. "No one but Lord Draygo would ride in that coach, and it is never used unless it is to take him on one of his errands."

"Then we have to go in now," Entreri said.

"It is still guarded," Effron started, but he was overrun by the others, all scrambling to prepare for their assault. By the time Effron had spoken his warning, Drizzt was already moving for the closing gate, the speedy Afafrenfere pacing him, and Ambergris, holy symbol in hand and a magical enchantment of dispelling glyphs and wards on her lips, moving right behind.

They simply couldn't miss this opportunity, Dahlia explained, she and Entreri sweeping up Effron in their passage.

Ambergris riffed off a series of spells in quick succession, first to detect magical wards, which she did, then several to dispel the potent magic she discovered about the gate.

As soon as she nodded, Drizzt shoved through the gates and led the way, again with the monk pacing him, toward the main door. On Effron's call, they veered left and sprinted around to the side of the building.

"Not trapped—not with magic," Ambergris assured Drizzt when they came to a small side door.

"No traps," Afafrenfere added after a thorough inspection, speaking of mechanical devices.

"Servant quarters," Effron explained, rushing up with Entreri and Dahlia.

Drizzt pushed through, now with Effron right beside him, guiding him along. They traversed a series of small rooms, bedrooms, and a kitchen and larder, and out through a heavy wooden door into an opulent dining room, one befitting a man of Draygo Quick's regal stature.

"This way," Effron prompted, and he and Drizzt led the way into an antechamber.

Ambergris and Afafrenfere came behind, with Entreri and Dahlia taking up the rear guard. They moved along another corridor and into the castle's main foyer and ballroom, a grand chamber with a high ceiling and marble floors that seemed a checkerboard of black and white tiles. Armored statues and meticulous tapestries lined the walls of the enormous room, which was split down the middle by a sweeping staircase that climbed twenty feet or more before veering left and right along balconies bordered by iron railings with decorated balusters wound into depictions of soaring dragons.

Drizzt started for the stairs, but Effron waved that thought away and pointed to a door opposite the hall from where they had entered. "The tower stair," he explained.

***

Effron knew many of the tricks and traps Draygo Quick had set up in his tower—many, but hardly all.

Sitting comfortably behind his crystal ball, having sent his coach out as a ruse, Draygo Quick alternately thought that he should punish the impudent young tiefling or thank him for delivering Drizzt so easily.

He watched the group progress across the checkered floor of the lowest floor's main room, and noted that this, too, was so perfectly convenient for him, for Effron and Drizzt, the only two of the group Draygo Quick cared about, had separated themselves from the others, moving several strides ahead.

The wretched old warlock had worried that this would be a dangerous encounter. Drizzt, Dahlia, and Herzgo Alegni's former champion, this Artemis Entreri, were all formidable, after all, and adding in a couple of former Cavus Dun bounty hunters made the powerful lord fear that he might lose many of his staff here, and perhaps a fair number of his precious pets, as well.

Though the outcome was never, in Draygo Quick's mind, in doubt.

And now, with the group charging in recklessly, thinking him gone from the castle, considerably less so.

Draygo Quick focused on the floor ahead of Effron and Drizzt and timed his command word perfectly, magically calling out through the crystal ball to the enchanted floor. The panel beneath the pair dropped open.

With amazing agility and reaction, Drizzt leaped and twisted, and might have gotten clear, or at least to the edge of the pit, except that he paused to grab at Effron.

The two tumbled from sight, through the floor and down a long slide, and the springs lifted the trapped panel back into place almost immediately.

The trailing four invaders skidded to a stop.

On cue, the suits of armor lining the hall began to move, and from above, gargoyles took flight, circling down slowly, and from the balusters of the balcony railing came miniature dragons, uncoiling and taking flight.

There was nothing to hold onto to slow the descent along the smooth, twisting slide. Drizzt tried to dig his heels in, or to find some jag with his reaching fingers, but to no avail.

Effron tried to cast a spell, but his words were lost in grunts and groans as he and Drizzt tangled and tumbled in the absolute darkness.

The descent finally ended with the duo crashing into a small, three-walled landing.

"Are you all right?" Drizzt asked.

"We have to get out of here," Effron replied. "Wraithform—"

His word was stolen by a cry of surprise as the floor fell out from under them once again. He and Drizzt dropped ten feet to land heavily on a floor of dirt and dry hay.

The darkness went away almost immediately. A low crackling sound overcame their groans, as the bars of their prison came alive with magical energy.

"By the gods, no," Effron gasped, rolling to a sitting position, but no farther, for he had landed hard on his legs and hips and they would not support him.

"What is it?" Drizzt demanded. Less injured, the drow rushed forward and drew his blades, and even dared to reach out and tap one of those sparkling bars with Icingdeath, only to have the scimitar blown from his hand as he went flying backward and to the floor.

"We are caught," Effron assured him. "New pets for Draygo Quick."

"Use your wraithform, then!" Drizzt told him through chattering, gritted teeth, but Effron, still sitting, shook his head.

"None of my magic will work in this cage. We are caught." He gave a helpless chuckle and added, "Like Guenhwyvar."

Drizzt wasn't listening, rushing around and inspecting every seam, every plank, every glowing bar of the magical cage. He shouted out for Entreri and the others, unwilling to admit defeat.

When he finally noted Effron again, the young tiefling was sitting on the floor, head down and despondent.

Drizzt didn't know if that defeated posture reflected immaturity or reality.

"Beware your feet!" Afafrenfere yelled, an obvious warning since they had all just seen the abrupt departure of Drizzt and Effron.

The monk moved quickly, running along the seams in the floor, so that if another tile fell out, he'd be able to dive one way or the other. He met the nearest charging armored creature with a flying kick that rattled the bones of the house defender, an animated skeleton, and sent it flying backward and to the floor.

Afafrenfere landed nimbly and spun right back to his feet, his right arm flying across to take aside the stabbing sword of the next attacker, his left palm snapping forward to ring against the chest plate with stunning force.

In rushed the armored attacker, another skeleton, stubbornly, but Afafrenfere dived past it, ahead of the stabbing sword, and he came up powerfully right beside the monster, hooking his arm under the skeleton's breast plate as he did and planting his foot firmly behind. Up and over went the armored skeleton, thrown into backward flight.

A third came charging in even as the first tried to stand once more, and again Afafrenfere was ready, executing a heavy double strike between its upraising arms. His goal was to shove the attacker back, to buy some room.

But this was no skeleton and it hardly budged, and those upraised arms did not reach out for Afafrenfere, but rather to reveal the monster's primary weapon.

The medusa removed her helmet.

Artemis Entreri went into a spinning assault, stabbing and thrashing to drive the ground attackers back, while Dahlia, staying carefully within the assassin's defensive perimeter, put her long staff to brilliant use, swatting the dragonettes and stabbing at the swooping gargoyles, each strike against the stone-like monsters filling Kozah's Needle with lightning energy.

She brought her staff down and in a horizontal swing at one skeleton that had slipped past Entreri's defensive spins to come at her, and her aim proved perfect, catching the monster against the side of its helm and launching it sideways—where Entreri's sword and dagger waited. Following through with the spin, Dahlia stabbed up into a diving gargoyle, and now let loose the building charge, the air above her exploding with crackling lightning, the gargoyle exploding into several pieces. Out arced the bolt, and several of the tiny dragons dropped like dead birds.

They had an opening now, and so they could find a more defensible spot, but when Dahlia looked ahead, she saw Ambergris running her way, staggering her way, head down and arms up shielding the dwarf's face. She saw Afafrenfere beyond the dwarf, standing absolute still in perfect defensive posture, hands raised before him.

And she saw past Afafrenfere, to his opponent . . .

"No!" Entreri cried out, and he leaped against Dahlia, trying to knock her to the ground, trying to do something, anything to turn her gaze.

But too late. He crashed against solid stone. The Dahlia statue slid only a bit, and Entreri crashed down hard to one knee and reflexively glanced where he should not glance, and this time, the medusa's magic found him.

He too became a statue, his flesh turning to stone, and he knelt and leaned there, joined with Dahlia, the last desperate try of a friend.

Ambergris wailed and stumbled past the pair, still ducking and covering, not daring to slow to swing up at the gargoyle assaulting her from above. She had resisted the medusa's devastating gaze in those first moments, but she knew that such an assault would reach out at her again, and she might not be so lucky the next time!

So she didn't dare slow, and surely didn't dare turn, accepting the clawing strikes of the gargoyle all the way back to the door from which she had come.

She went through, and the gargoyle went through right behind her, and the dwarf went for the door most of all, and took several more brutal hits for her efforts, one opening her skin from her shoulder to her ear.

She kept her back to the door, but put up her heavy mace, trading blow for multiple blows against the well-armed creature. The gargoyle hopped, its wide wings holding it aloft, as clawed hands and clawed feet raked in at the dwarf.

Ambergris accepted the gouging hits and focused instead on a single, heavy, two-handed down-strike.

Skullbreaker once more lived up to its name.

Blood dripping from multiple wounds, the dwarf had no time to pause and cast any healing, for the door at her back rattled with the press of castle defenders.

She darted away, through another door, then crashed through a third, again retracing her route. This door had a locking bar, which she promptly dropped in place, but she held no illusions that it would hold for long, or that the castle's defenders wouldn't have other routes to get at her.

Where had Drizzt and Effron gone? She couldn't do anything for the three turned to stone—there were spells of restoration to counter such magic, but they were far beyond Ambergris's power!

So she fled—not just the castle, for where might she go?—but fled the plane of Shadowfell itself. Ambergris couldn't shadowstep, and creating a gate as Effron had done was also beyond her experience, but she had her enchanted brooch, her Word of Recall, and she had set her sanctuary far, far away.

In the blink of an eye, the dwarf stumbled from Draygo Quick's castle into the room reserved for her at Sailor's Solace in Port Llast.

She spent many heartbeats just trying to even out her breath, and then many more trying to figure out her course. She reflexively turned east, toward the Silver Marches, her home and Mithral Hall. Perhaps she could go to Clan Battlehammer with news of Drizzt Do'Urden, who had once been their favored guest. Perhaps she could rally them to assault the castle in another plane, to launch a daring rescue.

The dwarf laughed at the absurdity of it. Three of her companions, including Afafrenfere, were gone, and the other two . . .

Ambergris thought of Draygo Quick; she knew much of his reputation. In that reflection, it seemed to her that Entreri, Dahlia, and Afafrenfere had been the fortunate ones.

A page in her book had turned, Ambergris realized, and with that, she took a deep and steadying breath and left the past behind, ready to find a new road.

But her old escapades might not so quickly let her go. Cavus Dun wanted her, and had the resources to find her and kill her.

Sometime later, after expending all of her magical energies to close the worst of her many wounds, she looked out her window at the small seaport opening below her balcony.

Cavus Dun would find her here, and easily, for she would surely stand out among the lesser folk of this small community. And here, she would find no allies powerful enough to ward such attacks.

She thought of Luskan, of Beniago and Ship Kurth. He would welcome her back. Perhaps he would put her aboard another of Kurth's merchant ships, out to sea. She found herself nodding. What better place for a fugitive dwarf to be?

The next day, Ambergris secured a pony and supplies and started out from Port Llast, traveling north.

Beginning the next chapter in a life gone mad.

CHAPTER 19

CURIOSER AND CURIOSER

"W HY'RE YE WALKIN'?" ATHROGATE ASKED. "BACK AND FORTH AND BACK again. If ye're meaning to dig a trench in the floor, get me a pick!"

"There's something afoot," Jarlaxle answered Athrogate.

"Well, have out with it, then," Athrogate replied, waggling his fat toes as he placed his feet comfortably on the ottoman, grinning as if that movement was directly in response to Jarlaxle's terminology.

"It will not much concern us," Jarlaxle replied. "Other than the trade agreement, which seems secured now."

"Eh?" Athrogate clearly hadn't expected that answer.

"It is an interesting time," Jarlaxle clarified. "I envy these Netherese lords in their endeavors and grand searches. Would that I had the time to join them!"

"Eh?" an even more confused Athrogate asked.

"Indeed," said Jarlaxle. "And I know that if we remain here any longer, I will surely be drawn into Parise Ulfbinder's work far more than I can afford. We will take our leave this very night."

"Eh?" Athrogate asked again, now seeming alarmed and not very happy.

"Indeed," was all that Jarlaxle would answer.

And that very night, Jarlaxle and Athrogate rode across the rolling ground of the region that had once been the great desert of Anauroch, Jarlaxle on his nightmare, Athrogate on his hellboar. Jarlaxle rejected Athrogate's desire to find a proper shelter, and instead camped out on the open plain. The two sat across an open fire, Athrogate cooking some fine stew, their magical mounts standing around as sentries.

"Could've stayed," Athrogate mumbled. He had been silent, but clearly annoyed, throughout the ride.

"There is something afoot," Jarlaxle replied. "Something important."

"Yeah, yeah, and it'd keep ye too busy and all that rot ye already said."

"You understand that Parise Ulfbinder was watching us in our room, of course," the drow replied.

"Eh?"

"That again? Yes, I assure you," Jarlaxle said, and he tapped his eyepatch to reinforce the strength of his claim, for that magical item was well-known to protect against telepathic or clairvoyant intrusions. "Something important is afoot. Something connected to the Spellplague and the fall of the Weave."

"Spellplague," Athrogate muttered. "I keep hearing that name, but I ain't much knowing what ye're talkin' about."

"As subtle as the darkness," the drow explained. "As quiet as the shadow. For some reason, with the fall of the Weave, we are bound to the Shadowfell and her dark minions."

"Aye, seen too many o' the damn shadow things. So what're ye thinking's happening, then?"

Jarlaxle shook his head. "Our friends of Shade Enclave might be making a move at domination."

"Of?"

"Everything?" Jarlaxle asked as much as stated. "They are spending great energy in examining the old gods. Parise asked me if Drizzt might perhaps be a Chosen of Lolth."

"Aye, he asked me a few things about that one, as well."

That news surprised Jarlaxle. "When did you speak—?" he started to ask.

"When yerself went to him th'other day," Athrogate answered. "He come to me right before yerself returned, wantin' to know about that damned ranger."

"And what did you tell him?"

"Unicorn lady, Mylickin' or something—"

"Mielikki," Jarlaxle corrected.

"Aye, that's me thinking. Heard Drizzt claim as much."

Jarlaxle nodded, but remained intrigued by the other theory, that Lolth secretly considered Drizzt her champion of chaos, and indeed, that rogue had lived up to the billing as far as the city of Menzoberranzan was concerned.

"So ye're thinkin' that them shadow lords're studying the gods and them Chosen such to find some plan o' attack against us all?"

Jarlaxle was impressed that Athrogate had gone so quickly to that reasoning, and he reminded himself that this particular dwarf was no fool, despite his nonsensical rhyming and frivolous laughter, particularly in matters of battle strategies.

"Be interestin' to see where we might fit into such plans of domination, eh?" the dwarf added, and Jarlaxle nodded.

Interesting indeed.

"It seems that many are interested in the rogue Do'Urden of late," Kimmuriel said to Jarlaxle a couple of days later, when Jarlaxle and Athrogate arrived in Luskan.

"Tiago?"

"He's a persistent one."

"Where is Drizzt?" Jarlaxle asked.

"In or around town, though laying low, I expect," Kimmuriel replied. "His boat arrived back in port some time ago, and he was aboard, but where he and his friends have gone, we cannot be sure."

Jarlaxle nodded. Keeping track of any band that included Artemis Entreri would not be easy, he knew.

"Do you think that the inquiries of this Parise Ulfbinder are in any way connected to Tiago's pursuit of Drizzt?" Kimmuriel asked. "Is it possible that the Netherese lords are trying to create a back-channel to the direct markets in Menzoberranzan?"

Jarlaxle shook his head. "Our agreement is fairly thorough," he reminded, and Kimmuriel, who had just negotiated that very contract could not disagree. "My sense is that Parise's interest in Drizzt extends only so far as to use Drizzt as a symbol of something larger."

Kimmuriel nodded as Jarlaxle spoke, revealing that he was of like mind. "There have been other inquiries by the Netherese," he explained.

"Of Drizzt?"

"No, none that I know of, but of others who have elevated themselves amongst the ranks of the mortals of Faerûn. Elminster, for one. It seems that our Netherese neighbors have taken a special interest in those who have distinguished themselves in the eyes of one god or another."

"The Chosen," Jarlaxle reasoned. "Or perhaps they hold an interest in the gods themselves."

"And our duty in any such a conflict?" Kimmuriel asked.

"Profit."

"And Menzoberranzan's role?"

"That is more interesting," Jarlaxle admitted, meaning that he couldn't begin to figure it out.

"If you are correct in your assumptions regarding their interest in Drizzt, then likely Menzoberranzan will be able to pick sides as is most convenient, but if you are wrong. . . ."

"If Drizzt is their focus, then perhaps their plans are also focused on our people."

"And in that regard, what then is our new agreement worth, to us and to the Netherese?"

"Let us be very cautious in the manner of goods we send to Shade Enclave," Jarlaxle decided. "And regarding any information we disclose. I do not believe that Parise means to move against Menzoberranzan, or against Bregan D'aerthe—to what end, after all? But let us make sure that we do not help them in whatever they think to accomplish."

"You will remain in Luskan for the time being?" Kimmuriel asked.

"You're leaving?"

"I will go to the city of the illithids," the psionicist announced. "Their hive mind will help us find the answers. If something grand is unfolding, then the sooner we understand it, the larger our profit."

"How long?"

"Who can tell with mind flayers?" Kimmuriel responded with a shrug.

Jarlaxle nodded.

"Drizzt Do'Urden," Kimmuriel stated.

Jarlaxle shrugged.

"He is here, as is Artemis Entreri," Kimmuriel clarified. "I trust that any contact you might find will be in the interest of Bregan D'aerthe, and not in the interest of Jarlaxle."

"They are one and the same."

Kimmuriel stared at him hard.

"Go," Jarlaxle said, waving him away. "I am no fool, and I recognize that the events unfolding could well be important. Where is Beniago?"

"He is around, surely in the city. He was quite useful in getting Drizzt far from Luskan for the last several months."

"Tiago again?"

"He is stubborn," Kimmuriel admitted. "But then, he is a Baenre, after all."

Jarlaxle Baenre grinned and bowed at the clever remark. "Tiago may well be stepping into something larger than he understands, and to his—and to all of our—detriment."

"As I said, he is a Baenre."

Jarlaxle could only chuckle in response.

"Well met, again," Jarlaxle said to Tiago Baenre when he found the young warrior holed up in an abandoned farmhouse just outside of Luskan. As Beniago had informed Jarlaxle, Tiago had several companions with him, including a brother and sister of House Xorlarrin.

Jarlaxle tipped his great hat, turning as he did in apparent deference to the drow wearing the robes of a priestess—Saribel Xorlarrin, no doubt—but in truth to let his gaze scrutinize the spellspinner standing beside her. Beniago had warned him specifically to beware the spellspinner known as Ravel Xorlarrin.

"You were not invited," Tiago said sternly.

"Nor were you, yet here you are, far from Menzoberranzan, far even from Gauntlgrym," Jarlaxle returned.

"I am Baenre. I go where I please."

"You're in Bregan D'aerthe territory, young weapons master. You would have done well to inform us of your intent."

"Bregan D'aerthe," Tiago spat with clear contempt.

"So you continue your hunt for Drizzt Do'Urden."

"This is none of your affair."

Jarlaxle grinned.

"Where is he?" Tiago demanded.

"I thought you just said it was none of my affair."

"You play dangerous games," said Tiago.

"I? Why, young weapons master, you are the one hunting a fellow drow, and without the imprimatur of Matron Mother Quenthel." The mercenary leader made a point to glance the way of the Xorlarrins as he spoke, and judging from their reaction, his words had hit a mark.

But Tiago remained obstinate, predictably so, given his bloodlines.

"Where is he?" Tiago demanded.

"I know not."

"He went forth on a boat—*Minnow Skipper* by name," Tiago said. "Now that boat has returned, and Drizzt with her, but he seems to have disappeared."

"You know more about it than I, apparently," said Jarlaxle. "I have only very recently returned from unrelated business."

"From where?"

Jarlaxle scoffed at the demand.

"You should consider my position," Tiago said to him. "My family and my rank. Matron Mother Quenthel will not be pleased to learn that Jarlaxle of Bregan D'aerthe hindered my pursuit of the rogue."

"What Matron Mother Quenthel will or will not say may well surprise you, confident one," Jarlaxle returned. "You pursue that which you do not understand."

"I am to fear him?" Tiago said with dripping sarcasm.

"Perhaps you are to fear the wrath of Lady Lolth should you succeed in your quest," Jarlaxle replied, again glancing at the Xorlarrins, and Saribel seemed to sway a bit at that surprising remark.

"You would do well to step aside and remain aside," Tiago said threateningly. "Already, I have seen too much of Jarlaxle."

"Perhaps I feel that I owed it to Matron Mother Quenthel to properly warn her misguided warrior before he ventures into a darkness he does not understand," Jarlaxle returned with a wry grin.

"You owe it?" Tiago asked incredulously. "You owe it to House Baenre?"

"Our finest client."

"And merely that, Jarlaxle?" Tiago asked, not hiding the implication that he knew more than he was letting on, and indeed, his sudden cockiness had Jarlaxle on his guard. "Is that your only interest in House Baenre, Houseless mercenary?"

Jarlaxle considered the specific wording of this sly young Baenre for a long while. Tiago knew the truth of Jarlaxle? Who else might know, then? His heritage had always been a secret even from most of the family. As far as Jarlaxle knew, only Gromph, who was one of the very few drow older than Jarlaxle, and the matron mother herself knew his heritage, along with Kimmuriel.

But Tiago's air of superiority was no false bravado, and it was clearly based on something Tiago knew that he should not.

"Step carefully," Jarlaxle said, and he bowed and turned on his heel, taking his abrupt leave, for he could not be away from this brash young upstart and his powerful friends quickly enough for his liking. Rarely had Jarlaxle found himself in a position of such a disadvantage.

He rushed back to Luskan, and found Beniago in short order.

But Beniago had no answers for him, for they still had found no sign of Drizzt and his five companions. The group had left *Minnow Skipper* when she docked, every one, and Beniago had traced them to a specific inn, even to a room they had rented for a private gathering.

But from there, nothing. It was as if they had simply disappeared.

The old drow mercenary—and he felt very old at that moment—could only blow a resigned sigh, for this was one of those rare occasions when events were outside of Jarlaxle's ability to control them.

Between the Netherese lords, Tiago Baenre and his hunting band, and the mysterious disappearance of Drizzt and his companions, too many wheels were turning in too many different directions for his liking.

CHAPTER 20

THE MENAGERIE

THE MOMENTS BECAME AN HOUR, THE HOURS BECAME A DAY, AND DRIZZT and Effron had nowhere to go. They broke out their packs in the small square of the magical cell, each side of which was no longer than a tall man's height.

In their packs, they had food and water for several more days, but their inability to get anything beyond the magical bars had the cell smelling rank, but soon enough, even that faded into the background of monotony, as did the low humming sound of the lightning magic infusing the bars.

After one night, or perhaps it was a day, of fitful sleep, Effron awakened to find Drizzt inspecting the bars. Icingdeath in his hand, Drizzt eyed the joints where the bars met the ceiling and the floor, and he even dared prod at one.

The shock sent him flying backward, to crash into the opposite bars, which sparked angrily and threw him aside. Sitting on the ground, his long white hair dancing wildly with the charge, Drizzt took a series of deep breaths, trying to recover his sensibilities.

"Not very bright," said Effron. "Amusing to watch, however."

"There must be a way out of here."

"Must there be?" the young tiefling asked. "Draygo Quick is a master in matters of imprisonment, I assure you. His menagerie is vast. I know of none who have escaped, humanoid or monster, and that includes your wondrous panther."

"We are not in stasis," Drizzt countered. "Are you so quick to surrender?"

That statement had Effron narrowing his gaze in anger. "You know nothing of me," he said in a low and threatening tone. "Were I quick to surrender, I would have done so as soon as I knew who I was—and what I was! Do you know what it is to be an outcast, Drizzt Do'Urden? Do you know what it is to not belong, anywhere?"

269

Drizzt broke out in laughter and Effron couldn't begin to sort out what the drow had found so funny. The tiefling watched as Drizzt crawled over to sit right in front of him.

"We seem to have time," Drizzt said. "Likely quite a bit of time, unless your mother and the rest can find us."

Effron studied the drow carefully, not sure what to make of him.

"Perhaps it is time we came to understand each other, for your mother's sake," Drizzt explained. "Let me tell you what I know of not belonging in my own home, or, as I thought for so many years, even in my own skin."

Drizzt told him a story then, one that began two centuries before in an Underdark city called Menzoberranzan. At first Effron scoffed at the seemingly meager attempt to create a bond—what did he need with this drow, anyway?—but soon, the young tiefling found himself scoffing less and listening more.

He marveled at the drow's descriptions of this decadent place, Menzoberranzan, and descriptions of his family in House Do'Urden, which seemed to Effron not so unlike life at Draygo Quick's castle. Drizzt told of the drow schools of study—martial, divine, and arcane—and the inevitable accompanying indoctrination they entailed. Effron found himself so drawn into the winding ways of Menzoberranzan, his imagination walking those shadowy streets, that it took him a long while to realize that Drizzt had stopped talking.

He looked up at the drow, staring into those lavender eyes, reflecting back at him in the dim bluish light of the glowing bars.

Drizzt told him another story, one of a surface raid where his companions had slaughtered an elf clan. He described saving a young elf child by smearing her with her own dead mother's blood.

Clearly affected by the memory, Drizzt's voice grew very low, so he was obviously startled, straightening quickly, when Effron angrily interjected, "Would that you had been there before Dahlia threw me from the cliff!"

An uncomfortable silence followed.

"You have not made peace with her," Drizzt said. "I had thought—"

"More so than my comment and tone would indicate," Effron replied, and he meant it. He lowered his gaze and shook his head and admitted, "It is hard."

"She's a difficult person sometimes, I know," said Drizzt.

"She loves you."

Effron noted Drizzt's wince, and came to think that perhaps the feeling wasn't mutual—which explained a lot regarding Drizzt's acceptance of Dahlia's dalliance with Artemis Entreri, after all.

"I was much like you when I left Menzoberranzan," Drizzt said, quickly regaining Effron's attention. "It took me many years to learn to trust, and some time after that to recognize the beauty and love such trust can bring."

He launched back into his story then, completing the tale of Menzoberranzan and completing, too, the tale of his own father and Zaknafein's ultimate victory over the miserable priestesses of Lolth. He detailed his journey through the Underdark, the road that led him, at last, to the surface world.

By that time, growling stomachs interrupted the tales, and the two went to their stocks. But Effron bade Drizzt to continue his tale through the meal, and all the way until they lay down once more for sleep—where Drizzt left Effron's imagination on the side of a cold mountain known as Kelvin's Cairn, with a promise to tell him of the greatest friends anyone could ever hope to know.

And they had plenty of time for Drizzt to finish his stories, as the days drifted past and no one, not Draygo Quick or his minions, nor Dahlia and the others, came to see them.

Then it was a tenday, and Effron, too, had shared his own tales of growing up in the shadow of Herzgo Alegni, and under the harsh tutelage of Lord Draygo Quick.

And they ran out of food and water, and still they sat, in their own waste, and both came to wonder if Draygo had just sent them to this place to be forgotten and to die in the near darkness and the monotonous hum.

"Our friends were likely victorious, but they haven't found us yet," Effron posited at one point, his voice barely a whisper, for he had no strength for anything louder. "Lord Draygo would not just leave me here to die."

Drizzt, lying on his back, wore his skepticism on his face.

"You were too important to him," Effron explained, echoing what he had told Drizzt on *Minnow Skipper*'s return journey to Luskan. "He wouldn't . . ."

Those were the last words Effron spoke to Drizzt in that cell, or at least, the last Drizzt heard.

When Drizzt awakened, he found himself in a different place, in a more typical dungeon cell with a dirt floor and stone walls. He was sitting against the wall, opposite the bars of the cell door, his arms chained up above his head, the other end of the chain spiked into the wall far above him.

It took Drizzt a while to sort out the changes in his situation, but one of the first things he came to recognize was not an encouraging thought: given his predicament and the change of venue, his friends had certainly not won out.

It was darker in here than in the other cell, the only light coming from the distant flicker of a torch set in a sconce on a wall many twists and turns from Drizzt's location. Before him on the floor, Drizzt noted a plate of food, that sight reminding him of how desperately hungry he was.

A pair of rats poked around the plate, which Drizzt could not begin to reach with his chained hands. Instinctively, a feral movement even, Drizzt kicked out at the rodents, chasing them away—and looking at his own legs and feet made him aware that he was naked now. His thoughts could hardly register the implications of that, or of anything, though, as he hooked his feet and toes and dragged the plate in closer.

Still he could not reach it with his hands or his face, for he could not lower his hands below his shoulders. He tugged futilely against the chains for a few moments, but then, driven almost mad by his hunger, he merely scooped the meal with his dirty foot and used his great agility to bring it to his mouth.

He managed to force the dry and foul-tasting stuff down his parched throat, barely, but after a single swallow, he had tasted more than enough, and so he just slumped back and thought of the world beyond the grave.

He forced himself to fill his mind with notions of Catti-brie . . .

"It is humbling, is it not?" came a voice, from very far away it seemed.

Drizzt cracked open one eye, and flinched away in the brighter light. The torch was right outside his dungeon cell, in the hands of an old and wrinkled shade.

"How it must pain Mielikki to think of her favored child in such a predicament," the old wretch taunted.

Drizzt tried to respond, but he hadn't the strength to force any words past his parched and cracked lips.

He heard the scrape of metal as his cell door opened, then was handled roughly as more food was shoved into his mouth, followed by foul-tasting water.

It happened again a short while later, then again sometime after that. Drizzt had little understanding of the passage of time, but it seemed to him that many days were drifting far, far behind him.

Despite the filth and the wretched taste of the sustenance they were forcing upon him, the drow found his strength and sensibilities gradually returning. Then the old shade was there again, but inside his cell, standing before him.

"What am I to do with you, Drizzt Do'Urden?" he asked.

"Who are you?"

"Lord Draygo Quick, of course," Draygo answered. "And this is my castle, which you assaulted. By the laws of any land, I am well within my rights to kill you."

"I came for Guenhwyvar," Drizzt replied, and he had to cough a dozen times in the span of that short response, from the dryness in his throat.

"Ah, yes, the panther. You'll not get her, of course, but then, you'll likely never leave this place." He paused and offered a sly look. "But then again, if you cooperate, then perhaps we will become great friends."

Drizzt couldn't begin to sort out that comment.

"Tell me, drow, who do you worship?"

"What?"

"Who is your god?"

"I follow the tenets of Mielikki—you already said as much," Drizzt replied in a hoarse whisper.

Draygo Quick nodded and put a hand to his chin contemplatively. "Perhaps I would do better to ask, who worships you?"

Drizzt stared at him curiously, and the old wretch chuckled, sounding almost as wheezy as Drizzt.

"Of course you cannot answer," he said. "We will talk again, and often, I promise," Draygo Quick said, and with a nod, he turned and left the cell. "Grow strong once more, Drizzt Do'Urden," he called over his shoulder. "We have much to discuss."

His cell door clanged shut and the torchlight receded. Drizzt watched the flickers trailing away down the outside hallway, then soon after heard another cell door scrape open, and the murmurs of the old warlock speaking once more.

Effron?

Drizzt leaned forward and craned his head—not to see anything, for that was obviously not possible, but to try to hear some of the words being spoken, if not the conversation itself.

He couldn't make anything out, but he heard a second murmuring voice, and recognized it as Effron's. He slumped back, sorting his thoughts. He looked at his chains and promised himself that he would find a way out of them.

Drizzt wasn't a victim.

Soon enough he would find his way out of this cell and to Effron's rescue. That was his vow.

"You were too confident!" Draygo Quick proclaimed to Effron, whose situation differed from Drizzt's only in the fact that only one of his arms was chained. "But then, that was ever your failing, was it not?"

Effron stared at him hatefully, but that only seemed to amuse the shade.

"You thought you knew all of my tricks and traps, but of course, I am no fool," Draygo went on. "Did you really believe that you could walk in here and simply steal away with the panther?"

"It was not my choice."

"You led them here."

"I did," Effron admitted.

"Your loyalty is touching."

Effron lowered his gaze.

"You have decided to wage war against me, and that is a foolish pursuit."

"No," Effron immediately retorted, looking back up, staring Draygo Quick right in the eye. "No. I decided to travel with my mother, and I needed to blind you to our movements, but only by taking the cat. I would not go against you, but I would be done with you."

"Interesting," Draygo Quick mumbled a few moments later, after digesting that information. "Let me tell you about your mother. . . ."

Drizzt pulled hard against the unyielding chains when he heard Effron's wailing from down the hall. At first he thought his companion was being tortured, but when that initial keening transformed into sobs, he realized it was something else.

It didn't take him long to figure out the implications of those sobs.

"Where is Dahlia?" Drizzt demanded the next time Draygo Quick appeared in his cell, some days later, he believed, though he couldn't be certain.

"Ah, you have heard the weeping of your twisted companion," Draygo Quick replied. "Yes, I am afraid that Dahlia and your other companions have met a most unfortunate end, and now stand as trophies in my hall."

Drizzt lowered his eyes, unable to even scream out in protest. He was surprised by how profoundly the news had hit him, surprised to realize how deeply he had come to value Dahlia's companionship. Perhaps he couldn't love her as he had loved Catti-brie, but she had become, at least, a friend.

And it wasn't just the loss of Dahlia that brought him pain in that moment, for his tie to his past, too, was gone. "Entreri," he heard himself whispering, and he couldn't deny the sense of loss.

And so too with Ambergris, of whom he was quite fond, and Afafrenfere.

"You have walked into something far beyond you, Drizzt Do'Urden of Menzoberranzan," Draygo Quick said, and it surprised Drizzt to hear a sincere tone of regret in the Netherese lord's voice. He looked back up, trying to find something in Draygo Quick's expression to reveal the lie of his concerns, but he found no such thing.

"To the detriment of all," Draygo Quick continued. "Of course I would defend myself and my home—would you expect anything less?"

"It would need less defending if you were not a thief and kidnapper," Drizzt retorted.

"Kidnapper? You walked into my home!"

"Of Guenhwyvar," Drizzt clarified. "You stole from me something which does not belong to you."

"Ah, yes, of course," said Draygo. "The cat. As I said, you have stumbled into something apparently quite beyond you, but perhaps there is hope for both of us. I do not think that I will have need of the cat when we are done, so perhaps you will find her companionship again."

The tantalizing carrot had Drizzt inadvertently leaning forward, before he realized the revealing posture and corrected himself, unwilling to let his thoughts go into the realm of false hope.

The Netherese lord would never let him go, he told himself, over and over again.

He would find himself repeating that silent mantra many times as Draygo Quick came to him each day, always with questions about Drizzt's past, about the priestesses of Lolth and about his life on the surface while following the tenets of the goddess Mielikki and the ways of the ranger.

Drizzt resisted those questions at first, but his stubbornness couldn't long hold, and some tendays later, he came to look forward to those visits.

For accompanying Draygo came the servants with his food, and that food greatly improved, and was fed to him far more tenderly and decently by a young shade, a child.

One day Draygo Quick arrived with a trio of burly guards. Two moved to flank Drizzt, reaching up for the chains as they did.

"If you struggle in the least, I will torture Effron to death before your eyes," was all that Draygo Quick bothered to say, and he took his leave.

The guards put a black hood over Drizzt's head and carried him from his cell, depositing him in a room somewhere within the castle above. They set him down in a chair, told him to remove the hood, to bathe and to dress.

"Lord Draygo will come to you soon," one said as they departed.

Drizzt looked around at his new home, a well-furnished, clean, and warm room. His first thoughts went to the notion of escape, but he quickly dismissed that possibility. Draygo Quick had Effron, and Guenhwyvar, and where might he go, in any case?

The Netherese lord had told him that he had walked into something far above him, and Drizzt didn't doubt the truth of that claim at all in that confusing time and place.

PART
IV

ICEWIND DALE

I found, to my surprise, that I had lost the focal point of my anger.

The anger, the frustration, the profound sense of loss yet again remained, simmering within me, but the target of that anger dispersed into a more general distaste for the unfairness and harshness of life itself.

I had to keep reminding myself to be mad at Draygo Quick!

What a strange realization that became, an epiphany that rolled over me like a breaking wave against Luskan's beach. I remember the moment vividly, as it happened all at once (whereas the loss of the focal point took many months). I rested in my chamber at Draygo Quick's grand residence, relaxing in luxury, eating fine food, and with my own small wine rack that Draygo's staff had provided, when I was struck dumb by my affinity toward Draygo Quick—or if not affinity, perhaps, then my complete absence of anger toward him.

How had that happened?

Why had that happened?

This Netherese lord had imprisoned me in the most terrible of circumstances, chained in filth in a dark and rank dungeon cell. He hadn't tortured me overtly, though the handling by his servants had often been harsh, including slaps and punches and more than a few kicks to my ribs. And wasn't the mere reality of my incarceration in and of itself a manner of grotesque torture?

This Netherese lord had set a medusa upon my companions, upon my lover, and upon my only remaining tie to those coveted bygone days. They were gone. Dahlia, Entreri, Ambergris, and Afafrenfere, turned to stone and dead by the machinations of Draygo Quick.

Yet, we had invaded his home ... that mitigating notion seemed ever-present in my mind, and only grew in strength, day by day, as my own conditions gradually improved.

And that was the key of it all, I came to recognize. Draygo Quick had played a subtle and tantalizing game with my mind, and with Effron's mind, slowly improving our lives. Bit by bit, and literally, at first, bite by bite, with improving food in terms of both quality and quantity.

It is difficult for a starving man to slap the hand that feeds him.

And when basic needs like sustenance dominate your thoughts, it is no less difficult to remember to maintain anger, or remember why.

Tasty bites delivered with soothing words steal those memories, so subtly, so gradually (though every improvement felt momentous indeed), that I remained oblivious to my own diminishing animosity toward the old warlock shade.

Then came the epiphany, that day in my comfortably-appointed room in the castle of Draygo Quick. Yet even with the stark recollection of the unfolding events, I found it impossible to summon the level of rage I had initially known, and hard to find anything more than a simmer.

I am left to sit here, wondering.

Draygo Quick comes to me often, daily even, and there are weapons I might fashion—of a broken wine bottle, for example.

Should I make the attempt?

The possibility of gaining my freedom through violence seems remote at best. I haven't seen Effron in tendays and have no idea of where or how to find him. I know not if he is even still within the castle, or if he is even still alive. I have no idea of how to find Guenhwyvar, nor do I even possess the onyx figurine any longer.

And even if I struck dead the old warlock and gained an escape from the castle, then what? How would I begin to facilitate my return to Faerûn, and what would be there for me, in any case?

None of my old friends, lost to the winds. Not Dahlia, or even Artemis Entreri. Not Guenhwyvar or Andahar.

To strike at Draygo Quick would be the ultimate act of defiance, and one made by a doomed drow.

I look at the bottles nestled in their diagonal cubbies in the wine rack now and in them I see that the promise of deadly daggers is well within my reach. Draygo Quick comes to me alone now, without guard, and even if he had his finest soldiers beside him, I have been trained to strike faster than they could possibly block. Perhaps the old warlock has magical wards enacted about him to defeat such an attack, perhaps not, but in striking so, I would be making a cry of freedom and a denial against this warlock who took so much from me, who imprisoned Guenhwyvar and cost me my companions when we came for her.

But I can only shake my head as I stare at those potential daggers, for I will not so fashion the bottles. It is not fear of Draygo Quick that stays my hand. It is not the desperation of such an act, the near surety that even if successful, I would be surely bringing about my own demise, and likely in short order.

I won't kill him, I know.

Because I don't want to.

And that, I fear, might be the biggest epiphany of all.

—Drizzt Do'Urden

CHAPTER 21

MIGHT AS WELL DRINK

B ENIAGO'S EYES IN THE CITY WERE CONSIDERABLE, OF COURSE, BUT LUSKAN was a large place, with many thousands of citizens and hundreds, at least, of visitors, particularly this time of year when the weather favored the sailing ships and the merchant trade was in full swing.

The reports filtering back to him over the last few days had caused concern for the Bregan D'aerthe agent. Drizzt had not been located, but other drow had—several, in fact. So many, in fact, that Beniago had come to wonder if Tiago and his Xorlarrin friends hadn't created some minor invasion, or if Bregan D'aerthe had started to operate more openly, and without informing him.

After eliminating that second possibility simply by asking Jarlaxle, Beniago had gone searching for answers.

The first he found, at least, had proved somewhat confusing, but somewhat comforting as well.

"They are not allied with Tiago," he reported to Jarlaxle.

"The group at the inn?"

Beniago nodded.

"The Xorlarrins, then," Jarlaxle reasoned, for they already knew that there were a couple of males among the group, and of the arcane persuasion, it seemed.

But Beniago shook his head. "These are not Xorlarrins, nor from Menzoberranzan at all."

"Then why are they here?"

"I walk in the guise of a human," Beniago replied. "Would you have me go and ask them? And after I do, would you bury me properly back in Menzoberranzan?"

"Sarcasm," Jarlaxle replied with a chuckle. "At last I have come to understand why I supported your ascent."

"Our next move?"

"I will deal with these unknown dark elves presently," Jarlaxle said. "I have word that Tiago is not in Gauntlgrym, nor are his ever-present companions, Ravel and Saribel Xorlarrin."

"You have spies in Gauntlgrym now? I am impressed." Beniago dipped a sarcastic bow.

"They are out hunting," Jarlaxle explained.

"On the surface hunting Drizzt, then."

"It would seem."

Beniago bowed again, more seriously now, understanding his role.

"Tiago carries his new sword and shield, no doubt," Jarlaxle said. "And is undisguised, I believe."

"He is too vain to wrap such magnificent items, particularly since they sing of his station," Beniago agreed.

"So find him."

Beniago nodded and left to do just that.

"Aye, but she's a tough life out there on the waves," the crusty old dwarf, Deamus McWindingbrook, explained. He grabbed his belly as he finished and let fly a great belch.

Ambergris giggled. "I been aboard, ye dope," she replied. "I seen the water, and naught but the water, through the whole o' me turn and to the curve o' the horizon."

"Not many of our kin and kind who'd take to that sight," remarked a third dwarf at the table, younger than the crusty old graybeard, but looking much like him both in weathering and because he was the other's son—Stuvie by name. He wore a blue cap, flopped over to one side, while his father wore a similar stocking cap of red. The younger's beard was yellow, as the older dwarf's had been not so long ago, before the salt and the sun and the years had turned it.

"Sailed to Baldur's Gate," Ambergris explained. She almost added in the rest of the itinerary, but wisely cut herself short, for she didn't want to give too many clues as to her previous visit to the city. She wasn't even using her name, appropriating instead the name of her cousin, Windy O'Maul.

Cavus Dun might be looking for her, after all, or worse, Draygo Quick.

And so it was that a journey out on the open seas seemed a fine idea to the dwarf at that time.

"Bah, Baldur's Gate's an easy sail," scoffed the younger of the McWindingbrooks.

"Aye, but I ain't been no lower on the Sword Coast," Ambergris lied. "But I'm hopin' to see the deserts o' Calimport."

Both McWindingbrooks crinkled their faces in disgust at that.

"Still!" Ambergris said with a laugh into their doubting expressions. "Ye can act like that because ye've seen it. But for meself, I ain't seen nothing but the halls o' Citadel Adbar, the road to Waterdeep, and the ports o' Luskan and Baldur's Gate. And I'm wanting to see more. Aye, so much more!"

"It'd be good to have another kin and kind aboard," Deamus admitted.

"Aye, and better that she's a she, and a pretty lass at that!" Stuvie added, and lifted his mug in toast.

Ambergris was quick to clap her mug against his, enjoying the compliment, the sentiment, and the possibilities.

She had to build her life anew. She had to escape all that was behind her, both emotionally and in practical terms. She had thought to return to Citadel Adbar, but given the news she would have to deliver, she realized that she wouldn't be well-received, and particularly not if the leaders of that dwarven complex came to realize that she might be leading a hostile Netherese lord their way!

This was the better route, and one she intended to make much more enjoyable.

She drained her mug and hoisted a second one, empty, up high, waving for the barmaid to bring another pitcher to the table.

The McWindingbrooks were paying, after all.

Hours later, two dwarves bobbed out of the tavern, walking shakily, laughing heartily, grabbing generously and both obviously quite drunk.

"That one?" Tiago asked his companions.

"That one," Saribel Xorlarrin replied, nodding. "Ambergris, by name. She sailed with Drizzt, and rode with him to Luskan from Port Llast."

The dwarves shambled past, not even noticing the dark figures in the deeper shadows of the alleyway.

"Here 'ere for swimmin' with bowlegged women!" the male said.

"And to sailin' with tall-masted lads!" the female lewdly added, and they rolled along, laughing and groping liberally. So enmeshed and enamored with each other were they that they clearly didn't even notice the three forms moving out of the darkness behind them.

Ravel glanced around, and seeing few others, began casting a spell. Tiago, Saribel right behind him, hoisted Orbcress, his spider web shield, and quick-stepped to close the gap.

"Ah, but ye do me well, me lady—" the male started to say, but he cut it short and began spitting instead, for he had walked into some sort of cobweb, the filaments filling his mouth. Indeed, both had walked into Ravel's web, the female more fully than he, and the magical creation, stretching from the building to their left to the street post to their right, grabbed on stubbornly.

Still spitting, the male dwarf pulled back and broke free, turning as he stumbled, and only then taking note of the fast-approaching dark elf warrior.

With a yelp of surprise, the dwarf drew a long and wicked knife from his belt. Having sailed the Sword Coast for most of his life, and having been trained by his father from childhood, Stuvie McWindingbrook was surely no novice to battle. He saw the approaching drow and his thoughts cleared immediately—almost, at least. He instinctively reached behind him with his free hand and shoved Windy defensively back, and thus, further into the web.

Then Stuvie executed a wonderful forward dive and roll, popping up to his feet and striking hard and fast and true.

The long knife struck the drow's shield, but if did not scrap or chime as it would have against a metal buckler, nor did it make a *thunk* sound as if it had knocked against wood. Rather, a muffled sound came forth, as if he had struck a thick blanket.

Stuvie hadn't expected the first strike to win out, but wanted to use it to merely bring that shield out to the side a bit, and in that regard, he succeeded. He retracted fast . . . or tried to.

His knife stuck to that curious shield.

"What?" the dwarf asked incredulously, and he yanked with all of his considerable strength, and did indeed tug free the blade. But as he fell back, he felt the bite of a fine drow sword.

It wasn't a mortal wound, surely, but still a painful one, a burning cut across his left shoulder.

Painful and burning.

Burning with poison.

Vidrinath, Tiago's sword was called, or Lullaby in the Common Tongue, for it was infused with the infamous drow sleep poison. The dwarf spun away. He called for his companion to flee, but his words were slurred. He lifted his long knife to defend or to strike, but his movement proved sluggish.

Tiago bull-rushed, shield leading, and the dwarf swung desperately. At the last moment, the drow leaped up high, but kept his shield down low, picking off the feeble stab. Up in the air, the drow reversed his hold on Lullaby and plunged the sword straight down as he descended.

The fine blade, nearly translucent, but sparkling with the power of inner diamonds and flashing reflections of the street lamps, drove home just beside the dwarf sailor's neck, clicking off his collarbone and sinking deeper, easily piercing muscle and gristle.

Down the street, having plowed through the thin webs of Ravel's spell, Ambergris shrieked in horror and ran off.

"Get her," Tiago scolded his companions. "Stop her!"

He tore out his sword as the dwarf crumpled to the cobblestones and didn't even bother to wipe the bloody blade as he took up the chase.

Vidrinath didn't need cleaning, for the fine blade would suffer no stains from the blood of a mortal. Swinging easily at Tiago's side, the blade began to smoke, the thick dwarf blood wafting away on the night air, as the life-force of the creature dissipated into the ether.

***

Ambergris turned down a side street and fell back against the building to catch her breath. She paused to listen, but then remembered the identity of her pursuers. She wouldn't hear the approach of dark elves!

She slipped quietly away from the street, her back still to the wall.

Then she was falling into blackness as the wall somehow disappeared behind her.

She found herself in a lightless bubble, an area of nothingness. She tried to retrace her steps but there was only blackness and a velvety wall before her and floor below her, with nothing to hold onto or to climb. She jumped and reached as high as she could, but there was nothing. Just a hole.

"Well, damn ye then!" she shouted. "Show yer miserable selfs and be done with it!"

Nothing.

The dwarf walked back a few steps, then bull rushed back at the wall slamming it full force. It gave before her, just enough to absorb her blow.

Nothing.

She took up Skullbreaker and went into a frenzy, swinging in the empty air and slapping at the walls. In short order, she put her hands on her hips, leaning her mace against her waist, huffing and puffing, and she realized that the drow were probably hoping for exactly this, that she would exhaust herself before they ever began the fight.

"Bah, ye fool," she scolded herself at last, and she cursed the whiskey, then focused and tried to remember the words to a simple spell.

Her magical light filled the small room, black-walled and ten feet square.

"They should be gone soon," came a voice from behind her, and Ambergris nearly hopped out of her boots. She whirled around, taking up her mace, to see a dark elf seated comfortably in the corner. He wore a blousy purple shirt under a sharply cut black vest and tucked neatly into fine black pants. An eyepatch adorned his face as he peeked out from under the brim of one of the largest hats Ambergris had ever seen, a great affair with one side pinned up tight and holding an enormous purple feather.

He seemed unconcerned at her aggressive stance and huge weapon, and he casually stood up, bowed gracefully, and said, "Jarlaxle, at your service, lovely dwarf."

The name sounded familiar to her. Had Drizzt mentioned this one? Or Entreri, perhaps?

"Ah, but who's Jarlaxle to be, and where's me Stuvie?"

"Stuvie? The dwarf who accompanied you out of the tavern?" Jarlaxle responded, and he shrugged. "Likely slain. The trio in pursuit of you are not known to be a merciful bunch."

"And what is Jarlaxle to them?"

"An enigma." He bowed again. "As I like it to be. And you are Amber Gristle O'Maul, of the Adbar O'Mauls, correct?"

"Windy," Ambergris corrected after foolishly and instinctively nodding.

Jarlaxle sighed and laughed and took a step toward her, and Ambergris lifted Skullbreaker higher.

"You traveled with Drizzt Do'Urden," Jarlaxle said, "a friend of mine. And with Artemis Entreri, who once was a friend, but now would likely kill me."

"Ye need not be worryin' about that," Ambergris said.

Jarlaxle looked at her curiously. "Come," he said a moment later and he took off his hat and waved it and the black walls around them dropped, simply folding to the ground to reveal that they were inside a windowless room. Ambergris looked at the wall near to her with puzzlement, thinking that it must have been the alleyway wall she was crouching along when she fell into this . . . whatever it might be.

"Do step aside," Jarlaxle bade her, and he motioned to the clear section of floor and followed her that way. Then he grabbed the edge of the "room" they had been in, which seemed more like a large bed sheet then, or perhaps a black tablecloth. The drow snapped his wrists and the whole of it seemed to shrink, and he repeated the motion a dozen times, lifted the small black cloth and spun it atop a raised finger, then tucked it neatly into his great hat.

"Why don't I need to worry about Artemis Entreri?" Jarlaxle asked.

"He's dead," Ambergris replied. "And so's Dahlia and me monk friend Afafrenfere." She could clearly see the crestfallen expression worn by Jarlaxle, and she knew it to be an honest reflection of shock and grief.

"And Drizzt?"

Ambergris shrugged.

"You will give me a complete recounting," Jarlaxle declared.

"And if not?"

"Oh, you will," the drow said, his tone suddenly changing.

The room's single door banged open then and a fearsome-looking black-bearded dwarf crashed into the room, a pair of adamantine morningstars strapped diagonally across his back, their heavy balls bouncing around his shoulders.

"Way's clear," he said. "Them dark elfs moved off."

"Clear all the way to Illusk?"

The dwarf nodded. "Come on, then, pretty lady," he said to Ambergris. "Let's get ye safe."

"Indeed," Jarlaxle agreed. "Safely in a place where you will tell me your tale."

Ambergris stared at him suspiciously.

"You will," Jarlaxle assured her, his tone deathly even, every syllable and inflection fully in control and brimming with confidence. "One way or another."

Ambergris swallowed hard, but eased her mace down to the ground. This one, or these two, had saved her life, no doubt, and she already understood that starting a fight with them might not be the smartest thing she ever did.

They were out across the town in short order, moving to the haunted region of Luskan known as Illusk. From ground level, it seemed no more than an ancient graveyard and ruin, but within those graves were secret tunnels that led to a subterranean section of the city that few knew of. Bregan D'aerthe had appropriated this place of late, turning the underground chambers into their hideout.

"Don't ye be worryin'," the rough-looking dwarf assured Ambergris a short while later when they walked around those chambers, dark elves all around, watching them curiously. "Ye're with Jarlaxle now, and none'll move against ye."

"So says . . . ?" Ambergris asked him leadingly.

"Athrogate o' Adbar at yer service, pretty lady," he said, dipping a bow.

"Adbar?"

"A long time ago," Athrogate explained. "Long afore yerself was born. I'll tell ye me tale, if ye're interested, but it'll be waitin' a bit, until Jarlaxle's done with ye."

"If I'm still alive, ye mean."

"Oh, but ye'll be alive, don't ye doubt, bwahahaha!" Athrogate roared. "Jarlaxle's a fierce enemy, but he's a fiercer friend, and he's been namin' Drizzt and Entreri among his friends for a century and more."

"He said Entreri wants to kill him."

"Bah, but a misunderstandin'," Athrogate assured her.

They came into a lavishly-furnished chamber, full of comfortable pillows and a grand hearth and a grander desk and chair. Jarlaxle waited as the dwarves passed him by, then shut the door.

"Every detail," he said to Ambergris. "And you can start by telling me why you went to the Shadowfell in the first place."

"To get the cat."

"The cat?"

"A friend o' Drizzt, ye call yerself?" Ambergris asked suspiciously.

"Ah, Guenhwyvar," Jarlaxle replied knowingly, but then he shook his head as if that made no sense at all to him, which of course, it did not. "All five of you went to rescue—"

"Six," Ambergris interrupted. "Effron the tiefling led us. Twas himself who told us that Lord Draygo had Drizzt's cat."

Jarlaxle's eyes widened, and Ambergris could see that he had found some significance in that notion, though what it might be, she did not understand.

The dwarf took a deep breath and got right to the point. "They looked into the eye o' the beast," Ambergris began, and she took her time and duly recounted that dark day in the Shadowfell. She noted the wince of this most curious drow when she told him of the medusa and the fate of three of her companions, particularly that of Artemis Entreri, and it seemed an honest reaction of grief.

"So what of Drizzt and this young tiefling, Effron?" Jarlaxle asked when she was finished, and after he had taken a long while to compose himself. "They fell through a trap in the floor, and then?"

Ambergris shrugged. "Out o' me sight and I was runnin' for me life."

"But did you hear from them? Were they crying out below?"

"Nay, I can'no say I did, but the fight was on in full and so I wouldn't've, even if they were screaming from just below the floor. Not that it's matterin'," she added, shaking her head. "Lord Draygo's not one to play with. I seen enough o' that one in me time with Cavus Dun—" She paused at that slip-up, and at the intrigue it brought to the drow's handsome face.

"You will tell me about that, as well," Jarlaxle assured her.

"Aye," the dwarf said with a nod.

"But first, finish your tale. Why do you say it doesn't matter?"

"Lord Draygo ain't known for mercy."

Jarlaxle nodded. "But as far as you know, they were alive when you fled the castle?"

"Aye," Ambergris replied. She lowered her eyes. When he put it that way, she sounded like quite the coward.

Jarlaxle nodded, his expression pensive.

"What're ye thinking?" Athrogate asked.

That broke the drow's contemplation. He stood up, and nodded. "See to her needs," he instructed Athrogate, then to Ambergris, he said, "You have done well, fine lady. In surviving that which few might, and you have done well in trusting me. Your words are most appreciated. We will speak again, and soon."

"And I'm yer prisoner?" she asked.

"You should remain here," Jarlaxle said. "In fact, I insist upon it. Those three who pursued you will be relentless, I assure you, and you cannot defeat them."

"So ye're *askin'* me to stay here?" Ambergris asked incredulously. "They're drow, ye're drow—"

"They won't come here," Jarlaxle assured her. "Even if they do, they'll not know that you're here, and surely would not move against you in this place, in any case."

"Others saw me come in."

"Trust him," Athrogate told her, patting her arm.

Jarlaxle nodded at his dwarf sidekick, then tipped his hat to Ambergris and sped out of the room.

"Parise Ulfbinder asked about Drizzt specifically," Jarlaxle said to Kimmuriel sometime later, in a different room but still in the bowels of Illusk. "This is more than a coincidence."

"Even so," Kimmuriel replied, allowing his skepticism to show through. Jarlaxle had presented him with quite a bit of information in the last few moments, and with a proposal that seemed quite risky—and risky to more than Jarlaxle!

"This is bigger than Drizzt," Jarlaxle reminded him. "The lords of Netheril suspect something of great significance, and they seem to be interested in those they believe favored by the gods, and suspect that Drizzt might be among that group, as a chosen disciple of Lady Lolth."

Kimmuriel laughed aloud—a rare event for him indeed—at that notion.

"I know you think it preposterous," Jarlaxle said. "Surely it would seem so, but then, wouldn't Drizzt Do'Urden prove to be the perfect instigator of that which Lolth most dearly craves? He brought a great share of chaos to Menzoberranzan, after all.

"Nor is it even important whether or not this particular theory of Drizzt is true," Jarlaxle added. "All that matters is that the Shadovar believe it might be true, and given the movements of the Spider Queen of late, we would be remiss to let this pass."

"By that reasoning, if you go and find that Drizzt is alive, and somehow manage to bring him back, would we not be bound to turn him over to Tiago Baenre, or to your sister who rules Menzoberranzan?"

"Even if we were so bound, I would not," Jarlaxle replied honestly and bluntly. "Nor would I allow you to do so."

"Yet you ask so much of me and of Bregan D'aerthe."

"Yes," Jarlaxle answered evenly.

"You are mad. The cost will be enormous—are you willing to pay that for *iblith?*"

"Yes—to both, and I assure you that I am mad in both meanings of the word."

"Then I should relieve you of any command."

"Nay, you should grant me this, with the full force of Bregan D'aerthe."

"And how will House Baenre and the ruling council of Menzoberranzan view such an action?" Kimmuriel asked.

"Draygo Quick has him because he believes Drizzt to be the Chosen of Lolth. What good citizens of Menzoberranzan might Bregan D'aerthe be if we allowed that to stand?"

Kimmuriel could only laugh again at the unrelenting stubbornness of Jarlaxle.

"Send me to Gromph, I beg," Jarlaxle said.

Kimmuriel looked at him skeptically. "What you seek from your brother is outside the boundaries of your argument."

"I demand," Jarlaxle clarified. "And I will pay my dear brother with my own coin."

"And any risk this addition entails will be borne by Jarlaxle alone."

Jarlaxle nodded in agreement, and Kimmuriel closed his eyes, summoning the psionic powers to do as Jarlaxle had requested.

Jarlaxle awaited the magical gate eagerly—indeed, as eagerly as he had looked forward to anything since he had traveled back to the pit in Gauntlgrym with Drizzt, Bruenor, Dahlia, and Athrogate to put the fire primordial back in its magical prison. Jarlaxle felt alive once more.

He understood the odds, and the likelihood that he was far too late for the sake of any of those who had gone to the lair of Draygo Quick.

But Jarlaxle liked long odds. Indeed, he lived for them.

CHAPTER

22

AGNOSTICISM

"T ELL ME OF YOUR GODDESS," DRAYGO QUICK BADE DRIZZT ONE MORNING as they sat for a shared breakfast. "This one you name Mielikki."

"Are you asking me to proselytize?"

Draygo Quick shrugged. "Perhaps you will convert me. Do you think she would have me?"

Drizzt sat back and stared at Lord Draygo for a long while. "I believe that god is that which you find in your heart," he answered finally. "Were you to find Mielikki in your heart, were her tenets to sing to you as truth, then it wouldn't be within the power of any god to have you or reject you. Were you to come to believe those tenets, then you would be of Mielikki."

"You act as though the gods are no more than names for that which is in your heart."

Drizzt smiled and nodded, and went back to his food.

"You truly believe that?" Draygo Quick asked, sliding his chair back from the table.

"Does it matter?"

"Of course it matters!"

"Why?" Drizzt asked calmly. He realized that he was perturbing the old warlock, and he found that he quite enjoyed it.

"How can it not?" Draygo Quick replied. "Are you positing that, were I to discover these tenets of Mielikki, I would become one of her flock no matter my past?"

"If you found the truth of her tenets, then your past would be a trial of your own conscience, or a matter of justice in retribution for any crimes, but nothing to the goddess."

"That's absurd."

"Then what do her tenets matter?" Drizzt asked. "If a god, any god, is deemed to represent the universal and divine truth, then once one finds and truly embraces that truth, he becomes in harmony with the god. To hold it any other way is to attribute to supposed gods petty failings like jealousy or bitterness. If that is the case, then why would I pronounce the ultimate goodness of any such being? And worse, then why would I hold forth a name embodying that which is in my heart when doing so would only reduce a truth I call divine to a level of mortal frailty?"

Draygo Quick, too, slid back his chair and leaned back, scrutinizing the drow. "Well played," he congratulated.

"It's not a game."

"Because your goddess is supreme?"

"Because reason lies in harmony with truth, else truth is a lie."

"Hmm," Draygo Quick muttered. "It seems a shame that you focused your training on the martial arts."

"I will take that as a compliment."

"Oh, it was," Draygo Quick replied. "Or a lament."

"Are you now to ask me to proselytize the glories of the Spider Queen?" Drizzt asked. "That might prove a more interesting conversation."

Draygo Quick laughed at the sarcasm. "Nay," he answered. "Consider this talk over our breakfast as one last angle I pursued in order to wrest from Drizzt Do'Urden the truth of Drizzt Do'Urden. I had thought that truth a marvelous irony, and perhaps it is, but more likely, I fear, you're as boring as your preferred goddess."

It was Drizzt's turn to laugh—at Draygo Quick. "As boring as the sunrise and the sunset," Drizzt said quietly. "As boring as the movements of the moon, the planets, and the sparkles of the stars. As boring as the food chain and the place of every living creature within the interlocking hands that so bind them. As boring as birth and death, the ultimate tenet of this reason and morality I hold as Mielikki."

"I'm a warlock—do you forget? Perhaps I do consider death a lie."

"Because you can pervert it?"

Draygo Quick sighed and stood up. "It matters not," he announced, "for I grow weary of this conversation. Indeed, I find that I have lost interest in all of our conversations."

"Then let me go."

The old warlock laughed at him, and ended abruptly with, "No."

"Then kill me and be done with it."

"Again, no," Draygo Quick replied. "You're wrong about the gods of Toril, Drizzt. They are very real, and much more than mere embodiments of this or that tenet or truth."

"That does not change that which is in my heart."

"Or your fealty to Mielikki?

"My fealty to the truth and justice I know, which have been named to me as Mielikki. That is not a subtle difference."

Draygo Quick waved his hands frantically to silence Drizzt and end the conversation. "I have reason to believe the coming years will bring great events in flux," he said. "As great as those that brought Toril and Abeir together. I believe that, and I fear it. As great as the Spellplague and the advent of shadow. And I believe that you may have a place in these coming changes."

"I will sharpen my blades," the drow said with unrelenting sarcasm.

"Your blades are irrelevant. But your gods are not."

"I don't recognize gods—"

"I know, I know," Draygo Quick said, patting his hands once more. "You know truths, and those truths were given a name."

Drizzt resisted the urge to poke Draygo Quick once more by reminding him that he, after all, had brought it up again.

"You tell me of the path you follow, of the signposts of truth that guide you," Draygo Quick offered as a parting shot. "And I believe your sincerity. But I know more in matters of the world than you do, Drizzt Do'Urden, and I expect that this road you walk is a deceptive circle that will serve that which you reject more than that which you embrace.

"There, Drizzt Do'Urden, is your pathetic truth. I listened to the tales, your tale, that you told Effron in the cell when you were first captured. It comforts you to believe that your precious Mielikki carried away your wife and the halfling to some place of divine justice. Perhaps they are with her now!" He cackled wickedly and finished, "Or perhaps that was the greatest deception of all from a demon queen admired for deception."

He paused there, on the edge of leaving, and Drizzt knew that Draygo sought a reaction from him, and for a reason beyond any simplistic personal satisfaction. The best tests of character and commitment always came in moments of great stress and the most revealing moments often came in times when a person was pushed to anger.

"I know only that which is in my heart," Drizzt answered, evenly, refusing to take Draygo Quick's emotional bait. "When I do not fail, that is all that I follow."

The warlock left in a huff.

Drizzt sat in the room for a long while, chewing on that most-curious conversation. He didn't believe that he was any kind of Chosen, or anything significant at all—to Mielikki or to the Spider Queen, not in any positive way, at least, regarding the awful Lolth.

But Lord Draygo, a shade of no small accomplishment or power, thought otherwise, and that gave Drizzt pause. Mielikki had taken Catti-brie and Regis in a profound and strange way, after all, riding their ghosts out of Mithral Hall on the back of a spectral unicorn, ending their insane misery. And it was Mielikki who had done that, and no deception of Lolth, Drizzt had to believe.

But wouldn't Lolth be more than gleeful to so deceive him?

He shook the thought away. Had it been the doing of Lolth, then surely one or another of her minions would have revealed the ruse to Drizzt to torment him all the more. Indeed, if Drizzt was as special to Lady Lolth as Draygo Quick had insinuated, then why hadn't the priestesses of House Xorlarrin discovered his true identity when he had been captured by them in the bowels of Gauntlgrym?

It made no sense—none of this did—to Drizzt.

But whether he accepted Draygo Quick's premise or not seemed a moot point, for in either case, he wasn't going anywhere any time soon, absent Draygo Quick's blessing. There was no escape.

And even if there were, where might Drizzt escape to?

"You come well regarded by my associate in Shade Enclave," Lord Draygo told the curious visitor to his castle that typically-gloomy and rainy Shadowfell afternoon.

"I do appreciate your granting me this audience," Jarlaxle replied, and he tipped his great hat.

"I would admit that I'm surprised. I had thought that you and Lord Ulfbinder had concluded the trade contract."

"Indeed we did, and it was easy to find a place of mutual benefit," Jarlaxle replied. "That is not why I've come."

"Do tell." There was more than a little skepticism in Lord Draygo's tone, Jarlaxle recognized, and he knew that he had to be careful.

"I have knowledge regarding one who has become your . . . guest," Jarlaxle explained, and he watched the Netherese warlock carefully, hoping that his information, now quite dated, would still hold true and that Drizzt was still alive. After hearing the tale of Ambergris, Jarlaxle had spared little expense in trying to gain information regarding the fate of her companions, but even for Bregan D'aerthe, the castle of Lord Draygo Quick remained quite a mystery. Rumors in Gloomwrought whispered of Effron Alegni and another prisoner, and given Ambergris's tale, that other had to be Drizzt.

"Do tell," Lord Draygo prompted again.

"I have known Drizzt Do'Urden for more than a century," Jarlaxle explained.

"Friends?"

"Hardly!"

"Comrades?"

"Hardly! I am from Menzoberranzan, after all, and survive at the suffrage of the ruling council, particularly the fancies of House Baenre. Drizzt Do'Urden is no friend to House Baenre."

"Then why are you here?"

"Your inquiry," Jarlaxle explained. "You wish to determine if Drizzt is in the service of the Spider Queen." The drow mercenary was taking quite a leap, he knew, but from what Ambergris had relayed regarding Effron's claim and their journey here, and those things he had gleaned from his time with Parise Ulfbinder, it seemed a reasonable jump.

And Jarlaxle's suspicions were confirmed by Draygo Quick, unintentionally and reflexively, as the Netherese warlock eagerly leaned forward in his chair, before quickly collecting himself and settling back comfortably.

"Your Lady Lolth?" Draygo Quick innocently replied. "Is there not a drow goddess more clearly aligned with the actions of the goodly ranger?"

"Drizzt professes allegiance to the tenets of Mielikki, who is no drow deity," Jarlaxle replied. "The question, however, has ever been, to which, Mielikki or Lolth, does he truly serve—in action if not in heart?"

Draygo Quick assumed a pensive pose and nodded several times. "That is interesting," he admitted, though still feigning a removed posture, as if he hadn't considered it before.

Jarlaxle smiled at him to let him know without doubt that the drow saw through the ruse.

"You can find no answer in your inquiries," Jarlaxle stated bluntly. "Not from Drizzt, nor from any priestess or druid. Unless you can directly speak to a goddess, you will find yourself in the same dilemma as the rest of us who have long pondered the truth of this curious rogue."

"Do tell," Draygo Quick prompted, dropping his façade.

"You are familiar with Lolth's handmaidens?"

The warlock shook his head.

"The yochlols?" Jarlaxle clarified.

"I have heard of them, but I am not familiar with them in any detail."

"May I?" Jarlaxle asked, removing his great hat and turning it over, reaching his hand inside.

Draygo Quick looked at him curiously, and skeptically.

"I assure you that the creature is fully under my control at this time," Jarlaxle explained, and he pulled forth a circlet of black cloth, then tossed it

297

to the side. It elongated as it went, widening into a hole ten feet in diameter as it set down on Draygo Quick's floor. Jarlaxle bade the warlock to follow him to the rim of this portable hole.

The two peered in, to see what looked very much like a small stalagmite of oozing mud, but with two branch-like appendages waving menacingly and a large central eye staring back up at them.

"A handmaiden," Jarlaxle explained.

"You would bring such a powerful creature of the lower planes into my residence without permission?" Draygo Quick asked angrily.

"There is no danger, nor any implications to you, I assure you, Lord Draygo," Jarlaxle replied. "The handmaiden is my guest and not my captive."

"And pray tell, what does the handmaiden say?"

Jarlaxle looked down into the hole and nodded.

"Tiago!" the yochlol shouted in a bubbling voice, watery and stony at the same time, which seemed quite apropos given its apparent physical composition. It raised one limb and shook it fiercely as it spoke.

"Drizzt!" it said with the same timbre, lifting its other limb and similarly shaking it.

"Relax, dear lady," Jarlaxle cooed, patting his hands in the air above the creature, which seemed to be growing quite agitated.

"Bwahahaha!" the yochlol cried ominously.

"What?" Draygo Quick asked. "Tiago?"

"Tiago Baenre," Jarlaxle explained, and hurriedly scooped up the portable hole, which became a piece of black cloth once more, and stuffed it back into place inside his hat. "A powerful noble son of the First House of Menzoberranzan. He has decided to take it upon himself to hunt down and kill Drizzt Do'Urden."

"With the blessing of the matron mother?"

"Ah, there's the rub," Jarlaxle replied. "Matron Mother Quenthel does not hinder him, but I suspect that she does not even know of his intent. He has a minor priestess of Lolth at his side, however, though surely Lolth would cackle with glee if she favored Drizzt in this fight. Irony, chaos . . . they are the calling cards of that vicious one, after all."

"Then how is this relevant? Why should I care?"

"This confrontation will bring the questions filtering around the rogue to the forefront, and will demand a resolution," Jarlaxle explained. "Consider, if Tiago Baenre kills Drizzt, and Drizzt is favored by Lolth, the fallout will be clear and swift. And if Drizzt kills a favored son of House Baenre, the House will react violently—or it will not, and that will prove quite telling, given the matron mother's relationship with the Spider Queen. Simply put, Lord Draygo, your imprisonment of Drizzt is denying me the answer to a question I have been asking for a century and more, and indeed, denying you the answer to that very question you ask."

Lord Draygo stared at him incredulously. "You presume much."

"You have him," Jarlaxle stated.

"So you have claimed."

"He is dead, then, and our discussion is moot," Jarlaxle replied, and he dramatically spun and waved his arm toward the room's doorway, and the descending circular hallway beyond that would lead back to the grand entry hall of the castle. "When first I entered, I noted your castle guard holding Taulmaril, Drizzt's bow, the bow used by Drizzt's dead wife. He would not part with it for all the gold on Toril, nor would he allow any other to wield it. If you truly do not know the whereabouts of Drizzt Do'Urden, Lord Draygo, then take care, for I assure you that there is a very dangerous drow ranger lurking about your estate, intent on, and likely capable of, killing anyone standing between him and that particularly bow."

Draygo Quick stared at Jarlaxle for just a moment, then gave a sharp whistle. The room's door swung open and a pair of Draygo Quick's attendants, warlocks both, judging from their robes, hurriedly entered the chamber.

"Escort our guest to the west wing dining room and see that he is fed," Draygo Quick ordered. "I will not keep you waiting long," he promised Jarlaxle, "but I have some business to attend to."

Jarlaxle bowed low and followed his escorts out of the room and down the tower stairs, crossing back over the checkerboard-floored grand hall—where he listened most attentively for any sounds from below—and into the dining room opposite, where he was left alone.

So his hosts believed.

Draygo Quick will speak with Ulfbinder, Kimmuriel telepathically relayed to Jarlaxle. *Perhaps even to Quenthel.*

Not Quenthel, Jarlaxle silently replied. *He has no means to get to her as of now. You have found them?*

Yes.

All of them? Jarlaxle asked, focusing his thoughts on the first word for clear emphasis.

Two alive, three as stone, Kimmuriel confirmed.

Jarlaxle winced, then sighed.

If Draygo Quick releases Drizzt, you will not execute the attack, Kimmuriel relayed to him in no uncertain terms. *Not for the sake of humans and an elf!*

Jarlaxle blew another sigh, then looked up and painted a disarming smile on his face as an attendant entered with a tray of food.

Do you understand? Kimmuriel demanded.

"Yes," Jarlaxle said enthusiastically. "Truly I had not realized the extent of my hunger."

Kimmuriel relayed that he understood the double use of the affirmation, and then he was gone from Jarlaxle's mind, likely to let his disembodied thoughts wander the ways of Castle Draygo some more.

Jarlaxle could only hope, as Kimmuriel surely was, that the powerful Netherese warlock was not attuned to, or familiar with, or prepared against, such psionic intrusions.

So far, at least, all seemed well. Now, given Kimmuriel's last order, all Jarlaxle had to do was figure out a way to ensure that Lord Draygo would not let go of Drizzt without a fight.

***

"The handmaiden was an illusion," Draygo Quick told Parise Ulfbinder through his crystal ball.

"Jarlaxle lied to you, then, and apparently for the sake of Drizzt Do'Urden," Parise replied.

"But why? Is Drizzt more aligned to Bregan D'aerthe than we believe?"

Parise shook his head. "I would guess that this is more personal than professional with Jarlaxle. He is a curious one, full of many layers of intrigue all working in concert to form a meticulous spider web. The whole of Bregan D'aerthe is, above all else, pragmatic. By all accounts, they are a professional, if brutal, organization. I cannot believe that they would risk such a lucrative potential as the deal we signed for the sake of Drizzt Do'Urden."

"Yet he has done just that," said Draygo Quick. "I did not mask my annoyance, and still he persisted."

"Then there is something more."

Draygo Quick shrugged and did not disagree.

"Dangerous creatures are these drow," Parise Ulfbinder added.

"Are you hinting that I should release Drizzt to them?"

"Nay!" Parise replied without hesitation. "I would advise just the opposite. Admit nothing and release no one, and then we will scrutinize the reactions of Bregan D'aerthe henceforth. If Jarlaxle's claims are grounded even remotely in truth, then his failed attempt to secure Drizzt's release will likely be taken up by a higher authority."

"House Baenre," Draygo Quick reasoned.

"It would seem as if they hold a greater stake here, given the involvement of this young Tiago."

"It would seem prudent for them to have me keep Drizzt away from that one."

"Who can tell with these curious drow?" Parise replied. "We seek information above all else, and holding tight our cards will bring us many revelations, I expect."

"Revelations or enmity?" Draygo Quick reminded.

"Either way, we will learn much. If they push harder, then we can hand him over, and perhaps learn even more in the subsequent events. If House Baenre bothers to come for him, then we can be confident that the Spider Queen is involved, and perhaps then this battle between Drizzt and Tiago Baenre, of which Jarlaxle hinted, will indeed prove instructive."

"Until then, we hold the upper hand," Draygo Quick remarked.

"Do we?" Parise was quick to ask. "You have studied the sonnet."

Draygo Quick started to respond, but again merely shrugged.

The old shade draped the cloth over the crystal ball again, severing the connection, then sat back in his chair and glanced over at the glowing cage holding the shrunken Guenhwyvar.

So many gains, it seemed to him, had proven to be no more than illusion.

CHAPTER 23

A TOWERING VICTORY

YOU SHOULD JUST LET HIM GO," JARLAXLE SAID TO LORD DRAYGO, THE two standing in the checkerboard entry hall.

Draygo Quick put on an amused expression. He had just bid Jarlaxle farewell, after informing the drow that they had nothing further to discuss.

"You will better find your answers in that case," Jarlaxle continued. "And truly, if Drizzt is so favored by one god or another, what gain to you to keep him prisoner?"

"You presume much," Draygo Quick replied, a phrase he had thrown Jarlaxle's way on several occasions. Indeed, in their hours together, the Netherese lord had never admitted that Drizzt was within his castle.

But Jarlaxle knew better, for Kimmuriel had found Drizzt, and the young tiefling warlock, as well, in separate locked rooms in the western wing of the castle. Kimmuriel had found the others, statues all, as well, in a room not far from this very spot.

"If I am errant in my suspicions, then of course—" Jarlaxle started.

"And you annoy me even more," Draygo Quick continued. "Do be on your way, Jarlaxle, before I am tempted to speak with Lord Ulfbinder and nullify our agreement. Do not come to me again unless you are invited, or unless your request to pay a visit is accepted. Now, if you'll excuse me, or even if you will not, I have much work to do."

Jarlaxle bowed low. Draygo Quick acknowledged him with just a curt nod, and walked off across the floor to the doorway that would lead him to his tower and private quarters. Jarlaxle watched him, then glanced back at the sweeping stairwell in the rear of the hall, climbing up twenty feet and breaking left and right behind decorated railings.

No shortage of Shadovar guards stood up there, looking back at him, including one holding Taulmaril and another, amazingly, standing at the top of the staircase with one of Drizzt's scimitars strapped to his hip.

He is taunting me, Jarlaxle thought, and in his mind, he could sense Kimmuriel's discomfort as clearly as if the psionicist were standing beside him and groaning. *Tell me when,* Jarlaxle bade as Draygo Quick exited the room.

There are guards at the door in front of you, and more outside as well, Kimmuriel silently warned.

Jarlaxle bowed to the stern-faced sentries on the balcony, conveniently sweeping off his hat as he did.

Do not kill the lord, Kimmuriel telepathically cried.

Then guide my opening salvos properly, Jarlaxle replied. His hand slipped inconspicuously inside the hat, gripping the edge of the portable hole.

"I'll not be using your door," Jarlaxle announced to the guards as he turned back as if to exit the castle. "I have my own gate available."

"Just be gone, as Lord Draygo instructed," the guard commander on the stairs, the one with Drizzt's scimitar, shouted down.

Jarlaxle smiled and pulled forth the portable hole, set his hat back on his bald head, and flipped the spinning and elongating hole in the general direction of the guards flanking the castle exit. The two widened their eyes in unison and hustled aside in fear, but the hole plopped down on the floor short of them without any overtly ill effects, and now seemed no more than an actual hole in the castle floor.

With the obvious distraction demanding the attention of all in the grand hall, Jarlaxle slipped his hand into a pouch and produced a small cube—and reminded himself that his brother Gromph had promised him all sorts of pain if he ruined this particular device.

Draygo is safely ascending his tower, Kimmuriel imparted.

Jarlaxle was already grinning, seeing the door sentries edging over to the curious pit, unable to resist the urge to peek in. The mercenary tossed the cube toward the door where Draygo Quick had exited, and turned back to the guards on the balcony.

" 'With abacus, by architect, by carpenter, and mason,' " he recited, sweeping his arm out with dramatic flourish, and at the same time tapping his House insignia to enact a spell of levitation and lift himself conveniently and prudently from the castle floor, he reiterated and elaborated his song:

> With all the tools and knowledge of structural design,
> "For shelter most beloved, for love of hearth and home
> "To build your private castle, to whom would you consign?"

Act now, you peacock! Kimmuriel screamed in his thoughts, which only made Jarlaxle smile all the wider.

"Might I suggest that all the tools
"The mundane numbers and physical rules
"For the truly brilliant must remain
"No more than province of common fools."

"A castle, and warmth, a true abode,
"For when one truly seeks a home,
"The wise call upon the greater souls
"Who wile their days with a nose in a tome."

"What foolishness is this?" the guard on the stairs demanded.

"Foolishness?" Jarlaxle echoed as if wounded. "My friend, this is no such thing." A yelp from behind him told Jarlaxle that the door guards had reached the edge of his pit and had glanced in. "Nay, this . . . this is *Caer Gromph!*"

Caer Gromph, the last two words of the incantation, rang with a different resonance than the playful mercenary's chanting verse, for they spoke not to the audience, but to the magical cube Jarlaxle had tossed. Upon absorbing those command words, spoken in that manner, the magic of the cube awakened. The ground beneath their feet began to tremble, though of course the floating Jarlaxle remained unperturbed above it, and Castle Draygo began to shake as Caer Gromph's roots reached into the floor, as the cube transformed into an adamantine tower, designed to resemble the stalagmite towers of the drow Houses of Menzoberranzan.

Up it rose, and widened, crushing and splintering the floor and substructure of Castle Draygo with its roots, blowing out the wall and prodding up under the balcony as its unyielding walls stretched, its adamantine tip piercing the ceiling of the grand room nearly thirty feet above the floor. The Shadovar guards lurched and tumbled under the thunder of the magical creation. One of the pair peeked over the lip of the portable hole and tumbled in, and the other soon followed as a yochlol-like tentacle reached up and aided him in his descent, accompanied by a shriek from the guard and a hearty "bwahaha" from the supposed handmaiden.

A thing of beauty was Caer Gromph. Lined with balconies and a circular stair running its length, top-to-bottom, and edged in faerie fire accents of purple, red, and blue, it seemed as much a work of abstract art as a fortress. But a fortress it was, complete with lines of arrow slits and a magical gate inside, and the moment the construct expanded, Bregan D'aerthe archers poured through the magical portal inside and to their protected posts. Before the many Shadovar had even pinpointed the source of the earthquake, crossbow quarrels flew forth from those arrow slits, coated with that insidious drow poison.

One who was not cut down by either the shaking or the volley was the guard holding Taulmaril, and indeed, because of the way the balcony had buckled, the male shade found himself protected from the hidden drow archers. Regaining his footing, he leveled the powerful bow and took deadly aim at Jarlaxle, who floated in place hovering just above the floor below and watched the swordsman on the now-tilted stairs.

He would never see the enchanted arrow coming, the archer knew, and he pulled back and let fly, the arrow flying true to the hollow in Jarlaxle's breast.

Draygo Quick was not amused as he tumbled backward down the circular stairs of his private tower. He collected himself quickly, hearing the doors above banging open and the frantic calls of his fast-approaching acolytes.

"Lord Draygo, what is it?" one cried, coming around the bend above him.

What, indeed, Draygo Quick wondered? What had that wretched drow done to him? Done to his castle?

The old warlock spun around and ran off the way he had come with surprising agility and energy for one of his age. He had barely gotten off the tower stairs and through the door to the anteroom, though, when he was met by another of his warlock acolytes, coming the other way, his face drained of blood, his eyes wide with horror.

"A . . . a tower, my lord!" the man screamed.

"The tower?" Draygo asked and glanced back the way he had come.

The acolyte shook his head frantically. "A tower!" he corrected, and he hustled back through the room's other door, opening the way for Lord Draygo to see the black adamantine wall of Caer Gromph.

"By the gods," Draygo Quick breathed. "Invasion."

He called his acolytes together, bade them to form as one on and around the stairs, and to defend to the death his tower and quarters. Then he sprinted off, back up the tower stair, rushing to his private rooms to put out the call to war. He burst through the door to his inner room, and there he froze, stricken with shock.

For flanking the pedestal on which rested the cage of Guenhwyvar were two most unexpected and unannounced visitors, tall humanoids with three-fingered hands and heads that resembled the bulbous ugliness of an octopus.

One turned his way, those tentacles waggling, arms waving, and a blast of psionic energy assaulted the warlock and jumbled his thoughts. He tried to fight through, instinctively enacting his mental defenses—and indeed, the inner willpower of the powerful old warlock proved superior to the attack. As he unwound the scene before him, his vision refocusing, he found a second shock, and a second accompanying psionic blast, to see his prized glowing cage break apart and Guenhwyvar, six hundred pounds of feline power, appearing atop the pedestal, which toppled under her weight. Draygo Quick surely recognized the visceral hatred in the panther's stare, and when she sprang, the warlock thought himself doomed.

But Guenhwyvar dissipated into mist in mid-leap, and that mist swirled and blew away, taking the beleaguered panther to her Astral home at long last.

Both illithids turned on Draygo Quick, and in the hands of the second, he saw the panther figurine. Both waved their ugly tentacles his way, and both similarly disappeared, into the ether.

Draygo Quick fell back, overwhelmed and terrified, full of fear and full of rage.

From the breaking railings came the dragonnettes, from the cracking ceiling came the castle gargoyles, and from the tower, in response, came a hail of drow fireballs, lightning bolts, magic missiles, and crossbow bolts.

Down below that level, the lightning missile slammed into Jarlaxle's chest, the sparkling explosion lighting the room in a blinding flash, and before the drow's vision had even recovered from that glare, a second hit right beside the first.

Jarlaxle looked down at his chest, then back at the archer, now with a third arrow leveled his way.

"You shoot well," he congratulated, and the Shadovar, clearly confused and shocked and horrified, let fly again, and again his aim was true.

And again, Jarlaxle took the hit without any apparent ill effects. Indeed, he wasn't even paying attention at that moment, reveling in the efficiency of his army, and the macabre beauty of smoking and burning forms of tiny dragons spinning down to the floor.

In leaped the swordsman, Twinkle up high and glowing fiercely. He brought it across in a powerful sweep, slashing the distracted Jarlaxle across the face.

But not a mark, not a speck of blood, showed in the blade's deadly wake.

"Have you ever heard of a kinetic barrier?" the drow asked innocently.

The shade howled and lifted the blade to strike again, and Jarlaxle made no move to defend. The blade struck him just an instant after he merely touched the shade guard, and in that touch, he released all of the killing energy of the three bowshots and the first scimitar strike that had been captured by the kinetic barrier Kimmuriel had enacted over him.

307

The shade's face fell in half. His chest exploded, once, twice, thrice, and he flew away behind a crimson cloud of his own spraying blood.

Twinkle did strike, but with minimal force, but still Jarlaxle was much relieved to realize that Kimmuriel still had his protective barrier in place.

The drow mercenary turned to the archer, a wry grin on his face. Jarlaxle dropped his levitation, touched down, leaped away and called forth the floating spell once more, his stride lifting him toward the distant balcony.

Frantically and foolishly, the archer fired off another shot, and another, and Jarlaxle felt the energy mounting around him once more.

A Shadovar body flew up out of the pit and plopped onto the floor. The second dead door guard followed closely, and both had been wrapped by one end of a fine elven cord.

Now the corpses served as anchors and out of the portable hole pit came Athrogate, no longer in the guise of a yochlol. The ferocious dwarf got his feet under him just as the castle's outside door banged open and more guards charged in.

"Taked ye long enough!" the dwarf roared in glee, his morningstars sweeping across to send the nearest shade flying away.

Athrogate grunted a moment later, though, and looked down as his arm, and the handcrossbow bolt impaled there.

"Hmm," he muttered. "Durned drow."

The air around him buzzed with more such darts whipping all around, most striking home on those Shadovar standing before him.

"Poison," slurred the closest, and Athrogate regarded him to see a bolt sticking out of the shade's cheek, just under the poor fool's left eye.

The dwarf reached up and tore the bolt free of the Shadovar's face, flipped it over, and put it in his mouth, where he sucked on it hard. Wearing an inquisitive expression, he tossed the bolt aside to the floor and swirled the venom around in his mouth, nodding his agreement with the assessment.

"Aye," he said after he spat out the poison and a wad of spittle. "And I'm bettin' that one hurt."

The Shadovar fell over to the floor, fast asleep. So did several others, but a few, at least, managed to fight through the waves of drow poison. Still, the poison slowed their movements and made their blocks and parries quite sluggish, and so Athrogate, who had of course built up a complete resistance to drow sleep poison in his decades beside Jarlaxle, waded through them with wild abandon, swatting them aside with his powerful morningstars.

Behind him, the drow warriors came forth from their fortress, though none moved to join the wild and unpredictable dwarf as he gleefully executed his own brand of carnage.

"Truly?" Jarlaxle asked incredulously as the archer put up Taulmaril for a point blank shot at him. He had already absorbed three other arrows on his journey to face this shade and showed no ill-effects.

The poor shade trembled so badly that the arrow slipped off the bow.

"Just give it over," Jarlaxle said, holding out his hand. He noted, then, that the Shadovar wore, too, a fabulous mithral shirt he had seen before. "Oh, and my friend's shirt, as well."

To emphasize his point, Jarlaxle turned to meet the swoop of a gargoyle, and released all of the stored kinetic energy into the creature, which verily exploded under the weight of the blow, leaving no more than a burst of tiny stones flying around to shower the balcony and the room below.

"Truly?" he again asked the shade, who desperately tried to set another arrow.

The fool finally caught on, and handed over the bow with a hand shaking so badly that Jarlaxle had to work hard to suppress a laugh.

"And the mithral shirt," he instructed. "And anything else you might possess that belonged to my imprisoned friends! Indeed, strip yourself naked then run around and collect all of their items, and I warn you that if any are missing, you will follow the fate of the gargoyle!"

The shade let out a little whimper, tossed a ring and some bracers atop the pile of clothing, then shuffled away, bowing with every step.

"All of them!" Jarlaxle shouted after him.

"Well met, Lord Draygo," the drow said to the startled warlock after he materialized in Draygo Quick's private room, right near where the illithids had been standing.

Draygo Quick eyed him both studiously and incredulously. The warlock considered his options, wondering mostly if those dangerous illithids were still around. There weren't many creatures in the known multiverse that could unnerve Draygo Quick, but he counted the octopus-headed mind flayers among that group, to be sure.

The door behind him opened and one of his students gasped.

Draygo Quick held up his hand to keep the young warlock at bay.

"Bid her to close the door and be gone," the drow instructed. "My associates and I have little time, and I would speak with you alone."

"Speak?" Draygo Quick replied suspiciously.

"Lord Draygo, be reasonable here," said the drow. "We are both businessmen, in the end."

"Kimmuriel," Draygo Quick breathed, and it all made sense to him. Kimmuriel Oblodra of Bregan D'aerthe was rumored to be a psionicist of considerable power, and that would explain his association with the mind flayers, the most psionically-gifted creatures of all.

"At your service," Kimmuriel confirmed.

"At *your* service, you mean," Lord Draygo replied. "You dare attack a lord of Netheril with such impudence? You dare enter my private quarters and steal from me, before my very eyes?"

"Your minion," Kimmuriel prompted, motioning to the door.

"And if I choose to allow her to stay, perhaps to call in others?"

"Then I will fade away from here, and you will have nothing to show for the losses you have suffered this day," Kimmuriel answered, and he held up the onyx figurine of the now-freed Guenhwyvar. "Alas, the considerable losses."

The implication that there might be some gain to be found here was hard to ignore. "Be gone!" Draygo Quick snapped at his acolyte after mulling it over. Should it come to a fight, that one wouldn't be of much help against this drow of such reputation, or against the illithids in any case, Draygo Quick knew.

"My lord!"

"Be gone!" Draygo Quick cried again.

"But the dark elves have taken the whole of the castle beyond this tower!" the woman cried. "And we are trapped here, blocked by an adamantine wall!"

Draygo Quick leaped up from his chair and spun angrily on the young female shade, his eyes wide and nostrils flaring. Rare were such outbursts from the composed and powerful lord, and this one had the desired effect, as the younger shade gave a squeal of terror and fled, slamming the door.

Draygo Quick took a few breaths to compose himself, then turned back to face Kimmuriel.

"How dare you?" he asked quietly.

"We have done you a favor, and the rewards will prove greater than the inconveniences we have caused," Kimmuriel replied.

"By attacking my castle?"

"Indeed, to provide you proper cover to the lord of Gloomwrought and your peers for the loss of Drizzt and the others, for of course, that is why we have come. The damage to your abode is no doubt considerable—that is

Jarlaxle's way, I fear. His belief is that the best way to end any battle is to win it quickly, with overwhelming force, and so, as usual, he has."

"If you think me defeated, you know little of Draygo Quick."

"Please, Lord Draygo, remain reasonable," Kimmuriel replied with clear condescension—or perhaps it was just supreme confidence, Draygo thought.

"Your castle can be repaired, and we will kill as few of the fools you employ as possible. So yes, there is a bit of inconvenience to you—but it need not be more than that, and surely not as tragic as it might become if you place your pride before your pragmatism.

"We have come at the behest of . . . well, let us just say that Lady Lolth will not be denied that which is hers. I doubt that you wish such a war as you might find if you follow the path of your pride."

"Lady Lolth?" Draygo Quick asked, and he didn't hide his intrigue. "For Drizzt?"

"It should not concern you," Kimmuriel said.

"Then he is Chosen."

Kimmuriel shook his head. "I make no such claim."

"But Lady Lolth—"

"Has her own designs, and only a fool would pretend to understand those," said Kimmuriel. "Nor does it matter. Here is my offer, and I will make it only this one time: Remain here in your private rooms while we finish our work. Stand down with your remaining forces—not that you have much choice in the matter, in any case. We will be gone soon enough."

"With treasures," Draygo Quick noted, and he nodded toward the onyx figurine.

Kimmuriel shrugged as if it should not matter.

"You wish to know whether Drizzt is favored by Mielikki or Lolth," the drow said.

"You possess that knowledge?"

"I possess insights that go to the question you hope to clarify by garnering that knowledge," Kimmuriel answered. "Indeed, I hold answers that will make the question of Drizzt Do'Urden's allegiance or favor irrelevant to you."

Draygo Quick swallowed hard.

"I have come from the hive mind of the illithids," Kimmuriel explained, and Draygo swallowed hard again, for surely, if any creatures in the known multiverse had any answers to the fate of Abeir-Toril, it would be that group.

"So we have a deal?" Kimmuriel asked.

"You will finish and be gone? And what else?"

"You will hold to the agreement that Jarlaxle forged with Lord Parise Ulfbinder."

"Nonsense!" Draygo Quick blurted. "You cannot wage war and smilingly sign a trade agreement in the same moment!"

"We did not wage war," Kimmuriel corrected. "We came to retrieve that which does not belong to you—"

"Drizzt and his companions assaulted my castle! By my right of defense do I claim those spoils!"

"And in the process," Kimmuriel continued, ignoring the rant, "we have saved you from the wrath of one far less merciful, or at least, of one far less interested in allowing you to continue to draw breath. This raid, Lord Draygo, has surely saved your life."

Draygo Quick sputtered, unable to even find the words to strike back.

"But we do not expect your gratitude, just your good sense," Kimmuriel continued. "We have provided you with cover, and I will offer to you an understanding of that which is happening between the Shadowfell and Toril beyond anything Drizzt Do'Urden might have provided."

"So you have done me a favor, provided me cover and saved my life," Draygo Quick said skeptically, "and you offer one more gift, and all in exchange for a few baubles and a prisoner?"

"I would hope for much more from you."

"Do tell."

"When I give to you my insights, you will understand that both of our respective groups, Bregan D'aerthe and you and your fellow lords of Netheril, will benefit greatly from our alliance."

"How do I know you are not lying to me?"

Kimmuriel's expression remained, as always, impassive. "Why would I need to do so? Your tower is full of unseen illithids, all eager to feast on the brains of shades. By my word alone are you and your acolytes protected."

"The illithids answer to a dark elf?" the warlock asked doubtfully.

"In this instance, yes."

The way Kimmuriel said it, so matter-of-factly, erased any doubts in Draygo Quick, and he realized that this offered deal was the best he was going to get.

"Good," Kimmuriel answered, and only then did Draygo Quick realize that the drow psionicist was reading his thoughts.

"I will return to you within a tenday," Kimmuriel promised. "For now, keep your minions in this tower if you wish to keep them safe."

Draygo Quick started to protest, but Kimmuriel turned around and walked away, right through the tower wall.

Lord Draygo fell back into his chair, full of venom, but full, too, of intrigue.

CHAPTER 24

AFTERSHOCK

D RIZZT WAITED, CROUCHED DEFENSIVELY, UNSURE OF HIS SITUATION. THE room had shaken violently—the drow couldn't imagine what had caused such a rumble. His thoughts shot back to the cataclysm that had flattened the city of Neverwinter, the volcano that had thrown him from his feet with its incredible shockwave.

Was this, then, some similar natural, or primordial, disaster?

Drizzt stayed on his toes, listening, watching, knowing that he might have to spring away on an instant's notice. Perhaps another earthquake would split the wall asunder and drop the ceiling. Would he be quick enough to get free of the crash? And perhaps such a leap and sprint would garner him his freedom beyond Draygo Quick's crumbling walls.

But then what?

Soon after, the drow heard running outside his door, and shouts of protest, followed swiftly by grunts and groans and the all-too familiar thud of a body collapsing to the hard floor.

"An attack," he whispered, and no sooner had the words escaped his lips than his room's door swung in.

Drizzt tensed, ready to attack. Then he gasped, his thoughts spinning in a jumbled swirl, so much so that he tried to speak out a name, but barely made a squeak.

"Wonderful to see you again, as well," Jarlaxle replied with a wry grin. "I have missed you, my old friend."

"What? How?" Drizzt sputtered. Aside from all the implications of this unexpected encounter, Drizzt had thought Jarlaxle killed in Gauntlgrym. The sight of this one, another tie to a long-lost time, overwhelmed him and he simply could not contain his relief. He leaped across and wrapped Jarlaxle in a great hug.

"Ambergris," Jarlaxle explained. "She alone escaped the castle of Draygo Quick, and she guided me back to this place."

"But you died in Gauntlgrym!"

"I did?" Jarlaxle stepped back and looked at his arms and torso. "I fear I must disagree."

Now Drizzt eyed him suspiciously. "This is a trick of Draygo Qui—"

Jarlaxle's laughter cut him short. "My suspicious friend, be at ease. Recall the day of your escape from Menzoberranzan those decades ago, after you and Catti-brie dropped a stalactite through the roof of House Baenre's chapel. Did I not show you then that I am a friend full of surprises? I will tell you all about the events of Gauntlgrym and beyond, but at another time. For now, let us leave this place."

Drizzt mulled that over for a few moments and knew then that this was indeed Jarlaxle, the real, living Jarlaxle, come to rescue him.

"The earthquake? You caused it?"

"You will see, soon enough," Jarlaxle promised. "But here." He pulled a pouch from his belt and upended it, and all sorts of items—a bow and quiver, a pair of scimitars and a belt to hold them, boots, a mithral shirt, a unicorn pendant, a pair of magical bracers—tumbled forth, though few of those could have even fit in the small belt pouch had it not been powerfully enchanted. "I believe this is all of your gear, but my many companions are searching in case we have missed anything."

Drizzt looked at the pile incredulously, but knew with only that cursory glance, of course, that something was indeed missing.

"And there is this," Jarlaxle said, and Drizzt snapped his gaze back up, to see the drow mercenary holding forth the ring fashioned of pure ruby that Drizzt had taken from the Xorlarrin wizard. "Do you know what this is?"

"A mage's bauble, I would expect."

Jarlaxle nodded. "And of no small power. Keep it safe." He flipped it to Drizzt, who caught it and slipped it upon his finger.

"And this," Jarlaxle added, and when Drizzt looked up, the smiling mercenary held that which he wanted above all else, the onyx figurine of Guenhwyvar. He handed it over to Drizzt's trembling hands.

"She is free now," Jarlaxle explained. "Draygo Quick's bondage of her to this plane is no more, and she rests comfortably in her Astral home, recovering, and awaiting your call."

Drizzt felt his knees going weak beneath him, and he stumbled back and fell into a chair, thoroughly overwhelmed. "Thank you," he mouthed, over and over again.

"We're not done," Jarlaxle explained. "We must be gone from this place."

"Effron—" Drizzt started to reply.

"Our next stop," Jarlaxle assured him, patting a pouch on his other hip, one similar to that which had held Drizzt's possessions. "Gather your gear and come along. Dress as we go and be prepared for battle, for the fight might not yet be fully won."

By the time the pair reached Effron's room, which was guarded now by Bregan D'aerthe warriors, Drizzt had his bow in hand, and all of his gear back in place. It was all he could manage to resist blowing the whistle to summon Andahar, so badly did he wish to see his unicorn steed once more. A sense of normalcy leaped at his heart and mind, and yet, at the same time, it all seemed even more strange now, like knowing the roads that would lead to a place where you had once lived, only to discover that it is no longer your home.

He just wasn't sure. More than anything, he wanted to bring in Guenhwyvar, wanted to find the constancy of her thick fur and muscular flank, but he knew that he should not. He recalled the last time he had seen her, so haggard and appearing near death, and decided that he would let a tenday pass, or more even, before he called to her.

He glanced up at the sound of a crash, and saw Effron's gear lying on the floor before the obviously-startled tiefling warlock.

"You killed Draygo Quick?" Effron breathlessly asked.

"You would like that?" Jarlaxle replied.

Effron looked at him curiously for just a moment, then admitted, "No."

Jarlaxle's smile and nod caught Drizzt by surprise, making him suspect that the drow's question might have been some kind of test. He let it go, however, for they obviously had more to do.

And indeed, Jarlaxle led them off immediately, back the way he had come, and soon to enter the grand entry hall. Drizzt and Effron could only stare in disbelief at the new addition of an adamantine tower, standing amidst the crumbled floor and wall as if some giant had thrown it like a spear into the structure.

"Well met again, elf!" Athrogate the dwarf roared, bounding over to properly greet Drizzt.

"You fell into the pit, in Gauntlgrym," Drizzt said. "Both of you."

"Aye, and taked me a year to grow back me beard, durned fire beast, bwahahaha!" Athrogate replied.

"I foresee many nights about the hearth, drink in hand," Jarlaxle said. "But those are for another world, not this one." He swept his arm out toward the open tower door. "Athrogate will show you to the gate."

"Gate?" Effron asked.

315

"To Luskan," Jarlaxle explained, and he pushed Drizzt and Effron along. "Keep beside them," he instructed Athrogate. "I will be along presently."

"Only if the elf puts in a good word for meself with that pretty young Ambergris," Athrogate said, and he tossed an exaggerated wink Drizzt's way.

Overwhelmed again—or still, actually—Drizzt could only nod stupidly and follow along. He put his hand on his own belt pouch then slipped it inside, needing to feel the contours of the Guenhwyvar figurine and the promise of a true friend recovered.

Most of the drow were gone now, but Jarlaxle wasn't finished. He kept the magical tower of Caer Gromph in place, and could only hope that Lord Draygo had taken Kimmuriel's words to heart.

Off Jarlaxle went through a series of small chambers in the back left corner of the grand entry. Kimmuriel had shown him the way and it seemed as if there would be few obstacles or sentries blocking him, but still he was nervous, more so than at any other point in this rescue mission.

It wasn't Draygo Quick causing the beads of sweat—so rare a sight!—on his forehead. It wasn't the prospect of guards, or even facing a brutal enemy he knew to be around.

No, it was the prospect of facing the one he hoped to save.

He wound down to the castle's substructure and moved along a long corridor to a trio of doors. Before them lay four more of Draygo Quick's sentries, bound and gagged, two awake and the others still under the effects of the drow sleep poison.

Jarlaxle tipped his hat to them as he stepped over them to the center door. He took a deep breath and he pushed through, taking care to softly close the door behind him. He had come into a large cellar full of low archways, connecting the massive stone supports for the castle. Fortunately, Caer Gromph hadn't sunk its roots into this portion of the castle.

Jarlaxle moved slowly, keeping close to the stone buttresses, trying to get a feel of the dusty and ancient catacombs. The smell of decay hung thick in here, and many crypts lined the walls, open to the main area, their skeletal remains lying in a state of eternal rest, many with arms crossed, others with bones fallen away. Rusty swords and tarnished crowns, tattered and decayed robes and crawly things flitted around the edges of Jarlaxle's lowlight vision, but the gloom was too complete for him to get an accurate view of the place. He crouched beside one of the low archways and pulled a little ceramic ball out of his belt pouch. He brought it up to his lips and whispered the command, then tossed it deeper into the catacomb.

The ball rolled and bounced and burst into flame as it settled, spitting sparks as it lit the dust around it, and flickering with the intensity of a torch, casting strange shadows all around.

"Come and play, pretty lady," Jarlaxle said quietly.

He froze in place and listened, and thought something or someone had shuffled behind another low archway not so far from him.

"Do be reasonable," he said, moving that way, but his words were more of an afterthought, for his concentration surely lay elsewhere.

He came up near that low archway and paused, shadows dancing.

Suddenly, one of those shadows wasn't a shadow, but the medusa leaping out at him as he spun around to meet the charge, her red eyes wide, her killing gaze falling over him.

Jarlaxle saw her in all of her awful glory, and he knew without doubt that only his eyepatch had saved him in that instance, that without its powerful dweomer, his skin would already be turning to stone. He called upon his innate drow abilities, his affinity to the magical emanations of the Underdark, and brought forth a globe of impenetrable darkness around him and the medusa, stealing her most powerful weapon.

At the same time, his left hand pumped, his bracer feeding him daggers to throw out at his foe, and he caught a dagger in his right hand as well, and snapped his wrist to elongate the weapon into a sword, which he put out before him, hoping to keep the medusa and her hair of living, poisonous snakes back from him.

When he didn't strike her with his prodding weapon, he thrust out further, and still hit nothing but the empty air, and he knew that his foe had slipped aside.

Totally blind and totally helpless were not the same thing with Jarlaxle. He had committed the area to crystal-clear memory, and now he moved without hesitation, slipping down and around to get under the archway, an opening no higher than his shoulders. He came out of the magical darkness as soon as he crossed under, throwing his back against the buttress stone.

He nearly faltered, however, for from this new vantage, he noted before him the man he had called a friend for decades,

Artemis Entreri stood perfectly still, of course, though he had surely been in the midst of movement when he had looked at the medusa. He was angled and up against Dahlia's side, as if trying to knock her aside, and it didn't take much imagination for Jarlaxle to picture the scene that had led to this tragedy.

The distraction almost cost Jarlaxle dearly, for he noted the pursuit of the medusa only at the last instant. He leaped away and spun around to face his nemesis, but not to look at her, instead leveling a wand at the level of her head. He listened intently to the hissing approach of her snakes as she moved into range to strike at him as he spoke the command word, then breathed a sigh of relief when that hissing abruptly ceased and he heard the medusa stumble backward.

Jarlaxle dared open his eye to see the powerful creature struggled and staggering, her head engulfing in a blob of viscous goo, and her hands, too, had become fast stuck as she had tried to scrape the sticky stuff away.

One of the snakes wriggled free of the goo, waving at Jarlaxle menacingly, though the medusa was too far away for it to strike at him.

Still, that freed serpent might guide his foe, he realized, uncertain of the relationship between a medusa and those snakes, or whether she might, perhaps, see through the creature's eyes. So he fired another glob at her, this one capturing her midsection and pinning her back against the side of the stone archway.

He thought to go and finish her off, but held back, figuring that perhaps Lord Draygo would be more agreeable in their future encounters if he let the wretched and powerful creature live. He watched for a few more moments, until he was certain that she was truly and fully caught.

Jarlaxle turned to the statues, and quickly located the third, that of Afafrenfere, not so far away. From another of his many pouches, the drow mercenary produced a large jug and set it on the floor halfway between the monk and the other two.

He took a deep breath, unsure as to whether this would work. Even Gromph, who had fashioned it for him, could offer no guarantees. And even if it did work, the archmage had warned, the conversion of flesh to stone, then back to flesh, brought with it such a tremendous shock to the body that many would not survive one or the other transmutations.

"Entreri and Dahlia," the drow whispered to himself, trying to garner his resolve. "Hearty souls." He looked at the monk and could only shrug, for he cared little for the stranger.

He popped the cork off the jug and stepped back as smoke began to pour forth, filling the area and obscuring his vision. His first indication that his powerful brother had succeeded was the sound of jostling, as Entreri and Dahlia, flesh once more, stumbled and tumbled, trying to extract themselves from the tangle.

Entreri cried out, "No!" and Dahlia merely cried out, and from the other side, the monk leaped into view, landing in a defensive crouch, one arm up to shield his eyes, the other cocked to strike.

"Be at ease, my friends," Jarlaxle said, stepping forward and scooping up the jug as the fog began to dissipate. "The battle is won."

"You!" Entreri cried, clearly horrified and outraged, and launched himself at Jarlaxle.

"Artemis!" Dahlia interrupted, and interrupted, too, Entreri's charge, blocking his way.

"You are quite welcome," Jarlaxle said dryly.

"Who are you?" Dahlia demanded.

"Jarlaxle!" Entreri answered before the drow could.

"At your service," Jarlaxle agreed, sweeping low in a bow. "Indeed, already at your service," he added, and he snapped his finger, breaking another magical ceramic torch. He dropped it to the floor as it flared to life, revealing the stuck medusa clearly to the others. Still she struggled against the stone buttress, one menacing snake coiled atop her goo-covered head.

"You would ask for gratitude," Entreri spat at him.

"Call us even, then," Jarlaxle replied. "Or leave our squabble for another time and place, when we are safely away from Lord Draygo and his minions."

Dahlia looked back at him, clearly alarmed, as did Afafrenfere.

"Come," Jarlaxle bade them. "It is time to go. You have been here a long time."

"How is this possible?" Dahlia asked, glancing all around at the unfamiliar catacomb. "We were in the room, the checkerboard floor. Drizzt and Effron fell—"

"They are well," Jarlaxle assured her. "They have already escaped back to Luskan."

"How long?" Afafrenfere asked.

"The three of you have served as decorations for Castle Draygo for many months," Jarlaxle explained. "For more than a year. It is the spring of 1466 on Toril."

Three stunned expressions came back at him, for even Entreri seemed sobered by the news.

"Quickly," Jarlaxle bade them. "Before the medusa wriggles free, or Lord Draygo finds us." He started away at a brisk clip, the other three falling in line.

Afafrenfere and Dahlia both gasped when they came back into the checkerboard entry hall, to see a tower construct blocking the far wall, but loudest of all, and most satisfying to Jarlaxle by far, was the resigned sigh offered by Artemis Entreri, who knew Jarlaxle well enough to not need any detailed explanations.

"Inside you go," Jarlaxle explained, stepping aside and motioning to the tower door and a drow soldier standing guard. "He will show you to the gate, and the gate will show you to Luskan."

"Ambergris!" Afafrenfere said. "I will not leave without her!"

"Your gallant dwarf friend was the one who led me here, of course," Jarlaxle replied.

"Effron and Drizzt?" Dahlia demanded.

"Likely with Ambergris by now, and yes, back in the City of Sails. Now, be gone, I beg."

Afafrenfere and Dahlia both looked to Entreri.

"Trust him," the assassin admitted. "For what choice do we have? And indeed," he added, staring hard at the most-hated Jarlaxle, "only because we have no other choice."

The monk and Dahlia started for the tower, but Entreri held back, and paced to stand right before Jarlaxle. "I have not forgotten what you did to me," he said. "Nor the years of torment I suffered because of your cowardice."

"There is more to the story," Jarlaxle assured him. "Someday, perhaps, you will hear the tale in full."

"I doubt that," Entreri replied with a snarl and he started after his companions. He glanced back a couple of times, but seemed more to be watching out warily for Jarlaxle, as if expecting the drow to stab him in the back—literally this time.

Jarlaxle said no more and just let him go. He had hoped that his daring, and expensive, rescue might put him on even footing with the man once more, but he had always known that hope to be rooted more in his heart than in his reason.

Artemis Entreri had been tortured for decades as Herzgo Alegni's slave, and Jarlaxle had little argument against the truth that much of Entreri's suffering had been his fault.

Artemis Entreri was not a forgiving man.

A signal flash in the tower's second floor showed Jarlaxle that the trio and the remaining guards had gone through the magical portal back to Toril.

With a quick chant, the drow dismissed the tower, which reverted to a mere cube on the floor, and more than a bit of Castle Draygo rained down from above as the intervening structure disappeared. The room's grand balcony crashed down in ruins. When the rumbling ended, Jarlaxle realized that he was not alone, and indeed it was Kimmuriel who walked in from the castle's far wing to scoop up Gromph's toy.

"Are you quite finished?" Kimmuriel asked with rare sarcasm, tossing the cube to Jarlaxle.

"You have brought Lord Draygo to an understanding?"

"He desperately desires the answers that I am uncovering in my commune with the illithids," Kimmuriel explained.

"And you are willing to supply those answers?"

"In the tumult of coming days, we will find a valuable ally in Lord Draygo Quick, and in his peers."

Jarlaxle looked around at the ruined entry hall and laughed at the absurdity.

"Allies, then," he said with a snicker. "Now pray open a gate that I might be out of this place."

"Indeed, but to Baldur's Gate and not to Luskan."

Jarlaxle looked at him curiously.

"Your role in this play is ended, my friend," Kimmuriel explained.

"Powerful entities seek Drizzt—"

"You need not remind me, but that is a worry for others of Bregan D'aerthe and not for Jarlaxle."

"Athrogate is in Luskan," Jarlaxle argued.

"I will return him to your side in short order."

Jarlaxle eyed his companion sternly, and even entertained a thought of betraying Kimmuriel here. It passed quickly, though, as Jarlaxle considered Entreri's reaction to him.

Perhaps it would be better Kimmuriel's way.

CHAPTER

25

THE JOURNEY HOME

E RE YE GO, ELF," ATHROGATE SAID TO DRIZZT AS THEY WALKED THE STREETS of Luskan. He handed over a folded cloak, which Drizzt immediately identified as a drow *piwafwi,* a most useful garment for concealment and protection. "Jarlaxle told me to give it to ye, and to tell ye to use it."

"Use it?"

"Aye," Athrogate said. "Ye got some powerful enemies huntin' ye, I'm hearin'. So use it, and get yerself long gone from Luskan in short order."

Drizzt stopped and turned to regard the dwarf directly. By his side, Effron, too, paused at that news.

"Where?" Effron asked.

Athrogate shrugged. "Back to Mithral Hall, mayhaps?"

Effron looked to Drizzt.

"Jarlaxle thinks I . . . we, should be gone from Luskan?" Drizzt asked the dwarf.

"Good advice," Athrogate replied. "Ye met some drow in Gauntlgrym, and them drow've figured out who ye be."

Drizzt sucked in his breath. "House Baenre," he muttered.

"What does it mean?" Effron asked.

"It means that you and I should part ways here, for your own sake," said Drizzt.

"Nah," Athrogate interjected. "They're knowin' yer friends, and they'll be findin' yer friends if not yerself. Jarlaxle tells me to tell ye to stick together, all of ye." As he finished, he nodded his hairy chin beyond Drizzt, who turned around to see Ambergris bounding toward him, her whole face smiling. She rushed up and threw a great hug over Drizzt, then gave one to Effron as well.

Then she embraced Athrogate, and it was apparent to the other two that these two had come to know each other quite well, and quite intimately. They broke the hug and shared a tremendous kiss, all sloppy and loud, full of fun and full of lust, as only dwarves could do.

"Ye got the caravan schedules?" Athrogate asked when they broke the embrace.

"Aye, north, south, and east, and a boat or two putting out soon enough," Ambergris replied, looking to her two returned friends as she spoke.

"A boat might be a fine choice," Athrogate offered with a shrug.

But Drizzt shook his head. "Caravans north?" he asked Ambergris, then added, "Icewind Dale?"

"Aye," Ambergris said, "that'd be the place north the drivers been speakin' of."

Drizzt looked to Athrogate. "Jarlaxle is sure of this pursuit?"

"Get ye gone, elf," the dwarf warned.

Drizzt nodded and tried to make sense of these sudden changes that had found him so unexpectedly. He had resigned himself to a life as Draygo Quick's prisoner, and likely to die there in the Shadowfell, in the room that had become his own world. And now he was free, and Guenhwyvar was returned to him.

But was he really free? House Baenre might soon make him wish that he was back in Draygo Quick's custody!

"Icewind Dale," he decided, for somehow it seemed the right choice to him, the place where he belonged. Few knew the ways of that tundra land better than Drizzt Do'Urden, though he hadn't been there for any length of time in a century and more. But yes, Icewind Dale. He felt a twinge of nostalgia at the thought, and felt at that moment as if he were going home.

Though Drizzt knew in his heart that no place without Catti-brie, Bruenor, Regis, and Wulfgar could ever truly be his home.

"Good 'nough, then," said Ambergris. "Wagons for Icewind Dale rolling with the dawn, and I'm thinkin' they'll be glad to take along the four o' us for guarding."

"The three of ye," Athrogate corrected. "I got me duties here in Luskan. But aye, they'll take ye, and they'll be glad of it." He reached into a side pocket of his vest and produced several parchments, then riffled through them and handed the appropriate writ to Drizzt. "Ship Kurth's recommending ye," he explained with a wink. "Whether ye take a boat or a wagon, we got yer imprimatur. Now put on yer durned cloak and get ye gone!"

There really was little more to say, Drizzt realized. "Extend my gratitude to Jarlaxle," he told the dwarf. "I had surrendered hope and he gave it back to me, and that is no small thing. Tell him that I hope our paths cross again, and not too many tendays from now. I would hear the tale of how you both survived the fall in Gauntlgrym, and I am confident that Jarlaxle has a hundred more tales to tell me of your exploits since that long-ago day."

"A hunnerd?" Athrogate said incredulously. "Nah, elf, a thousand! A thousand thousand, I tell ye! Bwahahaha!"

For some reason, given what Drizzt knew of Jarlaxle, that didn't sound like much of an exaggeration.

Ambergris, Drizzt, and Effron sat together that night in the back of an open wagon, one of a score that would begin the dangerous journey to Icewind Dale the next morning. As Athrogate had promised, the caravanners were more than thrilled to have the three along as added guards, for the road to Ten-Towns was fraught with peril and the reputation of Drizzt Do'Urden not so easily dismissed.

Drizzt put a hand on Effron's shoulder, trying to comfort the young tiefling as Ambergris related the last moments of Dahlia's life.

"All three saw the beast," she finished. "All three turned to stone. I got me out o' there, but only by the hair in me ears. He was waitin' for us, I tell ye."

"We certainly didn't catch Lord Draygo by surprise," Drizzt agreed, and he sighed deeply at the sad story, though he had already come to understand that Dahlia and the others were lost to him.

"It's my fault," Effron said, his voice thick with sadness. "I should never have led you there."

"Had I learned of your information at a later time, and that you knew of Lord Draygo's secret prisoner, I would never have forgiven you," Drizzt told him. "Guenhwyvar is a friend. I had to try."

"Aye, and all who went with ye, meself included, did so of our own accord," said Ambergris. "Ye did right," she told Effron. "That's the price of companionship and loyalty, and one not willin' to pay it ain't one worth walkin' beside."

"I deserted Draygo Quick's side and abandoned all that I knew, all of my friends and indeed my home, to find my mother's side," Effron replied.

"Thought ye did that to kill her to death," Ambergris reminded.

"I did it to learn the truth!" Effron retorted, a vein of anger entering his tone. "I had to know."

"And once ye did?"

"I found my mother's side, and now she is gone and I am alone."

Ambergris and Drizzt exchanged looks at that, and both asked together, "Are you?"

"Icewind Dale," Drizzt said. "When I was alone, so long ago, it was there that I found my heart and my home. And there I go again, and this time I am not alone, nor are you."

He patted Effron on the back, and the young tiefling gave him an appreciative nod.

A movement off the back of the wagon caught their attention, and a form, a female elf form—Dahlia's form!—leaped up onto the bed and skidded across to kneel before the seated Effron, whom she immediately wrapped in a huge hug.

"By the gods!' Ambergris cried.

"By Jarlaxle, I expect," Drizzt corrected.

"Indeed," replied Artemis Entreri, coming up to the back of the wagon beside Afafrenfere, who appeared quite glum, surprisingly.

Drizzt hugged Dahlia and nodded at the man. Ambergris scrambled back to greet her old Cavus Dun mate.

"Eh, but what's yer glower?" she asked the monk, who merely shook his head.

"How?" Drizzt asked. "You had been turned to stone, so says Ambergris." Entreri shrugged.

"I remember little," Dahlia admitted. "I saw the horrid creature, and then I was in the catacombs, Jarlaxle at my side and wearing his smug grin."

"Athrogate told us where to find you," Entreri added. "We are bound for Icewind Dale?"

"We are indeed," said Drizzt, and he felt light at that moment, so glad to see all three of his lost companions. Dahlia crushed him tighter in a hug, and he returned the embrace. She backed off just enough to try to passionately kiss him.

He kissed her, briefly, but he turned his lips away. "Effron, food for our friends!" he said exuberantly, injecting energy to cover up his revealing slip.

When he looked at Dahlia, though, he saw the pain there, and knew that his dodge had been unsuccessful. He hugged her tight again, but this time she broke the embrace and moved to take a seat in the wagon, pointedly on the other side of Effron and not beside Drizzt.

They were going to speak, and soon, Drizzt knew, and he wondered if his coming honesty with Dahlia would split the group apart. Perhaps it would, he realized, and so he knew that he owed it to her, to all of them, to have the conversation before they made the difficult journey to Icewind Dale.

The six moved off the wagon and to the campfire to share a hot meal then, but the talk about that fire was quite light, and often nonexistent, for in truth, they had little to talk about. Time had stopped for half the group, after all, and Drizzt and Effron's tales of their imprisonment by Draygo Quick offered very little content.

Ambergris took the lead in the conversation after dinner, recounting the last moments of the battle and explaining how she came to find Jarlaxle.

That part of the dwarf's story had Drizzt and Entreri perking up.

"Tiago Baenre," Drizzt whispered when the dwarf described Jarlaxle's rescue of her off the streets of Luskan. Given what he had been told by Athrogate, it made sense, and given that Tiago and his cohorts obviously knew the identities of Drizzt's companions, the news made him change his mind about his present plans.

He would not speak honestly with Dahlia until they were all safely away, for her own sake.

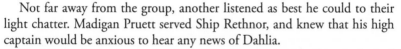

Not far away from the group, another listened as best he could to their light chatter. Madigan Pruett served Ship Rethnor, and knew that his high captain would be anxious to hear any news of Dahlia.

But Madigan wasn't sure that he'd relay this news to his Ship, for he had heard of another who had put out word on the street that he was looking for, and paying well for, any information that could be found regarding Drizzt Do'Urden.

Madigan Pruett had come out this night to deliver the last of Rethnor's supplies for the caravan. Now with this profitable opportunity before him, he decided that he would sign on with the caravan, but only as far as the southern entrance to the pass through the Spine of the World, a couple of days of travel if the weather held.

Then he'd take his information to the man paying well, a visiting wizard named Huervo the Seeker.

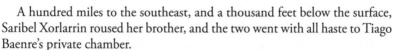

A hundred miles to the southeast, and a thousand feet below the surface, Saribel Xorlarrin roused her brother, and the two went with all haste to Tiago Baenre's private chamber.

Every night at her evening prayers, Saribel asked the handmaidens of the Spider Queen to guide her search, and on a more practical level, she had been charged with maintaining contact to the spies Tiago had set about Neverwinter, Port Llast, and other cities of the region.

"We must return to Luskan with all haste," Ravel Xorlarrin explained to Tiago.

"The dwarf has been located?"

"Better," said Ravel, and he looked to Saribel.

"Drizzt Do'Urden has surfaced, at long last," she explained.

Elated but not surprised, Tiago had been expecting this news since his near capture of the dwarf known as Ambergris. He moved from his bed, took up his clothing and armor, and fabulous sword and shield.

"He is with his companions, then," Tiago remarked.

"It would seem to be the case," Ravel answered.

"Gather them all, then," Tiago instructed, referring to the special force he had assembled for just this occasion, comprised of Ravel's closest spellspinners and warriors, including Jearth, the weapons master of House Xorlarrin. "We will take no chances of missing the heretic rogue this time."

"And House Xorlarrin will share in the credit?" Saribel dared to ask.

Tiago snapped a look at her, wearing a smile that he knew would surely unsettle the young priestess. He understood the source of her question: She would, after all, have to answer to her older and quite severe sister, Berellip, for her actions. Both Saribel and Ravel needed some assurance of gain for their House, given the risk they were putting forth.

"Share?" Tiago said with a dismissive laugh. "You will be mentioned prominently as the force I employed to carry out my great victory."

He kept his tone condescending, but knew, of course, that these two, his lessers, would be satisfied with that.

And so they were.

The next night, a force of more than twenty-five drow and a handful of driders, led by mighty Yerrininae and his wife Flavvor, moved north along the tunnels out of Gauntlgrym.

***

The wagons rolled at a swift pace. The weather had been dry and the road proved clear and hard, no mud or ruts wearing on the wheels.

For the first time in many months, Drizzt rode Andahar, and he felt grand up there on the unicorn's strong back, the wind in his long white hair. He put his hand to his belt pouch repeatedly, feeling the onyx figurine, longing for the day when he would call Guenhwyvar to his side once more.

"Patience," he whispered, reminding himself that Guenhwyvar needed her rest. She would be there, Jarlaxle had assured him, and Jarlaxle was rarely wrong.

He urged Andahar on more powerfully, cantering up around the lead wagon, then riding off down the road at a gallop to scout the way ahead. He let the unicorn run for some time, caring not that he had moved out of sight of the lead wagon. He was free now, riding along a road to a place he had known as home.

Andahar barely broke a sweat, thundering along with a smooth, long stride. Around a bend, they came to a long straightaway, lined with thick trees, and

Drizzt allowed the unicorn to move to a full sprint. Nostrils flaring, breath heaving in tremendous bursts, Andahar seemed all too pleased to comply, and now the sweat did bead on the unicorn's muscled flanks.

Two-thirds of the way along the run, Andahar eased up, and Drizzt sat up straighter, rolling his body in perfect balance as the gallop became a canter, became a trot.

Drizzt bent forward and patted Andahar hard on the neck, grateful for the joy of the run. He had just begun to urge the unicorn around when something caught his attention out of the corner of his eye, something large and black moving swiftly across the treetops.

Drizzt pulled Andahar up fully, and even reached for Taulmaril, until he recognized the pursuit.

A giant crow set down on the road in front of them, and the crow quickly became Dahlia, clad in her magical cloak.

"You might have passed a horde of highwaymen without ever noticing them," the elf scolded.

Drizzt grinned at her. "The road is clear."

Dahlia stared at him doubtfully.

"Fly along above the treetops, then," the drow told her. "Shadow my ride and show me the error of my judgment."

Dahlia considered the words for a moment, then shook her head and started toward Drizzt. "No," she explained, coming up beside him and lifting her hand for him to grasp. "I prefer to ride with you, behind you."

Drizzt pulled her up, and she came up very tight against him.

"Or under you," she whispered teasingly in his ear.

Drizzt tensed.

"If the road is clear, then they will not need us," Dahlia said.

But such a concern wasn't the source of Drizzt hesitance.

"What is it, then?" Dahlia said when he didn't reply, and when he didn't make any more intimate move toward her at all.

"It has been a long time," Drizzt started. "I spent months in the captivity of Draygo Quick."

"I would have traded places with you," the elf who had been turned to stone sarcastically replied.

"Would you?" Drizzt asked sincerely, and he glanced over his shoulder to look Dahlia in the face. "You were perfectly oblivious. In your mind and senses, there was no passage of time—tell me, when you were rescued, when you became flesh once more, did you think that months had passed? You said earlier that it seemed to you that you had gone in a blink from the entry hall to the catacombs, and instead of the medusa, you found Jarlaxle before you."

"It is no less unsettling," Dahlia said and looked away.

"Perhaps," Drizzt admitted. "Nor is it a competition between us."

"Then why start one?" Her voice grew sharp.

He nodded an apology. "The world has moved fast, and yet seems not to move at all," he said. "I fear that I lost much of myself in those months with Lord Draygo. I have to find that first before I can even entertain—"

"What?" Dahlia interrupted. "Before you can entertain making love to me?"

"To anyone," Drizzt tried to explain, but he realized that to be the wrong answer the moment the words escaped his lips, a point brought home only a heartbeat later as Dahlia slapped him across the face.

She rolled down off the unicorn and stood in the dirt road, staring up at him, hands on hips, looking very much like she wanted to kill him, or wanted to fall to the ground crying, for what seemed an eternity to poor Drizzt.

He didn't know how to react, or what he might do, and finally it dawned on him to get down from Andahar and go to the woman. But as he lifted his leg to dismount, Dahlia held up a hand to ward him away. She turned and ran off a few steps, throwing her cloak up over her head as she went, and then she was a giant bird once more, flying back to the caravan.

Drizzt closed his eyes, his shoulders slumping, his thoughts spinning, his heart pained. He couldn't lead her on. He did not love her—not the way he had loved Catti-brie, and despite the words of Innovindil, that love remained the standard for him, haunting him and warming him at the same time.

Perhaps he would never find such love again, and so be it, he decided.

He turned Andahar around and started off slowly back the way he had come, reminding himself that he had to handle Dahlia properly, for her own sake. He could not give her what she desired, but the Baenres were hunting, and he could not let her run off alone.

"I can hardly hear a word said to me," Afafrenfere said to Drizzt a few days later, when the caravan at last broke free of the high-walled mountain pass, to come out into the tundra of Icewind Dale.

"You will become accustomed to the wind," Drizzt shouted back at him, and truly the drow was smiling. Hearing the eternal wind of Icewind Dale in his ears again proved to be great medicine to Drizzt Do'Urden, healing him of the doubts and malaise that had infected him in the months of his captivity. He pictured the lone rocky pinnacle of Kelvin's Cairn, which was not quite visible yet above the flat plain, but soon would be, he knew. And that imagined view, the stars seeming as if they were all around him and not high above, brought to him an image of a smiling Bruenor, standing at his side in the dark night and the chill breeze. He thought of Regis, fishing string tied around his toe as he slept on the banks of Maer Dualdon.

Aye, this was home to Drizzt, a place of physical cold and emotional warmth, a place where he had learned to trust and to love, and he couldn't help but feel alive with the sound of the wind of Icewind Dale in his ears. He could hardly imagine the person he had become in the jails of Draygo Quick, so apathetic and hopeless.

He looked back to the caravan, to Dahlia in particular, who rode on a wagon with Artemis Entreri pacing his nightmare nearby, speaking with her. Drizzt imagined them in each other's arms, and hoped that it would become true. Because he could never truly return her love, he knew.

Drizzt turned Andahar around and paced back to the lead wagon. "Bryn Shander?" he asked.

"Aye, that's where we're bound."

"The roads will grow worse, for the melt is on, and the tundra mud is inevitable," Drizzt explained. "Another tenday before us, likely, if the weather holds."

The driver nodded. "Been this way many times," he explained.

"My friends and I will escort you to Bryn Shander's gates, but then I, at least, will turn away for Kelvin's Cairn."

"You will get your pay."

Drizzt smiled. He hardly cared, and had only wanted to inform the caravan of his plans.

"The Battlehammer dwarves for you, then?" the driver added, and Drizzt nodded. "I heard you were friends o' them."

"Proud to be called such."

"We've a wagon of goods bound for Stokely Silverstream's boys," the driver explained, and Drizzt was glad to hear that name again. "Might be two. I'll begin splitting up the goods when we camp tonight, sorting them that's for the dwarves, and you can guard those wagons to the mountain."

Drizzt nodded again and moved up front with Afafrenfere. He paced Andahar a bit faster after that, his conversation making him anxious to walk the ways of Kelvin's Cairn once more.

The next morning, soon after they were on the road again, the tip of that small mountain came into view, and Drizzt's heart leaped.

CHAPTER 26

THE SONG OF THE GODDESS

THE BEER, THE ALE, AND THE HONEY MEAD FLOWED FREELY IN THE BALL-room hall of Clan Battlehammer, beneath the rocks of Kelvin's Cairn. Dain Stokely Silverstream led the toasts, one after another, for Drizzt and the others of the drow's band, and so ridiculously effusive were the compliments that it didn't take long for the companions to recognize that they were as much an excuse as a reason for drinking.

Other than Drizzt, long a friend of the clan, Amber Gristle O'Maul got the bulk of the attention and praise, and truly, the female dwarf hadn't felt so welcomed in a long, long while.

Nor had she often found herself among so many peers in matters of holding one's liquor.

The celebration went on for many days, and both Drizzt and Dahlia were repeatedly pressed to recount their story of Gauntlgrym, describing the primordial, and most important of all, the fall of King Bruenor Battlehammer, patriarch and hero of the clan. The openness of Stokely and the others about the true identity of the dwarf who had gone by the name of Bonnego Battleaxe surprised Drizzt, and pleasantly so. The official story among the Battlehammer dwarves was that King Bruenor had died in Mithral Hall, decades before his actual demise, but this outpost of Battlehammers knew better, for they had been there, led by Thibbledorf Pwent, when King Bruenor, infused with the power of dwarf gods, had valiantly saved the day, heroically giving his own life in the process.

They knew the truth of Bonnego, and Mithral Hall almost surely knew as well—and thus, knew too that the cairn in Mithral Hall marking the grave of King Bruenor was an empty pile of rocks. But they'd never publicly admit it.

The absurdity of the open duplicity was surely not lost on Drizzt, but he found that he approved of the winks and nods, and that the Battlehammers celebrated the ultimate victory that had marked his dearest friend's demise came as a sincere and warm comfort to him.

"So how long're ye for the dale?" Stokely asked Drizzt a tenday later, when the two found a private moment outside the mining complex on the lower trails of Kelvin's Cairn.

"Perhaps forever," Drizzt answered, and he noted Stokely's approving nod and grin. "I've nowhere else to go that I can fathom, for nowhere else feels so much like home."

"Sure that meself's one to understand that! But I'm not thinkin' yer friends're of like mind. Amber, likely, and that monk fellow, but not so much th'other three, mostly that broken fellow."

"Are you so certain of that, or is it, perhaps, your own wishes to have Effron away?" Drizzt asked, and Stokely stiffened at the remark.

"Well, he is demon spawn, or devil spawn, or whatever durned tieflings be," the dwarf said uncomfortably.

"And I am drow spawn," Drizzt reminded.

Stokely could only shrug. "We ain't for kickin' him out," he said.

Drizzt laughed. "We'll not be staying here for long."

"Ye just said forever."

"Here at Kelvin's Cairn," Drizzt clarified. "Perhaps we'll set up in Bryn Shander, or maybe Lonelywood would be more to our liking. Dahlia and Entreri aren't overly comfortable with your tunnels."

Stokely narrowed his eyes.

"Inviting as you've made them," Drizzt quickly added, and he bowed to diffuse Stokely's growing scowl. "Dahlia is an elf, after all, and Entreri—"

"Not always a friend of the Battlehammers, eh?" Stokely interjected.

"Though no longer an enemy, else I would never have brought him here. Indeed, were that the case, I would not be traveling with him."

"Well, ye go where ye're needin' to go," Stokely said. "But if ye're staying in the dale, then ye best be visitin' me and me boys."

"Oftentimes," Drizzt assured him.

***

Later that same day, Drizzt, Dahlia, and Entreri rode out from Kelvin's Cairn for Bryn Shander, where the drow hoped they could begin to lay their longer-term plans. Afafrenfere saw them off, but remained behind to keep an eye on Ambergris and her unrelenting libations. Effron too, surprisingly, had declared that he would remain behind, and Drizzt discovered that Stokely had asked the tiefling to do so, that the two of them could spend some time alone and Effron could better explain his heritage. That notion struck Drizzt profoundly, and reminded him that Battlehammer dwarves were not nearly as xenophobic as many of the races of Faerûn. An open-minded Bruenor had long-ago befriended a rogue dark elf, after all, and now Stokely was apparently trying to carry on that tradition.

Drizzt's confidence that he had done well in leading his companions to this distant, seemingly-forlorn but ultimately-welcoming land only grew as he left the Clan Battlehammer complex.

Dahlia rode upon Andahar behind Drizzt, but the added weight did little to hinder the powerful steed and the trio made Bryn Shander that same day, though after the sun had set and the chilly wind began to blow more strongly. The city's gates were closed at the late hour, but the guards recognized Drizzt Do'Urden and were more than happy to grant him and his companions entrance.

"When's the caravan back to Luskan?" one asked as the strange and powerful mounts trotted between the western gate's small guard towers.

Drizzt shrugged, neither knowing nor caring. He dismounted from Andahar, bade Dahlia do the same, then dismissed the unicorn as Entreri released his nightmare.

"Our best choice is to enlist as scouts for the leaders of the city," Drizzt explained as the three made their way to the nearest tavern.

"How long do you plan on remaining here?" Entreri asked.

Drizzt stopped short and glanced around, ensuring that they were alone and would not be overheard.

"Jarlaxle recommended that we spend the rest of the season or more," Drizzt admitted.

"Sounds like a good reason to turn around and leave," Entreri replied.

"There are powerful forces seeking us—seeking me, at least—and they will find you, as well," Drizzt admitted.

"Draygo Quick," Dahlia reasoned.

"That is one."

"What do you know?" Entreri insisted.

"The drow from Gauntlgrym," Drizzt admitted. "They have come to realize my identity, I am told."

"Wonderful," Entreri muttered.

"What does this mean?" asked Dahlia.

"It means, welcome to your new home," said the dour assassin.

"When the trail grows cold, Jarlaxle will inform us," Drizzt said. "And there are worse places to live. Is there somewhere you would rather be?"

The pointed question elicited a curious response from Entreri: a shrug that came as an admission that indeed, this place was likely as good as any other.

"We have made some enemies, it would seem," Dahlia admitted. "Draygo Quick, Szass Tam, and now these dark elves. Is there a corner of the world far enough removed."

"If there is, we have now found it," Entreri remarked.

They drank for free that night, for Drizzt was recognized in the tavern, and their table was often visited by Bryn Shander citizens, offering drinks, or even a stay at their home if the trio were looking for accommodations, and asking Drizzt for stories of the long-ago days.

"To see a drow so welcomed," Entreri said sarcastically in one of the few moments when the three found themselves alone. "Truly touching."

"Stokely," Drizzt reasoned. "Apparently, our dwarf friends returned to Ten-Towns from Gauntlgrym with tales of heroism that were well-received. And I notice that you haven't refused the free food or drink."

"Free? I earn it by tolerating their insufferable intrusions," Entreri said. "I haven't killed any of them yet, so I deserve the food—and it is quite possible that the drink will prevent me from murdering any in the near future."

"If our time here is to be no more than a constant recitation of the heroics of Drizzt, then I will head back to Luskan and take my chances with Draygo Quick," Dahlia put in, drawing laughter from both Drizzt and Entreri—but Drizzt's mirth dissipated quickly when he looked at the woman, peering at him over the rim of her upraised mug, and realized that there was no small measure of truth in her joke.

"Tomorrow we go to the captain of the town guard and sign on," Drizzt said, changing the subject. "With our mounts, we can easily serve as scouts and couriers to the other communities. Who will outride us? Who will outfight us? We will find many nights such as this in all of the communities, I am sure. Not so hard a life."

Entreri lifted his glass in toast to that, though his expression showed it to be as much of a mocking gesture as any serious agreement. Drizzt accepted and welcomed that, however, knowing it to be the best he could expect from that one, and seeing that there really was a measure of acceptance in the assassin. Clearly, Entreri wasn't planning on leaving anytime soon.

Where the dour assassin was concerned, Drizzt took his victories where he could find them.

The innkeeper offered them a pair of complimentary rooms for the night, and promised to find lodging for them thereafter, though they'd have to pay—it was the busy season in Ten-Towns, after all. Drizzt graciously accepted the generous offer, and went back to his conversation with the others, when a complimentary dinner showed up at the table, to the cheers of all in the tavern.

"Insufferable," Entreri muttered, but Drizzt noted that Entreri ate quite eagerly.

They hadn't finished the meal before the next interruption, a middle-aged woman moving up to the table and fixing a grin on Drizzt.

"Ah, but you've heard the rumors, then," she said.

"Rumors?" Dahlia asked. She looked to Drizzt as she spoke, and he had no answers for her.

He looked at the woman more closely, a flicker of recognition in his eyes as he agreed, "Rumors?"

"About the forest, and the witch," she replied.

Drizzt's eyes widened. "I know you," he mumbled, though he couldn't remember the woman's name.

"My da was Lathan, who's been to the wood."

"Tulula!" Drizzt said. "Tulula Obridock!"

"Aye, but it's Hoerneson now," she said. "And well met again to you, Drizzt Do'Urden."

"What forest?" asked Dahlia. "What rumors?"

Again Drizzt felt her gaze upon him, but he could only shrug in reply, preferring to answer the second question and not the first.

"Iruladoon," Tulula answered. "A magical forest, 'tis said to be, appearing at its whim, so they speak."

"What is she talking about?" Entreri asked.

"Ruled by an auburn-haired witch and a halfling who lives by the lake," Tulula said.

Entreri and Dahlia turned directly on Drizzt, who sat staring at Tulula and seeming not to even draw breath at that point, clearly overwhelmed.

"Catti-brie," Entreri remarked quietly, nodding.

"The barbarian tribes have spoken of it of late," Tulula confirmed. "Seems my da wasn't so crazy, and more than a few of the folk have apologized for their jokes about crazy Lathan Obridock, and sure that they owed it to me!"

Drizzt ran his fingers through his hair. He didn't know where to begin, or what to think, even! He scrutinized Tulula and suspected, feared, that this was no more than a woman holding on desperately to her father's reputation. Did he dare allow his hopes to soar yet again?

"Ah, but the crazy Lady Hoerneson's captured you, has she?" said another patron, coming over and draping an arm affectionately across Tulula's shoulders.

"Bah for your own bluster, Rummy Hoerneson," she said.

"Your husband?" Drizzt asked.

"His brother," Rummy corrected. "As soon as I heard you were back in town, I knew Tulula would run to you."

"These rumors . . ." Drizzt started to ask.

"Nonsense and nothing more," said Rummy.

"Three have seen it!" Tulula protested.

"Three took your coins to say they've seen it, you mean," Rummy countered.

"They were speaking of it before ever did I see them," Tulula protested.

"Because they knew you would come running, purse in hand," Rummy said with a great laugh. "You've been looking for that forest since your da passed, and who can blame you? But a band of drunken barbarians looking for more to drink isn't anything to send this poor drow here swimming across Dinneshere!"

"What tribe?" Drizzt asked.

"Oh, don't you think it!" Rummy Hoerneson cried.

"Elk," Tulula explained. "Tribe of the Elk. They're following the herd back into the foothills, and came through to market. They'd be fair high up in the Spine of the World by now, I'm thinking."

Not even considering the movement, Drizzt reflexively turned his head to the southeast, for he knew well the route and destination of the caribou herds.

"Have you ever seen it?" he asked the woman.

"Went across Dinneshere only the one time with yourself, and again a few years later, when my da passed." She shook her head. "Never seen it."

"None ever seen it," Rummy grumbled.

"Catti-brie," Dahlia said, her tone terse, and she almost spat out the last part of the thought, aiming her venom at Drizzt, "long dead."

Drizzt swung his head around to regard her.

"Right?" she asked.

Drizzt just stared.

"You cannot even say it?" Dahlia asked incredulously.

Entreri gave a little laugh and Drizzt glared at him.

The tension growing thick around them, Tulula and Rummy offered quick salutations to Drizzt and his friends, welcoming them to Ten-Towns, then promptly hustled away.

"So, when do we head out to find the Tribe of the Elk?" Entreri asked when they were alone, and Drizzt glared all the harder—to no discernible effect.

"We are going, you know," Entreri said to Dahlia. "Or he is, at least."

Dahlia's glower more than matched the one Drizzt wore.

The drow relented and sat back. "Two of my friends were lost to me, many years ago," he began to explain.

"Your lover and a friend, you mean," said Dahlia.

Drizzt nodded, but corrected, "My wife. And yes, a friend. They were taken from us in an extraordinary manner—"

"I know the story," Dahlia said, biting through each word as it escaped her lips, and never blinking.

"You brought us to this forsaken land to chase a ghost?" Entreri asked, still seeming more amused than concerned.

"I have heard nothing of Iruladoon for many years until this very meeting," Drizzt protested. "Not in many years. Not since before I first ventured to Gauntlgrym."

"But you mean to go now," Dahlia said. She stood up and headed for the door, leaving Drizzt to stare blankly, overwhelmed and confused by the reaction.

"You truly are an idiot," Artemis Entreri said, laughing still some more.

Drizzt rose and started to follow Dahlia, and heard Entreri remark, "As you are about to prove yet again," as he moved away. That gave the drow pause, but only for a moment, and he hustled out the door.

Dahlia stood on the street with her back to him, her arms crossed over her chest as if she were chilly, though the night was quite warm. Drizzt moved up behind her and gently touched her shoulder.

"Dahlia," he said, or started to say, for she wheeled around and slapped him hard across the face.

"Why?" he managed to ask before her right arm swung again, and this time, the agile and strong Drizzt caught her by the wrist.

Across came her slapping left hook, and Drizzt caught that one, too.

"Dahlia," he pleaded.

She head-butted him, her forehead smashing into his nose, and as he staggered back, letting go of her wrists. She kicked up at him, aiming for his groin. He managed to turn his hip in and catch the foot on his thigh, but still it stung.

Dahlia pursued—in the moonlight, he could see tears streaking her cheeks.

A form rushed past Drizzt and intervened as Artemis Entreri cut off her advance and held her back, trying futilely to calm her.

"Fine, then, we'll go find your ghost!" Dahlia said. "And oh, but you can hug your dear dead Catti-brie, and would that her corpse freezes your heart forevermore!"

Drizzt held one arm out to the side helplessly, his other hand pinching his bleeding nose, as he tried vainly to begin to understand this outburst.

"Well, we leave in the morning, then," Entreri said, glancing back as he bulled Dahlia away. "A wonderful summer journey, I expect!"

Dahlia rode with Entreri upon the nightmare that next morning, leading the way back to Kelvin's Cairn to retrieve their other companions.

CHAPTER 27

SCRIMSHAW AND QUIET DREAMS

T HE SIX COMPANIONS MOVED OUT OF BRYN SHANDER'S EASTERN GATE THE next morning, traveling the Eastway, a fairly smooth and straight cobble-stoned road running from the main city of Ten-Towns to the easternmost of the area's communities, aptly named Easthaven. Ambergris drove the small wagon they had rented, Afafrenfere and Effron on the bench seat at her side, while Drizzt led the way upon Andahar, with Entreri and, notably, Dahlia following astride Entreri's nightmare.

They anticipated an easy day's ride to Easthaven, some dozen miles away, and understood that their road would grow more perilous and difficult after that, after they forded the swollen channel that ran between the two lakes of Lac Dinneshere and Redwaters. They wouldn't take the wagon past Easthaven, for the tundra beyond would undoubtedly prove too muddy, and Drizzt even hinted that Andahar and the nightmare might not fare well plodding around the unstable ground.

They spent only one very short night in the town of Easthaven, renting just a single room where they could store their supplies and take a short nap. They'd learned in that town that there was a ferry to take them from the town docks to the banks of Lac Dinneshere opposite the river, but alas, the captain would only offer the service before dawn.

"Too much fishin' to get done early in the morning," he explained.

So they were out before the dawn, the dark mound of Kelvin's Cairn looming before them as they boarded the wide and shallow boat tied to Easthaven's dock. The mountain shifted behind Drizzt's left shoulder as the ferry caught the morning breeze and glided to the east. The morning sun was just beginning to peek over the flat plain stretching before them when the ferry dropped its long gangplank, and the six companions walked off the boat to the eastern bank of Lac Dinneshere.

"We're going all the way to them mountains?" Ambergris asked, pointing to the south, to the Spine of the World range, the snow-capped peaks shining brilliantly in the dawn's light.

"Eventually," said Drizzt, and that surprising answer had all eyes turning his way. The drow guided those looks the other way, to the north along the large lake's shoreline.

"The Tribe of the Elk?" Dahlia asked. "Were you not seeking them to keep your pretty dreams of Catti-brie alive?"

Her tone had Entreri rolling his eyes, Afafrenfere and Effron looking on incredulously, and Ambergris sucking in her breath as if expecting an outburst to follow.

"Aye, and they be in the foothills, so ye said," the dwarf added, and she put a bit of jollity in her voice, something that was not lost on Drizzt.

He smiled appreciatively at the dwarf and nodded. "They will be in or around the foothills for a month or more," he explained. "But we seek them to confirm rumors, or their place in those rumors, at least." He looked back to the north again and nodded. "We can confirm a lot more in a day or so."

"Yer forest is up there?"

"So he hopes," Dahlia muttered.

Drizzt started off to the north along the shore, Ambergris and Afafrenfere moving close behind. Effron lingered, staying within earshot of Entreri and Dahlia.

"Why are we following him, then?" Entreri asked. "Let him chase his ghosts while we figure out if this place, Ten-Towns, is worth the trouble of getting here. Good enough to hide out with the drow chasing us, perhaps, but how long a wait—"

"No," Dahlia interrupted, and she started north along the shore as well. "I want to witness this. I want to see Drizzt find his ghosts, or surrender his hope. He owes me that much at least."

"Ah, true love," Entreri said wistfully to Effron as he walked past the twisted warlock.

Effron stood there staring for some time, trying to figure out what was happening, before he set off in pursuit.

※ ※ ※

The drow and drider caravan entered the southern end of the pass through the Spine of the World, moving steadily northward. When they had first started out from Gauntlgrym, Tiago Baenre had pushed them hard, eager to find his victory. But when they had learned of Drizzt's move to the north,

Ravel Xorlarrin had counseled Tiago to relax, and to set a steady and careful pace. Icewind Dale was not a large region, and was fully bordered by mostly impassable mountains and the unnavigable Sea of Moving Ice.

There was nowhere for Drizzt Do'Urden to run.

Riding Byok, his magnificent lizard, Tiago looked around at his band and took comfort. They were only thirty strong, but Tiago had little doubt that they could destroy all of Ten-Towns if the communities joined together to support Drizzt—though from everything he had learned of the place, that seemed quite unlikely. Ravel had brought his most powerful spellspinners, the same seven who had helped him develop his lightning web enchantment. Ravel was the youngest of the group, but they showed great loyalty to him.

And Jearth, weapons master of House Xorlarrin, had brought along his most experienced and skilled warriors, to say nothing of Yerrininae and the five powerful driders, including his consort, who flanked the procession.

Tiago regarded Saribel, riding a lizard not far from him, and her fellow priestesses. None of them were very old, he realized, and none as accomplished in their particular field as the spellspinners or the warriors. Still, Tiago found himself holding faith in this group—surely Matron Mother Zeerith Xorlarrin had eagerly enlisted her family in this hunt, with two of her children and her House weapons master riding along.

And all for Tiago's benefit. Drizzt was his trophy to claim, and the Xorlarrins knew it. For while Drizzt's head would bring glory to Tiago, the more important potential for Zeerith was the continued support of the Baenres as the Xorlarrins solidified their hold on Gauntlgrym as a sister city to Menzoberranzan.

No doubt many of the replacements now moving through the Underdark tunnels to bolster the force at Gauntlgrym were, in fact, Baenres or Baenre agents.

As he considered that, as he realized the bond that was strengthening between the two families, Tiago found his gaze lingering on Saribel. He had grown fond of this one, he realized, and she had learned to please him.

With his new weapon and shield, Vidrinath and Orbcress, and certainly with the head of Drizzt Do'Urden, Tiago had come to think his ascent to the position of weapons master in House Baenre would come quickly, likely immediately upon his return to the city. Even Anzdrel wouldn't be foolish enough to oppose him.

But now he was thinking that perhaps that wasn't the best course before him. Surely male drow would fare better in Gauntlgrym than in Menzoberranzan, for House Xorlarrin had always afforded their males positions of great power and influence compared to the other Houses.

Perhaps Tiago would serve House Baenre better, and serve himself better, if he remained in Gauntlgrym.

He veered Byok to the side toward Saribel, the other priestesses fading back when his intent to engage the Xorlarrin became obvious.

"I do not enjoy the World Above," she said as he approached. "I feel ever vulnerable here, with no walls in close and no ceiling preventing attacks from above." As she spoke, she glanced up at the towering mountain walls, and she shuddered, obviously imagining some archer up there, or a giant ready to drop rocks on them.

"Our prize is well worth the trouble," Tiago assured her.

"Your prize, you mean."

Tiago grinned at her. "Will you not share in my glory?"

"We are your raiding party, at your command."

"And you are no more than that?"

She looked at him curiously.

"My lover?" he asked.

"So is Berellip," she replied, referring to her older sister. "So are most of the females in Gauntlgrym, and a fair number in Menzoberranzan, I expect."

Tiago laughed and shrugged, but didn't argue the point. "Yes," he said, "but none of them, not even Berellip, could find the gain you will discover from this journey. Consider the glory I will know when I have returned with the head of Drizzt Do'Urden. My path before me will be my own to choose."

"Weapons master of House Baenre," she said. Tiago shook his head, but Saribel pressed on, "That has been the rumor since before we set out for Gauntlgrym."

"House Baenre will stake a strong position in your matron mother's desired Xorlarrin city," he replied. "Perhaps I will embody that position."

Saribel tried to remain calm, but her eyes widened, giving her hopes away.

"Perhaps I will take a Xorlarrin noble as my wife, joining our families in an alliance that will further both our aims," Tiago said.

"Berellip would be the obvious choice," Saribel said.

"My choice," Tiago emphasized, "would not be Berellip."

Saribel swallowed hard. "What are you—?"

"We will be married, our families will be joined," Tiago stated plainly.

"What?" came a question from the side, and the two turned to find Ravel listening in.

"You do not approve . . . brother?" Tiago said.

Ravel sat upon his invisible floating disc looking back at the Baenre, his expression shifting as he digested the startling news. Gradually a grin came to dominate his face—no doubt, Tiago realized, Ravel was going through the same thought process he had just realized, and coming to the same conclusion.

"Ah, brother," Ravel said at length. "It is good to be out on the hunt with you!"

"Particularly when our prey is cornered," Tiago replied.

"Well, hardly be callin' it a forest," Ambergris said, trudging through the scraggly trees above the small, dilapidated cabin on the banks of Lac Dinneshere. "Ye sure this be the place, then?"

The dwarf stopped talking and pulled up short when she regarded Dahlia and Drizzt, the drow crouched on one knee, staring down intently at his hand. No, not at his hand, she realized, but at something he held.

"What is it?" Dahlia asked.

Drizzt looked up at her, his expression blank, and he only shook his head, as if confused, as if he couldn't find any words at that moment.

Ambergris and Entreri arrived then, from different directions.

Drizzt closed his hand and rolled his fingers, gradually finding the strength to rise.

"What is it?" Entreri asked this time.

Drizzt looked at him, then over Entreri's shoulder, down at Effron and Afafrenfere, who were on the small dock before the old cabin.

"Drizzt?" Dahlia prompted.

"Scrimshaw," he answered, his voice hollow.

Dahlia reached for the hand, but Drizzt pulled it away quickly and defensively. His movement surprised her, and startled the other two as well.

Drizzt took a deep breath and brought his hand up, unfolding his fingers to reveal a small statuette depicting a woman holding a very distinctive bow, the same bow, it appeared, as the one currently draped over Drizzt's shoulder.

"Regis's work," Artemis Entreri said.

"Is that her?" Dahlia asked loudly, drowning out the assassin.

Drizzt stared at her blankly, hesitant to answer.

"Catti-brie?" she pressed. "Your beloved Catti-brie?"

"How'd it get out here?" Ambergris asked, looking all around. "Few been here in many years, I'm guessing."

"None, more likely," said Dahlia, staring still at Drizzt, her expression reflecting a deep and obvious discontent.

345

"Except when the forest is here, perhaps," Artemis Entreri said, and Drizzt took another deep breath, feeling as if he might simply topple over—or wondering if Dahlia might leap over and throttle him, given her expression.

"It is likely nothing more than coincidence," Drizzt said.

Artemis Entreri walked over and reached for the statue, but Drizzt kept it away.

"The foot," Entreri said. "The right foot. Should I have to tell this to you?"

Drizzt slowly upturned the scrimshaw, looked at its underside, the clutched it tightly against his heart.

"The 'R' of Regis," Entreri explained to the others.

"And how're ye knowin' that?" Ambergris asked.

"I have a long history with that one," the assassin chuckled.

Drizzt locked stares with him. "What does it mean?"

Entreri shrugged and held out his hand, and this time, Drizzt handed the statue over. Entreri studied it closely. "It's been lying out here for a long time," he said.

"And there's no forest to be seen," Dahlia added, rather unkindly.

"And the day's gettin' long," Ambergris remarked, looking back across the lake to the setting sun. "At least we'll be sleeping under a proper roof this night, eh?" She glanced down at the lakeside cottage. "Such as it is."

In reply, Drizzt rolled his pack off his back and let if fall to the ground.

Ambergris looked down at it, then back up to the stone-faced drow. "Like I was sayin'," she said. "Another fine night out under the stars."

Drizzt camped right there, sleeping on the very spot where he had found the figurine. None of his five companions went to the cottage, but rather surrounded him with their own bedrolls.

"Chasing ghosts," Dahlia muttered to Entreri much later on, the two sitting off to the side, looking back at Drizzt. The night was not cold and the fire long out, but the half-moon had already passed overhead and they could see the drow clearly. He lay back on his bedroll, looking up at the multitude of stars shining over Lac Dinneshere. He still clutched the figurine, rolling it over in his nimble fingers.

"Chasing her, you mean."

Dahlia turned on him.

"You can't rightly blame him, can you?" Entreri went on against that stare. "These were his friends, his family. We've all chased our ghosts."

"To kill them, not to make love to them," Dahlia said and looked back at the drow.

Entreri smiled at her obvious jealousy, but wisely said nothing more.

At first he thought it Andahar's barding, sweet bells ringing in the night, but as Drizzt opened his eyes, he came to understand that it was something more subtle and more powerful all at the same time, with all the forest around him resonating in a gentle and overwhelming melody.

All the *forest* around him . . .

When he had fallen asleep, he had done so watching the night sky and a multitude of stars, but now, from the same place, Drizzt could barely make out any such twinkling lights through the dense canopy above him.

He sat up straight, glancing all around, trying to make sense of it.

He was near a small pond that had not been there. He was near a small and well-tended cottage that had not been there, set against a low hill of hedgerows and flowers and a vegetable garden that had not been there. He pulled himself to his feet and considered his companions, all sleeping nearby, with one notable exception.

Drizzt moved to Dahlia and stirred her. "Where is Entreri?" he asked.

The elf woman rubbed a sleepy eye. "What?" she asked generally, her mind not catching up to the moment. She rubbed her eyes again and sat up, considered Drizzt somewhat blankly. "What is that music?" she asked, and then she looked around.

And then her eyes popped open wide indeed!

Artemis Entreri walked into view then and both regarded him curiously as he shrugged helplessly.

"No singer," he said, helplessly shaking his head. "Just a song."

He ended with a yawn, and eased back down to the ground.

"How far did you search?" Drizzt asked, but he too couldn't suppress a yawn as he fought through the words, for a great weariness came rushing over him then.

He looked at Dahlia, but she had slumped back to the ground and seemed fast asleep.

Magic—powerful magic, Drizzt knew, for elves were generally immune to such dweomers of sleep and weariness. Drow, as well, and yet Drizzt found himself on his knees. He looked around, and tried to fight it.

His head was on Dahlia's strong belly then, though he really wasn't aware of the movement that had put him to the ground. All he knew was the song, filling his ears with sweetness, filling his heart with warmth, filling his eyes with the sandman's pinch.

Dreams of Catti-brie danced in his thoughts.

CHAPTER 28

THE HERO OF ICEWIND DALE

"**H**AIL AND WELL MET," TIAGO BAENRE SAID TO THE GROUP OF GUARDS WHO had come running when the young warrior and his three dark elf companions approached Bryn Shander's western gate. He smiled as he spoke, attempting to be disarming here, but the group surely didn't relax in light of his tone and posture, for surely few cut a more impressive and imposing figure than Tiago Baenre. He wore black leather armor, studded with mithral and accented in swirling designs of platinum leaf. His belt was a cord of woven gold, tied at the hip and hanging down the side of his leg, like a tassel. His fine *piwafwi* was perfectly black, so rich in hue that it seemed as if the fabric had great depth, like peering hopelessly into a deep Underdark cavern.

But aside from the obvious fit and quality of his clothing, two other items quite clearly marked this drow as someone to be feared. Set in his belt, not in a scabbard but simply through a loop—for who would hide such magnificence as Vidrinath inside a sheath?—rested his amazing sword, its semi-translucent glassteel blade sparkling with the power of the inset diamonds, its curled hilt's green spider eyes staring at the guards as if it served as some sentient guardian familiar to Tiago. Set on Tiago's back, Orbcress was sized at that moment to be no more than a small buckler. Whatever its size, the shield spoke of powerful enchantments, for it seemed as if it were fashioned from a block of ice, and closer inspection revealed what seemed to be an intricate spider web encased within.

"Be at ease," he told the guard more directly with his halting command of the common language of the surface. "I have come in search of a friend, and am no enemy to the folk of Ten-Towns."

"Drizzt Do'Urden?" one of the guards asked, speaking more to her companions than to the visitors, but Tiago heard, and truly, no words had ever rung sweeter in his ears.

"He is here?"

"Was," a different guard replied. "Went out to Easthaven a few days ago, and meant to move out east from there, from what I heard."

"To where?" Tiago asked, and he tried hard not to let his disappointment show—and particularly not in the form of the anger that was suddenly bubbling up inside of him.

The guard shrugged and looked to his fellows, who similarly shook their heads or shrugged, having no answer.

"Not far, and not for long, likely," replied the woman who had first spoken Drizzt's name. "Might be to see the barbarian tribes, or might be to hunt. But he's sure to return soon enough. Nowhere to go east of Ten-Towns."

That calmed Tiago greatly. "Easthaven?" he asked as sweetly as he could manage.

"A day's ride down the Eastway," the woman answered.

Tiago turned to his companions, Ravel, Saribel, and Jearth, and all four wore perplexed expressions.

"To the east," another guard explained, and he turned back and pointed down the boulevard straight into the heart of the city. "Straight through and straight out Bryn Shander's eastern gate, to the east."

"Night is upon us," the woman explained. "You'll be wanting lodging."

Tiago shook his head. "I have arrangements elsewhere. This road, the Eastway, runs out from the other end of this city?"

"Aye," several answered.

Tiago turned and started back the way he had come, the other three drow moving in his wake, not one of them offered a parting word, or looking back, except for Jearth, whose duty it was to keep the rear guard watch.

"Drizzt Do'Urden," an excited Tiago whispered when they were out of earshot of the guards.

"Only days ahead of us," Ravel agreed.

"With nowhere to run," Saribel remarked, and all four dreamed of the glory they would soon know.

The small, flat-bottomed boat lurched and rolled, and the nervous captain looked at his three passengers, fearing they would punish him severely for the uncomfortable journey. But the seven of them, drow all, didn't appear at all bothered by the rolling; so dexterous and balanced were they even in this unfamiliar environment that they barely shifted as the deck was jolted repeatedly by the shock of uneven waves.

The captain glanced at the drow more than they regarded him, which gave him some comfort at least. These were proclaimed friends of Drizzt Do'Urden, but something about their demeanor didn't fit that description. Not that the captain knew Drizzt well, of course, having met him only once on this same ferry route, but the tales of the rogue drow were common about Ten-Towns, particularly Easthaven, which looked out onto the open tundra. Drizzt had been instrumental in forging the peace between Ten-Towns and the barbarian tribes a century before, and that peace held to this day, to say nothing of his legendary exploits in defeating the minions of the infamous Crystal Shard.

Even though few alive in Ten-Towns knew much of present-day Drizzt—indeed, only a couple of elves remaining in Lonelywood were even alive back in the time of Akar Kessell and the Crystal Shard—most would swing wide their doors for him. The nervous captain could hardly believe the same would be true for this particular group of grim-faced drow adventurers.

He was glad then, as he turned his craft around the last stony jut and into the shallow and somewhat protected cove on the lake's eastern shore. He dropped the single sail and let the current take them, locking the wheel and moving to the anchor and long gangplank set forward. He could typically secure the landing very quickly, having years of practice, but this day, despite the frothing waters, the captain had them in place and with the bridge to the shore up and steady faster than ever before.

He moved far aside, to the front corner of the craft, as the contingent of drow headed away.

"This is the exact location where you left Drizzt?" asked Tiago, coming near the end of the line, with only Jearth behind him.

"Same spot," the captain replied.

"A tenday ago?"

"To the day, sir."

"You will await our return in this very place."

The captain nearly choked on that. He had agreed to, and been paid for, taking them out here, but even with the rough weather, he wanted a day of knucklehead fishing. Indeed, in weather such as this, knucklehead trout were more likely to bite.

"But—" he started to argue, but the drow fixed him with such a stare that he knew that any contrary word from him would likely get him murdered, then and there.

"You will await our return," Tiago said again.

"H-how long?" the captain stammered.

"Until you die of old age, if need be," said Tiago. "And then you will return us to Easthaven's dock, or you will begin a circuitous ferry from that dock to this place as the rest of my force is brought forth."

The notion that there were more of these dangerous folk around had the hairs on the back of the captain's neck standing up. What had he stepped into here, he wondered and imagined a drow invasion force burning Easthaven to the ground!

Later that same day, the sun setting low, the captain breathed a sigh of relief when Tiago and the others stepped off his boat again, this time onto Easthaven's docks. They had found no sign of Drizzt out in the east, and had quickly realized the fool's errand of trying to pursue the rogue, who knew the region so much better than they, into the open tundra.

So instead, Tiago and a select few remained at the inn in Easthaven, with the bulk of their thirty-warrior force camped in an extra-dimensional space created by Ravel and the other spellspinners, ready for fast recall.

And they waited.

Another tenday passed. Tiago sent out tendrils—Saribel's priestesses—to Bryn Shander, and hired indigenous scouts to widen his network to encompass the whole of Ten-Towns, including the Battlehammer contingent living under the lone mountain. Ravel and his spellspinners, meanwhile, utilized their divination magic, while Saribel and her kind called out to Lolth's handmaidens for guidance in their search.

A month slipped by. Tiago hired locals to reach out to the barbarian tribes for word on the missing drow.

Another month passed, with no word of Drizzt, and indeed, even the extra-planar creatures the priestesses and now magic-users he had called upon could find no sign of the rogue. The season began its turn, where the mountain passes would fill with snow and cold, and Icewind Dale would again be isolated from the rest of Faerûn. By the time of the first snowstorm, no caravan moved along the single road connecting Icewind Dale to the lands south of the Spine of the World.

No caravan, perhaps, but the storm did not hinder the approach of a demonic balor, whose every monstrous stride turned the snowpack to steam.

A tremendous explosion rocked Bryn Shander's gate, crumbling the stones and shattering the hinges of the great doors, which fell in and were fast consumed by the demonic fires. A guard to the side of the devastation lifted her spear and threw, crying out for Bryn Shander, for Ten-Towns. The missile disappeared into the smoky shroud around the demon, but whether it had any effect or not, the poor sentry would never know. For as her spear flew out, the demon's long whip reached in, snapping around her torso. With a flick of his powerful wrist, Errtu yanked her from her feet and sent her flying from the wall, dragging her into the killing fires surrounding his great form.

He gave her not another thought, and waved forward three powerful minions, great glabrezu demons. Twice the height of a tall man, the bipedal, hulking creatures eagerly loped through the breach and into the city, each demon waving four massive arms. Two of those arms ended in giant pincers, powerful enough to cut a man in half, as one unfortunate Bryn Shander soldier discovered almost immediately.

"I will have the drow!" Errtu roared. "Send him to me now, or I will lay waste to your city!"

From a short distance south of the unfolding battle scene, Tiago and his minions, well-versed in demon lore, understood that the threat was not an idle one.

"A balor," Saribel said, her voice barely above a whisper.

"Hunting us?" a confused Ravel added.

"So it would seem," said Tiago. "And though I truly enjoy the spectacle of carnage before us, perhaps we should discern what this beast might wish with us. Nothing good, I expect, and so perhaps we will have to destroy it. A pity, really."

His casual attitude, so matter-of-fact and calm despite the formidable enemy on the field before them, had the others looking at the young Baenre with renewed respect, and inevitably nodding in agreement.

Tiago turned to Saribel. "Ward me from the demon flames," he instructed. "Ward us all. Let us strip this balor of its primary weapon."

While Saribel and her priestesses began the task, casting many magical protections over the group, Tiago gathered Ravel, Jearth, and Yerrininae to prepare the battlefield. Within a short while, Tiago rode Byok to the front of his column. He watched the huge balor follow the glabrezu into the city, a cacophony of screams echoing along Bryn Shander's wall, then started forward. He pointed to the wall, some twenty feet south of the destroyed gate, and kicked Byok into a run. The drow warriors and Saribel's priestesses followed quickly, Jearth guiding them. The mighty driders ran with the group for a short distance, but veered away to the west soon after, increasing their pace in a circuitous route that would take them north of the gate.

Ravel and his fellow spellspinners did not follow the others. They assumed their battle formation, with the noble drow serving as the hub of their "wheel." As the other five began their long incantation, Ravel cast the first spell, opening a dimensional portal from just north of their position to the area immediately before Bryn Shander's ruined gate. By the time he had finished that spell, the first sparks of mounting power began to crackle in the air around him.

***

Tiago Baenre guided his lizard mount at full speed to the base of Bryn Shander's tall wall, then leaped onto the stones and ran up so quickly that an onlooker might have thought the wall an optical illusion, and no more than a gently-sloping hill at best. Tiago gained the top of the wall quickly and ran along a short distance, taking in the scene of carnage before him while Jearth and the others gathered at the base outside the wall.

The citizens of Bryn Shander had come out in force to meet the assault of the demons, and to their credit, they did not break ranks as the mighty balor and the vicious glabrezu decimated all who came against them. A dozen warriors all at once charged a single glabrezu, off to the side of the main fighting, some bursting out of doors, tossing spears and demanding the creature's attention, while others leaped from the rooftops, throwing themselves atop the monster with flailing abandon.

A cloud of blood appeared almost instantly, and twelve warriors became ten, then six in short order. The glabrezu roared and struck hard, butting with its horns, biting with its canine maw, snapping with its deadly pincers. For all the damage it could cause, though, the sheer weight of the gallant citizens brought it to the ground, and the humans wet their spear tips and swords with demon blood.

"I will have you, drow!" the balor roared, and the greatest beast hardly seemed concerned by the fall of the one glabrezu. "Come forth or see them all destroyed! I have waited a hundred years!"

As it bellowed, the creature sent a wall of fire rushing down an alleyway, just as an arrow came forth. That arrow had little effect, and the poor archer's screams filled the air as the wall of fire ate him.

"Who is this balor to demand an audience so emphatically?" Tiago cried out, in the tongue of demons and not the common surface language.

The balor stiffened at the sound of the words in the distinct Menzoberranyr accent, and wheeled around.

Tiago started to ask another question, but the creature was apparently in no mood to converse—not with a solitary drow warrior, at least—and it lifted its whip in a spin around its massive horned head. Out lashed the weapon, and Tiago ducked behind his shield, and the magnificent web that was Orbcress spiraled as he did, and grew in size to fully wall him from the deadly bite of Errtu's whip.

"A hundred years is not so long a time, Drizzt Do'Urden!" Errtu roared, and threw a fireball Tiago's way.

The drow was already moving, though, running Byok along the narrow walkway toward the ruined gate, then down the outside of the wall, back to the field before Bryn Shander. He had barely registered the demon's words, barely begun to sort out that this creature was hunting not him, but Drizzt, when the beast charged back out of the city, its fiery whip snapping at Tiago once more.

At the same time, the great demon reached to the side with its sword hand, exuding a telekinetic power that lifted a boulder from the rubble of the broken gate.

Tiago blocked the snapping whip yet again, and started to call out, trying to strike up a conversation with this demon. But any thoughts he had of joining with the creature flew away from him as that boulder flew toward him!

He ducked behind the shield once more, and surely it saved his life, but the weight of the blow sent him flying from his mount with such force that it tore the saddle from Byok's back and sent the powerful lizard tumbling over.

A glabrezu lifted a Bryn Shander warrior into the air between its great pincers. The man's companion and dear friend cried out in denial, but to no avail.

The pincers closed and the poor warrior fell to the ground in two pieces.

"Drizzt did this!" the man screamed, throwing himself with abandon at the huge demon. He slashed and stabbed wildly with his sword, scoring a couple of solid hits before the creature backhanded him with the strength of a hill giant, launching him to the side.

Other warriors replaced him. From the balcony of a nearby building, a wizard lashed out with a lightning bolt, shocking and startling the glabrezu, weakening its preparedness as the other citizens came on.

To the side, the battered warrior cried out for his fallen friend, and loudly cursed the name of Drizzt Do'Urden.

Others joined in.

Tiago rolled a dozen times, trying to absorb the shock of the blow. He came around, his shield arm slumping low, his shoulder numb, just in time to see his prized lizard charging in fiercely at the balor.

"No!" Tiago screamed, but the lizard, as well-trained as it was, was hearing none of his commands. Byok leaped at the balor, forelegs raking, maw snapping.

But the balor's whip connected first, wrapping around the powerful lizard, and with frightening strength, the great demon tugged hard and defeated the lizard's momentum, sending Byok into a sudden spin to land hard amidst the flames at the balor's feet.

Tiago charged, screaming for his prized pet. He saw Byok bite up at the balor, and catch the whip arm, tearing demon flesh, but then the balor's greatsword swept down into the flames, and came up dripping lizard blood.

From the side charged Jearth and the others, a volley of javelins soaring in to sting the great demon. Two glabrezu came through the gate at the same moment, however, turning immediately to engage this new force.

Tiago winced with every strike as the battle in the flames continued before him. The balor stood up straight, towering above the flames, and lifted its whip arm, and Byok—grand and brave Byok!—was still attached, biting on ferociously. Ragged skin hung from the lizard's powerful maw, and Byok shook his jaws and the balor howled in pain and Tiago's heart leaped with hope.

But across came the demon's sword arm, and the sword it held proved vorpal, severing Byok's head cleanly. The lizard's body fell away into the flames. The head remained in place, locked onto to the balor's arm.

Tiago skidded to a stop and felt as if a hill giant had punched him in the gut. "Byok," he breathed and he retched as if he would vomit. He had raised that lizard from the day it had hatched, and had been magically attuned to it, much as a wizard might find and bond to a familiar.

"Kill it!" he cried in outrage, and looked to Jearth and the warriors, who engaged the glabrezu pair.

"Kill it!" he cried again, looking helplessly to the city gates and the force assembled just within, not daring to come forth.

"Hold!" the guard commander called out to the gathered forces of Bryn Shander. "Do not exit the city!"

He waved his hand, ordering archers back up to the wall. Who were these dark elves battling the demons?

"Allies?" he asked quietly, but aloud, and those around him could not offer an answer.

He looked to the north then, to another approaching force, and he swallowed hard with sheer revulsion and horror, and at the thought that Bryn Shander might well be in dire trouble no matter which side in this titanic battle proved victorious.

Tiago's plea was answered with a net of crackling lightning, hurtling through a dimensional gate to seemingly appear out of nowhere right beside the massive balor. The demon grunted in surprise as the net descended over it, brilliant flashes of lightning exploding all around, blinding all who looked on. Tiago continued to squint against the thunderous explosions, though, wanting to see this demon utterly destroyed, wanting to witness the retribution against the demon that had killed his prize lizard mount.

Sparks burst into the air, carrying the demon's flames with them. The balor tried to stand against the net, but the stinging lightning explosions drove it down, down, and it roared, maddened with pain.

The ground began to tremble, the lightning explosions came faster and faster until they crackled and boomed as a single, unending note of destruction.

The net fell flat to the ground, amidst the now-dying flames, where it continued to pop and spark.

But the demon was gone, and in the next instant, it was back again, but no longer under the net.

No, Errtu had teleported from the danger and now stood directly behind Tiago Baenre. Down came the balor's greatsword, and Tiago swung around and lifted his shield just in time to block the heavy swing. His shoulder went numb again, and his shield arm slumped. No single warrior could stand against a balor! And though this one was badly hurt, lines of lightning scars all around its head and torso, with one of its horns blown away completely, a balor was a creature of rage.

Errtu knew rage.

But so did Tiago, who had witnessed the death of Byok.

The balor swung again, but Tiago was quicker and dived aside. Out snapped the demon's whip, but Tiago rushed back in, inside the bite of the flaming weapon. Across came the demon's greatsword, but the drow's shield was there, and Tiago rolled around the hit and struck a blow of his own.

Vidrinath, forged in Gauntlgrym by the legendary smith, Gol'fanin, sliced through Errtu's flesh and muscle with ease, cutting deep into the balor's hip.

Tiago retracted, blocked another heavy swing, then stabbed straight ahead, skewering Errtu's belly, spilling guts and blood.

The balor lifted a giant, three-clawed foot and stomped down hard, and when Tiago dodged, Errtu kicked out and sent the drow flying aside.

The beast lifted its fiery whip, rolling its flaming length back over its shoulder. Stunned from the kick, Tiago reacted too slowly, and he tried desperately to roll around to get his shield in line to absorb at least some of the vicious blow.

Forward came Errtu's arm . . . almost.

For the beast froze in place, staring hatefully at Tiago, and curiously at the bulge that had just prodded into the front of its massive chest.

Not pausing to figure it out, Tiago put his feet under him, sprang up and charged, then leaped high into the air and brought Vidrinath down in a powerful overhand chop. The magnificent sword cleaved Errtu's head in two, right down the middle, and both halves flapped weirdly as the balor sank to its knees. Somehow, though it had no mouth left, the great demon issued a huge, agonized bellow, a cry of rage and denial, an echoing promise and threat, "A hundred years is not so long a time, Drizzt Do'Urden!"

Errtu melted into the ground.

Tiago looked past the charred spot to see Yerrininae standing before him, great trident in hand, the weapon dripping the blood and ichor of the slain balor.

"He thought you Drizzt," the drider said. "That is a good thing."

"Let the beast know it was Tiago Baenre who slew him," the young warrior replied. He knelt to the ground, for as Errtu's body had melted away, the only things left behind were the demon's sword and the head of Byok.

"The kill is mine to claim," Tiago insisted, gently stroking Byok's head. "The sword and whip are yours, mighty Yerrininae, and well-earned."

A cheer from behind turned Tiago around, just in time to see the last glabrezu fall before Jearth's warriors. To the side of that fight, the gathered folk of Bryn Shander stood in the broken gates, staring out, cheering, but tentatively.

Tiago understood their hesitance, surely, for not only had they seen the full extent of his drow force now, many more dark elves than they had expected, but a handful of horrid driders as well.

"Take your force and return to the camp," he quietly instructed Yerrininae. "This battle is won."

"There are more than a hundred potential enemies staring at you," the drider quietly replied.

"Not enemies," Tiago assured him. "Grateful peasants, more likely." He saluted the drider and walked toward the gate, motioning for the others to remain to the side.

"It would appear as if Drizzt Do'Urden has made powerful enemies of the lower planes," he said to the gathered folk. "You are fortunate that we were nearby."

They all looked at him, and he noted the glances south, to the rest of his force, and many more to the north, where the five driders had gathered and started away.

Tiago thought to reassure them, but he held his tongue, letting it all sink in, trying to see where it would all lead.

It started as a small clapping of a single person, far in the back of the crowd, but grew quickly to riotous cheering and calls of "huzzah!" for the drow heroes who had saved Bryn Shander.

Tiago and his band kept their encampment south of the city, but Tiago and the Xorlarrin nobles remained in Bryn Shander after the fight. Their coin was no good there any longer, with free food and drink and lodging for as long as they desired.

In the short time before their arrival on the field of battle, Errtu and the glabrezu demons had killed scores and had caused great damage to the eastern section of the city, and only the charge of Tiago had saved them, the folk believed, and so it was true.

"Oh, the irony," Jearth said one night in the tavern, lifting his glass in toast. "To think that Tiago Baenre would be hailed as a hero to humans on the surface world."

Tiago, Ravel, and Saribel all drank to that delicious twist.

They remained in Bryn Shander, awaiting word of Drizzt's return—and now Tiago did not doubt that the folk of Ten-Towns would aid him in his search. To further ensure their cooperation, the politic young Baenre began many rumors of his own, emphasizing that Drizzt Do'Urden had brought this demonic tragedy to Icewind Dale, and hinting that Drizzt had done so intentionally. As those whispers echoed and amplified through the streets of Bryn Shander, Tiago and his allies grew confident that the folk of Ten-Towns would not stand with Drizzt when he at last returned.

But the days became another month, and the season passed to spring, and then summer. Runners went to the barbarian tribes, and to the far reaches of Ten-Towns.

But not a word was heard of Drizzt Do'Urden and his five companions, and the last person to see them, the captain of the ferry, insisted that they had gone ashore exactly where he had placed Tiago's group.

Before the roads closed once more with the coming winter, Tiago and his force traveled south, through the Spine of the World and back to Gauntlgrym. Ravel and his spellspinners had left behind a prepared area to support a magical

R. A. SALVATORE

portal, though, which could get them back to Ten-Towns quickly. They used that magic many times over the next months, and even over the next few years.

But not a trace of Drizzt Do'Urden was to be found, not a rumor from the barbarians nor a sighting among the dwarves of Kelvin's Cairn, nor a visit to any of the towns of Icewind Dale.

The angry Tiago sent out tendrils across the northern reaches of Faerûn, sent hired scouts to Mithral Hall and the Silver Marches, bribed thieves in Luskan, and demanded of Bregan D'aerthe that they bring him to Drizzt. He invoked the power of House Baenre, and his aunt, the Matron Mother of Menzoberranzan, and even mighty Gromph, growing curious, joined in the hunt.

But none could find Drizzt, for he was lost, truly, even to Bregan D'aerthe, even to the eyes of Lady Lolth, even to Draygo Quick and the archwizards of Netheril, and to the great lament of Jarlaxle, who spent a king's fortune in the hunt, going so far as to enlist a host of spies to roam the Shadowfell.

And the years became a decade, and the legend of Drizzt lived on, but the body, it seemed, did not.

Drizzt had been taken by the wind, lost among the legends, a name for another time.

CHAPTER 29

THE LONG NIGHT'S SLEEP

MOONLIGHT.

A distinct beam reached down to the sleeping drow, penetrating the veil of his slumber, beckoning him back to consciousness. Lying flat on his back, Drizzt opened his eyes and focused on the pale orb high in the sky above him, peeking at him through a tangle of scraggly, leafless branches. He had slept for many hours, he realized, though it made little sense to him. For he had fallen asleep in the early evening, and judging by the moon, the night couldn't be more than half over.

Gradually the memories came drifting to him: the sound of sweet music, the return of Artemis Entreri to the camp, the overwhelming desire to lie back down and go to sleep.

The starlight stolen by the heavy canopy above . . . but now that blanketing canopy was no more.

Drizzt felt the thick grass at his side. But when he propped himself up on his elbows, he realized this immediate area was the only remaining hint of the lush forest in which he had previously awakened. He blinked and shook his head, trying to make sense of the scene before him. His five companions lay around him, their rhythmic breathing, the snoring of Ambergris, showing them to be fast asleep. This one area, perhaps ten strides in diameter, seemed exactly as it had been in the "dream," but everything else, everything beyond this tiny patch, was as it had been when first the six had come to this spot. No small, well-kept house. No pond. Exactly as it had been before his dream.

No, not exactly, for the snow lay thick on the ground immediately beyond the enchanted bedroom, but there had been no snow, nor any sign of an approaching storm, when they had come out from Easthaven.

Drizzt stood up and walked to the edge of the grassy anomaly. The moonlight was bright enough to give him a clear view as he inspected the snowpack, and from its formation, it seemed to him that the lower levels of snowpack, compacted and icy, had been in place for many tendays. He looked up at the clear sky, sorting the constellations.

Late winter?

But they had come out here from Easthaven just two days before, and in the early autumn.

Drizzt tried to sort it all out. Had it all been a dream? Only then did he realize that he still held an object in his hand, and he lifted it up before his eyes and confirmed the scrimshaw statuette of Catti-brie and Taulmaril.

"Entreri," he whispered and nudged the assassin with his foot. The dangerous man, ever a light sleeper, awakened immediately and bolted upright, as if expecting an attack and already prepared to defend against it.

And in an instant, the assassin wore the same expression, Drizzt knew, as was upon the drow's own face. He blinked repeatedly, face contorted with confusion, as he glanced around at the curious, impossible sight.

"The music?" Entreri asked quietly. "The forest?"

Drizzt shrugged, having no answers.

"A dream then," said Entreri.

"If so, then a common one," Drizzt replied, and showed him the scrimshaw. "And look around! Our encampment is in summertime, it seems, but the rest of the world is not."

They let the others sleep, both going out and breaking branches from the scraggly trees around the area so they could start a fire if winter closed in. They noticed, too, that the camp remained warm, summertime warm, but the air outside that small cluster proved wickedly cold, and a strong wind swept across the lake from the northwest. But that wind, like the winter itself, did not penetrate the magically protected area, almost as if that small patch of summertime grass existed in a different plane.

Drizzt started a fire and began preparing breakfast just before the dawn, and the others awakened, and each wore the same expression and remembered the sweet music in the summertime forest and asked the same questions and lacked the same answers. None of this made any sense, of course.

Any thoughts they might entertain of spending more time in this enchanted spot, to see if the forest returned, were lost with the break of dawn, for the daylight broke the enchantment fully, and the wind howled in at them, blowing snow stealing their summertime beds.

Drizzt alone heard the music again, then, but it was a different song, or at least, the closing notes to the previous song

The closing notes, the end. A sense of finality engulfed him, for he knew that he was watching this forest, Iruladoon, die away, lost to the ages forevermore.

"Across the frozen lake?" Ambergris asked, breaking the drow's contemplation.

Drizzt considered the words, then shook his head. He wasn't sure of the exact month, but he knew it to be late in the winter season, or early in the spring, and he had no idea how thick the ice might be.

"The same path that took us here," he replied, and he started to the south, moving down toward the even ground of the lake bed. "To Easthaven."

"Ye plannin' to tell us what's what?" Ambergris asked.

"If I had any idea what might be happening, I would," Drizzt replied.

"Well, ye seem to be knowin' our path," the dwarf protested.

"I know where our path is not," Drizzt clarified. "And it is not straight across the lake, with no cover from the wind, and where the ice might prove too thin to support us."

The dwarf shrugged, satisfied with that, and off they went, trudging through the snowpack, pulling their inadequate cloaks tight around them. Drizzt couldn't begin to sort out any of this mystery, but he was glad indeed that they hadn't awakened in midwinter, or surely they would have soon perished.

They were still moving along the lake bed, their progress slow, when the sun began to dip off to their right-hand side.

"We need to find a cave or a sheltered dell," Drizzt explained, turning from the lake and into the small foothills that lined the western shore of Lac Dinneshere. As the daylight began to fade, he moved to the top of one small hill, trying to get his bearings. To the south, he saw the lights of Easthaven, still many hours of walking away, but he noted, too, an encampment much nearer, nestled in the foothills. A barbarian tribe, he knew, and judging from the location and the estimated time of year, likely the Tribe of the Elk, Wulfgar's people, who knew the legend of Drizzt well.

He left his five friends in a sheltered vale near to the barbarian fires and moved in alone, breathing a sigh of relief when he determined that it was indeed the Tribe of the Elk. He entered with his hands upraised, unthreatening, and introduced himself clearly as many suspicious looks came his way.

One large barbarian wearing the garb of the chieftain stepped forward and paced right up to the drow, staring down at him from barely a hand's breadth away. "Drizzt Do'Urden?" he asked, and he seemed less than convinced. He lifted his weapon, a very familiar and magnificent warhammer, Drizzt's way. "What ghost are you?"

"Aegis-fang," Drizzt breathed, for surely it was indeed the warhammer Bruenor had crafted for Wulfgar a century before, and truly it did Drizzt's heart good to see the hammer in the hands of the leader of this barbarian tribe, a proper legacy for a great man of Icewind Dale.

"No ghost," he assured the man. He looked around, trying to find some face he might recognize, though he had not seen any of the tribe for some time. He spotted one large young man, barely more than a teenager with blond hair and sparkling blue eyes, one who immediately sparked some note of recognition in the drow.

But no, Drizzt realized. He was surely confused, and conflating this one with a barbarian he had known so many years before. The sight of Aegis-fang, the smell of Icewind Dale, the sound of the wind in his ears once more—it all seemed enough to transport Drizzt back those many decades.

"I have friends nearby, just five," Drizzt explained. "We're bound for Easthaven, but ill-equipped for the season. If we could spend the night . . ."

The chieftain looked around at his people, then back at the drow. "Drizzt Do'Urden?" he asked again, seeming unconvinced. "Drizzt Do'Urden is long lost to the world, they say, taken by the tundra many years ago."

"If they say that, then they are wrong. I passed through Easthaven only recently, coming out to find . . . well, you or some other tribe, to investigate rumors of a forest on the banks of Lac Dinneshere."

"Why would you seek us?"

"I was told that three of your tribesmen spoke of such a forest."

"I know of no such rumors," said the chieftain and he seemed to stiffen at the suggestion.

"I have heard this talk," interjected one of the others, an older woman. "But not for many years."

Drizzt glanced at her, but found his gaze drawn instead to the young man who reminded Drizzt so much of young Wulfgar, who, Drizzt suspected, might be a descendant of his friend, so strong, uncanny even, seemed the resemblance. The young man shied away from his glance.

"You are Drizzt Do'Urden?" the chieftain asked him directly.

"As surely as your hammer was forged by King Bruenor Battlehammer for Wulfgar, son of Beornegar," Drizzt answered. "A hammer named Aegis-fang, and etched upon its mithral head with the intertwined symbols of the three dwarf gods, Moradin, Dumathoin, and Clangeddin. I was there when it was forged, and there when it was given to Wulfgar—and indeed, with Wulfgar did I travel to the lair of Ingeloakastamizilian, Icingdeath, the white dragon, and there where I came upon this very weapon." As he finished, he drew out his diamond-edged scimitar, which he had named after the slain dragon, and held it up before the chieftain, letting the firelight catch the brilliant edge. He rolled it over in his hand to display the black adamantine handle shaped as the head of a hunting cat.

"Gather your friends," the chieftain said, nodding in recognition of the distinctive scimitar and smiling widely, for as Drizzt had hoped, the legend of Drizzt and particularly of Wulfgar, remained strong in the oral tradition of the Tribe of the Elk. "Share our fire and our food, and we will dress you warmly for the road to Easthaven."

"Long dead," said the young ferryman. "Drowned in '73. Saved the boat, but not old Spiblin."

The six companions looked to each other curiously, not knowing what to make of the strange words. They had made the southeastern corner of Lac Dinneshere, the egress point of the ferry, early the next afternoon, and luck had been with them, for not only was the water at this end of the lake clear of ice, but they saw the boat's sails not far off the shore.

"A good thing we didn't try to cross the lake, eh?" Amber remarked.

"The most dangerous season in Icewind Dale," Drizzt said. "The solid grip of winter leaves as fast as a shift in the wind, and the mud and thin ice left in its wake takes more to the grave than the snows ever could."

A signal fire had brought the ferry sailing in, but to their surprise, the captain was not the crusty graybeard who had dropped them at this spot only a few days earlier.

"There are several ferries from Easthaven's docks, then," Drizzt reasoned.

"Nay, just this one," said the young skipper.

"And the former captain?"

"Long dead, like I told you."

"Wait, you said '73," Afafrenfere put in.

"Aye, we speak of it as the Year of the Wave, for such a storm blew down from the north that half the waters of Dinneshere took the docks of Easthaven, and most of our fleet as well. Spiblin was too stubborn to run to higher ground, saying he'd save his boat if he had to die doing it. And so he did, to both. Eleven years, it's been since then."

"1484?" Drizzt asked, and behind him, Effron sucked in his breath. Drizzt turned around, to see the monk and the tiefling staring at each other.

"By Dalereckoning. It is 1484?" Effron asked the ferryman, who nodded. Effron looked back at the monk and said, "The Year of the Awakened Sleepers."

They disembarked the ferry at Easthaven's docks, and indeed these were not the same structures from which they had departed, though remnants of those "old" docks were still to be seen. They didn't even enter the town, though, despite the late hour, but instead brought forth the nightmare and the unicorn. Drizzt, Dahlia, and Effron on Andahar, the other three on Entreri's steed, they thundered off down the Eastway, making for Bryn Shander and

Kelvin's Cairn, determining that Clan Battlehammer seemed their best hope for answers.

Another riddle met them the next morning at Bryn Shander's gate, for they were denied entrance.

"No friend of Ten-Towns drags a demon in his wake, then runs off!" the captain of the Bryn Shander garrison shouted to them from the wall when he at last arrived to the summons of the guards. "What menace chases you here this time, Drizzt Do'Urden?"

"No menace," Drizzt replied, and he wanted to say much more, but found the words impossible to find. The city looked much the same, but he knew none of the guards, nor the captain, though he had met the captain on his last journey through the city, which seemed only a tenday previous.

"What demon?" Artemis Entreri asked when it became obvious that Drizzt was overwhelmed, and tongue-tied.

"A mighty balor, seeking Drizzt Do'Urden," the captain replied from on high. "And praise that Master Tiago was around, to slay the demon before our western gate!"

A huzzah went up from the other guards at the mention of . . . Tiago?

Entreri turned and stared open-mouthed at Drizzt and both shook their heads. "And pray tell, what year was this battle?" Entreri asked the captain of the guard.

The captain looked at him curiously.

"The year?" Entreri repeated.

"The very year my son was born," the captain answered. "1466. Eighteen years ago this coming fall."

"1484," Entreri muttered, doing the math.

"The Year of the Awakened Sleepers," Afafrenfere remarked.

"No wonder me belly's grumbling with hunger," Ambergris put in dryly.

"I have ever been a friend to Ten-Towns," Drizzt called out. "Something . . . strange has happened here. Beyond reason or all sense. I bid you let me enter, that I might speak with the ruling council, perhaps a gathering of all the towns—"

"Ride around, drow," the captain replied sternly. "Your previous reputation wards you from the wrath of the people, perhaps, but you have used up all your good will here. You'll not be allowed entry here, nor to any of the other towns, once word has spread of your return."

"I did not bring the demon—not knowingly, at least," Drizzt tried to argue.

"Go to the dwarves, then," the captain offered, and he winced as he spoke, as if trying to reconcile the Drizzt of legend with the Drizzt who had brought ruin to much of Bryn Shander with this shaken drow standing before him.

"Stokely Silverstream will have you, to be sure. Let him call a gathering of Ten-Towns. Let him plead the case of Drizzt Do'Urden."

The advice seemed sound enough, a pocket of clarity within this tumultuous, illogical sea of absurdity. Drizzt and Entreri dismissed their mounts and the six hiked off around the city, taking the southerly route. When they came to the western gate, they found it flanked by two stone guard towers, much larger than the meager structures that had been there when last they had passed through, still further confirmation that they had lost many years in their night of long sleep in the strange forest on the banks of Lac Dinneshere.

"It's true, then," Ambergris said, staring at the gate, for of course these could not have been constructed in the tenday they believed they had been gone. Before the gate and just south of it, was a wide circle of blackness, surrounded by a rock wall and with a small stone statue of a drow warrior, sword and shield upraised.

" 'On this spot did Master Tiago slay the demon,' " Afafrenfere read from the plaque beneath it. " 'And the snows will cover it nevermore.' "

"We have all gone insane, then," said Dahlia, shaking her head. "I have walked the planes to the Shadowfell, I have existed as a statue of stone, and now I have awakened from a slumber of eighteen winters? What madness this?"

She walked off a bit to the west and stood facing away from the others, hands on hips and head down.

"Madness indeed," muttered Entreri.

"But if it's all true, then Draygo Quick's long lost interest," Ambergris said, and she slapped Afafrenfere on the back and gave a great snort. "But why's the long faces?" she asked of them all. "None had family now gone, eh? We come to the dale to be rid o' Tiago's hunters."

"And Draygo's eyes," Effron reminded.

"Aye, and Cavus Dun, too," said Afafrenfere.

"So fugitives we been, and now one long nap's fixed it for us!" Ambergris said with a belly-laugh. "Slate's as clean as an Icewind Dale snowstorm, and every road's open!"

"You would dismiss this loss of time so easily?" Drizzt asked incredulously.

"Ye thinkin' ye know anything I might be doing against it?" the dwarf replied. "It is what it is, elf, and what it is is a blessin' more than any curse to any one o' us! Least-ways, that's what I be thinkin'!"

Effron nodded his agreement and managed a smile, as did Afafrenfere, but neither Entreri nor Drizzt could find the line of thinking to join in their relief, or whatever it was. The shock of this all had them both reeling, particularly Drizzt, who dropped a hand into his belt pouch and rolled a small piece of scrimshaw around in his fingers. They had found an enchanted forest, so it seemed obvious, and one where time had all but stopped through a long night's slumber. He had heard the song of Mielikki, so he believed, and had found a reminder to a long-lost friend.

But what did it all mean? How did it all make any sense, and what implications might he draw?

Overwhelmed, Drizzt led the others away from Bryn Shander at a leisurely, meandering pace. They got into the foothills of Kelvin's Cairn as night descended and, exhausted and overwhelmed, set their camp.

Drizzt didn't know it, but it was the night of the Spring Equinox, the holiest day in the calendar of Mielikki, in the Year of the Awakened Sleepers.

Drizzt got the fire burning, and Ambergris brought it to great heights. At one point, the dwarf giggled that she would surely "turn the night orange."

"Truly?" Effron replied. "I prefer purple!" With that, he cast a spell, and a colored bolt reached out from his fingers to the flames, his cantrip altering the color indeed—to purple.

"Bah for yerself and yer minor magic!" Ambergris huffed, and she cast her own enchantment, her divine magic overwhelming the warlock's tricks.

"Oh, indeed!" said Effron, and he went right back at her, and the flames fought their battle, shifting hue in a wild dance for supremacy. It became a game to her and Effron, to the amusement of Afafrenfere, who kept feeding more kindling to the blaze.

Even ever-dour Entreri, sitting off to the side and polishing his dagger, couldn't suppress a chuckle or two.

Because they were all free, Drizzt realized. This apparent and bizarre time-shift had only made the world a better place for these four fugitives. The dwarf and monk could go as they pleased with no fear of Cavus Dun, and for Effron and Entreri, the specter of Draygo Quick seemed lifted, and likely, too, the shadows of a hundred others with a vendetta against Artemis Entreri.

So, too, would this strange leap of years benefit Drizzt and Dahlia, he realized, but the elf warrior showed no mirth, sitting by herself, her expression grim, and glancing his way every now and again.

For Drizzt, there was just confusion. Had his sleep, had the enchanted forest, been a vision, a love letter to him from Mielikki? More likely, he realized, it had been a moment of closure. Awakening in the tiny secluded area of a land still grasped by the late winter signaled a farewell to Drizzt.

The forest was gone.

Somehow he knew that, in his heart and soul. The enchanted forest was gone, was no more, and so too were flown any ties to the world that had once been, before the Spellplague.

Thus, his past was gone, at long last.

He focused on that moment when the moon had opened his eyes, and thought it a passage. He thought of Innovindil (and stole a glance at Dahlia) and her insistence that an elf must live his life in shorter time spans, must reinvent his existence, his friends, his love, with each passing generation, to know vitality and happiness.

He glanced at Dahlia again, but his gaze inevitably lowered to his own hands, where he rolled a piece of scrimshaw over and over again.

By the time he looked back up, while the dwarf, monk, and warlock remained at play with the fire, Dahlia had gone to sit with Entreri, the two conversing privately.

Drizzt nodded, rose, and walked off into the night. He came to a high rock, overlooking Bryn Shander away to the southeast, and with the high peak of Kelvin's Cairn to the northwest behind him. He stood there, the wind in his face and in his ears, remembering what was and pondering what might now be.

"We're not staying," came Dahlia's voice behind him, and he wasn't surprised—by her presence or her message. "We'll go to the dwarves, perhaps, but for a short while only. We're to ride with a caravan out of this forlorn place at the earliest opportunity."

"To where?" Drizzt asked, but didn't turn to face her.

"Does it matter? A decade and more's gone by and our names have slipped past in the wind."

"You underestimate the memories of those with a vendetta," Drizzt said, and he turned in time to see Dahlia shrug, as if it hardly mattered.

"When we came here, you said it would be for the season. The seasons have come and gone fifty times and more. I've not thought of living my years out in the emptiness of Icewind Dale, and might any time prove safer for us to leave than right now, before rumors of our return filter to the south?"

Drizzt mulled over her words, looking for some way to argue the point. He was as confused as the rest of them, unsure of what had happened or what it might mean. Was it really 1484? Had the world passed them by while they had slept in some enchanted forest?

And if that was the enchanted forest of Nathan Obridock, the place named Iruladoon, then what of the auburn-haired witch and the halfling by the pond?

Drizzt couldn't help but wince as he considered the place, for there it was again in his heart, the knowledge that he had witnessed the very end of Iruladoon when he had awakened in the one warm spot amidst the last snows. He had felt the magic drain away to nothingness. It wasn't that the enchantment had moved along. Nay, it had dissipated all together. That place, whether it was Iruladoon or not, was no more, nevermore. He knew that with certainty, though he knew not how he understood it with certainty.

Mielikki had signaled to him that it was no more, that it was gone, and with a pervading sense of comfort . . . that it was all right.

"Are you agreed?" Dahlia asked impatiently, and Drizzt realized from her tone and her stance that she was reiterating that question for more than the second time.

"Agreed?" he had to ask.

"First caravan out," Dahlia said.

Drizzt chewed his lip and looked all around, but really tried to look within his own heart. Behind Dahlia loomed the blackness of Kelvin's Cairn, and it did not elicit a cold emotion within Drizzt—quite the opposite.

"We can have the life up here that we spoke of before we went to Easthaven," he said.

Dahlia looked at him incredulously, even laughed at him.

"It will be an easy life, and one of adventure."

"They wouldn't even let you in their town, you fool," Dahlia reminded him.

"That will change, with time."

But Dahlia shook her head resolutely, and Drizzt recognized that she didn't disagree with his particular reasoning, but rejected the whole premise.

"We're all for going, all five," she said. "Even Ambergris."

"To where?"

Again Dahlia laughed at him. "Does it matter?"

"If it doesn't, then why not here?"

"No," she stated flatly. "We are leaving this forlorn place of tedious winds and endless boredom. All of us. And I'll not chase your ghosts back to Icewind Dale again, if all of Menzoberranzan, all of the Empire of Netheril, and all the demons of the Abyss are chasing us."

"There are no ghosts left to chase," Drizzt whispered under his breath, for he knew it to be true.

But even with that, spoken sincerely, there was no compromise to be found within her, Drizzt realized. She saw Icewind Dale as a surrogate to Catti-brie for him, a place of those memories, and she would not tolerate it.

But nor could Drizzt lie any longer, to himself or to Dahlia. He felt a twinge of guilt in coercing her up here in the first place, but reminded himself that he had done so only to protect her from Tiago Baenre. But now that threat seemed distant, and Dahlia was right, there was no compelling reason for any of them to remain in Icewind Dale any longer.

Any of the other five, at least.

"It is best that you go," he agreed.

"That *I* go?" she asked, and a dark edge came over her voice and her posture. Drizzt nodded.

"But not you?"

"This is my home."

"But not mine?" she asked.

"No."

"So that you can chase your witch of the wood?"

Drizzt chuckled helplessly at that, for there was some measure of truth in it, he had to admit. Not literally, of course, but in this place, even without his old and dear friends by his side, he felt the warmth of hearth and home, and it was a feeling he would not allow to slip from his grasp yet again.

"Have I told you of Innovindil?" he asked, and Dahlia rolled her eyes. Drizzt pressed on anyway, though he remembered that yes, he had told her many stories of his lost elf friend. "Have I explained to you the idea that an elf who resides among the shorter-living races must live his life in bursts to accommodate their sensations of time?"

"Yes, yes, to let go of the past and press ahead to new roads," Dahlia said absently, as if long bored of that particular lecture.

"I seem to be ignoring Innovindil's advice," said Drizzt.

"Then let us leave in the morning."

"No."

Dahlia shrugged, clearly confused by the seemingly pointless reference to Innovindil, given his answer.

"Innovindil was wrong," Drizzt said. "Perhaps not entirely, and perhaps not for everyone, but for me, in this regard, I know now, and admit now, that Innovindil was wrong."

"In this regard?"

"Regarding love," Drizzt said.

"The auburn-haired witch of the wood."

Drizzt nodded. "My heart remains with Catti-brie. I gave it to her wholly and cannot take it back."

"She is dead a hundred years."

"Not in my heart."

"Ghosts are cold comfort, Drizzt Do'Urden."

"So be it," he replied, and he had never been more certain of his road in all of his two centuries. "I'm not saddened by this realization, by this admission that I remain in love with a woman lost to me a century ago."

"Saddened? I would think you insane!"

"Then I hope for you, dear Dahlia, for I wish you nothing but the best road, that one day you will understand my . . . insanity. Because I do truly care for you, as my friend, I hope that you will one day be so afflicted as am I. Catti-brie died, but my love for her did not. Innovindil was wrong, and I

371

will live my life happier in the warm memories of Catti-brie's embrace than in a foolish and impossible effort to replace her."

"So there is only one love? There can be no other?"

Drizzt considered that for a moment, then honestly shrugged. "I know not," he admitted. "Perhaps this is, at long last, the time when I will find closure. Perhaps there will come in my path someday another to so warm me. But I do not seek that. I do not need it. Catti-brie remains with me, very much alive."

He watched Dahlia swallow hard, and it pained him to hurt her—but how much greater would he be wounding her by living a lie out of cowardice?

"Then take our relationship for what it is," Dahlia offered at length, and there seemed to be a bit of desperation creeping into the edges of her voice.

"And what is that, a distraction?"

"Play," she said as lightly as she could manage, and she put on a too-wide smile. "Let us enjoy the road and each other's body. We fight well together and we love well together, so take it for what it is and let it have no meaning beyond—"

"No," Drizzt interrupted, though he could not deny that Dahlia's offer was enticing. "Not for your sake and not for my own. My heart and home are here, in Icewind Dale, and here I will stay. And here, you should not stay."

The crestfallen expression that enveloped Dahlia nearly had Drizzt running to embrace her, but again, for her own sake, he did not.

"You would send me away with Entreri?" she asked, and her eyes narrowed, and her facial woad seemed to heighten then, reflecting a growing anger. "He is a fine lover, you know."

Drizzt recognized that she was just lashing out here, just trying to sting him back for the rejection he had shown her. He did well to offer no response.

"I have shared his bed many times," Dahlia pressed, to which Drizzt merely nodded.

"You do not care?" Dahlia asked, her tone on the edge of outrage.

Drizzt swallowed hard, seeing this breakup devolving into a matter of foolish pride, and he knew that he should allow Dahlia to salvage some of that. Or should he, and again, for her own sake?

"No," he answered flatly. "I do care, but not as you imagine. I am glad that you have found each other."

"You are walking a dangerous path, Drizzt Do'Urden," Dahlia warned.

Drizzt wasn't sure how to take that at first. Was she referring to his own emotional state, given his dramatic choice? Was she taking up Innovindil's mantle of long-searching wisdom to appeal to him on some philosophical level?

She lifted her walking stick before her and snapped her wrists expertly to break it in half, into two four-foot lengths, and these she broke in half into flails—*"nun'chuks,"* Afafrenfere had named them—and sent them into easy spins at her side.

"You do not get to so easily dismiss me," Dahlia informed him. "I am not a plaything for the whims of Drizzt Do'Urden."

Drizzt thought better of reminding her that she had just offered to be exactly that, and instead focused on how he might diffuse this strange situation. "I seek only that which is best for us both."

"Oh, shut up," she said. "Shut up and draw your blades."

Drizzt held his hands out unthreateningly, as if that request was absurd.

"Diamonds do not move so easily from one ear to the other," she said. "And this one, the black diamond, is to be the most difficult of all." She began circling to Drizzt's left, moving up the incline near to the edge of the rock. "That is why I chose you, of course. Or do you still not understand?"

"Apparently, I don't—" he started to answer, his words cut short as he ducked and dodged back, one of Dahlia's weapons whipping suddenly at his head—and had it connected, it surely would have cracked open his skull.

"Dahlia!"

"Draw your blades!" she shouted back at him. "Do not further disappoint me! You were the one, the lover I could not beat! You were the one to serve me my just reward. You are a failure as a lover, as a man, with your precious witch ever in your foolish heart. Do not doubly disappoint me by failing at the one thing I know you do well!"

On she came in a rush, and despite himself, Drizzt found his scimitars in his hands as he fended the sudden, brutal attacks, the flails spinning in at him from every conceivable angle. Instinct alone had Drizzt parrying and twisting away from the assault, for his brain could not fathom the situation unfolding before him. Instinct alone had him countering Dahlia's movements, even striking out at her with a reflexive riposte after one clean parry.

Drizzt sucked in his breath and retracted his scimitar at the same time, horrified that he had nearly skewered Dahlia, to the point where blood had begun to stain her torn shirt.

She didn't seem the least bit bothered, though, and pressed the attack with apparent glee, swinging her right-hand flail back in at Drizzt's retracting blade. And when the pole struck the scimitar, Dahlia released some lightning energy, which coursed Twinkle and sparked into Drizzt's left hand and arm.

The drow's teeth clenched involuntarily, and it was all he could do to hold onto his weapon, the muscles in his forearm clenching and knotting under the tingling and burning sensation.

"Stop!" Drizzt yelled at her between the ring of his blades blocking her swinging poles. "Dahlia!"

His calls only made her attack all the more ferociously, however. She went into a spin, coming around with her flying weapon swinging across for Drizzt's head. He ducked the blow, then leaped as she turned a second circuit, this time bending as she came around and sweeping a backhand of her other weapon for his legs.

She had left him an opening. With him up high and Dahlia down low, Drizzt could have charged in and put her at a tremendous, likely insurmountable, disadvantage then and there, and indeed he started that way.

But he didn't lead with his blades. He hadn't the heart to cut her again, and instead tried to wrap her in a hug as she tried to stand back up, moving in too close for her to strike at him with those deadly flails.

She seemed to lose all strength then, and Drizzt reached out for her, hopeful that this insanity had come to its end.

Dahlia smashed her forehead into his nose and drove a knee up into his groin as he fell back, and before he had even fully straightened again, she lashed out at him once more with her weapons.

He blocked right with Icingdeath, left with Twinkle, then brought Twinkle across to block again to the right, and turned around away from Dahlia, coming around with Icingdeath angled diagonally to lift up her second attack from the left.

He dived under that raising nun'chuk, just ahead of her next trailing strike. He rolled easily to his feet, tasting blood from his smashed nose, and fell into a crouch as Dahlia turned to pursue.

But again, suddenly, she seemed to lose all strength for the fight, and her arms slumped to the side and she looked at Drizzt with a clear sense of helplessness, of anguish and sadness. She offered a shrug and a sniffle.

Then snapped her right hand, her nun'chuk lashing straight ahead like a serpent.

Drizzt fell for the ruse because he desperately needed to believe in the ruse. For all his training and all his speed and honed reflexes, Drizzt couldn't quite catch up to that attack. The nun'chuk's tip cracked into his forehead, knocking him upright, and Dahlia released the rest of Kozah's Needle's magical lightning, throwing him forcefully backward. He flipped off the edge of the rocky outcropping, spinning right over as he fell from the ledge. He slammed down on the sloping ground some ten feet below the rock, and bounced and rolled his way down the slope, crashing through brush, wet snow, and rocks alike.

He finally settled against a rock, his thoughts spinning, burning pain assailing him from many different wounds.

"Fool!" he heard Dahlia shout from above, and he knew she was coming for him. He couldn't see her, for she had moved to the trail behind the rock, but she continued her verbal tirade, "This is to the death, yours or mine! So fight better or be damned, Drizzt Do'Urden!"

Drizzt climbed to all fours, or to three, at least, for he wound up tucking his right hand in close to his chest. He looked down at the hand, already swelling and bruised around the thumb and index finger. He tried to clench his fist, but could barely move the fingers.

He spotted his dropped scimitar, Icingdeath, on the slope just up above him, and climbed to his feet to retrieve it.

Such waves of pain washed over him that he nearly fell back to the ground. As he recovered, he settled his weight onto his right foot and glanced down at his left leg, noting a bulge against the leather at mid-calf. Drizzt swallowed hard, amazed that he was upright at all, for in the fall, he had surely broken the bone in his shin.

Slowly he put his foot back to the ground and eased some weight onto it. Again the waves of pain assaulted him. He looked around for a splint, but heard Dahlia's approach and realized that he had no time.

He scrambled for his scimitar, retrieved it, and spun around to watch the woman's determined approach, her weapons swinging easily at her sides.

"You were supposed to win," she said through gritted teeth, tears streaming down her angry face. "In so many ways have you disappointed me!"

Her words didn't make any sense to Drizzt, and he could barely keep his eyes focused on her. He knew that she was coming closer, ever closer. He knew that he couldn't begin to fight her now. He had no speed and no balance, and the pain . . .

She was so close.

A dark form rushed by, carrying Dahlia with it off to the side.

"Enough!" Drizzt heard, Artemis Entreri's voice. He followed the sound to see the two of them, and only then realized that he was sitting once more, and was only looking out of one eye now, as the other was covered with the blood pouring from the wound on his forehead.

Dahlia struggled against the man, but Entreri held her back, talking to her, though Drizzt could not hear the words. But Entreri remained insistent—even in his desperate and dazed state, Drizzt could recognize that—and he pushed Dahlia away, step-by-step.

"Farewell," Drizzt heard him call back, and then something around them leaving Icewind Dale.

Drizzt couldn't be sure. His face was in the dirt by that time, and all he heard was his own pulse, pounding in his head, images both real and imagined intertwining in a place far removed from consciousness.

EPILOGUE

T HE STARS REACHED DOWN TO HIM, LIKE SO MANY TIMES BEFORE IN THIS enchanted place.

He was on Bruenor's Climb, though he didn't know how he had arrived there. Guenhwyvar was beside him, leaning against him, supporting his shattered leg, but he didn't remember calling to her.

Of all the places Drizzt had ever traveled, none had felt more comforting than here. Perhaps it had been the company he had so often found up here, but even without Bruenor beside him, this place, this lone peak rising above the flat, dark tundra, had ever brought a spiritual sustenance to Drizzt Do'Urden. Up here, he felt small and mortal, but at the same time, felt confident that he was part of something much larger, of something eternal.

On Bruenor's Climb, the stars reached down to him, or he lifted up among them, floating free of his physical restraints, his spirit rising and soaring among the celestial spheres. He could hear the sound of the great clockwork up here, could feel the celestial winds in his face and could melt into the ether.

It was a place of the deepest meditation for Drizzt, a place where he understood the great cycle of life and death.

A place that seemed fitting now, as the blood continued to flow from the wound in his forehead.

Ambergris stood with her hands on her hips, looking this way and that, fully perplexed. She turned to Afafrenfere, who could only shrug.

They saw the blood, the signs of the tumble, the signs of the fight, as Entreri had explained to them when he had returned to the camp, a thoroughly shaken Dahlia in his grasp.

But Drizzt was not here.

His leg was broken, Entreri had said, and his head bleeding badly, and indeed, the three of them, the dwarf, the monk, and Effron, easily located the spot where Drizzt had last stood against Dahlia simply by the amount of blood on the ground.

But he wasn't there, and there was no trail leading from that place, not a line of blood nor drag marks one would expect from a person with a shattered leg.

"Someone found him first," Effron offered.

"Someone flying, then," Afafrenfere replied, holding up his hands helplessly as he stood near the lone set of tracks in the snow leading from this place, the path of Entreri and Dahlia that had so easily led them out from their camp.

All three looked up, as if expecting a great bird or a dragon to descend upon them.

"Not hurtin' as bad as Entreri thought," Ambergris surmised. "He's a ranger, then, and with no small skill."

"But where would he go?" asked Effron.

"To the Battlehammer dwarves," Afafrenfere said, and the others nodded.

"We'll go by there and see," Ambergris declared.

"Entreri said we were to leave directly, and before the dawn," Effron reminded them, "to the east and south and out of the dale."

"Entreri's wrong, then," the monk said. "Drizzt wouldn't leave a friend in such a state, nor will I."

"Aye," the dwarf agreed.

Effron glanced back toward their camp, where Dahlia and Entreri were packing up the bedrolls, and couldn't suppress a wince. He was caught in the middle between his mother and the drow, and while he didn't want to go against Dahlia in these tentative beginnings of their relationship, he couldn't disagree with the reasoning of the dwarf and monk. Drizzt had been a loyal companion to him, had welcomed him after his "conversion," and indeed had become more than a mere companion to Effron. In the Shadowfell, in those days when they sat starving side-by-side, Drizzt had been Effron's friend.

And it wasn't a self-serving friendship, the likes of which had dominated every aspect of Effron's previous existence under the suffrage of Draygo Quick and Herzgo Alegni, but rather, an honest compassion, and welcome.

"To Stokely Silverstream and Clan Battlehammer, then," the tiefling agreed. "We owe Drizzt that much at least."

"Perhaps we're not to part with him, then," Afafrenfere said obstinately, and he, too, looked back toward the encampment, clearly uncomfortable with the report Artemis Entreri had delivered, clearly upset with the breaking of their band.

"Whole world's out there," Ambergris was quick to remind them, however. "Meself ain't one to stay in this place, not with all roads open. And it's been many years—who might be knowin' what we'll find out there?"

Afafrenfere looked to the dwarf, then back at the camp, and reluctantly nodded.

They did convince Entreri to veer northeast around the base of the mountain to the Battlehammer tunnels.

But the five would leave Icewind Dale, crossing through the Spine of the World pass and coming once more to see the skyline of Luskan a tenday later, with no word of Drizzt Do'Urden.

He had melted into the night, and they knew no more.

The warmth of the blood . . . the stars reaching down . . . on his knees against Guenhwyvar . . . floating up to become one with the stars, with eternity, with all . . .

The disconnected thoughts pulsed through Drizzt's consciousness.

Dahlia had slain him, because he wouldn't so kill her . . . Entreri intercepting, saving him, but not quite, apparently . . .

How had he come to this place, Bruenor's Climb, atop the thousand-foot peak of Kelvin's Cairn? His broken leg hadn't carried him here, could not have carried him here.

Why didn't his leg hurt?

He was drifting away then, and hearing once more the song—the same song he had heard in the enchanted forest on the eastern bank of Lac Dinneshere. The song of Mielikki, he knew in his heart and soul.

The song to call him home.

And who might be there?

His vision blurred. He put his head against Guenhwyvar's muscled flank, feeling the warmth and strength of the dear panther.

"Don't forget me," he whispered.

He heard the song, and the low moan of the panther, and a voice . . . a voice from long ago, from another time and another life.

His vision crystallized around that sound, for one fleeting instant, and he saw her again, his beloved Catti-brie, and a flood of happiness washed through him.

For she was with the song, and the song beckoned him to join.

The strength left him.

Guenhwyvar cried out, long and low into the Icewind Dale night.

And Catti-brie was there beside him, hugging him and holding him, and he knew that it was all right to let go, to let himself fall, because Catti-brie would catch him.